"Are you mad?"

With one swift tug, FitzHugh hauled her, naked and shrieking, from the tub.

Mellisynt tried to wrench her arms loose, desperate to cover herself. "How dare you storm in here and handle me so?"

FitzHugh's voice rose to a furious shout. "How dare *you* disappear like that, with no word to anyone? Have you no idea of the dangers in this land for a woman alone? Have you no sense at all?"

"I've sense enough to find my way back unassisted and unmolested," Mellisynt countered. "Unmolested until *you* returned, that is."

His long night of wanting and even longer day of worry came together with the force of two chargers colliding. A tide of need swept over FitzHugh, and he began to drag her toward the bed.

"I'll do more than molest you, wife. I'll make sure you don't have the strength left to go a-walking for many a day!"

Dear Reader,

Harlequin Historicals welcomes you to another sizzling month of romance. With summer in full swing, we've got four titles perfect for the beach, pool—or anywhere!

From popular author Miranda Jarrett comes another swashbuckling tale set on the high seas—*Mariah's Prize*, her next book in the thrilling SPARHAWK series. In this story, a desperate Mariah West convinces Gabriel Sparhawk to captain her sloop, never guessing at his ulterior motives.

Scottish chieftain Dillon Campbell abducted Lady Leonora Wilton as an act of revenge against the English. But one look into Leonora's eyes and it became an act of love, in *The Highlander* by favorite author Ruth Langan.

In Julie Tetel's stirring medieval tale, *Simon's Lady*, the marriage between Simon de Beresford and Lady Gwyneth had been arranged to quell a Saxon uprising, yet this Saxon bride wants more from her husband than peace.

And finally, if you liked Merline Lovelace's first book of the DESTINY'S WOMEN series, *Alena*, you'll love her second book, *Sweet Song of Love*. When knight Richard FitzHugh was called to battle, he left behind a meek bride given to him by the king. So who was the curvaceous beauty who now greeted him as *husband?*

Next month, our big book selection is *To Share a Dream*, a reissue by author Willo Davis Roberts. Don't miss this moving saga about three sisters who dare to build a new beginning in the American colonies.

Sincerely,

Tracy Farrell
Senior Editor

Please address questions and book requests to:
Harlequin Reader Service
U.S.: 3010 Walden Ave., P.O. Box 1325, Buffalo, NY 14269
Canadian: P.O. Box 609, Fort Erie, Ont. L2A 5X3

MERLINE LOVELACE

Sweet Song of Love

Harlequin Books

TORONTO • NEW YORK • LONDON
AMSTERDAM • PARIS • SYDNEY • HAMBURG
STOCKHOLM • ATHENS • TOKYO • MILAN
MADRID • WARSAW • BUDAPEST • AUCKLAND

ISBN 0-373-28830-1

SWEET SONG OF LOVE

Books by Merline Lovelace

Harlequin Historicals

*Alena #220
*Sweet Song of Love #230

*Destiny's Women trilogy

Merline Lovelace

After a career in the air force, Merline Lovelace especially enjoys crafting strong, decisive warriors who more than meet their match in the women they come to love. She admits to being swept off her feet by her own handsome warrior twenty-four years ago, and to a lifelong passion for historical novels.

Merline's own novels have been set in eras and locales as varied as Roman Britain and medieval France. Look for her next book, *The Siren's Call*, the last in the Destiny's Women trilogy, coming in September. In this tale of ancient Greece, a dashing Athenian sea captain finds his life turned upside down by the stubborn Spartan woman he carries off.

To my sister, Pam, for all the sweaters you loaned me, the guys you fixed me up with and the wonderful hours we spent devouring pizza and historical novels!

Chapter One

Lady Mellisynt of Trémont drew in a deep breath and raised wide, steady eyes to the towering stranger before her.

"I will wed with you, my lord."

"You understand you have a choice," he growled. "You may take your widow's portion with you to a nunnery. With such riches to buy your entry, you would enjoy a life of restful ease."

"I understand."

Piercing blue eyes, the color of a winter sky washed with rain, stared down at her. He had removed his helmet, revealing a lean, sun-darkened face and thick black hair threaded with faint traces of silver at the temples. Lines of weariness bracketed his mouth and eyes, and his dark brows drew together over a nose that had been broken more than once, by a mailed fist or an oaken staff. He looked exactly like the ruthless warrior Mellisynt knew him to be.

His jaw tightened, as if he had come to a decision that afforded him little pleasure.

"So be it. Summon your household priest and arrange for the betrothal ceremony within the hour. We'll leave for Nantes at first light on the morrow. I would have you safe within the city walls before I rejoin the duke."

Mellisynt nodded, her heart pounding. She knew well the knight's spoken words masked their real meaning. He intended to carry his wealthy prize to the city because he dared not leave her here. He feared she might repudiate their betrothal in his absence and seal herself within Trémont's formidable walls. He could not know she would have walked naked across a bed of hot coals to leave this place.

"Do you wish to wash and refresh yourself in my lord's—in Lord Henri's chambers? I will attend to you immediately I speak with Father Anselem."

He glanced down at his mud-spattered surcoat and leggings, then shook his head. "Nay, I must see to the keep's defenses while there is yet light. My squire will attend to my needs before I take you to the chapel."

Mellisynt stood silent while he took his leave and strode across the dim, cavernous hall. A cowering servant threw open the doors that led to the bailey, and for a moment the knight stood silhouetted against thin winter twilight. His broad back, made immense by his mailed armour and fur-lined surcoat, filled the doorframe. Sudden doubt swamped Mellisynt, and she drew her mantle tight around her shoulders. Sweet Mother of God, what had she done? He was so huge and stern of face! How could she have agreed to bind herself to such a one?

The door closed behind him, cutting off the light and plunging the hall back into its customary gloom. A rustle of activity at the far end of the great room stilled her incipient panic. She straightened, not wanting her people to see her fears. They'd been frightened enough at the appearance of a heavily armed troop whose fierce leader demanded entry by order of their overlord, the duke of Brittany. When the knight had identified himself as Sir Richard FitzHugh, their fear had turned to terror. Since war had broken out this summer, in the year of our Lord 1184, FitzHugh had left a trail of charred villages and subdued castles in his relentless wake. But on this cold November day, at least, he'd laid aside his sword and ridden alone up the steep incline to Trémont's gates.

Even from the high perspective of the castle walls, Mellisynt had seen at once the knight's raw strength. When she'd learned his business, she'd allowed him entry into the keep. And into her life. Surely such a man could give her the child she longed for. And he would remove her from Trémont. Were he twice as large and even more fierce, she would take him to husband for those two reasons alone.

She wrapped her arms tighter around her chest, knowing she should go to Father Anselem, but loath to move. Her eyes roamed the vast hall, now bathed in dark shadows lightened at intervals by flickering, pitch-soaked torches. Soon, she told herself, soon she would walk out of this keep that had housed her for most of her girlhood and all of her adult life. Soon she would be free of its gray stone walls. A rush of joy washed through her veins, stilling the last of her fears. With a steady step, she crossed the rushes to the narrow corridor leading to the chapel.

Father Anselem paced back and forth before a side altar, his embroidered chasuble slapping against well-padded thighs. Annoyance at being excluded from her meeting with the knight showed plainly in the scowl darkening his pudgy face.

Mellisynt paused in the shadows of the vestibule, took a deep breath, then stepped into the small chapel.

"'Tis indeed the FitzHugh, Father."

The cleric's breath hissed out and pale, watery eyes narrowed to spiteful slits. "The English bastard! The duke would wed you to the son of a common whore."

"Aye, the duke is ever solicitous of his subject's welfare," she agreed dryly.

At her sarcasm, the priest's face filled with the choleric red it habitually assumed whenever he dealt with her. "Mind your speech," he sputtered. "Brittany is your overlord, after all. It is his right to dispose of your person where he thinks best."

"Aye, just as he did when he bestowed me on Henri of Trémont." Try as she might, Mellisynt couldn't keep the scorn from her tone.

"'Tis your choice to take another husband," the priest snapped. "If you were a dutiful wife, you would accede to

Henri's dying wish and retire to the nunnery he chose for
you. The documents were signed, the fees agreed upon."

She shook her head. "Nay, I've had enough of walls."

"But think, my lady, think! To bind yourself to this
black knight!"

She folded her arms across her chest and met his agitated glare with a wry smile. "My experience of husbands
has not been such that I expect overmuch. This one will do
as well as any. At least he will give me children."

The priest strode forward, leaning so close she could see
the candlelight gleaming on his tonsured head. Her nostrils quivered at the mingled odor of incense and garlic he
always carried.

"This is God's punishment for your willfulness, woman.
If you had served Henri more faithfully, you might have
been blessed with a child of his loins. Then you need not
have taken a new lord, nor ceded Henri's lands and wealth
to this bastard."

"Nor put your comfortable living in jeopardy, Father?"

The priest's high color deepened, and he stepped back.
It had been many years since he'd left the primitive sim-
plicity of his Cistercian monastery to become Henri's confessor. And just as many years, Mellisynt suspected, since
he'd held to his vows of poverty and chastity. More than
one castle maidservant had born a babe with his pale eyes.
For a moment she enjoyed his sputtering indignation, but
then she sighed. As many uncomfortable hours on her
knees as this vindictive little man had cost her, he was not,
nor had he ever been, worthy of her spite.

"You need not fear as yet, Father. We leave at first light
for Nantes. 'Twill likely be some months before this war is
done, and FitzHugh turns his attention to ordering the liv-
ings within Trémont."

The cleric's face lost some of its mottled hue.

Mellisynt gathered her skirts to leave. "He would sanctify the betrothal this night, within the hour."

"'Tis not right," the priest muttered. "Henri's barely shriven."

"What's done is God's will, Father."

His mouth sagged as she recited the words he'd so often parroted to her. Before he could frame a reply, Mellisynt turned and left the chapel. Inside the keep, she stopped beside a pillar darkened with age. Soon, she told herself. Soon.

Shaking off the tight knot of disgust Father Anselem always raised within her, Mellisynt spurred herself to action. A quick summons sent four men-at-arms to the dank, locked cellars where Henri had stored his less valuable goods, with orders to locate her bride chests and bring them to her *solar.* When the panting men placed the chests in the center of her tiny room some time later, Mellisynt knelt beside them. She ran her fingers over the great iron hasps, then fumbled through Henri's heavy key ring to find the ones that would unlock her youth.

"Ahh, my lady, what colors!" her elderly maid gasped when the lid lifted to reveal a rainbow of shimmering silks.

Mellisynt reached out to stroke the rich cerulean and amber and crimson brocades. She tried not to think of the child bride who'd stood, excited and nervous, while a bevy of chattering maids fitted her trousseau. That girl had disappeared, along with the colorful gowns, within weeks of arriving at Trémont.

"Oh, no," the maid cried as she held a heavy damask outer robe up to the flickering oil lamp. "The worms have been at them. This bliaut is falling apart."

"Aye, so it is."

With a sigh, Mellisynt sat back on her heels. Her bride clothes, riddled with rot, seemed to symbolize her life. Like the rich, glowing garments, she'd been locked away these ten years and more to wither and decay. She reached out to stroke the figured silk. It felt cool and smooth under her fingertips. Despite its wretched condition, the emerald fabric shone in the weak light. Taking strength from its brave color, Mellisynt gave the maid a determined smile.

"Open the other chest, Maude. Mayhap we can find some gowns that careful stitching can make whole."

Between them, she and Maude salvaged two serviceable sets of robes. Knowing nothing of current styles, Mellisynt could only hope her bliauts, with their flowing, many-gored skirts and side-laced bodices, would not disgrace her in her new lord's eyes. The gowns would require careful stitching and patching to hide time's depredations, stitching that she and Maude would have to do by candle later that night. She spread them across a narrow wooden bench to air.

Buried in the bottom of one chest she found a chainse of fine bleached wool, still in its protective sheeting. She stroked the delicate gold embroidery embellishing its sleeves and hem. She was tempted to disrobe and don it now, if only to go to her betrothal with an elegant shift under her shapeless gray robe. At that moment, a breathless maid came running with the announcement that the FitzHugh awaited below. Mellisynt put the chainse aside, a smile curving her lips. Soon, she told herself, with a last look at the bright gold stitchery.

"And thereto I plight thee my troth."

FitzHugh eyed the still woman who knelt beside him as he slipped the heavy gold betrothal ring onto her thin finger. The folds of her old-fashioned wimple hung forward, hiding her face from view. As if from a distance, he heard his promise to care for her person and possessions echo against the dank chapel walls. His jaw clenched, and he released her hand. The priest gave a thin-lipped nod and continued the service.

Sweet Jesu, FitzHugh swore under his breath, if only the pompous cleric would cease his pontificating about the sanctity of marriage and a wife's duty. The man was dragging out what should have been a short exchange of promises into a high sermon. He should know this ceremony was a mere formality, a sop to the lady's estate and the power of the church. The duke of Brittany himself had signed the betrothal documents last eventide. FitzHugh had left immediately afterward to claim the lady. He didn't need this red-faced priest's sermonizing to sanctify what he already held as his own.

Cold from the stone floor seeped through his furred surcoat and into his bones. FitzHugh stifled a grimace. If he knelt much longer, the half-healed wound in his left knee would stiffen, and he'd be lucky to rise unassisted. He closed his ears to the cleric's droning and fastened his attention instead on a small tapestry hanging above the altar. Illuminated by tall candles, its rose, blue and gold threads glowed like jewels and added a touch of light and beauty to the dark chapel. The only touch, FitzHugh thought, shifting on the hard floor. Old Henri obviously hadn't shared much of his huge wealth with the church.

"And so, too, I plight thee my troth."

Lady Mellisynt spoke her vows in a low, steady voice. FitzHugh glanced down once more, but her bent head and heavy wimple obscured her face. His gaze caught only the tip of a short, rounded nose. He frowned, realizing that he had just joined his life to that of a woman he would scarce have recognized in a crowd. He tried to recall some distinguishing feature from their brief meeting in the dim, shadow-filled hall. The fact that he couldn't remember the color of her eyes, or even the shape of her face, added to his disgruntlement.

Nor could he discern much of her figure from the gray robe that hung, loose and formless, from her shoulders to trail the floor. Unadorned with even a single stitch of embroidery or patch of color, the gown completely enveloped the woman beside him. Lord Henri had spent as little on his wife as on his surroundings, FitzHugh thought with wry derision. And now the old man's relic, in the person of this same Lady Mellisynt, would bring all that hoarded wealth to him.

She was just the bride he needed, the duke had crowed. A rich widow, with no children, and no bothersome father or brothers to claim her estate. A recluse, from all reports, shut away from the world, caring for her elderly, infirm

husband. Not in the first flush of youth, certainly, but still
well within her prime childbearing years.

The duke had ruthlessly overridden FitzHugh's vehe-
ment assertion that he had no desire to take another wife,
his first having given him a taste of marriage that made the
bloody flux seem pleasant by comparison. At length, his
liege had admitted what FitzHugh had suspected all along.
In addition to rewarding his friend for faithful service,
Duke Geoffrey wanted to make sure a loyal vassal held the
border fortress of Trémont. FitzHugh shifted once more on
the stone floor, firmly suppressing the wish that the lady of
Trémont had chosen the cloister instead of marriage, and
so spared him the necessity of taking her to wife. 'Twas
done now; he'd make the best of it. He sent the priest an
impatient look, willing him to be done.

At long last, the friar granted them a reluctant blessing
and concluded the ceremony. Clenching his teeth against
the ache in his knee, FitzHugh rose and offered the lady his
hand. She placed her half-mittened fingers over his, gathered her voluminous skirts in her other hand, and rose. Her
fingers were cold as ice. Together, they walked through the
dim corridor and into the great hall. The small crowd of
FitzHugh's men and Trémont retainers who had been
hastily gathered to witness the ceremony followed.

Lady Mellisynt lifted her face to his. "I've ordered wine
and meats set out. If you do not object, I would ask my
people to join us to... to honor the occasion."

Her eyes were green, FitzHugh noted, flecked with bits
of brown and surrounded by thick sable lashes. They provided the only color in a pale face framed by an unbecom-
ing white linen chinstrap and headrail. The outmoded head
covering made her look older than the two-and-twenty
years he knew her to be.

"They are welcome," he responded, willing back a mind-
dulling weariness. Two savage days of fighting, followed by
a relentless ride to claim the widow, had sapped even his
endurance. He ached to shed his mail and tumble headlong into the soft bed he'd seen in old Henri's apartments,

but a lady of her rank deserved what little celebration this hurried repast would provide.

She stood beside him as they accepted the nervous good wishes of the castle folk and hearty congratulations of his own men. A stooped old knight who served as Trémont's steward was among the last to greet them. FitzHugh gave Sir Bertrand a brief nod of mingled respect and caution. He'd spent the previous hour with the man, reviewing the castle's defenses. The knight's knees might be bowed by age and years in the saddle, and his hands so arthritic that they would wield a weapon only with great pain, but FitzHugh didn't doubt he could still put a sword to good use, aches or no.

"Are you sure this marriage is to your wishes, my lady?" Sir Bertrand asked, with the bluntness of an old retainer. "I have not many moves left in me, but I would use them gladly in combat with this mountain disguised as a man, do you say the word."

The lady cast FitzHugh a quick glance, then turned back to the old knight.

"Nay, Sir Bertrand," she said, laying a firm hand on his arm. "There's no need to fight. I spoke the vows of my free will."

"Harrumph," the steward grunted, clearly not quite convinced.

"Truly," she told him. "I . . . I am well served."

"Well, if not now, ye soon will be," he muttered, running his eyes over FitzHugh's massive form. "At least that much will come of this hasty union."

The old man stumped away, and FitzHugh watched as a wave of color washed over his lady's face. Biting her lips, she stared straight ahead.

"Thank you, my lord," she managed after a few moments.

"For what?"

"For not taking umbrage at Sir Bertrand," she replied stiffly. "He's stood as friend and protector to me for many years."

"Why would I fault a man for holding true to his oath to serve you and Trémont? If he swears allegiance to me, as your lord, I will be well satisfied. I plan to leave him in charge during our absence. One of my own men will stand lieutenant to him."

A rueful smile curved her lips. "And your 'lieutenant' will see that your orders are obeyed, although Sir Bertrand is nominally in charge."

FitzHugh nodded, thinking that perhaps this pale, demure woman was not such a mouse after all. "I said I didn't fault him for holding true to you and Trémont. I did not say I trusted him completely."

"In any case, I thank you," she said once more.

"There's no need for thanks," FitzHugh told her. Weariness rasped through his voice like the sound of a rusty boot nail scraped across cobbles, making it sound harsher than he intended. "I know well enough a good soldier when I meet one."

Her green eyes flashed at his curt tone, deepening to a color that reminded him of a forest glen at the edge of a summer's night. Almost immediately, thick lashes swept down to brush against her cheeks. FitzHugh was left to wonder if he'd imagined the glow that had infused her pale face with something approaching comeliness.

He eyed her speculatively before turning to respond to the priest's greeting. Lady Mellisynt slipped away with a murmured excuse about needing to see to the tapping of another wine cask.

"I am informed that you leave Trémont immediately, my lord," the cleric offered, his sausagelike fingers wrapped around a goblet of wine as if he feared someone would wrest it from him.

"Aye," FitzHugh responded coolly. His knee still ached from this man's damned sermonizing. Moreover, he had little respect for one who appeared to value his dinner more than he did his flock.

"I've long kept the castle records and accounts," Father Anselem continued. "Henri, God rest his soul, entrusted me with most decisions concerning the business of the keep. I am prepared to continue such office for you, as well.''

"Such duties are usually a steward's responsibility," FitzHugh observed, taking a sip of his wine.

The priest bent forward, bringing with him a waft of garlic. "Lord Henri lost faith in Sir Bertrand. He intended to send him away. The man grew too particular in his attentions."

Father Anselem nodded across the hall, to where the old knight stood in conversation with the lady of the keep. The steward's stooped frame leaned over the Lady Mellisynt in a protective manner.

FitzHugh eyed the pair for a long moment, before turning back to the priest. When he spoke, his voice held a coldness that had set more than one man-at-arms to trembling. "My impression of Sir Bertrand is that he is a worthy knight."

"He is, he is," the priest sputtered, his color draining. "'Tis not his fault, after all. Most men are weak when a daughter of Eve beckons with warm smiles and sin in her eyes."

FitzHugh set his cup down on the wooden table with a slow, deliberate movement. "Do you imply that the Lady Mellisynt encourages him to dishonor himself and her?"

The cleric took a hasty step back, as if a chasm yawned suddenly at his feet. "Nay, she does not," he gasped. "No more than she did with any of the others Henri sent away. She cannot help what she is."

He stumbled backward as FitzHugh moved toward him with the silent menace of a panther.

"She is my betrothed wife, priest. I will hear no more of what rightly belongs in a confessional, if anywhere."

FitzHugh stood stiff and silent while the man scuttled away. A sour taste filled his mouth, and memories echoed in his mind of other, equally sanctimonious holy men reviling the woman who had born him for her loose, immoral ways. He picked up his goblet once more, draining it in one long swallow. His knee throbbed with a sharp, steady pain, his eyes felt gritty from lack of sleep, and his patience was suddenly worn thin.

The Lady Mellisynt cast him an uncertain look from across the hall. She began wending her way through dispersing servitors, scattered benches, and boar hounds rooting in the rushes. In her shapeless gown and confining head covering, she looked like a damn nun, FitzHugh thought. There was little in either her manner or her person to credit the wanton the priest had hinted at. If he hadn't seen that brief flash of green fire in her eyes, quickly hidden, he would have thought her too dull to raise any man's interest, let alone his rod. Yet now, for the first time, he found himself seeing her as a woman, not simply a widow.

"I ask your permission to retire, my lord. I have packing yet to do if we are to leave at dawn."

"Granted," FitzHugh replied, running his eyes over her impassive face. "I bid thee good-night."

He lifted her hand and gave it a quick salute. Her skin was soft and surprisingly warm under his lips. He caught a brief, elusive fragrance of gillyflowers. The old miser had trained his young wife well, he thought cynically. She didn't squander his coins on expensive perfumes of musk or sandalwood. As he watched her climb the winding stone staircase that led to her *solar*, FitzHugh wondered why the thought didn't bring the satisfaction it should.

Chapter Two

Mellisynt rose before dawn the next day. Shivering in the damp cold, she threw a thin wool mantle across her shoulders and knelt for her morning prayers. Hard stone cut into her knees and added fervency to her plea for God's blessing this day. Scrambling to her feet, she poked through the layer of ice crusting her water bowl and splashed her face. For a moment she toyed with the idea of summoning Maude to attend her, but excitement and years of habit quickly overrode the impulse. She'd dressed herself in the dark before tending to her husband for too many years to need any assistance from the old woman now.

Weak, gray sunlight drifted through the window slits as she pulled on layers of garments. Over a thigh-length linen tunic, she donned the embroidered chainse, reveling in the sinfully soft feeling of it. Its long, tight sleeves hugged her thin wrists and came down over the backs of her hands in decorated points. With a heady sense of anticipation, Mellisynt pulled on one of her refurbished robes. The heavy silk settled over her like a thick amber cloud. She tugged at the bodice ties, frowning at the extra folds of material around her waist. The gold brocade, shot through with colored threads, had once flattered her rounded, girlish figure. Now it hung as loose as a sack from shoulder to hips and dragged the stone floor. Her frown disappeared as she swished the material around, and a dimpled smile creased her cheeks. 'Twas more like a feed bag than a gown, but at least it had color other than the accursed gray she'd worn all these years.

Slipping on a pair of warm hose, Mellisynt slid her feet into serviceable leather boots. From long custom, she reached for the starched headrail and chinstrap lying on the wooden bench. Her fingers grasped the stiff linen, then stilled. She hated the constrictive head covering, but had long worn it at Henri's explicit wish. Drawing in a deep breath, she crushed the stiff fabric between her fingers. She opened her fist and watched the crumpled headrail fall, to lie like a broken blossom on the stone floor. Nudging it aside with one foot, Mellisynt tossed a light veil over her braided hair. A thin circlet of hammered bronze secured the veil over her forehead and her thick, coiled braids. She grabbed a heavy wool mantle and hurried out of the tower chamber without a backward glance.

FitzHugh awaited her in the inner bailey. Mellisynt stood on the steps of the keep, her eyes narrowed against the morning sun, and watched him approach. Sweet Mother, he was big! He strode across the cobbled bailey, carrying the weight of his chain mail as if it were no more than light cloth. Over the armor he wore a squirrel-lined surcoat in deep azure velvet, slit high on either side for ease in riding. The rich velvet was emblazoned on the front with a snarling black bear sewn in glittering ebony and gold threads. As he approached, a winter breeze ruffled through hair so dark it seemed to throw back the sun's light.

"Good morrow, lady wife."

He bent to give her the kiss of greeting, and his lips felt warm and rough against her skin. A faint aura of leather, damp wool and raw maleness teased her nostrils.

"Have you broken your fast?" she asked, swallowing.

"Aye, before the sun came up. Sir Bertrand and I wanted to inspect the men. We'll leave as soon as you're ready."

Her heart pounded. "I'm ready."

Mellisynt turned to take her leave of the men and women who had been her sole companions for so long. Maude, too old and too wedded to Trémont to journey with her lady, wept copious tears and fell into Mellisynt's arms.

Surprised at the painful tug it gave her to bid farewell to the castle people, she held Maude tight. She had dreamed of leaving this keep for so long she hadn't expected to feel any regret at all. Still, these people were all the family she had. She gave Maude a last hug and accepted Sir Bertrand's gruff farewell with a warm smile. As she turned to the priest, her lips thinned, then tilted upward in a determined curve.

"May God keep you, Father Anselem."

"And you, lady." His curt rejoinder held little affection. "Remember well all I have taught you."

"How could I not?" she responded, lifting wide, innocent eyes to his. "You've been most diligent in your instruction."

Father Anselem's brow creased, and the familiar red began to rise up the rolls of flesh swaddling his neck.

"We must make haste."

FitzHugh's deep voice spurred the priest to reluctant action. He laid his hands on Mellisynt's bowed head and muttered a brief prayer for her safety on the journey. He ended with the grudging hope that she fulfill her creator's purpose and proved more fertile in this marriage than her first.

Mellisynt added her silent, fervent prayer to his, then rose, as gracefully as she could in her heavy skirts and cloak. Her breath caught when FitzHugh took her arm and led her to the stone mounting block. A nervous fluttering began in her stomach as she eyed the caparisoned horse, held in place by a man-at-arms. Surely the animal was not as large or evil-natured as it appeared. Just because the gray gelding watched her approach with a small, mean eye, that was no reason to be afraid. And if it refused to sidle up to the block, despite repeated slaps on a huge, muscled rump, she shouldn't suppose it was as reluctant to take her on its back as she was to mount it. Mellisynt wiped her suddenly moist palms down the sides of her cloak.

"Help the lady mount."

FitzHugh's growled order to a waiting page made both the young boy and Mellisynt jump. The golden-haired youth moved forward to hold a wooden stirrup and looked at her expectantly. Taking a deep breath, she ascended the stairs. She slid her left foot into the stirrup, then whipped it out again quickly when the beast shied away.

FitzHugh's brows drew together as he walked around to heave his shoulder into the gray's far side. It snorted and sidled back to the block. Once more the page held out the stirrup. This time Mellisynt got her foot well in and both hands on the curved pommel before the horse danced away. Hanging on with grim determination, she managed to wrap her right knee around the wooden hook designed to give purchase on the precarious sidesaddle. Her buttocks landed in the leather seat with an audible thump.

FitzHugh glanced up, a look of pained resignation adding to the lines in his face, not quite erased by a night's sleep. Mellisynt managed a tight smile before he shook his head and turned away. He swung onto his own mount with a smooth grace that belied his size and the deadweight of his armor.

Mellisynt didn't look back as her horse clattered over the drawbridge. She couldn't, even had she wished to, since the swaying, shifting mountain of muscle under her claimed all her attention. Clinging to the pommel with both hands, she braced herself against the steep descent. Small, sharp stones rattled under her horse's hooves. Occasionally one pitched over the side of the track and down the sheer hundred foot drop to the river below. When her horse edged terrifyingly close to the side, FitzHugh jerked the gray in with a sharp oath and flung a hard look over his shoulder.

"By the saints, woman, can you not control your horse?"

"Nay," she said simply.

His dark brows furrowed. "How the devil did you get into the town to do your trading if you don't ride? Surely you didn't attempt a wagon or litter on this narrow path."

"I didn't go into the town," she answered with breathless distraction, peering at the sheer drop with the fascination a rabbit might give to the widening jaws of a serpent. She heard FitzHugh's disbelieving snort, but was too busy watching the perilous placement of her horse's hooves near the path's edge to essay any response.

Gradually the track widened enough for Mellisynt to relax and enjoy the soaring vista. The river Vilaine lay below them, a slice of silver meandering through winter-browned earth. All around her stretched a pale blue sky, unimpeded by walls. Her breath came in little excited pants that hung on the crisp air, like the puffs of clouds in the distance. When the cavalcade rounded the last turn and the road flattened out before them, she was almost sorry to lose the breathtaking view.

She was most definitely sorry when they had passed through the huddle of mud huts and timbered buildings that nestled at the foot of Trémont and FitzHugh quickened the pace. The beast beneath her broke into a canter, causing the saddle to slap against her with a jolting rhythm that jarred her teeth. Grimly Mellisynt set her jaw and tried to fit her body's movement to that of the horse, without notable success. Reminding herself that a little discomfort was a small price to pay for her freedom, she concentrated on the scenery once more.

By the second hour, she'd lost any interest in the view. Her sole focus was the gathering soreness between her lower extremities. With her mount's every step, the chainse, bunched under her thighs, rubbed against her skin. The thin wool, which had seemed so soft and fine only hours before, now scratched like the roughest serge. She shifted precariously, trying to ease her aching buttocks and sore thighs, only to shrink back in the saddle when FitzHugh cast her a frowning look over his shoulder.

"Are you all right?" he asked, a sharp edge to his voice.

The inclination to tell him just how not right she was slipped away. Mellisynt straightened her aching back.

"I'm fine."

"There's a stream up ahead where you can rest and refresh yourself."

A surge of relief rushed through her, followed immediately by doubt. She feared that once off this thrice-damned beast, she'd never be able to climb back on again.

FitzHugh drew up a short time later in a wide clearing crossed by a narrow, ice-encrusted stream. With a brusque order, he sent men to guard the road's approaches, then slid from his saddle and tossed his reins to his squire. Two long strides brought him to her side.

"I would suggest you stretch your legs and make use of the bushes while you may. We've many miles yet to travel."

Huge hands closed around her waist and lifted her easily from the saddle. Mellisynt opened her mouth to give thanks, only to close it on a squeak of dismay when her legs crumpled beneath her. She grabbed his surcoat with two fists to keep from tumbling to the rutted road. FitzHugh swept her up in his arms and carried her to the icy stream.

"I'm sorry," she said in a stiff voice as he set her down on a fallen log and bent on one knee to break the stream's crust with his dagger's hilt.

He paused in the act of filling a horn cup with clear, sparkling water. "The fault is mine, not yours. I should have inquired whether you are used to riding, and made proper arrangements."

He passed her the cup and leaned a forearm across his knee, watching as she sipped. The water slid down Mellisynt's throat with a sharp, painful coldness.

"I have no excuse for such carelessness," he continued slowly, "except that I've been so long in the company of soldiers and mercenaries I seem to have forgotten the simple courtesies women require. Rest a few moments, and I'll rig a pillion for you."

She stayed motionless, held as much by surprise as by the ache in her legs. The last thing she'd expected from this man, whose fierce demeanor matched his reputation, was forebearance. Her eyes narrowed against the sun, she watched as he bent at the waist for his squire to pull off his surcoat. Folding the furred velvet robe once, then again, FitzHugh strapped it behind his saddle. As he labored, Mellisynt ran her eyes up and down his body. In his thigh-length mailed shirt, with its hood pushed back around the strong column of his throat, he looked like one of the giants of childhood tales, all scaled in silver. If she'd searched throughout Brittany, she couldn't have found a husband more different from the thin-shanked, white-haired Henri of Trémont. The thought sent a thrill deep into her belly. Before she could decide whether the sensation betokened fear or joy, he returned to her side.

"Come, I'll take you into the bushes." One massive, mailed fist reached down for her hand.

"Nay," Mellisynt gasped, gripping the gauntlet and struggling to her feet. "I'll see to my own needs."

"There's no room for false modesty between us," he said, his patience obviously waning. "We are husband and wife, after all."

"We are not yet husband and wife," Mellisynt replied, lifting her chin. "I would have privacy."

Wide green eyes met narrowed blue ones in an unspoken contest of wills. FitzHugh took a step forward, then stopped abruptly as a shout rang across the clearing.

"Surrender your arms. You are surrounded."

FitzHugh whirled, his hand flying to his sword. He pulled it free of the scabbard and held it low in front of him, in a movement so swift and instinctive Mellisynt stepped back startled. Her legs wobbled under her, and only the sheerest effort of will kept her upright. A vicious curse seared her ears as FitzHugh reached back and grabbed her wrist in an iron vise. He gave a swift tug, pulling her behind his mail-clad body.

At the far side of the clearing, a band of foot soldiers stepped from behind the trees. Each man held a drawn bow, arrow notched, string taut. Their ranks parted, and a mounted knight rode forward. The morning sun glinted on his armor and his visored helmet. A gilded swan, silver on a field of gold, shimmered on his emerald surcoat.

"We wish you no harm. Yield the lady, and I'll allow you and your men to depart."

Mellisynt's heart slammed against her breast. Her fingers curled against the chill of FitzHugh's mail, and she sucked sharp, icy air into her lungs in a painful gasp. The rattle of metal behind her made her head jerk around. FitzHugh's men-at-arms drew up beside their lord, swords ready, shields high.

"I yield to no man." Her lord's voice rang sure and strong across the winter air.

"Then I will take her, FitzHugh."

Mellisynt glanced up at the man beside her. His blue eyes were narrowed against the sun, and his jaw was set in a rigid line. A muscle worked in his cheek, and a slow, dangerous smile lifted one corner of his lip.

"She is mine, Beauchamp. What I have, I hold."

"You'll not hold her long, bastard, nor Trémont, either. Prince Richard sent me to claim her and her lands for Normandy."

FitzHugh nodded to his squire, a solemn, brown-haired youth standing at his shoulder.

"Take the lady back to the horses, out of harm's way. Guard her well."

As she stumbled toward the rear with the squire, Mellisynt swung between fear and a slow, growing sense of outrage. She was beginning to feel much like a soup bone tossed to the floor between two snarling boar hounds. Her heart pounded, and she peered over the youth's shoulder to see how her fate would be decided.

The knight rode farther into the clearing, his horse lifting its hooves high to pick a way across the winter stubble. He stopped halfway to the small stream and raised his visor. White teeth gleamed through a thick, silky brown mustache, and his eyes fixed on FitzHugh with mocking challenge.

"My men ring the clearing. We outnumber you twice over. Surrender the lady now, without bloodshed, and go your way."

"She is my betrothed wife, Beauchamp. 'Twill take more than your puny force to wrest from me what is mine."

A surprised expression crossed the knight's face, visible even to Mellisynt's nervous gaze.

"Jesu, you wasted no time."

"And you wasted too much. You were ever one to dally late abed with the wenches."

At FitzHugh's lazy drawl, a rueful grin twisted the other man's face.

"Well, I suppose there's nothing for it. I shall have to make the lady a widow before she's yet again a wife."

"You may try, Beauchamp. Swords or lances?"

Mellisynt's breath caught in her throat as the knight slid his sword out of his scabbard and lifted the hilt to his face in a mock salute. Her frightened glance flew to FitzHugh. He stood straight in the morning light, his dark head bare, his mail glinting in the sun. He turned to take his shield from the man-at-arms who had brought it forward. To her astonishment, a grin creased his tanned cheeks. He looked for all the world like a man about to engage in a game of spillikins instead of a fight to the death!

Her eyes whipped to the other knight, now dismounted and advancing to the center of the field. He, too, wore a smile of gleeful anticipation. Holy Mary, they were enjoying themselves! Her life hung in the balance, her future, and these two thought 'twas a matter of sport!

A pounding echo of thudding hooves far down the road cut off her chaotic thoughts. FitzHugh caught the sound, as well, and paused in the act of pulling on his helmet.

"Reinforcements, Beauchamp?" he taunted. "Do you have so little faith in your skills you must call for help?"

"They're not mine," the other knight responded with a frown. He called a low command to his men, and they formed into two ranks, spread in a semicircle on either side of their leader. The front rank knelt, the rear stood with bows aimed over the heads of their companions. FitzHugh's men split into two groups and moved to either flank. Totally bewildered, Mellisynt watched the two opposing forces melt into one, all poised to meet the new threat.

"Come, lady," the squire said urgently. "You must get to the center, among the baggage horses. Your lord and this knight have fought together many times before. They will protect you."

Within seconds, Mellisynt found herself surrounded by a solid wall of men and horses. The two knights, both mounted now, all but blocked her view of the road. As the steady drum of approaching hooves grew louder, she clenched her fists into the folds of her wool cloak. Through the thin half mittens, her nails cut sharp crescents into her palms. Fear, sharp and metallic, rose in her throat. A sudden longing for the safety of Trémont's thick walls rose, only to be quashed instantly. She'd wanted to be outside those walls these ten years. She'd not whimper in terror at the first hint of danger. She unclenched her fingers, one by one.

A small troop pounded into the clearing. Three golden lions on a field of red were clearly visible through the mud spattering the leader's surcoat.

"My lord, 'tis the king's courier!"

FitzHugh nodded at his squire's relieved exclamation and slid the lethal shaft of hammered damascened steel back into its leather casing. The knight beside him did the same. Both waited while the messenger drew to a halt in front of them.

"The king demands an end to the war and has called his sons to England to negotiate peace," he said, panting. "Duke Geoffrey and Richard Lionheart have declared truce. Couriers ride to the far borders with orders to cease all hostilities."

Mellisynt felt a breath she hadn't realized she was holding rush from her constricted lungs.

The courier rubbed a weary hand over his face and turned to FitzHugh. "Duke Geoffrey is in Nantes. He asks that you come to the city straightaway so that he can witness your marriage before he sails with the evening tide. He bade me give you word if we should meet on the road.''

FitzHugh stared thoughtfully at the courier for a few moments, then thanked him with a silver coin drawn from the pouch attached to his leather sword belt. Turning to the knight at his side, he gave him a look that was half regret, half amusement.

''Well, Beauchamp, 'twould appear we must postpone our meeting.''

The other man leaned a forearm across his pommel. ''It would appear so. 'Tis just as well. The last time we met in the lists, you sent me tumbling from my horse.''

He hesitated, his rogue's smile fading. ''This is an accursed war. With you sworn to the duke, and me to the prince, I knew we'd have to meet eventually. I much dreaded it.''

FitzHugh nodded. ''I'm glad the war is done. Godspeed, Roger.''

The other knight raised his hand in farewell and wheeled his mount. He rode through the ranks, stopping beside Mellisynt. Merry brown eyes gleamed down at her.

''I'm sorry I was too late to keep you from pledging yourself to such an ugly, distempered rogue as FitzHugh. Mayhap I will see you at court and offer consolation on your lot.''

Mellisynt gasped at the laughing invitation in his eyes. She now understood FitzHugh's earlier taunt about this man's dallying with the wenches. His devilish grin and glinting eyes would turn any maid's head.

She stammered something in reply, and he was gone.

Her legs wobbly, Mellisynt leaned against one of the packhorses and waited for her turbulent emotions to subside. Truly, she had not anticipated that her first day outside Trémont's gray walls would be quite so full of excitement. The men-at-arms dispersed slowly to check gear and girths in preparation for departure.

After a few moments, FitzHugh approached her, his dark brows drawn together in what Mellisynt was coming to believe was his habitual expression. In the midst of her inner turmoil, she wondered what he'd look like if those chiseled lips once smiled at her. He took her arm in a firm grasp and led her aside, away from the men.

"Were you part of this?"

The low, growled question took her by surprise.

"Part of what?"

"This ambush. 'Twas well planned, my lady. Beauchamp knew he could not take you from Trémont once I secured it. He knew, also, I would leave half my force to garrison the castle. 'Twas logical he would try to take you while we were on the road."

Stunned, she stared up at the harsh planes of his face. "Why…why would you think I had aught to do with such a plan?"

"You were most anxious to go into the bushes alone. Did you expect him here, in this clearing?"

Mellisynt's jaw dropped. Recovering quickly, she closed it with a snap and gave him an icy glare.

"I will tell you once, my lord, and this once only. I knew naught of any ambush. I pledged you my troth, and I hold to my word."

His blue eyes narrowed on her face for a long moment. Mellisynt felt a surge of fury at his scrutiny.

"Is a woman's oath of so little value that you do not believe me?" she asked, her voice cold with disdain.

"I've found it wise not to place my trust in any woman's words, lady wife."

"I am not any woman," Mellisynt snapped. "You'd do well to remember that, if our union is to proceed."

A flicker of surprise crossed his face, as if a puppy had suddenly turned and bitten him on the ankle. His hand reached out to cup her chin, the mailed gauntlet bruising against her skin.

"Our union proceeds. You are mine now, and what I have, I hold. 'Tis the motto of my house. You'd do well to remember *that*."

Mellisynt blinked at the lazy menace in his voice. For a long moment, silence hung heavy between them. At last the hard grip on her chin loosened. Bending, FitzHugh swept her once more into his arms and headed toward his sorrel stallion.

"You have a most forward manner," he observed casually. "Did Lord Henri beat you often?"

Mellisynt's chin lifted. "Nay, never," she replied. Henri's way had been to lock her in her bare, stone-walled *solar* for days of fasting and prayer, but this arrogant knight didn't need to know that, she decided.

"Hold, Voyager," he ordered the huge destrier as he lifted her up onto the pillion rigged behind his saddle. His hands gripped her thighs, steadying her until she found a secure seat. With a terse order to hold fast, he mounted and set off at a loping canter.

By the time they crested the last hill outside Nantes, Mellisynt clung to him with aching, cold-deadened hands. Both legs were blessedly numb, and her feet felt like blocks of ice. She managed to ignore her discomfort enough to lean around FitzHugh's bulk and survey the sprawling city, displayed to advantage in the early-afternoon sunlight. A crenellated tower, a relic of an earlier age, stood in solitary splendor on a high hill, watching over the city below like a careful parent. The city itself was enclosed by high stone walls and crisscrossed with spacious streets. In the distance the Loire flowed, muddy and sluggish with winter's ebb as it wound its last few miles to the sea. Quays lined the river's wide banks and sported ships of every size and description, from fishing vessels to merchant transports.

A short time later, FitzHugh carried her out of the frost-filled air into a two-story timbered house on a narrow side street. Warmth from a roaring fire in the great room reached out to welcome her, and Mellisynt settled into a cushioned chair with a grateful sigh. Waiting servants brought cups of hot, spiced ale, and a rolled parchment for FitzHugh. He leaned toward the fire, straining to see the scribbled words, then rolled the document up with a snap.

"You have two hours, lady, before we must be at the abbey. The duke will stand witness for you, as he is your overlord, as well as mine. I am requested to meet with him immediately. Can you manage?"

"Aye," Mellisynt told him, knowing she had no choice. She prayed she'd have back the use of her legs by then. She would not face the duke weak and trembling, as she had so many years before. Her hands tightened on the chair arms as she recalled her long-held image of the flame-haired man who had laughed as he handed a frightened girl to Henri of Trémont for his use.

"Good," FitzHugh responded. "I'll leave my squire to assist you. Ian will escort you to the abbey when you're ready."

Mellisynt watched his broad shoulders disappear through the door, then rested her head against the chair's high back and released a long sigh. If ever there had been a bride who felt less like wedding and bedding this night, she'd be much surprised.

Chapter Three

FitzHugh led his small escort through the cobbled streets, his thoughts on the white-faced, wilting woman he'd just left. God's blood, he hoped she would recover from the grueling ride. He had no desire to take a limp, unmoving lump of flesh to his bed this night. Nor any night, he grimaced, thinking of his first wife.

His horse slipped on a cobble, dipping its powerful shoulders. FitzHugh shifted in the saddle and let the stallion find its footing. With deliberate effort, he forced his thoughts from his last wife to his next.

A thoughtful frown creased his brow as he remembered the pale, quiet woman who had exchanged vows with him last eventide. He was beginning to suspect there was a more complex creature than he'd first supposed swaddled in those baggy robes. The nagging suspicion that she'd known about the ambush would not be dismissed. Her eyes had sparked with a pure green flame when he challenged her, and she'd sworn she held to her pledge. Still, he had little faith in women's oaths.

As his troop clattered into the courtyard of the duke's château, FitzHugh shrugged off the aborted ambush. If the Lady Mellisynt had thought to avoid her fate, she'd missed the chance. He'd ensure she had no other in the future. He strode through the château's maze of corridors, his spurs clicking against white-and-black tiles.

"FitzHugh! I began to think you stopped to bed your rich widow before you wedded her!"

Geoffrey Plantagenet, duke of Brittany, earl of Richmond, fourth son of King Henry II and Queen Eleanor of England, detached himself from a group of battle-stained knights. He greeted his vassal with a slap on the back that nearly sent him to his knees.

"Nay, lord," FitzHugh ground out. Much as he loved Geoffrey, he often wondered how he'd survived their friendship. Tall, boisterous, possessed of his father's red hair and his mother's smiling charm, Geoffrey had the strength of two oxen in tandem, and the bullheadedness to match.

FitzHugh rolled his shoulders to ease the ache of Geoffrey's greeting. "We traveled more slowly than I had planned, as the lady was unused to riding."

"Well, if she was unused before to the feel of a horse between her legs, she'll soon grow accustomed," the duke told him, his voice booming. "To a damned rutting stallion."

FitzHugh shook his head at the laughter that rose around him. "More like the lady will refuse to let me in the same room, let alone her bed, if I don't get your final orders and retire to the baths. I've been so long in the saddle, my horse smells sweeter."

Geoffrey buffeted FitzHugh on the arm with high good humor. "Come, there's hot water aplenty in my chambers. You can bathe while we talk."

FitzHugh groaned in pure pleasure as he sank to his chin in hot, steaming water. Built especially to accommodate the duke's magnificent bulk, the tub took his long frame easily. Pages scurried out to clean his discarded armour and clothing while Geoffrey sprawled in a carved chair and surveyed his friend.

"Tell me true, Richard, is she bearable? I saw her only once, when she was but a mite. 'Twas a shame to give such tender flesh to Henri, but the old goat paid well for it, as you can imagine. How does she suit you?"

"She'll do." FitzHugh shrugged, then added dryly, "Though 'tis a little late to be worrying about it, after all but forcing the woman on me."

"You ungrateful sod," Geoffrey said, laughing. "Most men would jump at the chance for such a prize. And I know damn well you wouldn't have taken her, whether I wished it or nay, if you hadn't been satisfied with the woman."

FitzHugh merely grunted through the soap on his face. "I took her, but almost lost her on the road." He related briefly the aborted ambush attempt.

"You and Beauchamp! That would have been a contest worth seeing!"

"You wouldn't have thought the contest so sporting if I'd lost the lady and her lands to your brother," FitzHugh said with some dryness.

The duke waved a beefy hand, dismissing the possibility. "You've yet to lose in single combat, except to me, and then only because you held your hand. The woman's fate was as good as sealed." He paused, one brow arching in inquiry. "Why didn't you bring her here, to your apartments at the palace?"

"With your duchess and her ladies in the north, and you set to depart this night, I thought it best to settle her in someplace less grand."

"Hah," Geoffrey snorted. "You thought to avoid the trappings of a wedding feast and ceremonial bedding. You know full well those rogues out there, disguised as knights of the realm, would've filled your gut with meat, your head with wine and your lady with a disgust of all mankind by the time they were through."

FitzHugh grinned. "Aye, that thought did occur to me. I still remember the crack your own sweet-tempered duchess gave my skull when we carried you, drunk and slobbering, to her bed."

"'Tis a wonder I survived that bedding," Geoffrey recalled, his golden eyes gleaming. "The little witch has talons sharper than any falcon's."

FitzHugh ducked his head under the water, then began to soap the sweat and dirt from his arms and chest.

"Pull your thoughts from between your legs, my lord duke, and tell me where we stand on this matter of a truce. Do you yield the castles we've taken or wish me to hold them until the peace is settled?"

"We give them back. While you were off collecting your bride, I sent word to my brother that I'll restore his keeps, with suitable recompense, of course. The ransoms will make a goodly dent in the wealth he's collecting for his precious Crusade." Geoffrey smiled in grim satisfaction. "Richard Lionheart will think twice before daring to raise his sword in my lands again."

"He'll dare that, and more, when you threaten what is his," FitzHugh said quietly. "As would you."

The duke's smile faded, and he sprang up to pace the spacious apartment.

FitzHugh rubbed his scarred knee and listened with half an ear as Geoffrey began a lengthy catalogue of his older brother's iniquities. He was intimately familiar with the tangled web of strained loyalties and twisted allegiances that drove the Anjevin brood. He'd joined the royal household as a young man, having saved the duke's life in battle when they were both untried squires. Since that day, the bastard issue of a landless knight and the son of a king had been friends, as well as companions. For some twenty of his thirty-six years, FitzHugh had taken his sword and his heart willingly into battle beside Geoffrey. Only of late, as war followed insult and intrigue piled upon deception, had he begun to have doubts.

This latest war had added to his disquiet. Since Richard Lionheart had become heir to the throne of England, as well as to his ducal holdings of Normandy, Aquitaine, Maine and Anjou, he'd grown too powerful for his father's peace of mind. In an attempt to curb his strength, the king had commanded that he cede some of his lands to his youngest, landless brother, John. The Lionheart, of course, had refused. To enforce his command, the king had sent

Geoffrey to the Continent to take the disputed lands by force. In retaliation, the prince had struck ferociously into Geoffrey's own domains, savaging the land and luring border vassals to rebellion with promises of future gains.

Lords holding lands in vassalage to the two brothers had suddenly found themselves in the precarious position of having to choose sides between their next king and the emissary of the present king. 'Twas a tangled war of conflicting alliances, one that pitted vassal against overlord and friend against friend. It had raged for months, ravaging lands on both sides of the borders. Thank God the king had finally realized the fury he'd unleashed and demanded this halt to what was now a deadly feud between his sons. One that Geoffrey would someday carry further, FitzHugh feared, whatever the king's wishes. He closed his eyes and leaned against the headrest, wondering how he would choose if Geoffrey openly rebelled against his father. How could he choose between his king and his friend? He drew in a deep breath, reminding himself of all he owed the duke—including the rich widow even now awaiting him, he realized with a start.

"Jesu," he swore, hauling his dripping frame out of the tub. "If I don't move quickly, I'm like to keep the bride waiting at the abbey."

Geoffrey's eyes filled with laughter. "B'God, Fitz-Hugh, already you dance to the woman's tune. I grow anxious to meet her once more."

"Come and meet her, then. And hurry."

When he and Geoffrey and the duke's inevitable entourage crowded into the south transept of the abbey, it was empty of all save a patient bishop and his acolytes. Fitz-Hugh sent a page with a polite summons and took his place in front of the altar.

Lady Mellisynt and her escort arrived within moments. Coming forward at a slow, almost halting pace, she paused before the duke and sank into a shallow curtsy. It was a brief salute, the kind a serving maid might give a fat mer-

chant, not the obeisance a lady would give her overlord and
a prince of the realm.

FitzHugh's eyes narrowed at the deliberate slight, but the
duke ignored it. With a strong hand and a warm smile,
Geoffrey raised her from her curtsy.

"'Tis many years since last we met, my lady. How fortuitous that we do so again."

Her brow arched delicately. "Fortuitous, my lord? That
Henri of Trémont died and gave me once more into your
keeping? I suppose some might consider it so."

Geoffrey blinked at the irony in the lady's deliberate
words. Still, his charm had carried him through more than
one encounter with a difficult female. He smiled and led her
forward, toward the waiting knight.

"It grieves me that your marriage should be so rushed,
lady. When you journey to England, we'll celebrate with
feasting, and all due ceremony."

"This suits me well, my lord," Mellisynt told him, her
tone cool.

His smile slipped, and a hint of regal condescension
edged his voice. "But not me. Richard FitzHugh is my
friend, as well as my loyal knight. I would see him, and
you, fittingly honored."

"Let's just see the thing done," FitzHugh suggested
dryly.

The marriage took much less time than the betrothal had.
Within the hour, they were wed. With the prelate and other
vassals as witness, FitzHugh knelt, placed his hands between the duke's and gave homage for the fief of Trémont.
They then bid Geoffrey farewell and retired to share wine
and a hastily assembled wedding supper with the knights
invited to join them.

After a round of ribald toasts that brought a rush of
blood to Mellisynt's cheeks, the company settled down to
the serious business of eating. Servants carried a steady
parade of fragrant, steaming dishes from the kitchens below, and the knights' conversation picked up in volume
with the flow of wine and hot dishes. Having come from the

battlefield, the men were eager still to talk of booty and the satisfying ease with which the rebels' keeps crumbled under their determined assault. Caught up in the conversation, FitzHugh leaned forward, his bride all but forgotten.

Mellisynt picked at the trencher she shared with her new lord and listened to the talk of battles won and lost. Although she lived in a time when war was the accepted means of settling every quarrel, she had never experienced the violence these men seemed to relish. Henri of Trémont had paid scutage to his overlord, pleading age and infirmity as an excuse to avoid his knightly duties. He, and his wife, had stayed locked within his castle walls. The closest she had come to the edges of war were those heart-stopping moments in the clearing this morning.

Mellisynt listened to these knights' gruesome tales and tasted sparingly of the dishes set before her. She but sampled a bite of braised lamb served in a ring of truffles, artichokes and peas, and waved aside sauced sea bass and pickled herring. Only a bowl of delicate Bélon oysters tempted her. She pried a few of the flavorful, succulent mollusks from their half-opened shells and sopped up the sauce with a crust of thick wheat bread. The fire flickered low in the fireplace at the end of the hall, and still the men talked. Leaning both elbows on the cloth-covered table, she felt the weariness and emotion of the long day wash over her.

"Come, wife. I'd best take you to bed before you fall asleep in the sweetmeats."

Mellisynt blinked as a strong, firm hand took her arm and lifted her from the bench. A last round of hearty toasts and explicit advice followed them out of the main room. As they made their way down a narrow passage toward the private bedchambers, Mellisynt felt the glutinous oysters congeal within her stomach. Every stricture Henri had thrown at her, every virulent lecture Father Anselem had ever delivered on the subject of a wife's duty, echoed in her mind. She swallowed, telling herself that this husband was different from the first, that she could perform her duties without feeling the edges of her soul curl in despair. Even if his use of her body proved as loathsome as had Henri's, she would endure. She took a deep breath when FitzHugh closed the heavy wooden door behind them.

"Would you like wine?"

"Yes," she whispered. Flushing at her own timidity, she swallowed and said again, more steadily. "Yes, if you please."

FitzHugh's thick brows drew together as he poured a stream of amber wine into a silver goblet.

"There's no need to fear me, lady. I know I'm over-large, and not comely of face, but I won't hurt you if you give me no cause. Show yourself a dutiful wife, and we will contrive."

Mellisynt stiffened. Not yet wed three hours, and already he must needs instruct her in her wifely obligations. She took a deep, steadying swallow of wine. Placing the goblet on a high chest inlaid with ivory and gold mosaics, she nodded.

"I'll do my duty," she assured him in a level voice.

Reaching up, she tugged the veil from her head and pulled out the wooden pins that held her braids. Reddish ropes, thick as a man's wrist, tumbled down her back. Laying the veil across the chest, she began to work the ties that held her gown at either side.

"Do you wish me to ring for the women to help you prepare?"

Mellisynt looked up, surprise widening her eyes. "Prepare?"

"Forgive me, lady" came the sardonic reply. "I supposed you would wish privacy to ready yourself."

Uncertainty threaded through her. Was she supposed to don some special garment or apply some unguent? Henri had made her use what he called medicaments at first, but none had succeeded in sustaining the strength of his rod for very long. She'd not thought she would need such aids this night, with this man.

"I...I have no need... Nothing to prepare," she finally got out.

When FitzHugh shrugged, she shed her gown and chainse. Her hands reached for the edge of her undershift, then stilled. She cast a fleeting glance at the figure leaning against the far wall, his blue eyes surveying her body with interest, if not with the heated lust she'd often seen in Henri's avid stares. A shaft of feminine pique drove the unease from her belly. She might not have the soft curves of her youth, but her body was firm, and not totally despicable. She would not cower like some frightened virgin before his cool, assessing gaze.

Straightening, she pulled the shift over her head. The drafty air brought goose bumps to her naked flesh and puckered her nipples. Hastily removing her boots and woolen stockings, she climbed between the sheets. Her chin lifted a fraction as her eyes met FitzHugh's across the dim room.

He set his wine aside and crossed the room, working the buckle of his belt. Through half-lowered lids she watched him shrug out of the surcoat and the quilted gambeson beneath. He'd left off his mail shirt in honor of the occasion, she supposed. Untying the tapes of his chausses with quick, sure movements, he rolled them down, along with his braies. When he turned toward the bed, Mellisynt resisted the urge to shrink back against the pillows. In the dim firelight, he loomed huge and menacing. Where Henri had been all bone and white, withered flesh, this man was solid muscle covered with dark, curling hair. She dropped her eyes from his massive shoulders, down a chest marked by a tracery of faded scars, to a root lying thick and flaccid against his thigh. She bit back a gasp at its size.

FitzHugh tossed back the coverlet and slid into bed. The corn-husk mattress rustled and sagged with his weight. When he stretched his long legs out beside her, Mellisynt sucked in a ragged breath. Slowly she came up on her knees. Taking his manhood in both hands, she wet her lips and bent over him.

"What the devil are you doing?"

He grabbed her arm and jerked her upright. Mellisynt turned to him in blank astonishment.

"I but seek to raise your seed."

"Jesu," he swore. His grip on her arm tightened as he edged himself back to sit upright. "Just where did you learn that little whore's trick?"

"Whore's trick?" she gasped, pulling against the hurtful hold. Her uncovered breasts quivered with the cold and her awkward position. "I know not what whores do to swell a man's root! I know only that failure to rouse a husband is a sin. One I have done penance for often enough," she ended on a low, mutinous note.

A thunderous scowl darkened his features. "Do you tell me you were punished because your husband couldn't rise?"

Embarrassed and angry, she jerked her arm, but couldn't break his iron grip. His other hand shot out to take her chin and force her head around.

"Aye, my lord," she finally muttered. "I spent as many hours on my knees in the chapel as I did in my lord's bed."

Releasing her, FitzHugh threw the covers to one side and rose. With a hamlike fist on either hip, he growled down at her.

"Listen to me, lady wife. I don't need your mouth on me to make me swell."

He hesitated, then added, somewhat less forcefully. "Not unless you wish it. And from the look on your face, you did not."

Mellisynt wrapped the down coverlet around her chest and stared in bewildered consternation at the figure towering above her. Sweet Mother, did he give her a choice? After a long pause, she responded hesitantly.

"I will admit I went to Henri's bed with great reluctance. But that had much to do with the fact that he smelled like rancid cheese and oft made me gag."

She paused, biting her lower lip. A slow tide of heat rose up her neck, and she looked away. "Your scent is passing pleasant, my lord."

When long moments passed in silence, Mellisynt looked up to see a tinge of red coloring FitzHugh's prominent cheekbones. His mouth curled in a wry smile that altered the harsh planes of his face into something resembling handsomeness.

"I will admit to bathing and dousing myself in Geoffrey's costliest perfume in your honor." The smile widened into a lopsided grin.

To her amazement, Mellisynt felt an answering smile tug at her lips. In all her years, she'd experienced many emotions in the marriage bed. Fear, revulsion, anger, and stubborn resistance had often taken hold. But she could not remember ever feeling the least inclination to laugh.

"I, too, bathed," she told him, biting her lower lip.

"Well, then, wife, let us not waste all that effort. Lay yourself down, and mayhap we can pleasure each other without gagging."

FitzHugh slid back into bed and turned her stiff body against his. As his hands stroked lean flanks and small, high breasts, he tried to sort his jumbled thoughts.

When she'd first bent over him and taken him in hand, the priest's ugly insinuations had flashed through his mind. For a startled moment, he'd believed the widow had a wider knowledge of men than he'd suspected. Her blank surprise and mumbled explanation had soon put that notion to rest. She'd only done what her decrepit old husband had taught her.

Although FitzHugh's mind revolted at the thought of how she'd been made to service the aged Henri, his shaft stiffened at the memory of her soft, moist lips brushing him so intimately. Deliberately his hand closed over her breast and plucked at the hardened tip. When she gasped and arched under him, he bent to take the nipple in his mouth.

"Sweet Mother," she breathed.

He took his time, worrying the tender flesh with small, teasing nips, then laving it with his tongue. A tang of milky sweetness rose from her nipple, and the taste made his loins throb. Lifting his head from her turgid flesh, he looked down at her face. Wide, luminous eyes met his. He could see a question in their green depths, and curiosity, and the first smoky edges of desire. He bent and took her lips with his.

FitzHugh felt his blood begin to pulse with a slow, sweet heat as he sampled her. She might be too thin and pale to arouse a man with her looks, but by the saints, she tasted of warm, dark honey and sweet wine. He ran his tongue over the smooth flesh of her inner lips, then thrust against her teeth until she opened for him. FitzHugh explored her mouth, and his loins began to ache in earnest. He tightened his hold, crushing her breasts against his chest and her hip against his swollen member.

When she moaned and writhed under him, he slanted his lips across hers more fully and slid his hand down her belly. With one knee, he pried her legs apart, opening her center to his touch.

"Oh!" She jerked her head back, breaking the contact of their mouths.

Smug male satisfaction coursed through him at her startled reaction. She might have learned a few unnatural tricks from the old lecher she'd been wed to, but she bucked under his questing hand like an unbroken filly. FitzHugh buried his face in her neck, breathing in once more the elusive scent of gillyflowers and spring. His fingers rubbed against her core.

This time her gasp accompanied an involuntary shift of her hips, away from his hand. A muted cry pierced his absorption. He raised his head.

"Do I crush you?" he growled, his hand on her moist flesh.

"*Nooo....*" The single drawn-out syllable wavered in the stillness.

Even through the heat clouding his mind, he could hear the tears in her voice. With a slight shock, he realized it was not passion that was making her writhe under his hand. He levered himself up on one elbow, grimacing at the ache in his loins.

"What ails you, lady?" Sweat beaded on his brow from the effort of holding back, but he would not force her unless he had to.

"The saddle, my lord," she said with a small gulp.

FitzHugh frowned down at her. "Saddle? What saddle?"

Her eyes slid away in embarrassment. "The one that took the skin from my thighs."

His scowl deepened. Sitting upright, he thrust the coverlet aside and parted her legs. Even in the dim light, he could see the raw, angry skin that darkened each slender thigh.

"God's blood, why didn't you say something? We could have stopped and bound your hurts."

Embarrassed, she tried to close her legs against his hand. "You stressed the need for haste, and I didn't wish to slow us. In truth, I didn't feel the pain after the first few hours. My legs were numb."

FitzHugh felt the last remnants of desire drain as he eyed the fruits of his own carelessness. He cursed himself for putting her astride a horse when he could see she was no experienced rider. Christ's bones, he gave his veriest recruits more consideration than he'd given the woman he'd sworn to protect and defend! Stifling another curse, he swung out of bed and stalked to the door.

Shaking awake the page who slept on a pallet outside the threshold, he sent him scrambling with a terse order. He shut the door once more and crossed to the fire. With quick efficiency, he tossed wood shavings and dry logs onto the smoldering embers. While the fire hissed to a roaring blaze, he picked up a glazed ceramic basin and water jug and brought them back to the bed.

"Those blisters need tending lest they fester. Let me cleanse them."

"Nay," Mellisynt gasped, scurrying back, away from his looming presence. Embarrassment stained her cheeks, and she dragged the sheets across her chest.

"Don't be more foolish than you've been already," FitzHugh snapped. He leaned down, intending to lay her flat, but a sharp rap on the door forestalled him.

He strode to the door and took a shallow covered bowl from the young page. The boy craned his neck, trying to see around his lord's massive frame. Mellisynt had a quick glimpse of curious brown eyes and tousled golden curls before the door shut with a slam.

"This should ease the pain," FitzHugh declared, setting the bowl on the floor. He looked around, then picked up the chainse lying beside the bed. With one sure tug, he ripped it from hem to neck.

"My lord!" Mellisynt gasped, her eyes wide with dismay.

"Don't fear," he told her. "I've bound enough wounds on the battlefield to know what I'm about."

"Aye," she said weakly.

"Bare yourself and let me tend your hurts."

Hearing the hint of impatience in his voice, Mellisynt responded with great reluctance. Waves of mortification swept over her as his dark head bent to examine her injuries. The intimacy of her position shamed her to her core. She turned her face away, and he lifted first one, then the other leg, washing them with amazing gentleness.

After a few moments, he set the water aside and removed the lid on the bowl the page had brought. Mellisynt's nostrils flared as a nauseous odor, redolent of onions, fenster oil and sour mead filled the room. Her eyes began to water with the reek. FitzHugh plunged his hand into the oozing mess and turned toward her.

"My lord!" she shrieked, wriggling away. "You do not mean to put that noxious mixture on me!"

"I do. 'Tis the best poultice I know for saddle sores. My squire always carries a goodly supply when we travel. It should work as well on you as on the horses."

"Do not speak to me of horses!" Mellisynt muttered, refusing to move. "Truly, I thank you for your attentions, but the aroma makes my head spin."

A roguish gleam lightened the blue of his eyes. "Consider the odor punishment for your stubbornness in refusing to reveal your hurts earlier. Come, spread your legs."

Mellisynt measured the determination in those glinting eyes. Accepting defeat, she heaved a resigned sigh and pushed aside the coverlet.

The poultice brought immediate relief. She gave a low, thankful groan as the searing pain in her thighs eased to a slow burn.

FitzHugh's dark brows drew together. Without speaking, he wrapped clean linen over the salved area. His hands stilled finally, and he sat back on his haunches.

"You must have been in agony most of the day. How in God's name did you walk to the abbey and back?"

Her lips twisted into a wry grimace. "With great care."

At his considering look, she gave a little shrug. "I thought it was God's punishment for my eagerness to be gone from Trémont. I would have endured pain many times more severe to be away."

His eyes thoughtful, FitzHugh tossed the used rags into the bowl and set it aside. Binding each leg with clean linen, he finished the job with quick efficiency, then washed his hands with the remaining water in the jug. That done, he climbed back into bed. Stretching out his long legs beside her, he raised both arms to link his fingers under his head. Stillness descended between them, broken only by the hiss and crackle of pinecones in the flickering fire.

"'Tis clear you had no joy of your first husband." His deep voice drifted across the quiet. "But you had a choice this time. Why did you wed with me?"

Mellisynt turned her head toward him, her cheek brushing against the wool-stuffed pillow.

"The choice was you or a nunnery," she reminded him. "I spent most of my life behind Trémont's walls, my lord. I didn't want to spend the rest in a cloister."

"You need not have accepted those choices," he commented after a few moments. "You could have closed the gates and held Trémont for Prince Richard. He would gladly have taken you into his keeping for such a prize."

"I thought of doing so," she admitted, propping herself up on one elbow.

FitzHugh's blood began to pulse at the thought of how close it had been. If he'd left to claim the lady even a day later, he might have arrived at Trémont to find the gates closed and Beauchamp's pennant waving from its turret.

"But I had no way of knowing who Richard Lionheart would give me to," she continued candidly. "I decided I would as well take you. You are young enough, and strong, and you are a bastard."

He didn't move, yet his muscles seemed to harden under her very eyes. Mellisynt clutched the coverlet to her chest, aware that she had stumbled, badly. Hesitant, she tried to explain.

"Henri could trace his line back to Charlemagne, and even before. He boasted often that his veins ran with the purest, noblest blood in the land. Yet he was weak and infirm and could give me no children."

FitzHugh's face settled into sharp planes and shadowed angles. Despite his grim expression, Mellisynt forced herself to finish what she'd started.

"Many would scorn the fact that your mother was a leman, kept by your father for his pleasure, but she brought new, fresh blood to your line. I would pass that blood to my children." She paused, then continued on a low, throbbing note. "I want children, my lord."

For long moments, silence hung heavy between them. Mellisynt swallowed, certain she'd spoken too rashly. She rued her forward tongue, as Father Anselem had so many times, but could not unsay the words.

When the silence had stretched her nerves to wire thinness, FitzHugh finally drew down his arms. With one huge fist, he closed the bed curtains on his side, then reached across to draw them on her side as well. Darkness welcomed them.

"Well, wife, it doesn't appear we can do aught to make you a babe this night. Go to sleep."

Chapter Four

The next days passed slowly for Mellisynt. Accustomed to tending Henri from earliest cock's crow, she felt a nagging sense of guilt at staying abed, even if it was at her lord's express order.

FitzHugh was absent most of the time, seeing to his duties as Geoffrey's chief lieutenant. With the duke en route to England to meet with his father and brothers at the peace council, it fell to FitzHugh to disband the armies. The lords of Brittany dispersed to their various keeps, replete with booty taken from subdued rebels. The English vassals enfeoffed by Geoffrey in his mien as earl of Richmond grumbled as cold, damp mist closed the harbors and prevented their departure for home. FitzHugh spent as much time settling violent disputes between the bored, idle knights as he did finalizing the details for transporting over a thousand men, animals and camp followers back to England.

Mellisynt learned little of his responsibilities from FitzHugh himself. The few times he repaired to their rented house to see to her welfare and grab a hurried meal, he was preoccupied and curt. When he returned, most often late at night, he fell into bed with a grunt and was soon asleep. Although he would take her in his arms and curl her into him for warmth, he brushed aside her halting offer to perform her duties with a brusque order to heal herself first.

The little page, Bartholomew by name, supplied Mellisynt with most of her information as to her lord's activities. Shy and round-eyed, the youngster blushed when FitzHugh told him he was to see to his lady's care. Mellisynt guessed his age at around eight years. As unused to dealing with children as the boy was to a lady's company, she made awkward attempts to converse with him. He kept his eyes cast down, answering in one-syllable mumbles. She'd almost given up hope of drawing him out when she discovered a chessboard in the cupboard beside the bed. In bored desperation, Mellisynt moved to a low couch in front of the fire and began to place the pieces.

"Do you play, Bartholomew?"

"Some," he replied, his eyes shying away from hers. "Sir Richard has tried to teach me, but my moves oft try his patience."

Stifling the thought that most things tried her lord's thin patience, Mellisynt patted the couch. "Come, help me pass this dreary day."

It took more gentle coaxing before the boy shed his diffidence enough to seat himself on a low stool beside the couch. Cold, dismal rain splashed against the casement windows and filled the corners of the chamber with dampness. But, swaddled as she was in thick blankets and tucked close to the fire, Mellisynt felt a rare contentment. She smiled inwardly as the boy agonized over each move. Henri had not given her much joy in life, but at least his passion for chess had challenged her mind during her years at his bedside. Her hand passed over the bishop that would have placed the boy's king in check and, instead, moved a pawn forward.

"Have you served long with Sir Richard?" she asked idly.

"Nigh onto a year." Boyish pride glowed in his eager brown eyes. "My father is a freedman, a tanner. He like to pissed in his braies when the lord agreed to take me in service."

Mellisynt bit her lip. "Aye, of a certainty, he would be proud," she agreed.

Bartholomew had just moved a rook forward with reckless daring when a commotion sounded outside the windows. Dashing to the casement, the boy pushed it open to peer down into the street.

"There's a great train below, lady," he exclaimed. "I can't see the markings, but the horses' trappings are above order grand!"

Mellisynt began to gather the discarded chess pieces. Before she had them back in the board's fitted drawer, her chamber door opened and a diminutive figure draped in rich furs swept in.

"I bid you good-day, Lady Mellisynt. I am Constance, of Brittany."

The words rang with unconscious arrogance, but were softened by a smiling face framed by silver fox fur. While not beautiful, the lady's countenance shone with subtle rose tints and sparkling violet eyes.

"My lady," Mellisynt stammered, struggling to unwind the swaddling blankets.

"Nay, do not rise. I returned to Nantes this morn to find not only had my lord's most trusted vassal married in a shameful, hurried ceremony, but his wife was ill and abed in some damp little house. 'Tis why I came." She paused, her nose wrinkling delicately. "Do you have a putrid fever?"

Mellisynt shook her head.

"What is that evil smell?" Constance came forward a few cautious paces. "Tell me straight, lady, do you need the court physician?"

"Nay. The head groom, mayhap, but not the physician."

At the other woman's look of utter confusion, Mellisynt sighed. "My illness is naught but raw legs from an unaccustomed saddle. My lord doctored them with a remedy he claims is most efficacious with horses. In truth, it worked wondrously, but I fear this chamber will bear the scent of the cure for months to come.''

Constance stared, eyes wide with disbelief. After a moment, her mouth quirked, then opened in lilting laughter. ''If that's not typical of FitzHugh! He always did know more about horses than women.''

Her violet eyes alive with merriment, she studied Mellisynt from the tip of her hair to the toes peeping out from the twisted blankets.

''I've come to carry you to the château. Tell your women to gather your things.''

Mellisynt frowned, nibbling at her lower lip. ''My lord said nothing of moving.''

''Pah! He used my absence as an excuse to avoid the court. But I'm returned now, and will not have the wife of my husband's most loyal knight housed without. I've sent FitzHugh word that he may attend you this eve at the château. Come, a litter awaits below stairs.''

Mellisynt hesitated, having no desire for closer concourse with the duke or his court. Yet Geoffrey was gone, and his lady wife commanded her presence. She was debating what she should do when one of FitzHugh's men-at-arms rapped on the door of the chamber.

''Your pardon, milady.'' The man's Adam's apple bobbed nervously. ''Sir Richard sends word you are to expect the Lady Constance and should do her bidding.'' He gave the women a quick, awkward bow, then slipped out the door.

Constance grinned in triumph. ''There, you see! Even FitzHugh, stubborn as he is, bows to my authority—on some things. Come, my men will carry you down the stairs.''

Before she quite knew how it happened, Mellisynt found herself ensconced in a litter, the like of which she had never imagined, much less seen. Intricately carved and inlaid with gold leaf, it was drawn by a pair of perfectly matched bays. Heavy velvet curtains of rich burgundy shut out the rain, and high-piled furs kept her warm throughout the short trip. Still bundled in her confining blankets, she was carried up wide marble steps and settled in a high-ceilinged apartment.

"You'll be more comfortable in here," Constance told her briskly.

Awed by the magnificence around her, Mellisynt could only nod. Her eyes roamed over the vaulted, gilded ceilings, past the rich tapestries hanging on each wall, to the wide canopied bed draped in burgundy-and-gold cloth. She stood, uncertain, still cocooned in her blankets, while Constance shooed the male attendants out.

"Get you to bed," she ordered. "But first remove those foul-smelling bandages. I'll not have my fine linens imbued with Richard FitzHugh's horse poultice."

Wondering that such a tiny woman could be so domineering, Mellisynt obediently unwrapped her coverings and reached under her thigh-length shift to strip off the offending bindings.

"Take these and burn them." Constance held the bandages out at arm's length and passed them to a reluctant maid. Mellisynt swallowed a sigh as she watched the remains of her only good shift being borne away.

"I'll leave you now to rest. My maids will tend your hurts with a cream of my own making. I trust you'll find it somewhat more aromatic than FitzHugh's," Constance drawled. "When you feel well enough, you may join me in my *solar* during the afternoons. 'Tis when we have our entertainment."

She was gone in a whirl of color and a cloud of tantalizing scent.

Mellisynt submitted with embarrassed reluctance to the attendants' ministrations. Not even with her old maid, Maude, had she allowed any woman to tend her so intimately. She protested in vain that her hurts were sufficiently healed, but the duchess's word was law. Not one of the determined serving women would leave until she was seen to.

Red-faced, Mellisynt finally settled into the wide bed. The equally red-faced and exasperated maids left, but one returned almost immediately.

"There is a page without, milady. He says he is yours and would speak with you."

At Mellisynt's nod, she stood back to allow in a wet, thoroughly bedraggled young boy. Water dripped from his flattened gold curls and squished in his shoes as he crossed the room.

"Bartholomew! How came you here?"

"I walked behind your litter, lady."

"In this freezing rain? Why didn't you wait at the house until Sir Richard returned?"

The boy's lower lip stuck out belligerently. "My lord bade me stay by you."

Mellisynt's eyes widened, and she turned a pleading look on the maidservant still hovering by the door.

"I'll send dry clothes for him, milady."

She gave the woman a wide, grateful smile.

A runnel of icy rain ran beneath the mail covering FitzHugh's neck and slid down his back. The dampness added weight to the quilted gambeson beneath his armour and seeped into his bones. Wrapping his surcoat more closely about his body, he slumped, wet and weary, in the saddle. Sweet Jesu, if one more of Geoffrey's damned vassals challenged his authority to order the departure, he'd toss the lot of them into the Loire's muddy waters. As it was, half the ships scheduled to depart on the morrow were yet to be loaded. And now, instead of a quick meal and peaceful sleep in the quietude of his rented apartments, he had to wend his way through Nantes's crowded streets to the château to claim his rooms and his wife.

When he arrived at the palace, FitzHugh gave his horse, helmet and gauntlets into his squire's keeping and mounted the marble steps. After passing through a series of long, drafty corridors, he opened the door to his assigned apartments. He stopped short at the scene that greeted him.

Two children sat cross-legged before a blazing hearth, a clutter of half-filled plates around them. One of them FitzHugh recognized immediately. Bartholomew's golden curls, the bane of his existence and the butt of older pages' taunts, identified him. But it took a few moments longer to recognize his wife.

Her unbraided hair cascaded over her shoulders in a cloud of undulating chestnut waves. Startled green eyes stared out of a face as scrubbed and pale as any child's, and a voluminous white nightshirt enveloped her slender frame like an oversized tent. She held a roasted chicken leg in one hand and wore what appeared to be a smear of grease on her left cheek.

While FitzHugh stood frowning at the unfamiliar creature who scrambled up and offered him a hesitant smile, Bartholomew jumped to his feet and came to greet him. Accepting the boy's welcome with an absent nod, FitzHugh dismissed him.

"I see you are well settled," he said finally.

"Aye, the duchess has been most kind." Mellisynt crossed the tile floor on bare feet to help him disrobe.

"Get back to the fire," he growled. "My squire will attend to this."

"Nay, my lord, I can help."

He shrugged off her light hand. "I'm wet to the bone, and will drench you, as well. Leave it."

FitzHugh cursed his clumsy tongue as Mellisynt's thick lashes swept down over her eyes and she went back to stand beside the fire.

"I don't want you to take a chill," he offered in a gruff tone, as unused to explaining himself to a wife who would see to his comfort. In a heavy-handed attempt at humor, he continued. "I would not be a widower before I'm yet a husband."

Mellisynt's back stiffened. "I am well enough now to... to tend to your needs."

Her offended tone made FitzHugh pause in the act of shrugging out of his sodden cloak. He glanced across at the woman standing in bare feet and rigid dignity. God's bones, with her thick, unruly hair and wide green eyes, she looked like a stray cat, one whose fur had been stroked the wrong way. Leaping flames silhouetted her body through the wool nightshirt, and FitzHugh felt a sudden flicker of heat deep in his belly.

"Are you sure? Your hurts are healed?"

Her tongue darted out to wet her lips, and the flicker grew to a low flame.

"Aye," she said, her eyes steady on his.

FitzHugh studied her through heavy-lidded eyes and decided at that moment to consummate their union. In truth, he'd been hard put to restrain himself these past nights, when her slender frame had fitted itself to his and they'd shared their bodies' warmth.

His initial reluctance to take this woman to wife had faded the past few days. Despite her barely veiled dislike of the duke, and FitzHugh's own lingering suspicions of her loyalty, she'd shown no other signs of rebelling against her fate. While he couldn't quite bring himself to trust her, he had to admit she'd not tried to interfere in his ordering of Trémont's men and moneys. He was already benefitting from the widow's rich inheritance, having outfitted his men and hers with new weapons and armour. 'Twas time he lived up to his side of this marriage bargain, he thought, remembering her admission that she'd given herself to a bastard knight to milk the strength of his loins. His loins were more than ready to be milked, he decided grimly. They ached. Bellowing for his squire, he finished undressing.

In short order, he'd wrapped himself in a clean, dry robe and joined his wife in front of the fire. She resumed her seat, knees tucked decorously under the nightshirt, and spread an assortment of cold meats, pasties and cheeses before him. When she leaned forward to pour him wine, her hair swung down in a curtain of dancing russet and gold lights. FitzHugh gave in to an unconscious urge and reached out to touch the thick, silky mane.

"Your hair is most unusual in color," he told her, fingering the fiery strands.

"Aye." She sighed. "Father Anselem reminded me often that red's the symbol of sin and wickedness."

She paused, then took a quick breath. "I dislike mightily the head coverings I was used to wear, but will don them if the color offends you. Or I could dye my hair black, as is the fashion here."

"Nay, it's fine. 'Tis like the coat of a newborn colt I once helped birth, all slick and shiny and filled with copper lights."

FitzHugh let her hair fall and grimaced to himself at his gauche reply. Few ladies of his acquaintance would appreciate being compared to a just-birthed horse. For the first time he wondered if Lady Constance was right. The duchess had often, and at great length, insisted he would benefit mightily from more exposure to her court, where the troubadours sang of courtly love and knights fashioned poetic tributes to their ladies. FitzHugh had little time and less use for such pursuits. Still, he knew wellborn ladies had come to expect flowery phrases and smooth songs of praise. He glanced at his wife.

The Lady Mellisynt didn't appear offended at his less-than-poetic comment about her hair. Her lips curved in a small smile, and she passed him a dish of salted fish.

Through the screen of her lashes, Mellisynt watched her husband consume the contents of the heaped plate she placed before him, then explore the remains of the other dishes. And to think she had protested when the servants left such heaping platters as would have made Henri screech in protest at the excess! She ran an assessing glance down FitzHugh's massive frame, displayed to advantage in a short velvet robe and wool chausses. He bent one knee and rested an elbow on it while his strong white teeth cleaned a pheasant leg. Mellisynt's eyes lingered on his muscled calf and trunklike thigh, before skittering over the pouch cupping his manhood. She felt heat stain her cheeks as she remembered her first sight of her husband's maleness. An unfamiliar tingling began, low in her belly, and she glanced impatiently at the scattered dishes to see how much remained to be consumed.

When FitzHugh finished a short time later and pushed aside the empty plates, Mellisynt's shivery sense of anticipation dimmed somewhat. She'd had little joy in what passed between husband and wife in the past, but she reminded herself of FitzHugh's restraint the night of their marriage. Instinctively she knew she need not fear this man, who would put a woman's hurts before his own desires. Still, she couldn't control the strange trembling in her hand when he took it and drew her across the furs to his side.

"Are you cold?" he asked, his big fingers fumbling with the drawstring that held the neck of her borrowed nightshirt.

"No. Yes. A bit," she stammered.

She looked up to see amusement glinting in his shadowed blue eyes. Did this man always find humor in the bedchamber! she wondered. She sat still while he pushed the nightshirt down her shoulders and off her hips, then stopped wondering, stopped thinking at all, as he slipped an arm around her waist and brought her naked body onto his thighs. When he dipped his head and nuzzled her ear, she stopped breathing, as well.

"I will warm you, wife."

His breath filled her ear with hot, moist promise. He took the lobe between his teeth, as if to taste her very flesh, and ran his tongue around the outer shell. While his mouth wreaked its depredations on her ear, his hand began a slow, deliberate exploration, from breast to hip and back again.

Mellisynt hunched her shoulder and wiggled, trying to evade the half-sensual, wholly disturbing sensations. Held firmly in his lap, her front to the fire and her backside tucked against his thigh, she heard him suck in his breath sharply.

"By the saints, I hope you are truly whole," he rasped. "Lie down and let me check before we go too far to stop."

Flames hotter than any in the fireplace leapt into her cheeks. "Nay, my lord, I'm fine, I swear it. Your remedy worked well. Please!"

She grabbed the fist, covered with fine dark hair, that reached for her thighs.

"The formula is my own," FitzHugh told her with a touch of smugness as he laid her down on the furs spread before the fire, then covered her body with his.

Conditioned by past experience, Mellisynt held herself rigid and still. The few times Henri had managed to mount her, he'd snarled at her to lie quiet lest she sap his seed prematurely with her wanton movements. But as FitzHugh's mouth pressed against hers with hot demand and his hands toyed with her nipples, she felt an overwhelming urge to move against him. Her hands loosed their death grip on the pelt beneath her and lifted slowly, tentatively, to grasp his arms. Muscles bunched under her fingers, like thick ropes of steel sheathed in warm satin. She ran the pads of her fingers along his arms and over his shoulders. Following an instinct older than time, she shifted beneath his weight to cradle his root against her cleft.

With one hand beneath her head, FitzHugh held her steady while he took her mouth. Mellisynt tasted wine, dark and sweet, and a masculine hunger that was as unfamiliar as it was arousing. A slow, steady pressure began to build between her legs. To ease it, she moved against him, lifting her hips to his.

The hand in her hair tightened to a hard fist, and he drew in a ragged breath. Mellisynt's own breath caught as his other hand reached between their bodies to rub against her core. When he slid his fingers into her, she bucked in startled surprise.

"What are you doing?"

"Sweet—! Do you hurt?"

"No!" she gasped.

"Then lie still and let me ready you," he ground out, "because my sword must bury itself in your sheath soon or I will disgrace myself."

Mellisynt stared, wide-eyed, at the vaulted ceiling above her. She had a good idea what he meant by disgracing himself, and was no more eager than he to have it happen. Ceding to his command, she held herself still. For the space of three heartbeats. Then she writhed under his hand. And thrust her hips up to meet him as he entered her.

When he rolled off later, much later, Mellisynt lay bathed in a fine sheen of perspiration. Her breath matched his in its ragged unevenness. FitzHugh sprawled beside her on the furs, his bulk shielding her from the cold drafts, his shoulder pinning her hair. He bent one leg to rub absently at his knee.

"It seems I owe you yet another apology." His voice broke the stillness between them.

Mellisynt turned her head as far as her trapped hair would allow. "For what?"

His lips turned down in a self-mocking smile. "I've been too many weeks without release. In my incontinence, I did not bring you to your pleasure."

Her eyes widened. The silence between them lengthened. Finally she shook her head.

"'Twould appear I have much yet to learn of marriage with you, my lord," she said in a small, confused voice. "I thought myself well pleasured."

FitzHugh gave a low groan and rolled to his feet. Scooping her up, he carried her to the bed. Curling her back into his body, he wrapped a strong arm around her waist. Her breast rested in the palm of his hand, and he played idly with its still-sensitive peak. His other hand splayed possessively across her belly and tangled in the curls at the apex of her thighs.

Mellisynt sucked in her breath as his lazy fondlings grew more deliberate and began to stoke the fires she thought well banked. She stiffened against him, her buttocks push-

ing into his loins. To her amazement, she felt his shaft begin to harden against her.

Sweet Mother, did he think to spill himself yet again?
This same night? She tried to turn, but his hand tightened
on her breast.

"Be still, wife, and relax against my hand. You don't
need to work so hard this time. Do we give it time, my rod
will gain the strength to do its duty. Just close your eyes and
let yourself feel where my fingers play."

Mellisynt squeezed her eyes shut so tight she saw bright
points of light behind her lids. And then, when he entered
her, slow, rising stars. And, finally, a blinding flash of light
that tore a ragged moan from deep in her throat.

Her last thought, before she drifted off to sleep, was that
she'd better make her way to the chapel on the morrow. If
Father Anselem had chastised her for unseemly demands
on Henri, she shuddered to think what penance the priest
here would impose on a wife who required a husband to
service her not once, but twice, in one night!

Chapter Five

"Sir Richard!"

A loud pounding thrust them both into wakefulness. Darkness cloaked the room, except for a dim glow from the fire's embers. FitzHugh sprang out of bed, his hand groping for the dagger he'd laid beneath the mattress the night before.

"Sir Richard, a courier has just arrived. The news is urgent."

Mellisynt propped herself up on one elbow and watched as her husband stalked to the door, totally unconscious of his nakedness. When he flung it open, the oil lamp held by his squire wavered in the draft.

"What news?"

"The lord of Bellamy has broken the truce. He let a force of mercenaries into his keep, and they overran our garrison. Even now he barricades himself within the walls and defies all orders to surrender." Ian paused to catch his breath. "The duchess has called a council of all senior knights within the hour. She desires you attend her before the council."

"Tell her I'll be there immediately. And send the pages with my armor."

Mellisynt clutched the thick coverlet to her breast as FitzHugh threw logs onto the fire and used an iron rod to prod the smoldering embers into flames. Her clothes and his lay scattered before the hearth. As he bent to pull on his braies, two pages came with fresh clothing and armour. Bartholomew cast Mellisynt a quick, proud grin and he staggered in under the weight of his lord's precious mail shirt. Mellisynt suspected the forged iron links, threaded at intervals with silver gossets, weighed almost as much as the boy himself.

FitzHugh drew on his hose and his padded protective tunic, then knelt so that the two pages could lift the heavy mail shirt over his head and fasten the detached sleeves at the shoulders. Straightening, he threw the blue surcoat over his head. His long, blunt fingers fastened a sword belt low over his hips with the ease of long practice.

He strode for the door, the boys trailing behind him carrying gauntlets and shin guards. At the threshold he stopped abruptly, and Bartholomew crashed pell-mell into his back. With a muttered curse, he put the boy aside and came back to Mellisynt.

"'Twould do you better to stay with the duchess," he told her. "I know not how long I'll be gone. Draw upon her exchequer for your needs." He hesitated, then bent and brushed his lips across her cheek. "God keep you, wife."

"And you," she whispered.

FitzHugh followed the scurrying pages through the tall corridors. Flambeaux, set high on the walls in iron holders, cast patterns of light and dark on the smooth, tiled walkway. He was expected. A servant ushered him into a brightly lit *solar* where Constance paced. Geoffrey's chief minister for his French possessions, Roland de Dinan, a quiet, competent man of Breton birth, stood to one side.

Constance whirled when he entered. "That whoreson Bellamy! He waits only until Geoffrey is half across the sea before he recants his oath. You should have decorated the castle walls with his head when you subdued his rebellion the first time."

FitzHugh bit back a sharp reply and marshaled his patience. He knew well this tiny duchess was fiercer than any of the panthers in the king's menagerie when it came to her lands. Geoffrey had married into a line that had held Brittany since the Charlemagne's time.

"I will rectify the error," FitzHugh told her.

"I want not one of his blood to see the new moon," Constance seethed.

"He has children."

"Put them to the sword!"

FitzHugh cast a quick glance at the minister. Roland shrugged and shook his head.

"Sheathe your claws, lady," FitzHugh said, with the bluntness of long service. "The count has only daughters. You know as well as I, 'tis more sensible to use them to your advantage. Give the girls in marriage to loyal knights who will hold Bellamy's land for the duke."

Deep violet eyes narrowed to angry slits. "Do you dare to tell me how to manage my lands, FitzHugh? If you and that doltish husband of mine had treated these rebels as they deserved, we'd not now have to send out more men."

"Geoffrey knew beheading the captured rebels would only stiffen the resistance of those who yet held out. That so many had surrendered without battle proved him right. You should be glad the rebellion was put down with so little loss of lives and livestock, instead of shrieking like a fishwife over the loss of one cod's head."

Constance glared at him a full minute longer. FitzHugh folded his arms and waited for her temper to ebb, as it always did.

"Don't give my husband credit for such clear thinking," she said finally. "He may be wondrously brave and a born leader of men, but he has the brains of a stillborn ass."

FitzHugh shot Roland de Dinan a quick look, and both men smothered their grins. They'd heard Constance say the same words to her laughing, infuriating husband on more than one occasion. Unfortunately, they were true.

"'Twas you who curbed his bloodlust, even as you do mine," she conceded. "You've stood good friend to both of us these many years."

FitzHugh shrugged. "I owe Geoffrey much. And you, as well, my lady."

"The debt goes both ways. I was pleased Geoffrey had the rare sense to offer you Trémont's widow. Her wealth will help you restore that rambling ruin you claim as home."

"Aye," FitzHugh replied, noncommittal. He knew his tenacious hold on the small keep in England irritated Constance. She much preferred her native Brittany, and schemed endlessly to keep Geoffrey and his knights in France as much as possible.

"I like your bride, FitzHugh."

"She'll do well enough," he replied, itching to get back to the urgent business at hand.

The duchess's eyes narrowed at his offhand remark, but she followed his lead when he directed the conversation to the imminent council. FitzHugh gave her a list of the barons still remaining within quick recall of Nantes, and those yet awaiting transport. Although Constance would play no open role in directing the battle, FitzHugh knew she had a shrewder grasp of which nobles would respond than Geoffrey ever would. With Roland de Dinan's able assistance, they drew up an order of march. Lady and knights then repaired to the main hall for the council of war, in perfect accord on a battle plan.

The morning sun rose over the hills by the time FitzHugh led the advance guard through the city gates and headed north by east. He set a forced march, hoping to catch the wily lord of Bellamy before he could rally a force of any size to his side. The foot soldiers accompanying the mounted knights would have to trot to keep up, but FitzHugh knew they would do so easily. In their lighter mail and leather coverings, they could hold the pace longer than the knights, whose weighty armour wore down even their huge war-horses.

He felt a twinge of reluctance as the spires of Nantes faded in the distance behind them. For the first time in all his years of soldiering, FitzHugh regretted leaving a warm bed, and an even warmer wife. By all the saints, the Lady Mellisynt had surprised him last night. With her fire-kissed hair and uninhibited, untutored responses, she'd pulled the seed from his loins far sooner than he'd intended. Fitz-Hugh couldn't remember the last time he'd lost control like that.

He shifted uncomfortably in the saddle as his groin tightened at the memory of their couplings. The discomfort annoyed him. He was unused to experiencing a lingering lust for any woman, especially one who was his wife. As his well-trained war-horse set one heavy hoof in front of the other, FitzHugh found himself pondering the Lady Mellisynt. After a week of marriage, he still did not know her well, nor know for sure where she stood. Most women were apolitical, amoral creatures, he knew. They would do what served their needs, regardless of oaths or duties. As would many men these days, FitzHugh was forced to acknowledge. In these troubled times, loyalties shifted with the tide. He straightened in the saddle and forced his attention from such troubling thoughts to the coming offensive.

By sunset, the troop had covered half the distance to Bellamy. Couriers brought reassuring word that the disaffected lord was caught within his keep, reinforced by a strong force of mercenaries. FitzHugh gave the men a brief rest while he conferred with the other senior commanders.

"If we push through this night, we have him."

FitzHugh nodded at Simon de Lacy. The old knight was descended from a long, illustrious line of robber barons whose principal keep dominated a strategic trade route between Brittany and Normandy. The senior knight who was technically in charge of the punitive force in Geoffrey's absence, de Lacy had great courage, but little skill at organizing or planning. He was shrewd enough to cede military decisions to FitzHugh while retaining the appearance of leadership—and the greatest share of the spoils, of course. FitzHugh wished some of Geoffrey's other vassals were as cooperative.

"We can't expect to take Bellamy as easily as we did before," another knight grunted. "This time he's brought in mercenaries. Those bastard sons and ragtag ruffians will want the chance to take booty and rise in circumstance."

FitzHugh ignored the sideways looks the other knights gave him. He was too used to the jealousies of Geoffrey's more nobly born vassals to let the slur affect him. Besides, the man spoke the truth.

"If Bellamy's defenders ride out for battle, so much the better. We are stronger and better equipped," Simon de Lacy asserted.

"Aye," FitzHugh agreed slowly. "For that reason, Bellamy will probably curb them and use their strength to hold the keep until Richard Lionheart sends reinforcements."

"If he will," another man interjected. "With the peace documents all but signed, and both princes en route to England, will Richard send men to support Bellamy?"

"If it gave him a foothold in Brittany, he would," Simon said. "Peace documents between the Angevin brothers last about as long as it takes the ink to dry. We can expect to sit on our thumbs outside the castle walls until the prince's troops arrive to force the issue or Bellamy is starved out."

FitzHugh surveyed the ring of men gathered around old Simon. They were a colorful lot, in polished armour and furred surcoats decorated with heraldic devices in bright shades of gold and crimson and azure. But FitzHugh saw beyond their varied plumage and rich fabrics, to the hardened knights who wore, as well, the scars of many battles. These men owed Geoffrey forty days' service at arms each year, and they, at least, had held to their oaths. FitzHugh knew to a day how much service remained on each man's duty, and how difficult it would be to keep them beyond their allotted time. As great lords with their own lands to manage, they could not stay away indefinitely. It would take promises of further fiefs and riches to keep them here for very long. Geoffrey would not be pleased if FitzHugh allowed his forces to settle in for a protracted siege.

"Bellamy is of earth and timber construction," he said with quiet authority. "We'll take it by fire if the lord will not fight."

A long, heated discussion followed, but in the end FitzHugh's plan prevailed. By midmorning, he reined in his mount at the edge of the thick forest that surrounded the rebel keep. He gazed at the stronghold, set high on a mound of earth in the center of a broad clearing hacked out of the wood. Weariness and the throbbing ache in his knee faded as a slow surge of anticipation coursed through his veins. Within an hour he had the troops dispersed and the siege engines in place according to his will and Sir Simon's instructions. Within another half hour, he had Bellamy's contemptuous response to the order to surrender in hand.

Before the sun reached its zenith, the first balls of fire arced across the sky, trailing a shower of sparks from the catapults to the wooden palisade.

Mellisynt left the château's sumptuously appointed chapel, her head whirling. She'd skulked in her apartments for days, hesitant to leave, even to attend morning mass, because of a reluctance to visit the confessor. Finally, her conscience and long-ingrained habit drove her to seek out the priest. Her face burned as she remembered the list of offenses she'd whispered to the lean, ascetic prelate. Topping the list was the wanton way she'd responded to her husband!

Mellisynt knew full well the pleasure she had taken at FitzHugh's hands and lips was a grievous sin. Father Anselem had schooled her often enough on a wife's duty to receive her lord's seed without sinful, unholy passions. Especially when any kind of energetic response caused old Henri to spill himself prematurely, or lose his erection altogether. She knew by heart the passage from the book of penances, which punished the venial sin of desire within the marriage bed by forty days and nights of fasting.

To Mellisynt's amazed relief, the château priest had listened to her halting confession with a small smile. Such strictures against overindulgence and unseemly passion between husband and wife were intended to restrain men and lessen the burden of childbearing on women, he explained, as were the specified periods each month when no relations were allowed. Although he cautioned her against responding too immoderately, he sent her off with a light penance and the hope that she would soon bear the fruit of her marriage bed. Still stunned at the priest's leniency, Mellisynt wound her way through the maze of drafty halls.

Mayhap FitzHugh's seed had already taken root in her womb, she thought. A painful hope clutched at her heart. Her arms ached to hold her child, a tiny scrap of humanity all her own, to love without fear and without restraint. She hugged the thought to herself and continued, more slowly. After several wrong turns, she finally stood on the threshold of the duchess's *solar*.

Eyes wide and wondering, Mellisynt surveyed the colorful scene. Oil lamps augmented the light filtering in through rows of tall, leaded windows and illuminated a crowd of bright plumed courtiers scattered about the room. A richly gowned knight stood with one foot planted on a bench, picking out a melody on a strange, gourd-shaped instrument. Sleek greyhounds patrolled the room, their claws clicking against black and white tiles in counterpoint to the haunting tune. Used to floors covered by thick rushes, filled with fleas and the remains of bones thrown to the boar hounds, Mellisynt's eyes lingered on the clean, bright tiles. They gave the room an airy, spacious look. Bartholomew had told her they were an innovation from Moorish Spain and much copied in noble houses, even if they did make a page's life a misery. More than one youngster serving at the table had lost both his dignity and his lord's dinner when his pointed felt shoes slipped out from under him on the slick tiles.

Mellisynt drew in a quick breath as she surveyed the ladies' high-waisted gowns, trimmed in rich miniver and ermine and sable. Laced tight at the front to display the ladies' figures, the gowns gapped only enough to hint at the elaborate embroidered wool shifts underneath. Instead of fitted sleeves with pointed tips that served as half mittens against the cold, these ladies' robes sported cuffs so long that many had tied knots in the ends to keep them from dragging on the floor.

Trying to ignore the tongues of envy flicking up her spine, Mellisynt gathered her baggy gown in two firm hands and stepped into the *solar*. Constance looked up and smiled a warm greeting. "Welcome, Lady Mellisynt. Come, sit beside me and tell me how you fare."

"I am well, my lady," she replied, settling herself on a low, padded stool beside the duchess's chair. A buzz of interest rippled through the crowd. Mellisynt heard her name whispered, and FitzHugh's. Men and women alike surveyed her from head to toe, and she caught a flash of derision in more than one glance. She folded her hands together within the concealing swath of her gown and lifted her chin.

Constance saw the gesture and cast a frowning glance around her immediate circle. "You must excuse us, lady. The court's been shut away during these times of trouble. Any new face piques our interest. They would stare, even were you not the bride of FitzHugh."

Mellisynt turned questioning eyes at the woman's dry comment.

"We had long despaired of seeing him attached," the tiny, dark-haired duchess explained. "Tell me true now, are you well?"

"Yes, my aches are gone."

Mellisynt felt a twinge of guilt at the small lie, especially having just come from the confessional! If the truth be told, she carried a whole new set of aches. But this lingering soreness between her thighs had nothing to do with the horse she had ridden and everything to do with the man who had ridden her. She vowed to perish in flames, however, before she would ever admit to more pains of any sort.

"Well, while FitzHugh's gone you must rest and enjoy yourself. When he returns and carts you off to that dingy little keep he calls home, you'll have little enough time for pleasures.''

Constance patted Mellisynt's hand and introduced her to those within her immediate circle. After a time, the courtiers picked up their individual conversations. When the plaintive melody resumed and drifted across the hall, Constance called out to the player.

"Sing your rondeau for us, Sir Guy. I'm most anxious to hear the song you've composed to your mysterious love."

The golden-haired knight smiled and crossed the hall. Constance whispered to Mellisynt that Guy de Claire's songs had won him almost as much renown as his exploits in battle. Mellisynt ran admiring eyes over the glorious embroidered device on de Claire's red velvet surcoat. It depicted three gilded lilies on a field of green. But when her gaze dropped to the knight's feet, she felt her mouth fall open in astonishment. The knight wore shoes with the longest, most pointed toes she'd ever seen. The tips protruded a good half foot in front of him, and their straw stuffing thumped against the tiles when he walked. Laughter gurgled in her throat. She covered it with a choked cough and glanced hastily around the room.

Over the heads of the other courtiers, a pair of merry brown eyes caught hers. Set in a well-shaped head crowned by curling brown hair, they invited her to share her mirth. Their owner, a tall, lean knight with a luxuriant mustache, smiled conspiratorially.

Mellisynt gasped, recognizing the face at once. It was the knight from the clearing, the one who had tried to take her from FitzHugh. Her head whirled, and she wondered what a knight sworn to Richard Lionheart was doing at the court of Duke Geoffrey. Confused, she missed most of the troubadour's song. Only when his pleasant baritone deepened in pitch and intensity did his words register.

My love's face is as a new bloom'd rose,
Her breath as soft and fair as spring.
Yet within such beauty lies a heart

Cruel and unyielding to the one
Who has loved her long from afar.

The singer's expressive eyes lingered on the duchess's face. She smiled up at him and arched her dainty brows.

Yet only to her do I sing of my feelings,
Such is the love that keeps me discreet.

"La, Sir Guy," one of the ladies tittered, "you'd certainly better be discreet. The last lady you pledged yourself to had a most jealous husband."

The knight smiled. "A husband has no rights to his wife's true love, or cause to be jealous. Marriage is a dull business, after all."

"Especially when you're wed to a ten-year-old boy with pustules still marking his face," another woman chimed in grumpily. "Would that I had a lover my own age, one who doesn't bury his face in my breasts and call me Mama. I hope you win your lady's love, Sir Guy."

The lords and ladies of the court added their opinions as to the worthiness of de Claire's suit, debating whether the unknown lady should yield to his advances. Mellisynt's ears began to burn at some of the franker suggestions to the aspiring lover.

She listened to their badinage with growing amazement. Stories of the cult of courtly love and the persuasive songs of troubadours had reached even remote Trémont. But never in her wildest imagination would she have believed that men and women would discuss love and... and passion so openly. Her eyes rounded as she thought of what Father Anselem's reaction to such verses would have been, and the amount of time she'd have spent on her knees had she dared flutter her lashes at any man, as the duchess was now doing.

"What think you, Lady Mellisynt?" Constance turned, a mischievous light twinkling in her eyes. "You're the newest to the court, and most unbiased. Should Sir Guy win his lady's love?"

"Nay, my lady," Mellisynt protested, stammering. "I couldn't say."

"But surely you have an opinion?" the singer asked with a slight, mocking smile.

"Nay, truly. I know naught of love...of passion...of such emotions."

"Wed to the bastard FitzHugh, I'm not surprised," Sir Guy drawled.

Constance snapped her brows together, but not in time to stop the low laughter that rippled through the court.

Mellisynt straightened slowly on her stool and met the knight's malicious look with a steady gaze. She might know naught of the love he sang about, but she'd allow no insult to her lord.

"Indeed," she agreed coolly, "you *should* not be surprised. Little as I yet know my husband, I misdoubt he would countenance the adultery you espouse in your song. He holds true to his oaths of honor and virtue and loyalty."

A startled silence fell. The ugly word *adultery* seemed to hang on the air and clash with the concept of delicious, forbidden love. Sir Guy's grin slipped, then hardened into a thin, tight line.

"'Tis only a song after all," a lazy voice drawled. "And not a very good one, de Claire. You'll have to work on the last verse."

A tall, lean figure detached himself from the crowd and sauntered forward. Mellisynt looked up into the brown eyes that had mirrored her laughter only minutes before.

"I am Beauchamp, Lady Mellisynt. We met before, while you were...en route to Nantes."

"I remember," Mellisynt told him, her voice dry.

"FitzHugh and I shared a campfire more than once, before this latest war put us on opposite sides. Will you walk with me and tell me how the devil an ugly, distempered rogue like that convinced you to wed him?"

Mellisynt felt a smile tug at her lips. Where only moments before Sir Guy's sneering comments had raised her hackles, Beauchamp's good-natured insults invited mirth. She glanced at Constance for permission, then took his outstretched hand and allowed him to pull her to her feet. When the babble of voices rose behind them, Beauchamp gave her hand a friendly squeeze.

"I know not if you intended to put Sir Guy in his place, but 'twas well and surely done. He's most proud of his poetry."

Mellisynt glanced up and saw the silky mustache part in a smile.

"I would be careful, though," the knight continued. "However much he may look the languid courtier, de Claire has a swift, sure sword. He's long carried malice toward your lord for unseating him in a tourney some years ago. He's a prideful little cock. You'd best watch him."

Mellisynt gave a choking laugh. "Pray, excuse me. I find it somewhat strange to be taking advice from one who but a week ago crossed swords with my husband."

"Ah, but he wasn't your husband then." Beauchamp grinned, leading her to a window seat at the far end of the hall. "Had I been but a day sooner, mayhap he would not be, even now."

"What do you here?" Mellisynt asked, pulling her hand free of the knight's light grasp. "How came you to the court of your enemy?"

"Geoffrey was my enemy last week. With the truce, he's once again my overlord."

At Mellisynt's startled gasp, he leaned back against the stone window casing and grinned.

"I know, 'tis most damnably difficult to keep it all straight. Like many old families, mine stole or acquired by marriage lands scattered across all of France and half of England. I owe Richard Lionheart allegiance for holdings in Aquitaine and Anjou, and Geoffrey for holdings in Brittany. I came this week to renew my pledge to Constance, in Geoffrey's absence."

"And she accepted?"

"Aye, of course. Until this last madness, I paid my knight's fees faithfully to Geoffrey and fought beside him in many a skirmish. And beside your lord."

Mellisynt shook her head at the confused logic of men. How could they so easily forget the enmity of just a week ago? To be sure, she didn't forget or forgive her grudges as easily. She grimaced, thinking of the hard kernel of resentment toward the duke she'd carried in her breast for so long.

With a connoisseur's eye, Beauchamp watched the emotions play across the pale face before him. By the saints, there was something more to this little widow than just her reputed inheritance. Those lashes framed eyes of startling depth and intelligence, though she kept them shielded most of the time. His gaze flicked over her dowdy dress, discerning the trim figure beneath. He felt a fleeting regret he'd not carried her off and discovered what else lay buried under those absurd gowns. He hooked a finger under Mellisynt's chin and turned her face up to his.

"If I can do aught to help you, or ease your way at court, I would be honored."

"Thank you, my lord."

Mellisynt pulled her chin away and rose. Friendship was one thing. Allowing a man to put hands on her was another. She shuddered to think of the penance that small touch would have earned her at Trémont. With a tight smile, she drifted back to the crowd of courtiers and took a seat in a secluded niche.

She found it easy to stay in the background in the days that followed. Embarrassed as much by her outmoded wardrobe as by her naiveté concerning noble manners and mores, she dwelt at the fringes of the gay group surrounding Constance. She found much to entertain her in simply watching and listening. Beauchamp joined her occasionally, making her laugh with his droll interpretation of the court's antics.

Gradually, she grew more accustomed to, and less shocked by, the concept of a noble, physical love outside the vows of marriage. Still, however much the ladies might sigh over their chivalrous lovers and troubadours might sing of the purity of their passion, Mellisynt struggled with the whole idea. She'd experienced little love in her first marriage, to be sure, nor did she expect any in this one. Yet still she shrank from the thought of violating her holy vows.

The duchess treated Mellisynt with kindness, when she noticed her at all. The burdens of administering Brittany in Geoffrey's absence consumed most of her time. And word soon circulated that Constance quickened with her first child. Mellisynt offered warm congratulations, and sternly repressed a shaft of envy. Seated before the fire in her own apartments late one night, she wondered when she, too, would carry the spark of life within her. By imperceptible degrees, she found herself thinking less of the child she wanted and more of the process that would produce it.

Despite her stern admonition not to dwell on such carnal matters, memories of how FitzHugh had taken her there, on that very hearth, warmed her blood. Her face tingled with heat, as did her belly. Hugging her arms around her middle, she slid into bed.

She awoke the next morning to Bartholomew's hasty pounding on her door.

"My lady, Sir Richard returns this day."

Mellisynt scrambled out of bed and threw on a mantle to cover her shift. Her toes curled against the cold tiles as she ran to admit the breathless page.

"Truly, lady, a messenger just arrived and was closeted with the duchess. Word is that Bellamy surrendered after mere token resistance, and the lord's eldest was given as hostage."

"And he's taken no injury or hurt?"

Bartholomew's brows furrowed. "The lord of Bellamy?"

"Nay, Sir Richard!"

The boy shrugged. "None that were reported. Even if he's wounded, it can't be that bad, since he rides."

Mellisynt marveled at the page's cheerful unconcern as she dressed. Her own heart hammered, both in anticipation and in relief. Never having been exposed to the ravages of war, she had only a vague idea of the death and destruction it involved. The thought that her husband had been in the midst of such carnage made her queasy. Still, she'd married FitzHugh for his strength and vigor. She couldn't expect a man of his temperament to sit behind castle walls and hire mercenaries to fight his battles, as old Henri had.

The heralds announced FitzHugh's arrival just as the squires were clearing the boards from the noon meal. Constance herself headed the welcoming party that surged out onto the castle steps to greet him. She tugged Mellisynt with her to the front of the crowd.

"God's blessing, Sir Richard. Your safe arrival is as welcome as the news that you've taken Bellamy."

FitzHugh climbed down from his mount, his movements stiff and weary. He knelt to kiss the duchess's extended hand.

Mellisynt's little rehearsed greeting died on her lips as he rose, gave her an absent nod, then turned away. She watched him stride to a docile palfrey and lift down a heavily cloaked, hooded figure. Leading the figure forward, he stepped aside. The woman threw back her hood and knelt before Constance.

A collective gasp floated on the thin winter air. Mellisynt felt her own breath catch in her throat as she surveyed the most stunningly beautiful girl she had ever seen.

Chapter Six

"I am Isabeau of Bellamy, my lady. I come in surety of my father's obedience to your will."

The words identified the girl as a political hostage, but neither her voice nor her manner carried any hint of submission. She held her head high, its curling masses of blue-black hair catching the sun's light. Under delicate, arched brows, eyes the color of Brittany's storm-tossed seas met those of the duchess squarely. Her skin was smooth and white, with rose tints where the winter cold had kissed it. As the silence about her lengthened, the girl's tongue came out to wet one corner of her red lips, but she displayed no other sign of nervousness.

Constance gave her head a slight shake, as if rousing herself from a trance. Holding out a hand, she lifted the girl to her feet.

"Your father is fortunate to have so beauteous a daughter to send as hostage," she said, a hint of acid in her tone. "Mayhap you can soften the duke's fury with your recreant sire. When Duke Geoffrey returns, we shall decide your fate, and that of your father."

The duchess turned to give FitzHugh a warm smile. "Attend me later, when you have rested and soaked the chill from your bones. The rest of the knights will have returned by then. This night we shall have a special feast in honor of your victory."

Mellisynt stood quietly while her husband gave orders to the troop to disperse. When he turned and started, as if surprised at her presence, she forced a greeting through stiff lips.

"I bid you welcome, my lord."

FitzHugh bent down to press a quick salute on her chilled cheek.

"Thank you."

Turning to lead the way inside, Mellisynt told herself she should be grateful that he had returned whole. 'Twas silly to expect effusive greetings from one who looked as tired and drawn as he did. Still, she felt a small niggle of feminine pique at the absentmindedness of his salute. Inside their rooms, she gave the servants orders for immediate hot water and went to help him disrobe.

"You don't need to sully yourself with my dirt," he told her, unbuckling his sword belt. "My squire will be here shortly."

"Nay, 'tis my duty," Mellisynt told him. She reached for the hem of his sodden surcoat.

FitzHugh shrugged and bent at the waist so that she could pull it off. She had laid it across a bench and was tugging at his heavy mail shirt when Ian arrived. The squire was as muddy and tired-looking as his lord, but he was well trained in his duties. He gave Mellisynt a respectful nod and stepped forward to finish the disrobing. FitzHugh grunted when his mail shirt came off, then quickly shed the rest of his clothes. A short time later he folded his bulk into a round copper tub, giving a low groan of pleasure as the hot water soaked into his chilled skin. The squire departed to clean his precious mail and heavy sword.

Mellisynt moved forward to kneel beside the tub. Picking up a rag, she spread it with soft soap and began to cleanse his back.

"Sweet Mother!"

"What?" FitzHugh opened his eyes and threw a quick glance over his shoulder.

"You have a bruise the size of a pomegranate on your back. 'Tis discolored and embedded with bits of mail."

"God's bones," FitzHugh cursed. "'Twill cost a fistful of silver pennies to repair that mail."

"'Twill cost more to repair your back, should it fester," Mellisynt responded tartly. "Lean forward, so that I may cleanse the wound."

With steady fingers, she picked the twisted bits of metal out of his inflamed flesh. While he finished his bath, she sent a page for ointment and clean linen. Positioning her lord before the fire, she doctored the lesion.

As she bent to wrap linen bandages around his chest, FitzHugh glanced down at his wife's neatly braided auburn hair. The memory of its thick, silky feel teased at his mind and chased the weariness from his body.

When she finished, he pulled on dry clothes with a grateful sigh, then crossed to his discarded surcoat.

Pulling a small leather pouch from a side pocket, he held it out.

"Here."

Her eyes opened wide.

"'Tis your bride gift. I had not time to find something suitable sooner." He pushed the pouch into her slack hand.

She opened the drawstring and gasped when a heavy gold brooch tumbled into her palm. Golden wires, twisted together to the thickness of a man's little finger, formed an intricate knot around a glittering square-cut emerald. Mellisynt touched the gem's faceted surface with trembling fingers. When she lifted her eyes to his, they glowed a brighter, deeper green than the stone.

"I've never had such a gift," she breathed.

Embarrassed, he shrugged. "The lady of Bellamy was most reluctant to part with it, but I thought you would like it."

The glow left her eyes like snow melting under an early spring sun. Thick black lashes swept down to hide her gaze from his view. FitzHugh placed his knuckles under her chin and tipped her face to his.

"Do you disdain the pin because it was taken as booty?" he asked, a harsh edge to his voice. "You need not. Bellamy knew he placed himself at risk when he broke his sworn oath to Geoffrey. He's lucky he lost only his possessions, and not his head."

Her closed, still face pricked at his pride. He had nothing to offer this woman but what he earned by the strength of his arm.

"I will not have you scorn what trinkets I choose to bring you. Such booty is the prize of battle."

"And you ever fight the duke's battles."

The disdain in her voice took him aback, then lit a slow anger in his gut.

"Aye," he told her, the word a soft warning. "I do."

She tried to jerk her chin away. His grip tightened.

"And you will wear the baubles I bring you from such battles."

Rebellion flared in her eyes before her dark lashes swept down to hide them from his scrutiny. She held herself rigid and unmoving while FitzHugh studied her set face. Finally his hand loosened. He scowled at the red marks on the fragile skin of her jaw. Annoyance at her stubbornness and anger at himself for marking her so roughened his voice.

"I must give the duchess my report. I'll see you at the evening meal."

When FitzHugh entered the main hall with Constance some hours later, he scanned the crowded benches for his lady. Irritation at his mishandling of her earlier lingered in his mind. Instead of setting up her stubborn back, he should have drawn her out, explored the reasons behind her simmering dislike of Geoffrey. FitzHugh had let pass her barely veiled discourtesy to the duke at their wedding, ascribing it to the stress of the day, but now he wondered at Mellisynt's animosity. Was it but a woman's resentment at being used as a pawn? Did it run so deep she would betray the duke, and her husband, given the chance? Surprised at how much the thought disturbed him, FitzHugh moved through the milling throng.

He spotted Mellisynt seated on a crowded bench beside a plump older woman. He started toward her, then stopped, a disbelieving scowl settling on his face. His wife wore a plain amber gown, unadorned by any touch of color. And bare of all jewelry. She dared scorn his gift. He felt the muscles beside his jaw tighten, and he moved forward once more.

A low, musical greeting stopped him halfway across the hall.

"God give you good even, Sir Richard."

After two days of travel in Isabeau of Bellamy's company, he would have recognized her voice blindfolded. And her scent. She wore a heady musk, redolent of the East and exotic nights. FitzHugh turned and acknowledged her greeting.

"And you, my lady. Are you settled and housed to your liking?"

Isabeau pouted prettily, a mischievous sparkle in her aquamarine eyes. "I'm put with three young girls. They are but children, in service to the duchess. I would rather be with women my age, to learn the secrets of the court and the choicest gossip."

FitzHugh felt his face relax into the makings of a smile. "I misdoubt you'll ferret out the gossip, regardless of your roommates. You have but to flash your eyes and you'll have all the courtiers at your feet, as you did half my troop."

"But not you, my lord," she murmured, slanting him a coquette's look from under kohl-darkened eyes. "You seemed most impervious to my charms."

FitzHugh bit back a grin at the chit's precocious femininity. In truth, her antics had kept him quietly amused throughout the two-day journey from Bellamy. His troop had barely ridden out of her father's keep before the supposed prisoner began testing her wiles on his men. His squire, Ian, had all but fallen off his horse helping the girl to dismount when they stopped to rest. More than one begrimed man-at-arms had tugged his forelock in bumbling awe at her sultry looks and luring smiles.

"Nay, Lady Isabeau, a man would have to be dead to be impervious to your wiles. But you should practice them on someone younger, less graybeard."

"Surely you, who made your fortune in the lists, know how much more challenging it is to attempt the harder target," she purred. She placed a soft white hand on his arm. "Please, will you not share a trencher with me? I know none of these people here, only you."

FitzHugh glanced over at his wife. She caught his look, lifted a haughty eyebrow, and turned away to speak to the woman beside her. With a slight shrug, he escorted the girl to a nearby seat. He'd deal with the Lady Mellisynt later.

Not even Isabeau's innocently provocative remarks could keep FitzHugh's attention from wandering as the meal progressed. As promised, Constance had turned the occasion into a banquet in honor of the returning knights. Doughty old Simon de Lacy, the senior vassal present, sat beside the duchess in the place of honor. Squires in puffed sleeves and pointed shoes served to the sound of pipes as course followed course and minstrels entertained the chattering crowd.

More used to simple soldier's fare than heavily spiced sauces and towering pasties in the shape of castles and cathedrals, FitzHugh had soon had his fill. He stretched his long legs under the table and recognized anew why he avoided Geoffrey's court whenever possible. A man couldn't even eat his supper without some damned doves bursting out of a pie and flapping around his ears.

He gave muttered thanks when Constance called for the boards to be cleared, the silverware counted and the leftovers distributed to the servants. Working the ache out of his left knee, he rose.

"Will there be dancing, do you think?" Isabeau sounded more little girl than budding woman in her excitement.

"Unfortunately so."

Her smile slipped at his disgruntled reply, and FitzHugh relented. "I believe the dancing master has some new steps to show the court. Come, I'll take you to him so you can meet him before the music begins."

From the corner of one eye, Mellisynt saw FitzHugh lead the Lady Isabeau to a far alcove. His dark head was bent over shining curls of a similar shade, and the chit smiled up at him shamelessly. Mellisynt clenched her fists in the folds of her skirts. An emotion as unfamiliar as it was fierce rushed through her. Only after a succession of deep breaths did she recognize the feeling for what it was. Jealousy. Pure, unadulterated jealousy.

Startled by the intensity of her disquiet, Mellisynt tried to banish it. What did it matter to her, after all, if FitzHugh chose to dally with this girl? She was welcome to the brute. Mellisynt rubbed her still-tender jaw, trying to whip up the anger and resentment she'd felt but a few hours ago, when he'd tried to impose his will upon her. But the anger wouldn't come. Instead, an insidious hurt wrapped its coils around her heart.

She traced a pattern in the table's cloth with the tip of one finger and berated herself for feeling hurt. So Fitz-Hugh had been kind on occasion? So he'd been most thorough in their coupling, teaching her more about her body in one night than Henri had ever managed in all his years of fumbling? So he employed his hands and mouth in ways that left her feeling breathless just to think on them? She mustn't attach too much importance to their physical activities. 'Twas a natural function, after all, an expected part of marriage.

Theirs was a political joining, she reminded herself. He wed to secure lands and wealth, she to escape Trémont's walls and take a babe from his seed. FitzHugh was but fulfilling his duty when he took her to his bed. Just because she'd enjoyed the experience mightily, that was no reason to feel this searing jealousy when he smiled down at an overripe, forward piece of baggage.

"I see FitzHugh has brought us a pretty child."

Mellisynt glanced up from her study of the woven tablecloth to see Roger Beauchamp at her shoulder. She followed his bland look to where FitzHugh and the girl stood in intimate conversation with another courtier.

"The Lady Isabeau is passing beauteous," she agreed.

"But still a child," he said, dismissing the court's newest addition with a lazy smile. "Not to be compared with—"

A fanfare from the balcony above cut him off. The household seneschal stepped forward and thumped the tiled floor with his staff. Murmurs of delight greeted his announcement of the rigaudon, a gay, rollicking dance new to the court.

"Come, lady, I would partner you in this dance." Beauchamp took her hand in a warm, sure grip.

"Nay, my lord, I do not dance."

He ignored her urgent protests. With a steady tug, he brought her to her feet. Mellisynt tried to hold back, but, short of throwing herself to the floor, she couldn't stop him. Grim-faced, she caught her heavy skirts up over one arm and took a place in the ring of dancers.

"Just listen to the music and step with it," he told her, his voice light and teasing. "And try not to look as if you swallowed a bowl of curdled milk."

Mellisynt gave an involuntary laugh, then looked helplessly about as the music sounded and the dancers began to circle. The woman to her right stumbled into her.

"Move!" the woman snapped, giving her a little shove.

Mellisynt caught Beauchamp's wide grin and moved. Slowly at first, then with gathering confidence as she began to discern the pattern. Her eyes followed the dancers' nimble movements, watching how the ladies managed their swirling skirts, and the men their long, pointed shoes with grace and skill. In line with the ladies, she took a few skipping steps across the tile. Gradually she caught the rhythm, and her movements became more elaborate. When she executed a dipping, swaying turn in time with her partner, she gave a little laugh of triumph.

"Well, well," Beauchamp murmured, surveying her flushed face and glowing eyes. "There's fire under that demure exterior."

"'Tis only breathlessness, my lord," Mellisynt responded, laughing.

When the first round ended, she tingled with unaccustomed pleasure. She'd never danced before in her life. Indeed, Father Anselem had often decried the evil of such abandoned activity, and had once read a text from the bishop of Rennes expressly forbidding dancing in the church aisles by peasants. But, by the saints, it made her heart gallop and her blood race most feverishly.

Beauchamp bowed low over her hand. "Your grace and spirit are delightful, my lady. Will you dance the second round with me?"

"Nay, she will not."

Mellisynt felt the hairs on the nape of her neck lift at FitzHugh's deliberate drawl. Her pleasure evaporated, and a sick feeling rose in her stomach. She swallowed and turned to face her husband.

"I was about to refuse him, my lord."

"Good." FitzHugh's blue eyes glinted. "I would not have my wife in the company of such a smooth-tongued, pretty-faced courtier."

"Then you should guard her better." Beauchamp's light, mocking voice drew her husband's gaze. "The lady's too charming to be satisfied for long with a heavy-handed dolt of a husband such as you, FitzHugh."

Mellisynt gasped and cast her husband a frightened look. "He's . . . he's but making sport. Please, my lord, I wish to retire. May we leave now?"

She bent to gather the weight of her skirt, and completely missed the startled look the two men exchanged above her head.

"Has this churl in knight's clothing been bothering you?" FitzHugh asked, frowning.

"No! No, I swear!" She clutched his arm.

Beauchamp straightened slowly. "By all the saints, FitzHugh, I knew you lacked address with anything not on four legs. But to cause such unease in just a week of marriage is something of an achievement, even for you."

"Begone, Roger," FitzHugh told him quietly, his eyes on Mellisynt's white face. He took her arm and started to lead her toward the dim corridor. Beauchamp took an involuntary step forward.

FitzHugh gave the other knight a hard, level look. "I'll see to my wife, Beauchamp."

After a long pause, the younger man nodded once, stiffly, then stood aside.

FitzHugh could feel the tremor in her arm as he guided his lady through the dim corridors. Icy drafts whistled along the vaulted ceilings, raising acrid gusts of smoke from the flickering flambeaux. He knew full well, however, that it wasn't the cold that made the lady tremble. He glanced down at the woman stumbling along beside him. She was pale and pinched of face now, but just moments before he had seen her laughing up at Beauchamp with a beguiling liveliness. Like creeping, insidious tendrils of mist, the castle priest's words crept into FitzHugh's head. Was this woman the wanton the fat little cleric had hinted at? Did she laugh so merrily with other men to lead them into dalliance?

He dismissed the idea immediately. Mellisynt's untutored responses during their coupling told their own story. Thoughts of that night, and the way her trim, taut body had arched against his own, hesitantly at first, then with growing enthusiasm, crowded out the priest's ugly insinuations. They also made FitzHugh revise instantly the punishment he'd decided upon for his wife's insolence in rejecting his bride gift. First, however, he needed to deal with the fear still darkening her eyes.

He released her when they entered their apartments. Ian was polishing an assortment of armour beside the fire, and was sent from the room with a quick jerk of his master's head. The door closed firmly behind the squire, and FitzHugh shot the bolt.

"Tell me what makes your hands shake so and your face pale," he ordered softly.

His wife whirled to face him. "Nothing. Nothing, I swear. 'Tis just the cold."

"It can't be nothing and the cold, both. Make up your mind, lady wife."

Moving slowly, so as not to frighten her more, FitzHugh crossed the room and poured wine into chased silver goblets. He swirled the rich Burgundian red around in one cup a few times, then handed it to the still, pale woman before him.

"Tell me," he ordered.

The wine splashed over the rim onto Mellisynt's gown. Taking a deep breath, she plunged into speech.

"He only touched me in the dance, my lord, I swear it! I tried to refuse, but did not want to make too much disturbance with my protests. There was nothing else between us, upon my soul."

"I didn't think there was."

His calm response brought her up short.

"You didn't?" Disbelief and fear edged her voice.

"Nay. I saw you clearly across the hall. Beauchamp has a well-deserved reputation with women, but even he couldn't manage to seduce you in a crowded hall while prancing around in circles like a silly jackanapes."

FitzHugh could see her tension ease with his casual words. Some of the rigidity flowed from her body, and the fright from her eyes. He went forward to lead her to the chairs before the fire, then halted abruptly when she stumbled backward, away from him.

His eyes narrowed, and then he moved toward her again with a steady, unhurried tread. Taking her arm, he settled first her, then himself, in the chairs.

Mellisynt sat stiff and uncomfortable, chewing on her lower lip. Her eyes stared unseeing at the snapping fire while her mind churned with FitzHugh's last words.

"Did you really not take umbrage at my dancing with Sir Roger?"

"I did not."

His calm words gave her pause. That he was not jealous of the handsome, devilish Beauchamp reassured her. Perversely, it also added to her little store of hurt. Telling herself that she should be glad this husband viewed their marriage dispassionately, as a business arrangement, Mellisynt stared into the fire.

"I take it Sir Henri objected to such activities rather strenuously?"

She flashed him a wary look. He sprawled, loose and long-limbed and totally at ease.

"Aye," she said, slowly.

"Or to any activity that put you in the way of other men?"

"To any other men at all," she admitted finally. "He was most..."

"Jealous of his young wife," FitzHugh finished when she seemed disinclined to.

"Aye." She sighed, then relaxed against the padded chair back. "I lost count of the number of men he had banished from the castle and his lands because he thought they gave me too warm a look, or because they dared to kiss my hand. Men whose livelihood depended on Henri's goodwill were turned out with their families to starve."

She turned her head and regarded him steadily. "Some took more than just his ill wishes with them. One poor knight swilled too much ale and pressed on me the embraces he thought my infirm husband could not. He carried away two broken thumbs and a fine web of lash marks on his back."

FitzHugh stretched his long legs out and crossed his ankles. "I cannot fault Henri for that. Any man who dared insult you so would fare far worse at my hands." He paused as a log crackled and gave off a shower of sparks. "And you? Did you not take some hurt from his jealousies, as well?"

Her mouth turned down in a rueful smile.

"No, no real hurt. Just fasts and penances, and they were scarce noticeable among all the other days and weeks I spent on my knees. I seemed to collect such punishments regularly."

"Aye, I would guess that you did."

Mellisynt decided to ignore his observation. A slumbrous silence descended, punctuated only by the hiss and crackle of the fire. Finally, driven by curiosity, she turned to him once more.

"If you were truly not angry, my lord, why did you sound so...so harsh when you came upon us?"

"I didn't say I was not angry. Just that I was not disturbed by your dancing."

Mellisynt straightened, her brows drawing together in confusion. "Then what caused your anger?"

"Your willfulness, lady wife."

"What?"

FitzHugh took a slow sip of wine. "You heard me."

"What willfulness?"

"Did I not tell you I wished you to wear the bride gift I brought you?"

"Aye," she said, caution threading her voice. "But you didn't say I should wear it this night."

One dark eyebrow quirked. "Do you truly mistake my meaning so?"

Mellisynt felt the heat of the fire on her cheeks. "No."

"I thought as much." He set his wine aside and folded his hands across his stomach.

She waited, her breath caught in her throat, while the silence stretched between them. When her nerves could bear it no longer, she broke the stillness.

"All right, I admit my temper ran away with me! I didn't wear the brooch because I hated that you won it on...on the duke's business."

FitzHugh surveyed her thoughtfully. "Aye, I thought as much. Tell me why you carry this hatred for Geoffrey in your breast. He is your overlord, as well as mine."

"Aye." She sneered. "And a fine protector he is, too. He would sell a child to one like Henri of Trémont, then ride off with his pockets full of gold and nary a backward glance, like the veriest whoremaster."

The simmering resentment in her voice startled even Mellisynt. She sat back, her hands grasping the wooden chair arms, expecting FitzHugh's censure for such disrespect.

To her surprise, he simply nodded. "'Tis the way of the world, to arrange marriages that bring the most advantage. Geoffrey gave a girl in his wardship to the lord of a strategic castle, one that guards his borders. Just as he gave you to me, to hold and protect that same castle."

His even, measured tone, and the steady way he regarded her from beneath his dark brows, took much of the heat from Mellisynt's argument. All that was left was the pain of her lost youth. The tight knot of resentment, buried so long in her heart, loosened, but did not completely disappear.

"And you, my lord, would do the same? If we have daughters, will you give them to any man who can bring you gold or lands? Will you care if they ever again see the sun or hear a voice raised in song?"

FitzHugh frowned, and Mellisynt saw a flash of uncertainty cross his face. This stern warrior had not thought in terms of daughters, only sons, she realized.

"Is that what you endured?"

Mellisynt brushed aside her years at Trémont with an impatient hand. "Aye, but I don't seek your pity. I want only your understanding." She paused, taking a deep breath. "And your pledge that you will not use our daughters so, should we have any. I ask your promise that you will allow them joy and . . . and love in their marriages, if possible."

His blue eyes settled on her face in a considering look. At length, he shook his head. "Love is an ill-defined emotion at best, found only in the troubadours' songs. Like you, I've seen little enough of it in my life. If we find trust and respect, and a touch of lust, in our marriage, we may count ourselves fortunate.''

He held up a hand when Mellisynt would have protested. ''I can't promise that the husbands chosen for our daughters will bring them more. But I do promise that I will consult with you before entering into an agreement for our children, do you wish it.''

Mellisynt's eyes widened in stunned surprise. That FitzHugh would grant her a say in the disposition of their children was beyond anything she'd imagined or hoped for. The knot of anger she'd carried for so long loosened even more.

''Aye,'' she breathed. ''I wish it.''

She slanted her husband an assessing look. His forbearance astounded her. For a man of his fearsome reputation in the field, he'd been remarkably restrained with her throughout their short betrothal and marriage. Except for his spurt of anger earlier, when she'd refused his gift, he'd treated her with respect and gentle hands. And that one incident had been as much her fault as his, Mellisynt decided magnanimously. Thinking to reward his remarkable promise with one of her own, she smiled across the small space separating their chairs.

''I apologize for letting my temper lead me to spurn your bride gift this eve. I'll wear it in all graciousness, if you will pardon my willfulness.''

''No.''

Her smile slipped. ''No?''

''No, 'tis not enough.'' He turned his head. ''You must learn that I don't make unreasonable demands, and those I make I expect to be obeyed. Take off your clothes.''

''What?''

''Do you have a disorder of the ear, as well as a willful temper, wife?''

He rose with a loose-limbed grace that belied his size and reached for the buckle of his belt.

Mellisynt sprang up. ''You puling caitiff! You would beat me?''

"The idea does hold some appeal," FitzHugh replied.
"Now take off your clothes, loose your hair and lay yourself down in the bed before I decide to do so."

Chapter Seven

Mellisynt awoke the next morning feeling most properly chastised. And wondrously well used. She was discovering there was much more to this business of coupling than she'd ever dreamed possible. Lifting the deadweight of Fitz-Hugh's arm from her chest, she slipped out of bed. Muscles she had never known she had protested as she groped her way through the dark to the pile of clothing scattered about the floor. She pulled her shift over her head, grateful for its thin warmth, then wrapped FitzHugh's discarded surcoat around her like a blanket. With a small groan, she sank down beside the hearth and began to feed the banked embers bits of kindling. Propping her chin on arms folded across her knees, she watched the coals begin to glow, then catch the kindling in tiny flames.

Sweet Mother of God, how she ached. A heat having nothing to do with the small, hissing fire suffused her face. Who would have thought a man's body could be the instrument of such exquisite punishment? That it could stretch and invade and fill her until she thought she'd burst? Only to be withdrawn and replaced by hands and lips that drove her to panting, sweating, groaning madness. For the first time, Mellisynt had experienced a male in full rut, a magnificent, sleekly muscled, powerful male who sought to demonstrate his dominance in the most elemental way possible.

Her face burned as she remembered FitzHugh's deliberate assault on her senses, his slow, determined pacing, her own gasping panic as he pushed her into a vortex of sensation the like of which she'd never dreamed of, let alone experienced, in all her life. She would have felt shamed by her wild, uninhibited responses if his low, rasping moans hadn't grown in volume toward the end until they matched hers, and he seemed to lose control of his own movements. What had begun as a lesson for one had ended in an explosion of erotic sensation for both.

As she studied the dancing flames, Mellisynt began to understand the courtiers' preoccupation with this business of love. To combine such . . . such passion with a fine, noble dedication of one's heart to another must surely be a worthy goal, even if unattainable.

With a small groan, she struggled to her feet. Shrugging off the heavy surcoat, she reached for her discarded robe.

"The aches ease with time and repeated effort."

She jumped and clutched her gown to her chest. Turning, she discovered her husband stretched comfortably in bed, his head pillowed on his hands.

"Do we repeat last night, I will not ache. I will be dead," she told him with a grimace only half feigned.

White teeth gleamed in his stubble-darkened face. "'Tis how many refer to the act of joining—*la petite mort,* the little death."

"There was nothing little about it, as I recall."

Her tart rejoinder brought what looked suspiciously like smug satisfaction to his face. She turned away, unwilling to pander to such masculine conceit. Pulling on her much-worn amber bliaut, she attacked its tangled ties with cold, stiff fingers.

"Did Henri force you to robe yourself, thus, in such shapeless rags?"

She glanced over to find him surveying her gown with distaste.

"Nay, he had me dress in gray wool habits so nunlike that at times I near forgot I was not a bride of Christ." Her fingers stroked the faithful yellow silk. "This was one of the gowns I brought with me to Trémont as a bride. 'Tis a bit outmoded, but has use yet in it."

The mattress stuffing rustled as FitzHugh brought his arms down and pushed aside the covers. Magnificent in his nakedness, he crossed the room. Faint fingers of dawn creeping through the high windows painted his body in shadow and light. Mellisynt ran new, experienced eyes over his massive torso and swallowed. Sweet Mother, what he could do with...

"Did the lickpenny you were wed to teach you his miserly ways?" His voice rumbled in her ear like a distant summer storm. "Why do you not buy yourself new gowns? The markets here in Nantes have goods from the four corners of the world."

Mellisynt looked up at him, her eyes wide. "I didn't think... I didn't know you wished it."

His brows knitted. "List to me, lady wife," he began. "I'm not Henri of Trémont. I—"

Mellisynt's indelicate snort interrupted him. "If I were not already aware of that, my lord, last night would have certainly made it clear."

She flicked a quick glance down his chest, lingered for a moment at his loins, then brought her gaze back to his face once more. His lips twitched, and he turned away to pick up his braies. Mellisynt surveyed two taut white buttocks with considerable attention. When he had covered them, and other parts of similar interest, he turned to face her once more.

"I'm no weak old man, lady. I'm fully capable of managing my most valued possessions, whether they be lands or armour or war-horses or wife. I don't require you to dress in rags to discourage overardent swains."

Mellisynt stiffened. "I'm not sure I care to be considered a possession of somewhat lesser worth than your horse, my lord."

One corner of FitzHugh's mouth lifted. "That's because you know nothing of horses, let alone destriers. A good one is much more difficult to obtain, and takes far longer to break in, than a wife.''

He laughed outright at her indignant gasp. "Much as I value them, however, I will not have my horses better caparisoned than my lady. Outfit yourself as befits your station. Spend your coins on whatever women's fripperies you wish.''

"I would spend my coins most willingly," she snapped, "had I any."

The glint of amusement faded from FitzHugh's eyes. "You have moneys. Use them."

"I hesitate to contradict you and risk another lessoning, but I cannot use what I do not have."

"Do you imply I've misused your inheritance, Lady of Trémont? That I've denied you your portion?" His slow, dangerous drawl made the hairs on Mellisynt's arms prickle.

"Nay!" she protested, confused by his sudden hostility.

He took a deliberate step forward. "For most of my life, I've had little but the strength of my arm and my honor to claim as my own. It's held me steady in a world filled with men who twist with the wind and break their sacred oaths on the least provocation. I'll not have you imply that I dishonored myself, and you, in greed for Henri's estate."

Mellisynt gaped at his grim countenance. "I did not think you denied my portion. It's yours, after all, to manage for me and mine."

For a long, hard moment, FitzHugh glared down at her. His jaw worked, and he made an obvious effort to rein in his anger. "Did you not read the betrothal documents? Your revenues are in your name, to use as you see fit."

Mellisynt thought of the parchments lying at the bottom of her traveling basket, totally incomprehensible to her untutored mind. She swallowed, and shook her head.

Disgust wiped the anger from FitzHugh's eyes. "Do you not know which manors were put in your name? How much of the forestry fees and shearing tariffs come to you?"

Mute, she could only shake her head once more.

FitzHugh swore, low and long and colorfully. "We'll go over the documents this night. You need to know what is yours, and what comes to me to manage. For now, know that you have a goodly income of your own. You may spend it as you please."

"But I have no coins, nor silver marks," Mellisynt protested in muddled confusion.

"Did I not tell you to draw upon the duchess's exchequer?" he bit out, exasperation and impatience drawing his brows together in a familiar scowl.

"Aye." Her voice wavered, then gathered strength. "But I did not do so, not realizing I had moneys of my own nor wishing to spend your coin without permission."

FitzHugh expelled a long drawn-out breath. "I'll give you coins enough to take care of your needs until you are comfortable with managing your own accounts."

Mellisynt nodded, her thoughts churning. The idea that she had rents and fees and income of her own, to do with as she would, astounded her almost as much as Fitz-Hugh's assumption that she could manage these moneys herself. And on top of those startling revelations, visions of bright silks and thick furs danced in her mind.

"I'll visit the markets this day, my lord."

He paused in the act of attaching the tapes of his chausses to his braies. "I recall your mentioning that you went little into town before. Are you used to haggling and buying?"

"Nay." An eager gleam entered her eyes. "But I'll learn."

"Mayhap you should take another lady with you, to show you the best shops," FitzHugh suggested. He paused, his shirt dangling from one hand. "Or take the girl, Isabeau. She's new to the court, and knows few other women as yet. No doubt she would enjoy a visit to the markets. And she is most pleasingly dressed. She can show you the latest styles."

Mellisynt bit her lip and turned away while her lord finished dressing. Her amazement at discovering she was mistress of her own funds and the shivery anticipation of exploring the shops had slipped away by imperceptible degrees.

"I still don't see why we couldn't have taken a litter."

Isabeau lifted one velvet-shod foot, protected by a heavy wooden patten, over a pile of snowy slush and gave her companion a disgruntled glare.

Mellisynt sent a silent prayer to the Virgin for strength. "I told you. I would not keep the men-at-arms standing about in the cold all day while we dawdled in the warmth of the shops."

"So instead we must pick our way through this— Oh!"

Isabeau jumped back as a shower of snow fell from the steep roof overhead. Pulling her fur-lined cloak closer, she hugged the inside of the narrow walk. The little page, Bartholomew, pressed into service with another youngster to carry whatever bundles Mellisynt might acquire, smothered a laugh. The two boys fell back when Isabeau whirled on them.

"You little toads, I'm tired of your snickering and laughing. If you don't know how to treat a lady with respect, I'll learn you right enough." She started toward them with one hand upraised.

Mellisynt sighed and put herself between the irate beauty and the unrepentant boys.

"Such agitation will leave lines upon your brow," she said mildly. She hid an amused grin as Isabeau halted in midstride and smoothed the anger from her face.

Having spent a full afternoon with the spoiled beauty and the two high-spirited boys, Mellisynt had learned quickly enough to handle them. She pandered to the girl's vanity and ignored all but the most outrageous of the boy's giggling pranks. 'Twas a wonder she'd managed to make any purchases at all, between admiring how a succession of colors looked against Isabeau's fair skin and keeping one eye on the boys as they enjoyed their unexpected freedom from the esquire who served as tutor and trainer.

"The little wretches," Isabeau muttered.

"They're just children, only a little younger than you yourself," Mellisynt commented, not for the first time that long afternoon. Indeed, at times she'd found the boys more mature, and certainly more companionable, than the budding girl-woman.

"I'm far from a child." Isabeau sniffed. "I would have been wed a year and more ago if my betrothed hadn't taken an arrow in the neck at Limoges. I had prepared all my bride clothes, too. 'Twas most inconvenient."

"No doubt your betrothed thought so, as well," Mellisynt commented.

Isabeau's delicate eyebrows drew together, and then she shrugged. "I met the man only once, at our betrothal. Now the duchess is to pick another husband for me, one who will hold Bellamy in my father's stead. I hope she chooses soon."

Mellisynt hoped so, too, most fervently, and continued her plodding path through the slush. She and Isabeau had just stepped around a pile of snow-covered garbage when a cacophony of shouts and high-pitched yelps made them both jump. She turned to see Bartholomew and the other page drop their bundles and hurl themselves at a milling, shouting group of street children. Both boys rapidly disappeared in a flurry of fists and thrashing legs.

"Holy Mother! What in heaven's name—?" Mellisynt thrust her own bundles into Isabeau's arms and picked up her skirts in both hands. Her pattens slid on the wet cobbles as she ran across the street and tried to make some sense of the swirling mass of shouting boys. Plucking at one ragged mantle, she tugged at it with both hands. A stocky urchin stumbled back and fell against her. Mellisynt and the boy both landed on their backsides in the slush.

Picking herself up with grim determination, she waded into the fray once more. She lost her veil and felt the pins slip from her hair as she struggled with the teeming mass. After a few breathless moments, she caught hold of Bartholomew's collar and managed to yank him upright. The other boys fell back at her fury.

"What in God's name are you about?" She jerked the boy's collar so hard his golden curls danced.

"They were stoning him," Bartholomew gasped.

"Him? Who?"

"Him."

He held out a begrimed hand and pointed to a huge, furred creature the size of a small pony, tied to a stone wall. The dog, if it was one, was the sorriest-looking animal Mellisynt had ever seen. Mud coated its brindled coat, half of one ear appeared to have been chewed off in a long-ago fight, and every rib stood out in stark relief against its ragged hide. One of its hind legs was missing, and it stood awkwardly on the remaining three. A rope cut cruelly into its neck and was tethered to a ring bolt in the wall.

"Whose dog is this?"

Keeping a firm grasp on Bartholomew's collar, she surveyed the assembled crowd. In addition to the boys, the circle around them now included interested passersby and shopkeepers drawn out into the street by the noise. Isabeau hovered at the edge of the crowd, a disgusted expression on her face.

"'Tis naught but a stray," one of the boys answered in a surly voice. "He's been digging in the garbage heaps and making a nuisance of hisself."

Mellisynt chewed her lower lip. No more than Bartholomew did she like to see a poor creature tormented. But a maimed animal such as this could not earn its keep, and was of no use to anyone.

"He's been hurt, Bartholomew."

"Yes, but see how he still manages on three legs. He's game, my lady. Look at his eyes."

She did, and knew at once it was a mistake. The hound's great brown eyes seemed to fasten on hers with a pathetic dignity, as if it sensed a savior from its torment but was unwilling to beg for salvation.

"He's filthy, and flea-ridden," Isabeau put in, shouldering her way through the crowd.

"So would you be if you had to sleep in the streets and eat garbage," Bartholomew told her indignantly.

"This is absurd. Leave him and let us return to the château, Lady Mellisynt. It's cold, and my shoes are wet."

Mellisynt looked from Bartholomew's pleading eyes to Isabeau's furious ones, and then to the crowd that surrounded them. The teeming mass waited with avid interest for the next act in this little drama. She bit her lip, then glanced up hopefully as a clatter of iron-shod hooves echoed over the heads of the crowd. A standard-bearer with Brittany's pennant rode into the square, followed by a troop of mounted men. When she recognized the unmistakable figure in the lead, she felt a rush of relief.

"What in the name of all the saints goes on here?"

FitzHugh's furious voice thundered across the winter air. He pushed his mailed hood back and surveyed the scene with a disbelieving scowl. Beside him, Sir Roger looked over the crowd, a grin of unholy amusement on his face.

Mellisynt's surge of welcome relief at the sight of her lord faded at the stunned incredulity on his face. Suddenly conscious of her straggling hair and mudstained cloak, she essayed a hesitant smile.

FitzHugh nudged his mount forward, parting the crowd. His eyes glinted dangerously as they scanned the throng, then came to rest on her.

"Would you care to tell me why I find my lady in the midst of a street brawl, with mud on her knees and face, surrounded by a bunch of ragtag ruffians and merchants?"

Mellisynt swallowed. Like leaves scattering before a cold wind, the crowd began to disperse, glancing nervously at the dark knight as they slipped away. Bartholomew moved closer to her side, and the other page scrambled to his feet.

"'Twas the dog, my lord," Mellisynt replied, with what dignity she could salvage. "The boys were stoning it, and Bar—and we thought to save it from such a fate."

FitzHugh's eyes slid to the animal, and a pained look crossed his face.

"You appear to have accomplished your goal, at least for the moment. Come, I'll take you back to the château." He reached down to lift her up before him.

Mellisynt looked at the mailed fist, then flicked a quick glance back at the hound.

"No, my lady," FitzHugh told her softly. "Geoffrey would not be best pleased were I to add such a creature to his kennels."

She stiffened at the name, and FitzHugh silently cursed his blunder.

"We would not have to add him to the castle runs," Mellisynt offered, her chin high. "We can send him back to Trémont, when he's been tended to."

"Aye, my lord." Bartholomew stepped forward confidently. "I'll tend him myself till he's well enough."

"You'll be too busy seeing to your own hurts to worry about anyone else's," FitzHugh growled. "If this is how you care for your lady, you haven't learned much at your trainer's hand. I'll make sure he applies his lessons more forcefully."

The boy's face crumpled, and Mellisynt laid a protective hand on his shoulder. FitzHugh did not miss the instinctive gesture. Nor was his simmering anger proof against the unconscious plea in his wife's wide green eyes. His irritation began to subside.

In truth, until he'd rounded the corner and discovered his lady in such straits, he'd been feeling an uncharacteristic sense of goodwill toward her. He'd left their chamber sated—replete, in fact. He'd never dreamed that this pale, slender woman would light such fires in his blood that they'd all but consume him. That his deliberate assault on her senses would send his own reeling. He suspected his attempt to demonstrate his absolute mastery had missed its mark.

As he surveyed Mellisynt's mud-streaked face, he could see it had. 'Twas obvious her spirit was intact, if the combination of appeal and stubborn determination filling her eyes was any indication. A grudging respect dawned. To have lived the life she had and kept her courage bespoke a stronger woman than he'd first supposed her to be. He shook his head, wondering at the nature of a woman who would wed a baseborn knight to get a child, one who would take a rascally page and a flea-bitten mongrel into her heart.

Isabeau interrupted his thoughts, stepping forward with her arms full of bundles and a thoroughly disgruntled look on her face.

"For pity's sake, my lord, I've stood here in this snow and wet too long as it is because of that misbegotten cur. My feet are frozen. Please, take us back to the castle."

"Beauchamp, see to the Lady Isabeau." FitzHugh leaned a forearm across the pommel and kept his gaze locked on his wife's dirt streaked face.

Beauchamp kneed his horse forward.

"Come, wench, 'tis clear this is a family discussion."

Leaning down, he wrapped a strong arm around the girl's waist and hauled her, packages and all, into the saddle before him. Flashing a wry grin over the beauty's dark head, he kicked his mount into a loping canter.

"My lord!" Isabeau gasped, struggling for purchase. "You go too fast! I cannot get my seat!"

Beauchamp tightened his hold, savoring the press of her full breasts against his arm through thick layers of clothing. Her bottom cheeks, soft and full and lush, bounced against his thigh. A wicked grin split his face. "Nay, girl. You most assuredly have your seat. I can feel the full weight of it, and very solid it is, too."

Isabeau's mouth dropped. "How—how dare you address me so!"

"When you get to know me better, you'll find I dare most anything, child."

"I'm not a child!" Isabeau snapped back.

* * *

Mellisynt swept into the great hall that evening, fully recovered from her street adventure. She glanced around the crowded room, looking for her husband's dark head above the milling throng. As she stood on tiptoe, one hand braced against a tall column, a lilting laugh floated across the air. Turning, Mellisynt saw the Lady Isabeau in the midst of a group of admiring courtiers. The elegant, golden-haired knight whose poetry so enchanted the court hung over the girl. He was as finely dressed as always, in a tunic of golden velvet and shoes so long and pointed they brushed Isabeau's very skirts.

"Nay, Sir Guy," Isabeau cooed, "I'm not yet ready to accept an *entendedor*. I've not been at court long enough for any knight to do duty as aspirant or supplicant, let alone be permitted to dedicate songs to me."

She softened her rebuff with a provocative smile that promised so much more than a girl her age and single status should.

"You're a cruel, heartless beauty," de Claire said with a sigh, lifting her hand to stroke it sensuously.

"Nay, she's just a silly, overpadded wench."

Mellisynt jumped at the mocking voice just behind her. She shushed Beauchamp with a smothered laugh, praying that his words hadn't carried to the group surrounding Isabeau.

They had. Guy de Claire stiffened. Isabeau turned, fury flaring in her huge aquamarine eyes.

"Sir Guy," she choked out. "Mayhap I would accept a suitor, if he were able to assure that ill-bred knaves do not bandy about comments on my person."

"None shall, my lady," de Claire said. He moved past Isabeau, putting the girl behind him with a steady hand.

Mellisynt's embarrassed amusement drained at the sight of the knight's face. His mouth curled in an evil smile that matched the feral gleam in his eyes. She suddenly remembered Beauchamp's warning after her own clash with de Claire, that the knight masked a vicious temper behind his courtier's facade. Glancing worriedly up at the man beside her, she discovered a devilish glee dancing in his brown eyes. Beauchamp was enjoying this, she realized, dismayed. The idiot didn't appear in the least daunted at the prospect of taking a dagger in his gut right in the middle of the duchess's crowded great room!

De Claire moved forward with a sinister grace that belied his elegant appearance. Mellisynt bit her lip, then gathered her skirts and made as if to move out of his way. In the process, her foot came down firmly on the tip of his pointed shoe. The man's eyes widened in surprise as his weight shifted. He wavered, then fell forward over his own feet and hit the tiles with a crash that made many of those nearby jump. Muffled oaths sounded, then gave way to sputtered laughter as the courtiers saw Guy de Claire, count of Almay, sprawled flat on his face.

De Claire levered himself up on one knee. His murderous glare told Mellisynt that wounding a knight's dignity was a far worse crime than disparaging his poetry. Evading Beauchamp's restraining hand, she rushed forward.

"Oh, Sir Guy, I'm so sorry. I swear, I'm as clumsy as a cow." She bent to take hold of one arm and help him rise. He shook off her hand.

"You did that apurpose, you little—"

"Do you address my wife, de Claire?"

The hairs on the back of Mellisynt's neck stood on end at the lazy menace in FitzHugh's voice. He pushed his way casually through the crowd, and stepped around his wife. With a firm hand, he set her to one side, out of the circle of his sword arm. Beauchamp moved up on silent feet to stand beside him, and the courtiers at the scene backed away.

The count straightened, his lips lifting in a sneer.

"'Twould appear you've taken an awkward wife, Sir Richard."

"Nay, de Claire," FitzHugh drawled. "'Twas you who tumbled to the tiles, after all. You can't seem to keep your balance on your feet any better than you keep your seat in the tourney."

A tide of red swept up the count's neck. "Bastard!"

"'Tis most unchivalrous of you both to discomfit a lady so." Constance swept between the men. With her dainty figure and haughty brow, she was every inch the duchess. "I'm sure the Lady Mellisynt does not wish a simple accident to cause such a disturbance."

"Don't intervene in this, my lady," FitzHugh warned.

Constance stiffened, and ice dripped from her voice. "Do you think to order me in my own castle?"

FitzHugh swallowed a curse. He knew Constance when she assumed that frigid mien and drew the dignity of her rank around her like a shield. If he persisted now and took satisfaction of de Claire, the damned woman wouldn't hesitate to call the castle guards down on them both. In a fit of temper, she'd once kicked a drunken Geoffrey from her bed and locked him naked in the corridor.

FitzHugh straightened slowly. He had no desire to have the long-simmering quarrel between him and de Claire end so farcically. Besides, Constance was well within her rights to keep order among her husband's vassals. Reining in his anger, he bowed to the tiny duchess.

"Forgive my presumption. Sir Guy and I will resolve this matter at another time and place."

Her eyes shooting violet sparks, Constance moved to de Claire's side. Deliberately, she took his arm. The rigid knight sent FitzHugh a look of hard promise over the duchess's head, then allowed her to lead him away.

"I'm sorry!"

"'Twas not your lady's fault."

Mellisynt and Beauchamp both spoke as one, then stopped. The knight flashed his rogue's smile and bent over Mellisynt's hand.

"I thank you for trying to save me from the folly of my words, my lady, but 'twas not at all necessary."

"No," Mellisynt replied, nerves sharpening her voice. "You would have much preferred to spill his blood right here, on the duchess's Moorish tiles."

He grinned. "Well, if I do not, FitzHugh will most like to do so, and soon."

She turned and laid a hand on her husband's arm. "I would not have you at daggers drawn over this silly incident, my lord. Truly, I was most clumsy."

"Aye, you were," FitzHugh agreed.

Beauchamp smothered a laugh at her openmouthed indignation.

FitzHugh nodded. "Very clumsy. Although I applaud your intent, don't intervene again in the affairs of men. You could get hurt."

Mellisynt's eyes narrowed to glittering green slits. She turned away with a swish of her skirts and plopped down on a nearby bench, determined to ignore the two men who stood behind her and conversed casually, as if near-bloodshed in the midst of dinner were a most common occurrence, and one of little import.

Later, after the servants cleared the boards from the evening meal and the crowd began to mingle, Constance moved to Mellisynt's side.

"I saw your attempt to intervene between Beauchamp and de Claire," she murmured. "That was well done, even if your method was a trifle crude and had unexpected consequences. What caused the disturbance?"

Mellisynt hesitated. "Sir Guy took exception to Beauchamp's . . . ah . . . comments about the Lady Isabeau."

"I knew it," Constance said, seething. "Men take almost as much pleasure in fighting over a woman's skirts as trying to get up them!"

Her eyes roved to where Isabeau, still somewhat flushed, held her usual court. "I need to do something about that one."

Chapter Eight

"I tell you, you must go!"

Constance tapped an angry foot against the floor. The staccato beat matched the tempo of FitzHugh's furious pacing.

"Is this a ruse?" he ground out. "Do you think to send me away because of last night's little farce with de Claire? If so, you but delay the inevitable. And make me look the fool."

"Don't be more pigheaded than you usually are," the duchess snapped. "I know you and de Claire will settle your quarrel, however little sense it makes to have you both spill your brains over something this trivial. But you will not do it here. And not while Geoffrey needs you." Her voice faltered on the last words.

FitzHugh stopped in midstride. He couldn't remember hearing Constance of Brittany's voice tremble before.

"Tell me quickly this news you have that necessitates my immediate departure."

"A ship just docked with messages from Winchester," Constance said, her eyes shadowed with concern. "Geoffrey writes that he will repudiate the truce."

"What! How could he be so ill-advised? We need this truce as much as does Richard Lionheart, to regroup our forces and garrison the castles on the border with loyal men."

"I know that, and you know that!" Constance all but shouted. "But Geoffrey is all arage at the peace conditions. He's expected to make reparations to Richard's damned Crusade chest. The king fears to offend the church."

"So Brittany is to bear the cost of the war, instigated by the king himself to keep Richard Lionheart in check." FitzHugh shook his head.

The duchess nodded glumly. "Geoffrey refuses to accept the conditions. He hates his brother, and swears he'll see that dour-faced sodomite in hell before he'll give him the kiss of peace."

Despite himself, FitzHugh grinned. "Calm yourself, Constance. King Henry demands this truce, and he'll get it. He pulls his sons' strings most skillfully."

"I know, God rot his soul. Henry plays one son off the other for his own ends. Damn the whole Angevin brood, devil's spawn that they are!"

"Do you forget that one sits in your belly?"

FitzHugh watched, amused, as Constance softened both her stance and her furious expression. She placed a protective hand on her stomach and turned troubled violet eyes up to his.

"Nay, I do not forget. That's why I ask you to go to England. Geoffrey needs your steady head, or he'll forswear my child's birthright in this mad game he plays with his brother and father. I would go myself, but I dare not risk my babe in a winter crossing."

"I'd not allow you to take such a journey," FitzHugh told her gently. "You know I'll go."

She came forward and placed a small white hand on FitzHugh's arm.

"Aye, I knew you would. I'm…frightened, Richard. The old king moves his sons about like pawns on a chessboard. He doesn't realize the hatred he stirs. It festers within them all. Of late, Geoffrey carries under his bluff exterior a bitterness so vile it eats at his very soul."

"Aye." FitzHugh nodded slowly and covered the duchess's hand with his own. "I've seen it take hold more, and more."

"You're closest to him, Richard. His only real friend. He needs you. Go to him and convince him to accept this truce so that Brittany can recover from its wounds."

Shaking off her uncharacteristic soberness, she essayed a gamine grin. "And then you can take your lady to that moldy old keep you call home and use her riches to bring some civilization to the place."

FitzHugh laughed. He'd first seen Constance as a tiny, indomitable seven-year-old when she arrived in England to meet her boisterous betrothed. She'd made no secret then of her preference for Brittany's windswept shores and majestic forests over England's damp clime. Nor did she now.

With the ease of long friendship, FitzHugh chucked her under her chin. "As you command, my lady."

"Oh, and I have a favor to ask of your wife," Constance added. "I would have her take the Lady Isabeau to England, and chaperone her most closely while I arrange a match for the minx. I'm thinking of Simon de Lacy. His wife died last year, and he needs someone to warm his old bones in bed."

"De Lacy? You'd give that child to a battered old warhorse like him?"

Constance snorted inelegantly. "Child! If she's not bedded soon, she'll melt from the heat between her legs."

She stopped and drew a breath. "'Tis why I thought to send her with you and the Lady Mellisynt. I need to remove her from court before the wench causes a riot. Your isolated holding will serve as well as any I can think of to keep her from mischief."

FitzHugh shrugged. "As you will. I'll leave you now and make the necessary arrangements."

He strode back through the drafty corridors, his face grim. Geoffrey's recklessness worried him far more than he would reveal to Constance. Even before this latest, accursed war, his hot-blooded friend had chafed more and more at his father's heavy hand.

The king was long used to controlling his vast domains in England and France, and to controlling the sons who would someday inherit them. Like a master puppeteer, he made them all dance and jerk on the strings he pulled. FitzHugh knew in his heart, however, that this time the king had gone too far. His decision to curb Richard Lionheart's power by devolving some of his lands on young Prince John had set the brothers at war. The king himself sent Geoffrey forth to battle on behalf of John, yet expected him to pay for the costs of that war. No wonder the duke now rebelled.

FitzHugh threw open the door to his apartments, still deep in troubled thought.

"Shut the door!"

"My lord, look out!"

A wet, hairy body threw itself forward with a hundred and more pounds of determination.

FitzHugh staggered back, his arms instinctively clasping the struggling shape. They went down in a flurry of water and foaming soap.

"Sweet Mother! Ian, help me haul him off. Grab his tail, Bartholomew, and pull."

Mellisynt locked both arms around the dog's huge neck and tugged.

"Stand aside," FitzHugh snarled. Keeping a tight grip on the panting beast, he staggered to his feet. "And shut the damned door before I loose him."

His squire hastened to comply.

"Sit! Be still, you misbegotten spawn of Satan!"

The dog cast FitzHugh a wary look and hunkered down on his one hind leg.

"Well! Of all the ungrateful creatures," Mellisynt gasped, tucking a wet straggle of coppery hair behind her ear. "I've fed him enough to keep a starving family for a year, physicked his hurts, and prepared him a bath, yet the cursed beast ignores *my* every command."

"Mayhap your orders lack a note of authority. As mine obviously did when I told you this hound was to be confined to the stables."

FitzHugh's voice carried soft, silky menace. He felt a stab of savage satisfaction when his wife blinked and wiped wet hands down the sides of her drenched gown. Ian and Bartholomew exchanged nervous glances.

"Well, he did spend the night in the stables...." Mellisynt began, somewhat hesitantly. "But the head groom says he took most violent exception to the presence of stable cats. He broke the rope holding him to chase one tom and, um...upset the horses somewhat."

FitzHugh closed his eyes, imagining the havoc this three-legged monster would wreak running through the stalls of destriers trained to kill and maim with tooth and hoof.

"No one was hurt, my lord," Mellisynt assured him. "At least not very seriously. But the groom sent me a message this morning, most earnestly requesting that I remove him immediately. So I brought him here. Just to feed and bathe him, I swear."

"And then what will you do with him?" FitzHugh inquired carefully.

"Well, I'm not exactly sure. I thought to hire a man to take him back to Trémont. With my own coins, of course."

She gave him a saucy grin that made FitzHugh's dark brows shoot up.

"He needs some care before I can send him on such a journey," Mellisynt continued blithely.

"Surely among the hundreds of servitors who see to the duchess's every need, you can find one to take care of this beast. You need not sully your hands with him yourself."

She took her lower lip between small white teeth and glanced down at the dog, who was dripping water and lather on the tiled floor in majestic unconcern.

"I'm sure I could, my lord. But his eyes have such a sad dignity. I don't mind taking on his care. I...I am used to spending my days attending to infirmity, and feel the lack of any useful occupation."

FitzHugh expelled a long, slow breath. "You'll not have the time to care for him, nor anyone else. We sail on the morning tide for England."

"We do?"

"We do. Ian, get you gone and start packing my gear and equipment. And take that imp with you."

Grabbing Bartholomew's shoulder, the squire hustled out with an air of palpable relief.

FitzHugh waited until the door slammed shut behind them before moving toward the bed. Shedding his soaked surcoat, he rolled up the sleeves of his linen shirt. Mellisynt eyed him warily as he walked across the room.

"Come, let's finish bathing this monster from hell while I tell you what necessitates our departure. Then we'll deal with your rashness in disobeying my orders as it deserves."

In the dark hours before dawn, Mellisynt snuggled deep in her new fox-lined cloak and settled herself more comfortably in the litter. With the ease of practice, she ignored Isabeau's low-voiced complaints. After her brief taste of court life, the girl was predictably unhappy at being bundled off to what had been described to her as the far end of the earth. Even Isabeau's complaining presence, however, couldn't dim Mellisynt's delicious sense of well-being.

She grinned into the fur brushing against her chin. FitzHugh had been surprisingly gentle with the dog, and satisfyingly less than gentle with her. Her face heated as she recalled the strength of his body pressing into hers, and its hard, driving demand for response. She'd been ready this time, though. This time she'd met him thrust for thrust, and wrapped her legs around his muscled thighs. This time there had been no one-sided dominance, no one-sided effort. Neither she nor FitzHugh expected love in the marriage bed, but what they shared would do very well, very well indeed, she decided.

Bitter cold whipped along the dark streets and snaked through even the thick curtains of the duchess's litter, adding to Isabeau's lists of complaints. Mellisynt had not been best pleased when FitzHugh informed her she was to spend her first winter in her new home chaperoning Isabeau of Bellamy, but in the face of the duchess's explicit request, she could hardly refuse. Not without admitting a most unworthy jealousy, one that she struggled to contain. 'Twas not the girl's fault that men, including her own husband, smiled down at her like besotted oafs.

They arrived at the dock just as the first fingers of dawn began to poke through the dark clouds blanketing the sky. Mellisynt climbed out of the litter eagerly, lifting up her heavy skirts and even heavier cloak to keep them from the garbage-strewn filth lining the wooden piers. Isabeau descended, muttering at the cold. A thin, shivering maid, pressed into service by Constance to see to their needs on the journey, huddled beside them and surveyed the scene with wide eyes. The girl started when FitzHugh's massive figure strode down a wobbling gangplank toward them.

Mellisynt felt a strange thrill clutch her heart at her husband's approach. In the weak, windswept dawn, he looked like a dark warrior descending from the clouds. His huge shoulders all but blocked the sky from her view, and his arms, whose strength she knew well, swept her up in a swirl of skirts.

"You're just in time, lady wife. The horses are stowed, and the shipmaster wishes to leave immediately. Come, I'll get you aboard." He headed for the narrow plank. "I'll be back for you, Lady Isabeau."

A deep, mournful howl, of approximately the same timbre and volume as the great cast-iron cathedral bell that awakened Nantes's citizens each morning, stopped him in his tracks.

FitzHugh's arms tightened to ominous bands of steel.

Mellisynt swallowed and met his disbelieving eyes.

"I tried to leave him behind, my lord, I swear! But he must have sensed my leaving. He wailed most loud and long each time I stepped out the door."

A muscle at the side of FitzHugh's jaw clenched and unclenched rhythmically. Eyeing it with some fascination, Mellisynt hurried on.

"I could not quiet him! He roused half the castle with—" she paused as another deafening howl rolled across the morning mist "—with that. Constance threatened to have him skinned and fed to her pet panthers did I not silence him."

FitzHugh spoke, slowly and deliberately, through gritted teeth. "If that cur comes anywhere near my horses, I'll personally cut out his liver and use it for fish bait."

"Aye, my lord."

The shipmaster greeted the addition of a three-legged beast who added his own deep braying to the din of departure with something less than enthusiasm. Secured by a stout rope to the rail surrounding the raised upper deck, the creature appeared to find his first sea voyage as exciting as did his mistress. Isabeau went below to the warmth of the shipmaster's cabin, but Mellisynt leaned over the upper rail, fascinated by the bustling activity below. Her eyes widened as seamen scrambled to untie the mooring lines and maneuver the three-masted barque out into the river's current. Others climbed like nimble monkeys up into the rigging. Within moments, the swift-flowing Loire, rushing its last few miles to the sea, caught the ship.

As they swept past the docks, rays of early-morning sunlight broke through dark, scudding clouds and painted the city with a patchwork of shadows and gilded spires. Mellisynt stood at the rail, her cheeks stinging with cold. She pulled the fox-lined hood up around her face and watched Nantes's steep-roofed, timbered buildings slip by. Every surge and dip of the ship as it danced with the river's rolling waters thrilled her. This was the way to travel, she decided. Not atop some hard-backed, mean-spirited animal whose every step jolted the very bones in her body.

A dim memory teased at her mind, one of sunlight dancing on a sparkling sea. A man's strong arms tossing her into the air. A woman's lilting laughter as she splashed through the waves. Mellisynt tried to capture the vague, half-formed images that were all she had of her parents. Her father had been a minor knight with holdings along the coast, she knew that much. She knew, as well, that both parents had died of an inflammation of the lungs that had swept away many souls one bleak winter. She'd been taken into a remote castle of her father's overlord, the young duke of Brittany, who later offered her as Henri of Trémont's third wife. Strange how the memory of those long years at Trémont no longer sent a shiver of resentment through her, Mellisynt mused. With the sun and the sea once again tugging at her senses, she felt reborn, as if she'd found the future she'd thought was gone. Clasping the rail, she threw back her head and drank in the life-giving sun.

She was still at the rail when Isabeau came up some time later to take the air. The stuffy cabin made her head ache, she claimed.

"Oh, look, Isabeau! 'Tis the sea."

The wind whipped Mellisynt's hood back as the barque rounded a bend and entered the Loire's wide estuary. Ahead of them, gray-green waves slapped against black rocks on either side of the channel. When the ship caught the tide's ebb, the master shouted an order and men scrambled aloft. Massive sails unfurled, and the ship leapt across the tossing waves.

"How it rolls and swells," Mellisynt exclaimed, holding on to the rail with mittened hands.

"It . . . it does, indeed," Isabeau agreed weakly.

Tendrils of hair whipped at Mellisynt's cheek and she threw back her head to toss them from her eyes.

"'Tis like riding the wind." She laughed. "Look how those clouds race across the sky, as if the devil himself were chasing them."

A low groan, barely heard above the wind's roar, made her turn. Isabeau slumped back against the sheltering cabin wall, her face as white as the rabbit fur framing it.

Mellisynt crossed the small, sloping space in two quick strides. "Are you ill, child?"

"Dreadfully," she moaned, then added, in a weak, pathetic voice, "I'm not a child."

With one arm around the girl's waist, Mellisynt moved toward the stairs leading to the shipmaster's cabin. Casting a quick, regretful glance back over her shoulder at the foamy sea and scudding clouds, she led Isabeau down the narrow stairs.

The next four days became a blurred confusion of tossing seas and violent illness. Dark clouds piled one on top of another, and fierce rains lashed the ship. They were blown far south and west, into the Atlantic, adding two extra days to the journey as the shipmaster beat back toward the Channel against heavy winds. Isabeau grew more miserable with each passing day. She retched constantly—dry, racking heaves that left her weak and sobbing. FitzHugh came several times to check on them, but found himself routed by the girl's pathetic moans and Mellisynt's snapped order to come in or get himself gone, but in either case shut the door. The little maid sent to see to their needs proved less than useless, succumbing to seasickness within hours of their losing sight of land. Mellisynt found herself in a familiar role, nursing and coaxing and bathing patients' faces with a steady hand.

The ship's cook proved a most welcome companion. A tiny, wizened old man with a gray patch over one eye and three prominent teeth in an otherwise empty mouth, he brought dry ship biscuits, thin soups, and a cold brew steeped from chamomile leaves. Between them, Mellisynt and the little man forced the protesting patients to down what liquids they could.

They sailed into Portsmouth harbor on the last day but one of November. Mellisynt left Isabeau's bedside for the first time in four days and climbed up the narrow stairs. Holding her elegant cloak close to cover her stained, wrinkled gown, she breathed in fresh air in great, welcome gulps.

Ships of all shapes and sizes and numbers of masts filled the quays of England's busiest port. Voices carried across the waters in strange tongues and accents. A steady stream of carriers, bent almost double by the huge casks and bales on their backs, made their way toward the stone warehouses across from the docks. A thin drizzle hung on the air, coating the ships and buildings with a gray sheen.

"How do you fare?"

Mellisynt managed to give her husband a tired smile. In truth, she felt like something rats had gnawed upon. "I'm fine, my lord."

"I've arranged for rooms at a nearby inn, where you and the other women can rest while we finish unloading. We're but a few hours from Winchester. Will you be able to travel this day?"

Mellisynt studied the crease between his thick, dark brows, made deeper than usual by tiredness and the worry she knew he harbored.

"Aye," she replied. "Do you think we are arrived too late? Will the duke have repudiated the truce already?"

"I don't know. The documents are to be signed tomorrow, at the great feast in honor of Saint Andrew. Mayhap there is time yet to reason with Geoffrey."

FitzHugh stared across the docks, his thoughts far away and most uncomfortable, if the troubled look in his blue eyes was any indication. He rubbed his forehead with a tired hand.

"I'll send men to carry Isabeau and the girl above decks. Do what you can to restore them as quickly as possible."

"We'll be ready when you come for us, my lord."

Mellisynt vowed to tie Isabeau and the maid on their horses, if necessary. The brief, worried look that had crossed FitzHugh's face, normally so set and authoritative, had communicated the depth of his concern far more than he realized.

Their bedraggled party arrived late that evening at the great castle of Winchester, once the seat of the Norman kings, to find it a scene of incredible chaos. A distracted household seneschal groaned at their unexpected appearance, claiming there was not a square inch of empty space within the castle. Not only had the king come to wear his crown at the Feast of Saint Andrew, but he had brought Queen Eleanor from her comfortable captivity to lend support to the reconciliation of their sons. In addition, their daughter Matilda and her husband, Henry the Lion, duke of Saxony, swelled the ranks. The Lion had made war upon his overlord, the Holy Roman Emperor Frederick Barbarossa, and had been exiled from his duchy.

Eventually an exchange of silver pennies won the weary travelers entrance to the castle. Ian, the men-at-arms, and the pages went into town to find a place to bed themselves and the beasts down. The hound's protesting howls echoed across the courtyard as they dragged him away.

Impatient to find Geoffrey, FitzHugh bade the women rest that night. Mellisynt was more than willing to follow her lord's directions. Too weary to take in much of the magnificent castle, she led a still-weak Isabeau and their little maid to the dormer room they would share with six other women. Straw pallets crowded the floor, with trunks and baskets piled high in every corner. 'Twas obvious each of the room's occupants had emptied her wardrobe for the trip to court.

Glancing around at the scattered silks and veils, Mellisynt thought of her brief foray into Nantes's shops. With their sudden departure, she'd had no time to have new gowns made. Her purchases of fine velvet, soft Alexandrine paile and rich purple asterin, all still wrapped in their protective coverings, awaited the seamstress's hands. Sighing, she shed her travel-stained amber robe and joined Isabeau on the pallet they would share.

Chapter Nine

The next afternoon, Mellisynt left Isabeau to the chattering company of the other women and followed a page through Winchester's high, vaulted halls to answer her husband's summons. He awaited her in a deserted garden. Wind whistling over the stone walls lifted bits of leaves and tossed them across brick paths laid out in concentric circles. Black-limbed rosebushes, brutally pruned against the winter cold, thrust their stumps toward a lowering gray sky. Snow hung heavy in the air, and Mellisynt tugged her furred cloak more closely around her.

FitzHugh had discarded his armour and wore only his thick gambeson under his blue surcoat. He waited patiently, one booted foot propped on a stone bench, an arm across his knee, and an austere expression on his face that made the winter garden seem even more bleak. He turned and straightened at the sound of her approach.

"God give you a good day, lady wife."

He bent and brushed a light kiss across her cheek. His lips felt warm against her cold skin, and their rough, velvety touch sent a tingle down Mellisynt's neck.

"And you, my lord."

"I'm sorry to drag you out into such inhospitable surroundings, but I would speak with you in private. The castle is so crowded, there's not a corner where we wouldn't trip over two others' feet."

Mellisynt dismissed the wind biting at her cheeks and nose with a negligent wave. "Have you spoken with the duke? Does he still hold firm to his intent to repudiate the peace?"

"I've spoken with him," FitzHugh responded dryly. "At some length. He was not best pleased that the duchess sent me here."

At Mellisynt's questioning look, his lips lifted in a sardonic half-smile.

"He'd planned on my presence in Brittany to hold his borders and rally his forces if he abjured the truce."

"So your coming has upset his scheme," Mellisynt breathed, trying to suppress a dart of satisfaction at Geoffrey's discomfiture. She'd thought she was beyond her grudge against the duke. "He will have to accept the terms now."

"A rational man would," FitzHugh admitted, "but Geoffrey's heart often overrules his head. 'Tis why I wished to speak with you. If things go as I suspect they might, you may have to make your way to Edgemoor alone. Peter St. Bressé will escort you. You know you can trust him."

Mellisynt nodded slowly. St. Bressé served as FitzHugh's lieutenant, and had traveled with them from Brittany. He was a good man, respectful and polite.

"I've arranged passage on a merchant ship to carry you and your escort from Portsmouth to Edgemoor. My uncle serves as steward during my absences, and will hold you safe. If I do not return, he'll help you manage your inheritance until you are resettled."

His words sent a shock jolting through Mellisynt. The rest of his detailed description of what she might expect on the journey north fell on deaf ears. Her mind reeled at the thought that he might not return. The possibility of losing this man, who had come so recently into her life and was now such a major part of it, overwhelmed her. The idea that she might never again feel his callused hands on her, or his teasing, tantalizing lips, just when she'd come to crave them, rocked her to her core. To think she had wanted marriage to this mighty warrior for his strength and vigor! Of a sudden she wished FitzHugh were every bit as thin and wizened and cowardly as old Henri had been.

She moistened dry lips with the tip of her tongue. "Must you go if it comes to war once more?"

FitzHugh shrugged. "If I can't deter Geoffrey from this course, he'll find himself facing the combined arms of his father and brother. I'm sworn to him, and must follow."

Mellisynt struggled to keep her voice steady. "But if Geoffrey forswears his oaths to his father, to whom he's given homage twice over, for Brittany and for Richmond, why are you bound to follow? Doesn't the fact that he breaks his pledge release you from yours?"

For a moment she feared he might take offense at her probing into these tangled affairs of men. In all her years at Trémont, she'd never dared question Henri so, nor to challenge his dealings. But here, in this windswept, barren garden, with dried leaves rustling at her feet and the sharp, coppery taste of fear on her tongue, she felt the need to know the man behind the fierce, hawk-faced exterior. She wanted to understand his reasons for leaving her, to understand what drove him.

FitzHugh stared down at her, his eyes almost opaque in their silver blueness. He pondered her question, his dark brows drawing together in the characteristic half frown that Mellisynt now recognized so well. A sudden urge swept through her to reach up and stroke away the lines creasing his forehead.

"Some would consider Geoffrey's repudiation of his allegiance to his father sufficient to absolve them of their oaths." FitzHugh spoke slowly, as if testing the sound of his words on his own tongue. "Each man must decide the course of his own honor in such circumstances, as we did in the last war. Should he hold to his sworn lord, or to his lord's overlord? Or to the rightness of the cause? My loyalty to Geoffrey goes beyond any oath of fealty, and I will follow him."

He tilted up her chin with a gentle, gloved fist. "I didn't mean to frighten you with such dire forebodings, but 'tis best you know how things stand."

At her troubled look, his somber look lightened. "You'll be safe at Edgemoor, with my people. Remember, what I have, I hold."

Mellisynt forced herself to respond to the teasing note in his voice. "Aye, so you told me. I also seem to recall I fall just below your war-horses on your list of possessions to hold."

A lopsided grin lifted one corner of his mouth. "Does that still rankle? Will it help you to know that I'm reconsidering the priorities on my list? I've found that even Voyager, as well trained as he is, can't perform certain necessary services for me. Like this."

He bent and brushed his mouth across hers. The air had chilled his lips and taken the rough warmth from them. A sharp desire flared within Mellisynt to taste that warmth once more. When he would have drawn back, she wrapped her arms around his neck, holding his mouth on hers. Her fingers tangled in the soft, springy hair of his nape. Opening her lips, she drew him into her.

FitzHugh accepted her invitation most willingly. His tongue met hers in a slow, sweet duel, and his arms tightened around her body until they were two taut bands pinning her against him. Stretched on tiptoe, her arms locked about the massive column of his neck, Mellisynt felt a growing need that half embarrassed, half thrilled her. She moaned deep in her throat and tilted her face to allow him more access.

Widening his stance, FitzHugh settled her weight in the cradle of his thighs. Mellisynt rubbed her hips against him shamelessly, frustrated beyond belief by the thick layers of clothing between them and by the surging lust that fired her blood. They hadn't been alone since their hurried departure from Nantes, and the urge to take him into her, to join with him, arced through her. Angling her lips across his, she deepened the kiss, demanding and taking all he had to give.

FitzHugh tore his mouth from hers. "Damnation, woman," he growled, "if you wish to show me how much more versatile is a wife than a war-horse, I wish you'd chosen another time, another place. There's not a private corner to be found anywhere in this castle."

Mellisynt clung to him, her breath crystallizing on the air in little puffs of vapor. She knew her eyes mirrored the rising need she saw in his, and made no effort to disguise it.

He gave a savage groan, then reached down to catch her under the knees. Striding to a protected corner, where the castle walls formed a V that cut the wind, he stood her upright and thrust her back against the wall. His body cocooned her in a tiny pocket of warmth. Reaching under his surcoat, he fumbled with the ties of his chausses.

"I don't believe we do this," he muttered. "I disremember the last time I had to take a woman against a wall."

"Good," she told him fiercely. "I don't wish you to remember the last time. Only this time."

She pushed his hands aside and burrowed under the layers of his clothing to find his stirring shaft. Enclosing him in both hands and a casing of soft fox fur, she quickly brought him to hardness.

"Jesu," he breathed, reaching for her skirts. "You'd best take my rod while you can. This cold will unman me do we play with it too long."

Mellisynt gave him a wicked grin. "You forget I've been taught well how to bring a husband to his duty."

Sinking to her knees, she took him into the hot wetness of her mouth. FitzHugh swore in startled surprise and braced both hands against the corner walls. When she had him primed to her satisfaction—her most admiring satisfaction—she slid up his length and lifted her skirts.

"Now, husband," she panted.

"Now, wife," he promised, lifting her hips and surging into her wet heat with a force that rocked her back against the stone.

Cushioned by layers of wool and fur, Mellisynt reveled in his fierce assault. She wrapped her arms about his neck once more and struggled to fit her body closer to his, despite the clothing bunched between them. FitzHugh flexed his thigh muscles and thrust upward, withdrew, and thrust again. She buried her face in his neck, breathing in the scent of his skin. Driven by an overpowering, primitive need, she sank her teeth into his taut flesh.

FitzHugh responded with all the force of his powerful body, pinning her against the stone over and over again with fierce, rhythmic movements. Mellisynt tried to clench her thighs against the sensation building in her lower belly, but his torso held her open, exposed, vulnerable. When she closed her eyes and threw her head back against the wall, FitzHugh bent and put his lips to her throat, nipping and sucking at the tender flesh. One of his hands slid from under her thigh and wedged itself between them. Fumbling beneath the folds of cloth, he found her center and began an erotic, maddening massage. The pressure at her core tightened, darkened, then shattered into a thousand blinding splinters of light. A ragged groan tore upward from deep in her throat. Within moments, he echoed her harsh moan, and she felt his hot seed flooding her.

FitzHugh braced his weight on one arm while he held her with the other, waiting for the tide of sensation to ebb. Gradually, reluctantly, he returned to the world around them. Cold singed the rims of his ears. A gust of wind hit his back and ruffled the hair at his neck. He felt himself slide from his wife's wet, slick depths, and forced himself to step back. Mellisynt's skirts fell, and she leaned against the wall with a languid smile.

"You'd best cover yourself before you freeze," she suggested, her eyes on his depleted manhood. "I would not have you permanently crippled."

FitzHugh's bark of laughter echoed in the deserted garden. Grinning, he stuffed himself back inside his clothes.

"You little witch—if I am crippled, you have only yourself to blame."

His voice rumbled with good-humored teasing as he took her arm and led her toward the wooden door to the castle.

"Are you so desperate to get the babe you desire that you must make your husband service you on the coldest day of the winter, in a public garden?"

Mellisynt felt a shock of startled surprise. She stumbled beside him, her steps guided by his, her thoughts whirling. She only half heard his smug, satisfied bantering. Dazed, she realized that she hadn't once associated her driving need to couple this day with its possible results. As they entered the hall, heat washed over her, generated as much by the roaring fire in the stone hearth as by her own rushing emotions. By the saints, when had she submerged her desire for a child in her desire for this man? When had she stopped seeing him as the means to give her a babe to love, and begun to see him as someone to love in himself?

Love? What did she know of love, she wondered wildly? What she felt for FitzHugh had none of the sweet, tortured nobility the troubadours sang of. She wanted him in a most basic, primitive way. Was it just desire? Or lust? Was she truly the evil daughter of Eve Father Anselem had so often decried, out only to satisfy the cravings of her flesh? Her head swam with confused thoughts. She ached for a quiet corner, for time to herself to sort through the emotions roiling in her. When FitzHugh stopped at the entrance to the women's quarters, she lifted dazed eyes to his.

"Don't fret, lady wife," he told her gently. "Remember, what I have, I—"

"Yes, yes," she said, interrupting him, anxious to be away from his overwhelming presence. "What you have, you hold."

"I've decided to revise the order of my holdings. You definitely rank above my destriers. With a little more work, you might even replace my prized damascene sword in my affections."

He kissed her lightly on her nose. "I'll send someone to escort you and Isabeau to our place at the feast this eve."

Bemused, Mellisynt made her way to the dormer room and opened the door. Waves of noise and color washed over her. The tiny room was filled to overflowing with chattering ladies and maids, while open baskets and trunks spilled silks and velvets of every shade onto the floor. A cluster of women vied for the thin light by the window, spreading bottles and vials and horn boxes of cosmetics in a dazzling array. Laughter rang across the room as women dug through their finery and called to each other to admire this piece or that. The cloying fragrances of musk and sandalwood and Cyprus oyselet filled the air, accompanied by the tinkling of perforated golden perfume balls.

"Where have you been?" Isabeau demanded, grabbing Mellisynt's hand and pulling her toward their corner of the room. She didn't wait for a reply, which was just as well, since Mellisynt couldn't for the life of her think of one that would not burn the ears of a young virgin.

"We've but a few hours to prepare for the feast," Isabeau complained. "This ninny the duchess sent to attend us knows naught of applying soot. You must help me."

Mellisynt blinked and looked at the hapless maid. The girl wrung her hands, tears obviously not far away. Mellisynt dismissed her with a kind nod.

"I don't wish to disappoint you, Isabeau," she responded, turning once more to the impatient beauty. "But I know naught of soot, either. Ah, where do you apply it?"

Isabeau's red, ripe mouth twisted down in a disgusted moue. "To the brows and lashes, of course." She shoved a small round mirror into Mellisynt's hands. "Here, hold this to the light, and I'll do it myself."

Mellisynt watched, fascinated, as the girl took a small goathair brush and dipped it into a ceramic pot. With sure strokes, she lengthened and darkened the line of her brow, then dusted her lashes until they gleamed like raven's wings against her alabaster face. That done, Isabeau rummaged through her pots and opened another. The sweet scent of roses drifted above the other, heavier fragrances wafting about the room. Vigorously she rubbed dried petals against her cheeks to augment their natural bloom.

Holding the mirror steady so that Isabeau could complete her toilet, Mellisynt glanced around the room. Her eyes fell upon naked limbs and exposed skin as women bathed and readied themselves. The spicy scent of bay leaves and hyssop, used to subdue the body's odors, filled the air, along with the sharp tang of quicklime as one woman applied it to her upper lip to remove unwanted hair.

"There," Isabeau commented. "That should do it."

Whatever "it" was, it was most certainly done, Mellisynt thought. The girl glowed with color and vibrant life. While Isabeau fiddled with the pots and jars, Mellisynt slowly, unwillingly, turned the mirror in her hands and surveyed the face illuminated there. If the cold and Fitz-Hugh's vigorous attentions had put any color in her face, it had faded well away. Her skin stretched tight across her cheekbones, pale and taut. Her brows and lashes were thick and dark, but lacked the lustrous shine of Isabeau's. And although her lips looked swollen and slightly red from the kisses so recently pressed on them, they did not pout with cherry ripeness. With a small sigh, Mellisynt put the mirror aside. Isabeau's hesitant voice broke into her musings.

"I don't wish to offend you, my lady, but I have some skill with paints and brushes. Do you wish it, I would be happy to add a daub of color to your face."

Mellisynt stared at the girl in surprise.

Isabeau shrugged. "'Tis little enough to repay you for your kindness to me on that accursed ship, when I was so ill. I...I thank you for that, my lady."

Realizing that gratitude sat most uneasily on the beauty's shoulders, Mellisynt smiled. "You're most welcome. And I thank you for the offer, but in truth, there's not much that paint and powders can do for this face."

Isabeau tilted her head, and a determined gleam came into her sea-green eyes. The smile she gave Mellisynt was all woman.

"You underestimate yourself...and me," she chided.

Two hours later, Mellisynt pinned the emerald brooch to her mantle with shaking hands. She'd been stripped, scrubbed, pumiced in places she blushed to recall, sprinkled with more herbs and scented flowers than she could count, and dressed in borrowed linens from the skin out. Having found a cause worthy of her not inconsiderable energy, Isabeau had taken charge of preparing Mellisynt for the banquet as if she were the main course instead of one of the throng of lesser knights' dependents who would fill the lower boards.

"Here, let me help you." Isabeau brushed Mellisynt's hands aside and fastened the emerald securely to the green velvet of her own second-best bliaut, loaned out for the occasion.

"Do you mind that this brooch was your mother's, and would have been yours?" Mellisynt asked, gazing down at the dark head bent before her.

"Of course I mind." Isabeau sniffed, her fingers busy with the clasp. "But I count the emerald well lost if it brings me a wealthy husband in return. One who will shower me with many more jewels than this, and who will be so besotted with my looks he'll be easy as pudding to manage."

Mellisynt took the girl's hands in a loose hold. "Don't count on a husband's wealth alone to bring you joy. I can speak of that from experience."

Isabeau shrugged and drew away to pin her own mantle across her shoulders. "I don't expect joy of a husband, my lady. Only comfort and luxury."

Curious, Mellisynt eyed the younger girl. "And love? Do you not expect love in your life?"

"Of course. But that will come from the knight who wins my favor. Who proves himself worthy to wear red in my honor, showing he's won my regard with his reverence and poetry."

Isabeau's eyes took on a dreamy, faraway look. "When I don a yellow gown and proclaim my acceptance of a lover, it will be for someone strong and handsome and most devoted to me. Not for a mere husband," she finished, straightening.

Mellisynt followed the girl out of the emptying room, confusion wrapping its insidious coils around her once more. In the face of Isabeau's conventional scorn for a husband's regard, Mellisynt hesitated to admit, even to herself, that she had primped and powdered herself for FitzHugh. She recalled the judgments rendered at the duchess's courts of love, which proclaimed it impossible for a man to revere a wife he could have at will. A slow flush added to the tint of roses on her cheeks. If a husband couldn't cherish his wife who came readily to his bed, what must he think of one taken up against a stone wall in broad daylight! Nay, not taken even. One who wrapped her legs around his hips and all but drained the seed from him with her writhing. Shaken, she trailed after Isabeau and the other women, hardly hearing their excited exclamations as they entered the huge, vaulted hall and made their way through the milling masses.

The page FitzHugh sent to guide them to their seats elbowed his way through the crowd, making space enough for the two women to follow him. After a low-voiced argument with another page, punctuated by fierce scowls, scandalous name-calling and a stealthy kick on the shins, he convinced the other to squeeze the occupants of a bench together enough to make room for the ladies. Mellisynt wondered briefly how FitzHugh's solid bulk would fit on the packed seat, then abandoned all thought entirely as a blaze of trumpets signaled the arrival of the high table. She surged to her feet with the rest of the crowd, breath caught in her throat, as the men and women who ruled her world made their entrance.

From her position far down the hall, she could just make out their features. There was no mistaking the king, of course. Even if he hadn't been wearing a gem-encrusted crown, Henry's robust figure and flaming orange-red hair would have identified him. Although he'd passed his fiftieth year, Henry strode forward with the legendary, furious energy that exhausted all those around him. Mellisynt had heard stories of courtiers left to find shelter as best they could under hedgerows while their demonic king galloped far ahead, often covering a hundred miles and more in a day's travel.

But for all the king's vibrant presence, it was the queen who held everyone's avid gaze. Some eleven years older than Henry, Eleanor still bore traces of the fabled beauty that had elicited the passionate love and implacable fury of two kings. Her gossamer veil drifted as she walked calmly to her seat, showing ebony hair only lightly streaked with gray. Her blue gown fitted tight around waist and hips still slender, despite the birthing of ten healthy children. A wide embroidered belt, studded with gleaming stones, encircled her hips, from which dangled an assortment of precious pendants—silver scissors, an enameled mirror, a pouch of soft leather, and the inevitable vented golden ball filled with aromatic scents. Noticeably absent was the usual dangle of keys, symbol of a woman's power as chatelaine. Eleanor had lost her keys, as well as her freedom, some twelve years earlier, when she'd incited her young sons to an abortive rebellion against their father.

Mellisynt was so struck by this first glimpse of the woman who had won, and lost, kingdoms and who had introduced the world to the concept of courtly love that she didn't hear FitzHugh edge his way through the crowd to her side. She jumped when his hand closed over her elbow, and a deep, husky whisper stirred the hairs by her ear.

"Watch the smile on Geoffrey's face. If it slips, you will know the worst."

She tried to turn, but FitzHugh's grip tightened and held her facing forward. The king raised his hands for quiet and began to speak. Mellisynt strained to hear, but his words were lost over the vast length of the hall and the shifting crowd.

"What does he say?" she whispered furiously over her shoulder.

FitzHugh bent and placed his lips close to her ear. "I pray he says that his sons have agreed to peace. And that he's given them each new honors in recognition of their valor and strength of arms.''

''New honors? What new honors?''

A full-throated roar drowned out his reply. It began in the front ranks, among those closest to the high table, and swelled as it rolled down the length of the great hall. The bright banners hanging from the rafters high above fluttered, adding to the sensation of sound and movement that swept over Mellisynt like a tide. While the noise still thundered about the hall, the king turned and motioned two figures forward. Mellisynt recognized Geoffrey instantly. Even over the heads of hundreds of courtiers, the duke's golden-red hair and handsome face stood out. By contrast, Richard Lionheart, duke of Normandy, count of Maine and Anjou, lord regent of Aquitaine and heir to the throne of England, appeared dark and forbidding. Richard had his mother's raven hair and high cheekbones, but none of her smiling charm. He was somber and serious, his square jaw set and eyes steady under dark brows.

The crowd quieted when the two brothers faced each other. FitzHugh's hand tightened on Mellisynt's arm until she thought the bones would break, but she dared not pull away, nor to disturb in any way the ominous stillness that settled gradually over the vast hall. It was as if five hundred people held their breath, waiting, wondering.

And five hundred people, Mellisynt included, let out a relieved sigh as Geoffrey and Richard leaned toward each other, pressed their lips each to the other's cheek, and then returned to their seats. FitzHugh's hand loosened, and he let out a little grunt of satisfaction.

''Why did he change his stance?'' Mellisynt whispered as she scooted her hips sideways against the well-padded ones of the matron next to her to make room for her husband.

FitzHugh took a long draft from the two-handed cup set before them. He closed his eyes while the liquid flowed down his throat, as if savoring some exotic elixir instead of a hearty, clove-spiced wine. When he had drained the cup, he turned and related what he knew in a low voice well covered by the din all around them.

"The king offered Geoffrey the chance to lead his men against Toulouse. To recoup the reparations paid to Richard's Crusade chests. I was not sure Geoffrey would take the obvious sop."

Mellisynt's eyes rounded. The house of Toulouse had battled that of Anjou for centuries, but she'd not heard that hostilities had broken out again. "The count of Toulouse has declared war?"

"Nay," FitzHugh said, a wry grin twisting his lips. "But he will as soon as he hears that King Henry claims Montauban, which guards the entrance to the Valley of the Garonne, and the rich Toulouse farmlands. We sail with our armies within the week to besiege the city."

"The lands surrounding Montauban have been part of Toulouse for generations!" she exclaimed. "By what right does the king now claim them?"

"None, in truth, although he cites a distant ancestor who married a sister of the present count's grandfather."

"Why on earth would he try to press such a specious claim?"

"So that Geoffrey might go to war and win back the spoils he had to cede to Richard."

Mellisynt's spoon clattered to the boards. She swiveled in her seat to stare at her husband. He sat there, calmly spearing chunks of roasted boar from the serving platter with his pointed dagger, as if unconcerned that a whole city, if not an entire province, would soon be ravaged as part of a political game. She thought of her probing questions to FitzHugh in the garden earlier, and of her heady belief that she might come to understand him. She knew now that she would never grasp what drove men, particularly the breed of men who called themselves warriors. While her mind churned with visions of bloody battle, and of FitzHugh's inevitable role in it, the object of her concern appeared most satisfied with the situation.

"How can you be pleased that there will be fighting again so soon? I thought you wanted peace for Brittany... time to recover from the last months of war!"

FitzHugh's brows rose at her vehemence. "This *is* peace for Brittany. We take the battle to the Garonne, far from Breton borders, and King Henry will augment our forces with levies of his own. 'Tis an honorable solution to Geoffrey's dilemma. We fight Henry's battles this time, and the king will bear the brunt of the cost."

"But not the brunt of the injuries. Nor the deaths. That will be your charge, yours and that hotheaded idiot you call a friend. He would—"

"Be silent, woman. I'll not have you speak of my overlord in such a voice, nor in such a setting."

The sudden ice in FitzHugh's voice halted Mellisynt's tirade in midsentence. She took her lower lip between her teeth, struggling to overcome the anger that swamped her. Did FitzHugh not see how he was being used? How Henry, and Geoffrey, and all those other highborn rogues at the head table used the assembled knights to their own purposes? They would sally forth, their banners blowing bravely in the wind, their armour shining, to war with another lord as powerful and grasping and hungry as himself. And for what? For hope of booty, for spoils, for lands. For riches.

Mellisynt felt hysteria rising up in her. Was her life ever to be controlled by men who desired riches? First one who sucked coppers from serfs and hoarded his silver in deep cellars. Then one who wed a woman he'd known less than an hour to gain her inheritance and who would spill his blood eagerly to advance his estate. She lifted her cup with shaking hands.

The rest of the long evening passed in a blur. Mellisynt nodded politely when FitzHugh commented on her appearance, expressing his appreciation of Isabeau's efforts. She stood silent while the girl flirted with him after the boards were pushed aside, practicing the smiles and slanted looks that soon had a flock of colorful, hefty young knights surrounding her. Mellisynt refused a halfhearted offer from FitzHugh to join in the dance, sensing his relief in his lighthearted comment that one his size looked much the fool galloping around a room to some damned trumpets.

The press of bodies and noise soon began to close in on her. After the storm of emotions she'd been through this day, she longed for a quiet corner, a place to sort through her troubled thoughts. Yet when FitzHugh drew her into a side alcove on their way back to the dormer hours later, she clung to him, not wanting to think, not wanting to listen to his murmured instructions for the trip north. Not wanting to hear his whispered farewell.

Chapter Ten

Although neither Isabeau nor the little maid succumbed to illness, the journey north proved far more tedious for Mellisynt than the voyage from Nantes. This time they sailed aboard a lumbering merchant ship, stopping at every major port to unload and take on new cargoes. Isabeau delighted in the merchantman's slow, plodding progress, as it gave her a chance to explore the busy markets in the port cities they visited.

Mellisynt accompanied the girl while she wandered through merchant halls more richly decorated than most castles. She waited patiently while Isabeau exclaimed over woolens as soft as clouds from the hinterlands and fingered trinkets and silks coming in from abroad. But she couldn't generate any interest in the luxuries that Isabeau sighed over.

In truth, she was surprised by her lack of enthusiasm. For so many years she'd bemoaned her dull, shapeless robes, and the meanness of Trémont's furnishings. Now she had the splendors of the world at her fingertips, and the means to purchase what she would, yet little tempted her. In the darkness of her curtained bed aboard the merchant ship Mellisynt admitted that much of her ennui had to do with the absence of a certain oversize knight, one whose harsh visage and less-than-gentle manners should not occasion the improper thoughts they did. Her mind returned over and over again to the desolate garden of Winchester

Castle, and to the explosion of heat and light FitzHugh's hands and mouth had wrought within her. She tossed and turned in her narrow bed until Isabeau called out crossly that she should take a purge to still her disquiet humors.

Her only relief from the half-formed longings that tormented her was the boisterous company of her younger companions. FitzHugh had commended Bartholomew to her care, along with the sorry hound who seemed to believe he was her second shadow. Hobbling about the deck with surprising agility, the dog attached itself to her by day and howled outside her door by night until she perforce had to grant him entry. Over Isabeau's angry protests, the hound took up residence in the small cabin, sprawling across most of the floor space between the bunks and relegating the maid to a pallet outside the door.

As the ship lumbered north, Mellisynt searched for activities to keep a lively, mischievous youngster occupied. Freed from his duties as page by his lord's absence, Bartholomew harried the shipmaster unmercifully. Once the boy had to be hauled down bodily from the tangle of ropes he'd climbed to, high above the decks. Another time he was fished out of the garbage-strewn waters beside the docks, when his eagerness to help release the ropes sent him tumbling overboard. In desperation, Mellisynt borrowed the captain's ivory-and-malachite chess set, then a set of spillikins carved by one of the seamen. When those diversions failed to hold Bartholomew's attention for long, she cajoled the boy into helping her identify the coastal landmarks they passed. He perched on a stool beside her on the upper deck and shared what sketchy details he knew of the coastal towers and cliffside keeps visible from shipboard.

"Look, my lady," he exclaimed one crisp, sunny morning. "'Tis Orford Castle."

Mellisynt gazed up at massive walls of stone and shell surrounding two circular towers. Rising high above the coastal marshes, the towers commanded a superb overview of the sea-lanes they had been built to protect.

"'Tis the king's own castle,'' Bartholomew informed her, obviously proud of his smattering of knowledge. "We stopped there when I first journeyed south with my lord. See, the king's standard flies above the walls. Do you see the lion crest, and the golden R on the pennant below?''

Mellisynt turned to stare at the boy. "What is this R? Is it the symbol for King Henry's name?''

"No,'' Bartholomew told her, scornfully. "It stands for *Rex*. For *King* in Latin,'' he explained.

"Do you recognize this symbol? This Latin letter?''

"Aye, of course. The pages all spend an hour a day with the priests. 'Tis part of our training.'' The boy's mouth screwed up in disgust. "I'd much rather be practicing with the lance or bow than translating verses from the psalter.''

Mellisynt stared at Bartholomew, not really seeing his wind-tossed golden curls or his dirt-smudged face. Instead, she thought of the rolled parchments buried deep in her traveling baskets, those indecipherable documents that gave her financial independence and made no sense to her at all.

"Do you read them, these verses in the prayer books?''

"Aye, of course.'' Bartholomew preened like a feathered cock. At her fascinated look, he amended his bold assertion. "Well, I try, most seriously. Father Vincent has worn out any number of switches, beating the lines into my hide.''

"If I show you some parchments, can you tell me the words and letters?''

A look of doubt compounded with dread crossed the boy's face, but Mellisynt ignored it. She remembered the night FitzHugh had gone over the betrothal documents with her, explaining sources of rents and incomes. She'd tried to grasp all the details, but within moments her head had begun to spin. He'd finally rolled the parchments up with an exasperated sigh, assuring her that she could rely on the clerics at Edgemoor and his uncle to help her with financial matters. Mellisynt stared across the sluggish waves at the castle slipping slowly past, imprinting the brave *R* from the pennant on her mind. Never again, she swore, would she allow any cleric to hold sway over her. Never again would she be helpless and bound by ignorance in her own keep. Not if she could help it.

Brushing aside Bartholomew's vociferous objections with ruthless determination, she kept him pinned to her side for an hour each day thereafter, poring over the betrothal documents. It was soon obvious the boy had large gaps in his education, but he struggled manfully over each letter, his tongue caught between his teeth and his brow puckered in concentration. Once or twice, when they met an impenetrable word or obscure conjugation, they appealed to Sir Peter for help. St. Bressé's education was not much better than Bartholomew's, and his obvious unease at deciphering words soon won his release from their impromptu classes.

Isabeau laughed scornfully at the sight of a grown woman taking lessons from a reluctant, grubby-faced tutor and declined to join their sessions. She whiled away the slow journey by poring over the treasures purchased at various ports and experimenting with new, exotic cosmetics.

Mellisynt watched uneasily when Isabeau sidled up to Sir Peter, fluttering darkened lashes and laying a white hand on his arm. The serious, unsmiling young knight had but recently wed, she knew, and his wife awaited them at Edgemoor. She didn't interfere, however, since St. Bressé bowed respectfully whenever Isabeau approached and listened most attentively to her pouting comments, but gave no overt sign he was succumbing to the girl's charms.

Finally, on the day the sun entered the sign of Capricorn and the darkest day of winter descended, they sailed up the river Humber's wide estuary and anchored at Kingston upon Hull. Mellisynt huddled on deck in the damp mists, her fur cloak drawn tight around her face, and watched their trunks and baskets being unloaded. They would continue their journey north overland.

With his customary careful attention to his duties, Sir Peter planned the trip in easy stages. He also arranged for a spacious, horse-drawn litter to carry the ladies over the rough roads, which met with Mellisynt's enthusiastic approval. Brushing aside her warm thanks, he explained that Sir Richard had given him most strict instructions not to mount her on any of his valuable horses.

Five days later, Mellisynt's heart thudded with excitement at the first sight of the keep that would be her home for those months spent in England each year. Edgemoor held true to its name. Set atop a high mound of earth not far from the rocky, windswept coast, it looked out over the desolate moors and dales of northern Yorkshire. Here, on the roof of England, Mellisynt sensed that nature was as yet unsubdued. The sky seemed wider and closer, the land harsher. The red sandstone keep appeared starker and more forbidding than the elegant stone castles to the south. This land suited FitzHugh, she decided. It exuded the same raw power, the same untamed ruggedness as her lord. Gazing up at the Edgemoor's high walls, she understood her husband's oft-stated disdain for the luxuries of the royal courts. He belonged here, in this wild land, holding it for the king and the duke against predators from the sea and raiders from the north.

As the massive timber gate swung closed behind her and walls of red stone topped with sharpened timbers surrounded their party, Mellisynt marveled at her excitement. She felt none of the suffocating sense of imprisonment she'd endured within Trémont for so many years. Mayhap it was the sea-laden breeze that lifted the edges of her cloak and blew away the odors of a crowded keep, leaving a tangy scent of salt in her nostrils. Or the cheerful jumble of roving livestock, barking dogs, boar pits, stables, dovecotes and servants' huts that jammed the outer yard, so different from Trémont's austere, shadowed grounds. This keep teemed with life, and with people, she noted, as she climbed out of the litter.

It appeared that every soul in the great hall and from the surrounding farms and villages had gathered to welcome their new lady, or at least to gawk at her. Keeping her cloak gathered close about her, Mellisynt surveyed the assembled crowd with some consternation. While she struggled to find words of greeting, a tall, well-muscled youth detached himself from the group beside the hall's entrance.

"God keep you, Lady Mellisynt. I am William, son to FitzHugh. My father sent word of your coming and bid me travel to Edgemoor to welcome you."

Mellisynt's heart leapt into her throat as she surveyed her son-by-marriage. FitzHugh's voice had roughened with pride when he'd told her of his oldest, William, now two-and-ten years of age and a squire in service to Lord De Burg, justiciar of England. But nothing in her lord's gruff description of the boy had prepared her for blue eyes that sparkled with life in a tanned face surrounded by black curls the exact shade of his sire's. Or for the dimpled smile that William must have inherited from his dam.

"My brother, Geoffrey, is page to Lord Ranulf, earl of Chester, and could not come north to greet you. He would add his most reverent welcome were he here."

From what FitzHugh had told her of young Geoffrey, godson to the duke, Mellisynt doubted his greeting would be reverent. Her lord had described his younger son, not yet nine years of age, as the greatest scamp ever to spring from any man's loins. With a silent prayer that she would breed such sons, Mellisynt smiled and held out her hands.

"I thank you for taking time from your duties to welcome me. Will you stay long?"

"Nay. Lord De Burg leaves soon for Ireland with the king, and I go with him." William puffed a bit at his own importance, then flashed her a boyish grin. "But I have three days' respite, and would show you about Edgemoor. We can cover much ground in three days, with good horses under us."

Mellisynt stifled a groan. Swallowing, she turned to greet the elderly, white-haired man who came forward.

"Hail, lady. I am Alymer, uncle to Sir Richard and defender of the keep in his absence. He bade us make you comfortable in your new home."

Mellisynt blinked as the hawk-faced man bent and brushed his lips across her cheeks in the kiss of welcome. Sweet Mother, did all the men in her husband's family have the same massive frame and chiseled countenance? Although Alymer's hair was silvered and his belly slightly rounded with age, he still towered over her.

"Thank you, Sir Alymer."

"Nay, not Sir." He led her forward. "'Tis plain Alymer, late of Swanley, now of Edgemoor. And this is my wife, Hertha."

The last vestiges of Mellisynt's nervousness faded when Dame Hertha came forward. As round as she was tall, the woman had the friendliest smile and the merriest eyes Mellisynt had ever seen. Hertha bent her head in a quick obeisance, all three chins wobbling vigorously, then detached a huge ring of keys from her wide belt and held them out.

"We're most pleased to welcome our new chatelaine, my lady."

Feeling slightly overwhelmed by the sudden acquisition of so many new relatives, Mellisynt took the ring from her pudgy hands with a warm smile.

"I accept the keys, but would beg you not to relinquish your place or your duties. I need your help and guidance in learning the ways of Edgemoor."

The woman beamed, as if she'd been given a great honor, not been asked to continue what must be a crushing burden. Although Edgemoor was considerably smaller than Trémont, with fewer outlying farms and dependents, Mellisynt knew well that the task of ordering its daily living would require all her energy and skill. She truly welcomed the older woman's experience and apparent willingness to continue in her role. Mayhap Hertha's assistance would give her time to master the frustrating parchments.

She turned, beckoning Isabeau forward to introduce her to the others. Leaning gracefully on Sir Peter's strong arm, the girl picked her way over the rough ground. Mellisynt heard a small gasp from the ranks of the women behind Hertha and glanced toward the sound. A slender, plain-faced young woman stared at Sir Peter, jealousy written in every bone of her rigid body. His wife, Mellisynt thought with a sigh. Suddenly the winter months, when they'd all perforce be enclosed within the keep's round walls by snow and frost, loomed long and fraught with unforeseen dangers.

"I don't care what the losses, you will take them forward!"

"For God's sake, Geoffrey, listen to your words," FitzHugh snarled. "You would sacrifice these men to your damned pride."

Rage glittered in the duke's golden eyes. "'Tis not my pride that makes you balk, bastard. 'Tis that you might not win such fat ransoms in open battle as you do by besieging half-defended, petty little keeps."

FitzHugh sucked in his breath. His eyes narrowed on the red face glaring at him from across the wooden camp table. He planted two mailed fists on the table and leaned forward, making no effort to disguise his fury.

"Do you accuse me of cowardice, of shirking battle, my lord duke?" he asked softly, dangerously.

For long, tense moments, friend faced friend. Hostility arced between them. An even deeper red washed over Geoffrey's cheeks. Angevin temper warred with the ties of friendship, and the struggle showed plainly on his expressive face. Outside the tent, normal camp sounds filled the soft spring air, but inside only the harsh, rasping breath of duke and vassal cut the thick stillness. Beads of sweat ran down Geoffrey's temples. With a low growl, he straightened and dashed the stinging salt from his eyes.

"Oh, be damned to you, FitzHugh. You know I would as soon see myself in hell as believe you false to me and your oaths."

Chagrin softened the hard lines of his face, and he gave a rueful smile. This time, however, the calculated charm failed dismally in its aim.

FitzHugh straightened slowly. Rage still spread its icy tentacles in every vein, and he didn't trust himself to speak. In truth, he didn't trust himself not to lean across the small table and knock his friend to the dirt floor. Never before, in all the years of their friendship, had Geoffrey questioned FitzHugh's honor. And never before had FitzHugh allowed anyone to do so and remain among the living.

As if sensing that this time he'd gone too far, Geoffrey unclenched his fist and reached out to grasp FitzHugh's arm. His fingers pressed mail deep into flesh and bone with the iron strength of their hold.

"Richard, 'tis the accursed heat and my own distemper speaking. And this damned game we play with Toulouse. We've spent nigh on four months chasing that slippery old fool around half of France. I've lost what little patience I possess in the process."

FitzHugh stared down at the hand gripping his arm with such painful intensity, thinking that for the first time in many weeks he could agree with Geoffrey. The duke *had* lost his patience, and much of his perspective, in the prosecution of this war. Not satisfied with besieging Montauban, their primary objective, Geoffrey had widened the battle and sent FitzHugh deep into Toulouse.

For months now, they'd fought against overwhelming odds as the crafty count of Toulouse lured the invaders deeper and deeper into his lands. He left burned villages and fouled wells behind so that the invaders had to spread themselves thin to forage for sustenance. Now Geoffrey wanted to divide his forces still further, and send half of them west, to the flat, fertile plain of the river Garonne, where Toulouse was thought to have retreated, while the rest went south to lay siege to the capital. FitzHugh had left his men encamped in a protected vale while he rode furiously back to Geoffrey's camp. He would know what drove this madness before he took even one archer one step farther. He pulled his arm free of the duke's hard grip.

"We achieved our objective in February, Geoffrey. Tell me truthfully why you still push forward, against all odds, against your own knights' best advice. We're private here, just the two of us. What devious scheme have you in your brain now?"

The duke flushed once more. "Why do you think it devious to want to press forward? Why don't you see the advantages of subduing once and for all a wily foe who's long harassed our borders?"

"Because taking Toulouse has no long-term advantages, man! This province is a buffer between the Angevin lands and the French king's domains. Do we take Toulouse, King Philip will be on us with every knight he can call to service or hire out of hand."

FitzHugh paused, and the suspicion that had taken hold in these last bloody weeks hardened into certainty.

"Unless," he continued slowly, watching Geoffrey's eyes, "you have assurances from Philip that he would welcome you as ally. Unless you think to align yourself with him against your father."

Geoffrey's golden eyes slid away. He turned and paced the length of the tent. FitzHugh felt a coldness creep down his spine. Had his friend forsworn himself?

"Nay," Geoffrey finally answered with a troubled frown. "I've made no promises to Philip, although 'tis true he would have me help him throw off my father's dominion on the Continents. He's offered men and supplies to aid us in this campaign, but I've not accepted."

He paused, and for a moment FitzHugh glimpsed the tortured man within the hulking, boisterous shell.

"They have me on a rack, Richard! One pulls this way, one that. I would be my own man, not my father's puppet nor Philip's tool."

"No man is entirely his own," FitzHugh replied deliberately. "All of us have ties, to God, to our liege. You've sworn to your father, you hold Richmond through him and

Brittany through Constance. You owe nothing to Philip, nor would you gain by playing his game. He would use you for his own ends.''

"I know, I know!" Geoffrey kicked a camp stool angrily. He strode about the spacious tent, agitation robbing his person of its normal fluid grace. "'Tis why I want to take Toulouse, despite my father's urgings to desist. I want to show him and Philip that I can do it! That I need neither of them to jerk my strings. That I'm as fit to rule my own lands as Richard Lionheart does his."

There was a certain twisted logic in his thinking, Fitz-Hugh admitted. Mayhap if Geoffrey showed strength and independence, he would become a force to be reckoned with in his own right. One that could help mold a precarious balance of power on the Continent. If that was truly his goal.

FitzHugh rubbed a weary hand across his eyes. He wanted to believe Geoffrey. He wanted to push aside the remnants of anger from his friend's harsh accusations of moments before, to recapture the trust and boon companionship that had been theirs until Geoffrey's inner devils began to twist and push him into recklessness.

"Lead this foray, Richard, and we have Toulouse. Once he's taken, I will negotiate honorable terms and withdraw, I swear it. I want not the lands—only to show myself capable of taking them."

FitzHugh stared at his friend for a long moment, doubt and suspicion battling with the need to trust. Finally, slowly, he nodded.

FitzHugh dragged his arm across his eyes to clear the blood and sweat, and tried desperately to get his bearings. Waves of noise rose all around him, battering at him with the force of a blow. The screams of dead and dying, the hoarse shouts of the foot soldiers and the wild shrieks of wounded horses, the sound of steel ringing against steel and arrows twanging into padded leather all beat at his ears. He ducked as a crossbow bolt whistled overhead. The cut on his forehead reopened as it slammed against his helm. A stream of fresh blood poured down, blinding him once more.

With a vicious wrench on the reins, he checked Voyager's plunging advance. He dared not push forward when he couldn't see whether the figures before him were those of his own men or of Toulouse. FitzHugh had led this bold charge at the center of the count's waving line. He knew his foot soldiers had swept forward with him, but at what pace? Were they behind him, or had he penetrated the enemy's line in this last, mad charge and now was surrounded? Swearing, he wiped furiously at his eyes. When his blurred vision cleared, he identified his mud-covered squire just beside him, and a solid phalanx of his own men behind Ian. He let out a ragged, relieved breath and set his spurs to Voyager once more.

"*À moi! À Bretagne!*"

His hoarse shout barely carried over the roar of battle, but the wave of men followed him forward. The ground was awash with mud churned out of the spring-softened earth by a thousand slashing hooves, and with the gore of half as many trampled bodies. FitzHugh charged at the wavering center line even now folding back against its own flanks. He leaned forward over his mount's shoulder, cutting and slashing as the Voyager surged forward.

Another bolt whistled through the air. With a sickening thud, it drove through the barding covering the destrier's neck. As Voyager screamed and went down, forelegs thrashing, FitzHugh tried to kick his feet free of the stirrups and throw himself sideways. Not quite fast enough, he landed in the mud, one foot trapped under his mount.

The tide of men swept over them both. FitzHugh planted one foot against the saddle and pushed, struggling desperately to free himself from the mortally wounded horse. More fallen knights died from being crushed by their own mounts or trampled by oncoming forces than from battle wounds. He gasped in relief as Ian fought his way through the rush of men to his side. The squire flung himself from his own horse, grabbed his lord's mailed arm, and heaved with all his might. FitzHugh's foot slid out from under the now-still destrier. Without pause, he mounted Ian's horse, leaving the squire to fight his way back to the handlers responsible for the spare mounts. Sword in hand, blood streaming from the cut on his forehead, fire and fear and icy fury coursing through his veins, he charged forward.

Within an hour, it was over. One by one, the count's surviving knights surrendered their standards and their swords. Gradually the roar of battle subsided, until only the screams and sobbing cries of wounded men and beasts carried on the April air. FitzHugh pushed his mailed hood back and surveyed the battlefield wearily. From his position on a small rise, he could see most of the flat plain enclosed by the winding river. The remnants of the count's armies were spread in a thin line along the water's edge, with the bulk of FitzHugh's forces between them. Bodies lay scattered across the devastated plain in grotesque piles alongside fallen horses, abandoned weapons, slaughtered farm animals and burning huts. It was a scene of incredible carnage, one he should be used to but wasn't. Surveying the aftermath of battle with aching eyes, FitzHugh cursed Geoffrey.

"Do we send the captured knights back to Montauban?" A begrimed knight, one of Geoffrey's lesser vassals, slumped wearily in his saddle and awaited instructions.

"Aye. The duke will decide where to incarcerate them until the ransoms are paid. See that the scribes record who was taken, and by whom, so the moneys are distributed fairly when they're received."

"And the count?"

"I'll meet with him myself and take his pledge. Prepare a tent where he may rest until we restore order and see to the wounded."

The man nodded and rode away.

FitzHugh rubbed a weary hand across his eyes, inadvertently grinding filth and blood into his wound. Jesu, he was tired. He slumped against the cantle, sheathing his sword for the first time since the bloody battle began. His eyes swept the littered plain, and he wondered again, deep in his soul, if such slaughter was worth the price of Geoffrey's pride.

A small field of clover at the edge of the plain, miraculously unscathed by churning hooves or flaming arrows, caught his attention. Its verdant color was a breath of life amid the stench of death. In the late-afternoon sun, it glowed green and rich, and reminded FitzHugh most forcefully of his lady's luminous eyes. Of how they, too, had glowed with life and passion in a bleak winter garden.

That scene, and others involving a curtain of russet hair and a slender body, had filled FitzHugh's mind more often than he cared to admit these last months. He shifted in his saddle, wondering how one slight, pale woman should have taken hold of his thoughts—and his desires—with so firm a grip. How the image of her awaiting him at Edgemoor had become such a talisman through these months of war and death. It was as if she lured him, drew him home. Never before had he felt such an impatience to be done with the business of battle and seek the softness of a woman's arms.

The realization that he and Geoffrey would return at last to England spurred him to action. As the blazing sun sank into the red-tinted river, clogged with the carcasses of men and horses drowned in their frantic attempts to escape, FitzHugh sent an exhausted courier to summon the senior knights and begin the wearisome process of restoring order after the madness of battle.

Ironically, FitzHugh's very victory became the instrument that delayed his departure for England yet several more months. Geoffrey's successes alarmed his brother Richard Lionheart, who began to mobilize his forces. King Henry himself came to France in late April when the rumor spread that Richard was about to attack Brittany. The king rode across his vast domains at a frenetic pace, bearding first one son and then the other in their respective camps.

In return for his assurance that he would not war with his brother, Geoffrey won full cognizance over the duchy of Brittany and the county of Nantes. He planned a triumphant return to his capital city of Rennes and sent word to all his barons that there would be a great assize the following month.

As holder of the fief of Trémont, FitzHugh was required to attend the great parliament. Sweltering in ceremonial robes under the June sun, he paraded with the rest of Geoffrey's barons through the streets of Rennes. During many a late-night session, he helped the duke forge reforms modeled after those King Henry had implemented in England, designed to curb the barons' independence. Geoffrey's blazing personality and sheer stubbornness forced each measure through the assembled parliament. One by one the fiercely independent Breton lords bent a stiff knee and pledged fealty to the triumphant duke.

By the time the great assize disbanded and the business of implementing the new reforms was done, June had become July, then August. FitzHugh's impatience to be gone grew with every passing day.

"By the saints, 'tis good to be back in the north again!"

Geoffrey slewed sideways in the saddle to face the sea and let the cool breeze ruffle through his sweat-flattened hair. They'd ridden hard since landing two days ago, pushing horses and men, following the coast road north. Just a half hour before, they had splashed across the estuary that marked the beginning of FitzHugh's own holdings.

Below them, waves crashed against the rocks, sending a fine spray up and over the cliffs. Sunlight danced on a dark emerald sea, reminding FitzHugh anew why he clung to these wild lands and the small keep that guarded them. Here, with the rolling moors to the west and the crashing sea to the east, the rest of civilization seemed far away. Here, the burdens of fealty and honor and finding balance in a world of intrigue slipped away. Here, he was home. And here, too, his wife awaited him.

FitzHugh pictured her in the great hall of his keep, her hair demurely veiled and her slim figure clothed in gowns of soft, rich color. He saw her coming forward to greet him with a chatelaine's solemn dignity, to offer him the kiss of welcome. Fingering the pouch at his waist, where a count's ransom in pearls nestled, he visualized how he would drape the ropes of translucent beads around her pale throat in full view of the assembled keep, to show the esteem in which he held his new wife. And how he would remove them slowly, seductively, in the privacy of their room.

"I'm glad I decided to go first to Richmond," Geoffrey said, his booming voice breaking into FitzHugh's musing. "If we had stopped at Winchester before coming north, as my father desired, Constance would have cut off my nose."

"Or your manhood," FitzHugh commented lazily. "She oft swears 'tis the most useless part of your anatomy."

Geoffrey's laughter rang out across the cliffs, and FitzHugh grinned in return. Although both men still carried the scars of their bitter argument in their hearts, FitzHugh's victory, Geoffrey's triumphant assize and the passage of time had helped heal the wounds.

FitzHugh wiped a trickle of sweat from his brow. They'd removed their protective wool surcoats and mailed tunics as they penetrated deep into his lands. Still, the hot August sun beat mercilessly on his sweat-dampened light linen shirt.

"Christ's bones, look at that."

FitzHugh turned in the direction of Geoffrey's wide-eyed stare. Squinting against the sun's dazzle, he searched among the rocks that lined the shore below them.

Geoffrey pointed, "There, where the sand and waters meet."

A figure splashed out of the shallow waves, her white shift lifted high above long, shapely legs. Even from this distance the men could see how the wet cotton clung to her breasts, outlining them in perfect detail. A trill of joyous laughter carried across air as she turned and beckoned to two dark heads just visible in the rolling waters.

"B'God, FitzHugh, if that's one of your villeins, I claim an overlord's rights." Geoffrey's eyes raked the woman's back, lingering on the lush rear clearly delineated by the wet fabric.

One of her companions broke out of the waves and dashed toward shore. FitzHugh's eyes widened in disbelief as he saw the boy's golden curls, unmistakable even from this distance. The second figure emerged and spread three shaggy legs wide to shake the seawater from its massive body. A wave of booming, ear-splitting barks rolled up the cliffside.

Geoffrey flung out an arm and gave FitzHugh a good-natured blow that knocked him sideways in the saddle.

"You've kept this juicy morsel well hidden, you selfish wretch. Send for her this night. I'd like to see her at somewhat closer quarters."

"And so you shall," FitzHugh told him dryly. "You will excuse me, my lord, while I go inform my lady wife that her overlord requests her presence at the keep."

Chapter Eleven

Mellisynt sat atop a sun-washed rock, her knees drawn up
and her chin resting on crossed arms. She watched as Bartholomew and the hound raced along the rocky shore. The
boy shouted in exuberance at his release from his tutor's
stern regimen while the dog jumped and echoed his joy with
deafening abandon. She smiled at their lively antics and
sturdy figures, thinking how different both child and hound
were from when they'd first come into her life. The three of
them had grown so close these last months, as winter gave
way to spring and spring softened into summer.

With Alymer and Dame Hertha to help in Edgemoor's
operation, for the first time in her adult life Mellisynt had
had time to enjoy her surroundings. William, her son-by-
marriage, had taken her in hand the first week, introduc-
ing her to FitzHugh's main tenants and nearby vassals. Although she groaned each time she recalled the long rides
with the energetic, boisterous youth, she'd been grateful for
his cheerful introductions.

After William left to return to his training, she'd ven-
tured forth with FitzHugh's uncle as guide, tentatively at
first and then with growing confidence. She'd visited tenants, brought herbs from the keep's store to ailing serfs,
doled out precious seed corn to start the spring plantings.
And with each task, she'd explored the wild beauty of her
new home. Whether drenched with freezing mist, lashed by
spring storms or, as now, bathed in a rare haze of hot sun,

the land drew her. After so many years within Trémont's walls, she soaked up the sky and moors like one long-starved.

Her most special time was that spent by the sea. With Dame Hertha's motherly, indulgent cooperation, Mellisynt would slip away from her chatelaine's duties and coax the tutor to release his reluctant pupil. Like a lodestone pointing to the North Star, she and Bartholomew and the hound would head for the rock-strewn coast. They claimed this rough stretch of shore as their own. Out of sight of the keep and the fishing docks to the north, they romped and splashed and grew brown from the sun's rays. Here Bartholomew forgot his page's dignity to become a child once more, and the hound raced the waves as if he had four good legs, not three. And here Mellisynt sat and spun her dreams.

Dreams that centered around the hazy face of her husband. Mellisynt shifted on the hard rock and settled her chin once more. He would come soon, his brief message had said, with the duke. Even the thought of Geoffrey's presence could not dampen the surge of joy she'd felt at the courier's news. She'd gone straight away to lay out her finest robe, fashioned with Isabeau's assistance and trimmed with exquisite embroidery. She would await him on the steps of the keep, she decided, cool and composed, and overwhelm him with her new finery.

A slow smile crept across her face. No doubt she would overwhelm him with her need, as well, once she had him within their curtained bed. Sweet Mother, but these nights had been long. How could one stern, harsh-faced knight have wiped out years of disgust of the marriage bed in just a few short weeks, and then left her, craving his touch? Mellisynt felt a tingling, low in her belly. Soon, she told herself, soon he would be home to satisfy that craving.

She knew she should be back at the keep, overseeing the cleaning and the preparations for their arrival. But ever since that messenger had ridden into the yard yesterday morn and delivered the stained parchment, she'd been unable to concentrate on the tasks at hand. The courier had said he thought the others were but a week behind, and she'd drifted about thereafter in an abstracted way. Even Isabeau, no lover of household chores, had finally exclaimed that she would instruct the cook herself rather than risk salted pudding and sweetened meat from Mellisynt's muddled directions. Isabeau and Dame Hertha had shooed her from the keep with instructions to let the sea breeze blow the hot choler from her body.

So far, at least, the breeze had failed miserably in its task. Even a swim in the cold sea waters had not washed the heat from her loins. Under the damp shift, her breasts tingled and her thighs clenched together in a vain attempt to still the pulsing need between them. Soon, she told herself, soon.

Her lids drooped in languid anticipation, then flew open at a startled shout far down the shore. Scrambling off her perch, Mellisynt searched for the boy amid the scattered rocks. Her heart leapt into her throat when she saw him running frantically toward her, the beast loping beside him. Behind them, far off in the distance, a lone horseman guided his mount down the steep shale path that led to their cove.

Sweet Mother, how had the man slipped past Alymer's guards? They'd had some trouble with bandits a few months past, but FitzHugh's uncle was certain he'd cleaned them out. Her blood pounded now with fear. Had the marauders returned? Had one of the bandits seen them alone and unprotected on the beach? She squinted into the distance, but the rider was too far away for her to make out more than a hazy outline and the faint sheen of the horse's roan coat.

"My lady," Bartholomew panted, "we must hie back to the keep. I don't recognize the horse."

"Come, we'll run along the shore. Mayhap we can round the curve before the tide cuts it off completely."

Abandoning her robes, she grabbed the boy's hand and lifted the skirts of her wet shift. With the hound loping beside them, they raced for the far cusp of the cove, where the cliffs jutted right out into the sea. Already waves dashed against the red sandstone, sending towers of spray up into the blue sky. The waters receded, then swept in once more to cover the narrow strip of sand at the cliff's base. Mellisynt swallowed convulsively as the undertow tugged at her ankles, then staggered when an incoming wave slapped at her thighs. Bartholomew stumbled, thrown off balance by the rush of the sea. Frantic, Mellisynt tugged on his arm with both hands, hauling him bodily out of the sucking sand and water. The hound raced back and forth, woofing in the shallows. Mellisynt cast a quick look over her shoulder and gasped. The rider was bent low over his horse's neck, his face obscured by the flying mane, galloping along the rocky shore, straight at them.

Realizing they could not outrun him, Mellisynt dragged the boy through the swirling water toward the cliffs. Mayhap they could find footholds and climb up, out of the man's reach. Her breath rasped in her throat as she struggled with Bartholomew against the tide's pull. Spray flew in her eyes and coated her tongue, salt vying with the sour taste of fear. She couldn't see through the blur of water stinging her eyes, but pushed forward blindly.

Halfway to the cliffs, they felt the pounding of the horse's hooves behind them and heard a ragged shout from the rider. Mellisynt couldn't make out his words over her own panting breath and the hound's furious barking. She stumbled and cried aloud when her bare toes hit a submerged rock. Bartholomew tugged his hand loose.

"I'll stop him, my lady! You go on!"

"Nay!" she screamed as he darted away from her, right into the path of the oncoming horse. The steed swerved violently and reared, its hooves pawing the air above the boy's head. Mellisynt heard a violent oath, then a splash as the hooves came down again, clear of the small body. The horse leapt forward, straight for her. Before she could turn or run, the rider leaned down and wrapped a hard arm around her waist, jerking her off her feet.

Her breath left with a whoosh as she slammed against the rock-hard body of her captor. Her nose smashed into his chest, while the sharp bend of his knee dug into her stomach. Unable to move, unable even to breathe, Mellisynt opened her mouth and bit into the flesh under the linen shirt.

"Jesu, woman!" he roared, jerking the horse to a halt. Ungentle hands yanked her sideways across the saddle.

Mellisynt barely heard the words over the furious pounding of her blood and the hound's frantic growling. She struggled to free herself, twisting and slipping on the wet saddle.

"Be still!" he thundered, pinning her body against his.

She shook her head to clear the glaze of salt water and soaked strands of hair plastered to her face. Shock swept through her.

"FitzHugh?" she screeched.

"By all the saints, woman, is this how you greet your—"

His furious shout was cut off as a brown body hurled itself through the air and crashed against them, knocking them both from the saddle. Man, woman and beast landed in three feet of swirling water.

FitzHugh struggled to stand, hauling Mellisynt up by one arm. It took the dog a few seconds longer to regain his precarious balance.

"Hold, you hound of hell!"

FitzHugh's enraged command stopped the animal in its tracks. It quivered with coiled tension, fangs bared and growls emanating from deep in its chest. Bartholomew gave a relieved shout and splashed forward, wrapping his arms about the beast's neck to still the reverberating snarls.

"My lord! 'Tis you!"

"Aye," FitzHugh snapped, dragging Mellisynt behind him. He reached for the reins of the nervous, skittering horse. "I wish to God you'd recognized me earlier and saved us all a dunking."

Mellisynt couldn't speak. Her throat swelled tight, whether from the residue of fear, or shock or sea water, she knew not.

"We had word you wouldn't leave Winchester for yet a week," Bartholomew cried, prancing happily alongside as they splashed through the surf toward the rocks. "Everyone is most anxious for your arrival. Word of your victories has spread across the north. All the squires brag and boast of your wins. We can't wait to hear of the battle."

They stumbled the last few feet to shore. FitzHugh's rough hold on his wife's arm loosened, and he swung her around to face him. His eyes traveled from her sodden hair, its dark red tendrils streaked with bits of brown kelp, down the slender column of her throat, to linger on the heaving breasts barely veiled by the wet, clinging linen.

"Did you really cut the count's armies in half, like a sword slicing through soft brains?" Bartholomew's voice was filled with glee at the gory thought. "Did you send them—"

"You'll hear the details in good time," FitzHugh said, interrupting him. "Get you gone, boy."

"But—"

"Now!"

FitzHugh tore his eyes from the rigid tips of his wife's breasts, thrusting against the wet material, to survey the lad's crestfallen face under its cap of wet golden curls.

"I would...speak with my lady wife. Go, and take that murderous cur with you. Ask my uncle to see to Duke Geoffrey's comfort until we return, and I may find something in my baggage of the battle that is yours to keep."

"Truly? What? A sword? A captured banner?" Bartholomew danced on one foot in his excitement.

Obviously confused, but willing to enter into the sport, the hound jumped up and added his booming voice to the child's eager, pelting questions.

The stallion jerked his head up at the din, almost tearing the reins from FitzHugh's grasp. He cursed and turned to soothe the beast.

"Bartholomew, take the hound and go," Mellisynt croaked, finding her voice at last.

The child opened his mouth to protest.

"Now!" Lord and lady spoke in unison.

The boy blinked at their vehemence and wrapped his arm around the dog. He trotted a few paces down the shore, then turned back, a hopeful expression lighting his face.

"A shield, mayhap?"

FitzHugh's low growl sounded remarkably like those the hound had uttered just a few moments earlier.

Mellisynt felt a bubble of laughter rise in her throat. She bit her lip, trying to hold it back.

"You think this amusing, lady wife?"

She glanced up to see FitzHugh's blue eyes glinting down at her. Beads of water sparkled on his dark lashes and trickled down his cheeks. A bit of seaweed dangled from one ear.

"Aye, my lord husband," she gasped unsteadily.

His brows drew together. "You will not find it as humorous when I skewer that damned hound and serve it *en brochette* to the gyrfalcons."

"No, my lord," Mellisynt replied, putting a hand over her mouth to hold back her giggles.

He scowled down at her. "I am not at all used to being unhorsed, and the fact that it was accomplished by a three-legged, lop-eared, sorry excuse for a dog rankles. You will not repeat this event to Geoffrey."

Mellisynt's laughter broke through. Whooping, she bent and wrapped both arms about her waist. When she could catch her breath, she glanced up to see a rueful grin lifting one corner of her husband's chiseled lips. His reluctant smile set her off again. Choking with laughter, she sank to her knees.

FitzHugh followed her down to the sand, a suspicious rumbling sounding deep in his chest.

When her gulping laughter finally slowed to occasional hiccups, Mellisynt wiped her eyes with a sand-encrusted hand. She lay back, propping herself on her elbows. Above, the sky stretched endlessly blue, and white-winged gulls dipped and floated on the breeze. FitzHugh settled himself beside her. For long moments they absorbed the sea and the sun in rare silent companionship.

Feeling wonderfully at ease, she turned and smiled up at him. "'Tis . . . 'tis not at all the greeting I had planned for you."

He reached out and brushed the sand from her cheek, his white teeth gleaming. "'Tis not exactly the welcome I had envisioned, either."

Mellisynt's heart began a slow, steady thumping. Holy Mary, how had she ever thought him stern and hard of face? Water dripping from the dark hair curled on his forehead and ran down his high cheeks and blunt, square chin. She ached to catch the tiny rivulets with her finger, or her tongue, or any other part of her body she could press against his face. And his eyes, sweet Mother, his eyes glinted with a light that rocked her knees, much as the swirling waves had moments before.

He turned at a sound from the still-restive horse. Mellisynt gasped in shock. A red, angry wound, poorly stitched, ran from the corner of his hairline back into his scalp. She lifted one hand to touch the edge, only to draw back when he jerked his head away.

"It burns," he told her with a grimace. "From the salt water."

"Good God, I doubt it not. Come, we must get you home so that I may rinse it and ease the sting."

He caught her before she could scramble to her feet.

"Nay, my lady. I fear there's yet another part of me that burns far worse. One that needs attending immediately."

Her eyes widened in alarm, and she ran them quickly over his body. She saw no other visible wound. She did, however, see his shaft standing rock-hard and rampant against his soaked chausses. Her mouth opened.

"Oh!"

"Oh, yes, or oh, no?" he inquired casually, reaching out one tanned hand to stroke the tip of her breast.

Mellisynt jumped as if seared with a redhot iron. Sitting up straight, she studied the glinting blue light in his eyes. Disbelief and a slow, insidious hope warred in her chest.

"You...you wish to couple here? In...in the sun and open sky?"

"Yes, here."

His voice lowered and washed over her with the slow, rhythmic pull of the waves. "I would have you here, where the emerald sea matches the color of your eyes and the sun heats your flesh to warm silk."

Mellisynt swallowed. "Now?"

"Aye, now. After these long months, I do not care to wait." His hand took possession of her breast once more, kneading gently, rubbing against the puckered tip.

"Nor do I, my lord."

She followed her husky whisper with a sinuous movement that stretched her damp length alongside him. But if Mellisynt had thought this was to be a slow, sweet joining such as she had dreamed of all through the long winter nights and hot summer days, she was soon disabused of the notion. The same hard arm that had lifted her from the surf once more wrapped around her waist. With a quick, fluid movement, FitzHugh rolled over, pressing her into the sand with all the force of his massive body. His head swooped down and captured her mouth in a fierce, consuming kiss.

Responding to his rough urgency, Mellisynt locked both arms around his neck and strained against him. She ground her lips into his, her need rising in hot waves. She reveled in the taste of salt and raw male hunger. Her fingers curled into his neck, feeling the soft, springy hairs and smooth skin under their tips. She opened for him eagerly, taking his tongue into her mouth and exchanging thrust for thrust, taste for taste.

When he tore his lips away to bury his face in her neck, she groaned and tugged at his hair to bring his mouth back to hers. A growl of pure, primitive passion surged up from deep in her chest.

FitzHugh lifted his body from hers enough to insert his hand between them and rip her soggy shift from neck to waist. A warm, callused hand covered her breast, shaping it to his satisfaction. His eyes feasted on her soft flesh. He bent to partake of the feast, then grunted when a sharp stone cut into his elbow.

Dislodging the stone, he tossed it away. A grin tugged at his lips. "Do you think we shall ever get to couple in our own bed, without rocks or cold winds to distract us?"

"Oh, yes," Mellisynt breathed. "But later. Later."

Impatient, she pulled his head back down to her breast.

Mellisynt rode home wrapped in the warmth of Fitz-Hugh's cloak, cradled against his strong body. As the timbered walls of Edgemoor rose into view, she felt her husband's arm tighten around her waist and shared his sense of homecoming. Her delicious languor dissolved as they neared the great gates and she saw the crowd that spilled out of the hall to greet them. With all her soul, she longed to turn her face into FitzHugh's chest, to pretend she didn't arrive home wrapped in her husband's cloak, her hair straggling down her back, with sand and seaweed decorating all parts of her body. Her face burned, and she sank back into the encircling protection of her husband's arms.

"My lady!" Dame Hertha's shocked voice, and the way in which the rotund little lady completely ignored her nephew, told her she looked even worse than she feared.

"Lady Mellisynt!" Isabeau gasped, her delicate brows arching in disbelief. "You . . . you've lost your shoes!"

Biting her lip, Mellisynt struggled for an answer. Behind her, her lord's chest rumbled with suppressed laughter. Before she could frame a coherent reply, FitzHugh swung down from the saddle and tumbled her into his arms. With the crowd trailing behind them, he strode up the stairs and through the open door of the great hall. A cluster of men gathered around the central hearth turned at their noisy entrance.

"Well, it appears you found your sea sprite, FitzHugh."

Geoffrey waved an ale tankard in greeting. Alymer turned, his jaw dropping in amazement as his nephew crossed the hall with a shapeless, cringing bundle in his arms. The men surrounding the duke parted, and their amused chuckles added to the heat coursing across Mellisynt's face. She succumbed to the embarrassment washing over her. With a groan, she buried her face in FitzHugh's chest.

"Aye, my lord, I found her. And, as we're both a bit waterlogged, I would beg your indulgence a while longer before we join you at table."

"Go, go," Geoffrey boomed. "We've waited this long while you played in the sand, we can wait a few moments more."

FitzHugh pushed through the milling crowd and crossed to the far end of the great room. A maid scurried to open the door in the wooden screen that divided the lord's quarters from the rest of the hall. Dame Hertha and Isabeau squeezed in with several other women before FitzHugh could kick the door shut.

"Put her down," Hertha commanded, "and get you gone while we attend to her. Your squire and servants await you in our quarters above stairs. You'll find hot water and fresh clothes laid out there."

FitzHugh grinned at the woman as he let his now-squirming burden slide to her feet. "'Tis a sorry welcome you give the lord of the manor, Aunt, casting him from his own chambers the very moment of his return."

"If you behaved more like a lord and less like a rutting dog, you could expect a more gracious welcome." Hertha's twinkling eyes softened the edge of her voice. "Go now, go! Get you bathed and made presentable. We've held dinner until the joints are charred as it is. Do we delay much longer, the men will like to be rolling beneath the boards with the ale they've drunk!"

FitzHugh allowed himself to be pushed from the room. Before the door even slammed shut behind him, the women attacked Mellisynt. Hertha pulled the wet cloak from her shoulders with an exclamation of disgust. Maids reached to strip away the remains of the sodden shift.

"My lady!" Isabeau's luminous aquamarine eyes rounded, then swiftly narrowed. "You do not even wear your gown!"

Mellisynt had not thought her face could heat any further. "I left it on the rocks while I swam with Bartholomew earlier. It, ah, washed away on the tide while I...while we..."

"While you welcomed your lord home," Hertha finished for her, bustling her shivering frame into the tub. She placed a firm hand on Mellisynt's head, grabbed the soap with another, then paused. A knowing woman's grin spread across her dimpled cheeks. "I disremember the last time I saw the boy looking so smug and cocksure. You must have given him quite a ride!"

Mellisynt went under the surface and came up sputtering, as much from the idea of anyone calling FitzHugh "boy" as from the water streaming over her. She tossed her wet hair out of her eyes and grinned back at Hertha.

"Well, I think it's disgusting." Isabeau scowled as she fiddled with the pots and jars she pulled from a small wooden chest. "Such conduct is hardly what one expects from a lady."

St. Bressé's plain-faced young wife glanced across the room, her almond eyes filled with malice. "How would you know the manner in which a lady attends her husband? 'Till you have one of *your own,* you should be less free with your opinions."

Hertha rolled her eyes heavenward, and Mellisynt groaned. Not again! If there had been one twisted thread in the fabric of their lives these last months, it was the unceasing, unremitting enmity between Isabeau and the wife of FitzHugh's lieutenant. Mayhap if the woman had not made such an issue of the knight's attentions to the girl when they first arrived, or if there had been some other man of sufficient rank and address in the keep for Isabeau to practice her charms on, the matter would have died. But the girl had needed no more than one hissed warning from the lady to keep away from her husband to begin a stubborn, determined flirtation. The result was constant, running warfare, which now flared again.

"I'll have a husband soon enough," Isabeau shot back. "I doubt not the duke brings word of a fine alliance. The duchess promised to settle my betrothal as soon as the troubles in France subsided."

"Hah! 'Tis more likely the duchess has forgotten you exist. Or sent you here because she wished to wash her hands of so frivolous and forward a maid. If maid you be," St. Bressé's wife muttered.

"Why, you suet-faced—"

"Enough," Mellisynt ordered through a froth of soap.

Isabeau slammed her pots down and advanced on the other woman, hands on hips.

"You're sour with jealousy, and with good reason. You can't hold your lord's interest, let alone arouse his passion. You have not the beauty nor the wit nor the—"

"Enough, I said!" Mellisynt rose and sluiced the soapy residue from her skin. "Lady Katherine, see that the cooks are ready to serve, if you please. I will be done forthwith."

She waited until the door slammed behind the angry woman, then turned to the girl. "Isabeau, will you work the magic of your pots and jars for me once more, and quickly?"

Still fuming, her cheeks bright with color and her eyes sparkling with brilliant blue fire, Isabeau crossed the room.

When Mellisynt paused just outside the lord's chamber a short time later, her high color came from a mixture of Isabeau's pots, tingling anticipation, and an embarrassed reluctance to join the boisterous group of nobles at the far end of the hall. She smoothed nervous hands down the line of her gown. The shimmering amethyst silk had been her most expensive purchase those long months ago in Nantes, and she'd fashioned it into a deceptively simple robe. Pulled snug against her upper torso by side lacing, it showed off her slender figure admirably. Under the outer robe she wore a soft linen shift, its sleeves and slit neckline embroidered with gold and purple designs. Mellisynt knew the gown's color added much to the warm glow her skin had acquired from these weeks in the sun. She reached up to straighten the thin circlet of beaten gold that held a gauzy veil over her braided hair and took a deep breath, causing her breasts to strain at the tight silk.

This was how she'd wanted to greet her lord, in her fine new robes and sun-deepened color. She chewed on her lower lip, thinking that all her careful planning for his return had gone for naught. Still, she wouldn't have traded one moment in the sand for all the rich robes now nestling in her chest. She looked up and saw FitzHugh coming toward her, his dark head visible above the crowd. He stood out among the throng of guests and household knights by his sheer size and by the richness of his red velvet tunic. Mellisynt felt a queer thrill at seeing him in a robe she'd fashioned with her own hands, as if it marked him somehow as hers. She lifted her gaze from the standard emblazoned on his chest, over the massive shoulders, to the sharp planes of a face that somehow had come to symbolize to her the essence of male beauty.

Their eyes met and held. The cheerful babble filling the room seemed to fade away, the other figures to blur. In that instant Mellisynt felt something flower deep within her, something achingly beautiful and strangely unfamiliar. Something that made her breath catch and her heart thump painfully. Something that lifted her lips in a small, private smile for her husband alone.

FitzHugh stopped before his wife, his stunned gaze moving from the translucent veil over her gleaming russet hair, down the glowing planes of her face, to the soft curves of her breasts, rising and falling delightfully in their casing of violet silk. He thought of all the images he'd carried of her in his mind—of a pale, still bride, a thin, uncertain bedmate, a mud-covered virago rescuing an animal any half-wit would have left to his fate. And he thought, as well, of the golden body stretched beneath his just hours ago on a rock-strewn, sandy shore. None of those vivid images did justice to this vibrant, glowing woman.

A fierce possessiveness, deeper than any he'd ever known, gripped him. He wanted to claim her, to mark her as his own. He fought to subdue this primitive urge, disturbed by its intensity. Jesu, he already owned the woman, and had proclaimed his possession most blatantly this afternoon. Shaking off the strange feeling, he bent over her hand.

"God give you greeting, lady wife."

"And you, my lord. I bid you welcome to your home."

She dipped her head in an elegant little bow, for all the world as if she'd not welcomed him, most energetically, just hours earlier.

FitzHugh restrained his smile, recognizing her need to regain her dignity. He reached into the leather pouch at his waist and drew out a tangled skein of pearls.

"I meant to give you these earlier, but was . . . somewhat distracted. Now I'm ashamed even to offer them, so pale and lifeless are they beside your lustrous shine."

Mellisynt gasped as he unwound the knotted ropes. He wrapped them once, twice, and then once more, around her neck. Still the heavy rope hung to her waist, gleaming luminescent against the purple of her gown. She ran her fingers over their milky smoothness.

"My lord, 'tis a king's ransom!"

"Well, a count's, at least. I will admit it was a difficult decision. I had to choose between these and another destrier to replace Voyager."

Her eyes flashed up to his in genuine concern. "Did you lose your horse? In battle?"

"Aye," he replied, rubbing a knuckle lightly down her nose. "The loss was most grievous. I sustained it with the knowledge that he no longer topped my list of most valued possessions. You've moved up a notch, lady wife."

"Harrumph!"

Mellisynt's indelicate snort sounded very much like her equine rival's. FitzHugh laughed and took her arm to lead her to Geoffrey.

Seated at the far end of the boards with the other unmarried maidens, Isabeau felt a mounting sense of irritation as Mellisynt greeted the duke, then took her place at the high table. Jaw clenched, she saw the men bow and kiss the lady's hand, and heard their extravagant compliments on her beauty. When FitzHugh's dark head bent intimately toward his wife's, Isabeau threw her silver eating knife to the boards with an angry clatter.

She'd spent all these months shut up in this miserable keep with only dolts and churls to toy with. Now the duke and Sir Richard were here and she was seated with a bunch of straw-headed, giggling girls. To make matters worse, the men seemed fascinated with the lady of the manor and just ignored *her!*

Isabeau forgot Mellisynt's many kindnesses these last months. She forgot her own growing affection for the woman who had befriended her. All she could think of was how the Lady Mellisynt was garnering the adulation that should come to her. She shot the high table another venomous glance, her teeth grating as even the duke managed to wrest a smile from the lady of the manor. Christ's wounds, were all the men in this hall blind? Could they not see that Mellisynt was *old* under her paint and simpering smile? And skinny as a reed, to boot!

"Is not Duke Geoffrey a man among men?" the maiden next to Isabeau asked, her dreamy eyes glued to the far table. "I've never seen hair like that on a man. Thick and silky, and halfway between flame and sunlight."

"He's most handsome," another girl agreed, "but Sir Richard is fearsome strong, and not at all hard to look upon. Would that such a one as he asked to wear my colors in a tourney."

"Bah!" Isabeau muttered, thoroughly put out with these silly girls when men, real men, sat so far away. "You'd be lucky if the swineherd asked to wear your silks."

"Why, I do believe the Lady Isabeau is upset because the duke brings no betrothal agreements for her," the first girl said, tittering. Thoroughly unpopular with the female portion of Edgemoor's occupants, Isabeau was a frequent target for their malice. "Could it be that no man wants you?"

"You know better than that," Isabeau cooed. "Why, your own betrothed assured me just last week that he'd never seen eyes so bright nor skin so fair as mine." Her mocking gaze swept the rash of pimples on the other girl's chin.

The maid's sputtering retort was lost as the door at the far end of the hall opened and a band of men entered. Straggling groups had been arriving all evening, coming to meet with the duke as he traveled through the north. Isabeau's eyes brightened at the interruption. Mayhap this latest group would bring a knight more to her interest, one who would appreciate genuine beauty when he saw it. She scanned the men-at-arms and squires, dismissing them immediately as unworthy men. Her gaze fastened on a pair of wide shoulders covered in a jeweled tunic of sapphire blue. Sitting up straighter, Isabeau wet her lips with a quick sweep of her tongue. She tilted her chin over one shoulder, the better to observe the knight and show the thick sweep of her sooty lashes.

Her carefully seductive smile faltered, then disappeared completely as Sir Roger Beauchamp strode past her without the slightest flicker of recognition or interest. He went forward to kneel before the lady of the keep. Isabeau couldn't hear his low greeting or Mellisynt's delighted reply over the fury ringing in her ears.

Chapter Twelve

"Sir Roger!"

Mellisynt greeted him with unaffected pleasure and reached up to give his cheek a kiss of greeting. She drew back, startled, when he turned his head at the last moment and her lips brushed the silky softness of his moustached mouth.

His warm brown eyes danced over her face.

"Now *that* was worth the long ride through some of the most desolate country this side of the Holy Land! If FitzHugh must hide you away up here, those who aspire to your regard should at least be allowed to claim a kiss after such a ride."

Mellisynt blinked in confusion. In the last months she'd forgotten most of the conventions of the game of love played at court. That Sir Roger would suggest he was a contender in the first phase of chivalrous love, in which knights worship their ladies from afar, surprised her.

"You may aspire all you wish, Beauchamp, but if you kiss my wife again, I'll break your head."

Sir Roger laughed and gripped FitzHugh's outstretched arm. "I see your absence hasn't improved either your disposition or your manners. Don't you know 'tis most unfashionable for a husband to discourage his lady's admirers?"

"Hah, Roger, you know FitzHugh never was in fashion, nor will he ever be!" Geoffrey joined them and threw his arms around Beauchamp.

Mellisynt watched, wide-eyed, as they pummeled each other's backs in that strange greeting ritual men reserved for their boon companions. The three knights stood in a loose circle, part of, yet isolated from, the rest of the room, bonded by experiences only another warrior could understand. She stood back, forgotten for the moment, and studied them.

They were so alike, all tall and well muscled and tanned from their days in the saddle. And yet they were each so very different—Geoffrey boisterous and fiery-haired and quick-tempered, Beauchamp smooth and polished, with warm brown eyes and curls any woman would give her right arm for. And FitzHugh. Ah, there was a man, she thought, so dark of hair and brow, so lean of face, with eyes that made her melt inside when they filled with laughter, or passion.

"From where do you come?" FitzHugh asked, leading them all back to the table. Beauchamp had been with the duke's forces in the early stages of the campaign against Toulouse, but had left when one of his holdings in England had been ravaged by a rival baron.

"From Winchester, by way of Richmond," he responded, attacking a tough ham joint with strong white teeth. "Your wife sends word, my lord duke, that your balls, and mayhap your life, are forfeit if you don't show your face immediately at Richmond."

Geoffrey choked on his wine. "Christ's blood, we landed but two days ago and rode straight here." He wiped the drops from his chin and turned to Beauchamp eagerly. "How is she?"

"Big! Evil-tempered as a bloated sow!" Beauchamp smiled with wicked glee. "Very pregnant, and most unhappy you're not there so she can vent her ire on the one who caused such discomfort. I expect your homecoming will not be quite as loving as you anticipate."

Geoffrey's face fell. "Hell and damnation! Don't you dare laugh, FitzHugh! After your frolic with your water sprite this afternoon, you'll no doubt find yourself in the same predicament nine months hence."

Beauchamp's brows rose as Mellisynt blushed a fiery red. When he opened his mouth as if to comment, she shoved a bowl of sweet plums across the board and all but ordered him to taste them. To her relief, he complied with nothing more than a teasing grin. After a moment, he dug into the pouch at his waist and passed her a small parchment.

"I almost forgot. The duchess charged me to bring you her message, my lady."

Mellisynt's fingers shook with excitement as she broke the seal and spread the square of thin vellum on the table. Taking her lower lip between her teeth, she peered at the script, trying to decipher its whirls and flourishes.

"Shall I read it for you?" FitzHugh asked, his low voice for her ears only.

"Nay," Mellisynt replied. Her finger moved across the inked lines with painstaking slowness. A few more moments passed, and then she looked up, triumph lighting her face.

"Constance sends her greetings. She wishes me to attend her when her time comes. She would have the company of her countrywomen in the birthing of her first babe."

FitzHugh's brows rose, and a glint of respect dawned in his eyes.

"Well done, my lady."

His soft-spoken words suffused Mellisynt with a glow of pride. Dismissing with a mental wave of her hands the many agonizing hours she'd spent with Edgemoor's priest, she basked in her lord's admiration.

"You are a woman of considerable talents, lady wife. What other surprises have you in store for me, I wonder?"

Before she could compose herself to answer, the duke claimed FitzHugh's attention. Mellisynt floated through the rest of the meal and the entertainment that followed on a cloud of joy.

Spurred by the duchess's command, Geoffrey left the next morning for Richmond, taking most of the knights with him. With the duke's disturbing presence gone, Mellisynt blossomed. Ever afterward, she would remember the weeks that followed as among the happiest of her life.

She preened in her new gowns under her husband's appreciative gaze, and shed them eagerly each night when she joined him in their curtained bed. Shyly she acknowledged the small improvements she'd made to the keep—the tapestries she'd acquired to brighten the walls, the rugs scattered in place of rushes, the dried herbs hung from the rafters to freshen the air.

But her moment of glory came one drizzly morning when she sat with her lord and his uncle, going over the tallies for the year. Confidently she accounted for the portions of grain set aside for malting, for seed corn and for bread-making. She knew precisely the number of bags of flour processed through their mill, the quantity of hides cured, the tuns of ale brewed. And with each accounting, FitzHugh's approving smile warmed her soul.

While Mellisynt glowed, however, Isabeau glowered. The girl waylaid FitzHugh on more than one occasion, desperate for male attention. Although he smiled and teased and flattered her, he seemed preoccupied. Unused to such treatment, she redoubled her efforts. One fine afternoon, Isabeau sought him out in the stable yards and begged him prettily to accompany her on a walk to gather violets for perfume-making.

"Nay, not this day. I promised to take the Lady Mellisynt sailing. She has found an old coracle, and will likely drown herself if I do not show her how it works."

He gave her a gallant bow and strode away.

Isabeau clenched her fists in fury, her eyes on his broad back.

"You'll make no hay with that one," a lazy voice drawled. "He's too besotted with his wife."

She whirled to find Beauchamp leaning against the stable wall, the familiar mocking grin she'd come to hate lifting his lips. Why did this man ever taunt her, and make her feel the clumsy maid?

"That must discommode you." She sniffed, lifting her nose. "Your attentions to the Lady Mellisynt must wait until FitzHugh's attentions wane. She doesn't have the skill to manage more than one lover at a time."

Beauchamp levered himself off the wall and came forward. "Don't impugn the lady with your own impure thoughts."

"Impure!" Isabeau gasped. "You dare say that to me, when you all but drool over her hand!"

"'Tis but a game, child, as well you know."

Isabeau ground her teeth. Goaded, she closed the small space between them and planted herself before him, hands on hips, bosom heaving.

"I...am...not...a...child!"

Beauchamp's laughing eyes slid from her face down to her chest. "Mayhap not," he conceded. "But not yet a woman, either."

"I'm more woman than you know what to do with!" she screeched.

"Ah, Isabeau—" he grinned, sweeping her into his arms "—such silly challenges only prove what a babe you are."

Her foot drew back to kick him soundly on the shins. Beauchamp laughed again and bent her backward, off balance, over his arm. Her foot flailed only air. Burying a fist in her hair, he brought her face up to his and stilled her indignant shrieks with a long, hard kiss.

When he released her her breaths came in gasping pants—whether from fury or sheer surprise, she knew not. She stared up at him, struggling for breath and for the words to wither him on the spot. Before either came, he turned her about and gave her a sound slap on the rear that sent her stumbling toward the keep.

''Go play with the other maids, girl. You're too trouble-
some to be let loose in the yard.''

Red-faced and seething, Isabeau ran from him.

Still piqued, she joined a group of riders in the outer
bailey the next day for a hunt. FitzHugh had arranged it the
night before, as much for his guests' entertainment as to
provide meat for their table.

''Don't you wish to accompany us?'' he asked Mellisynt
when she came to see the chattering group of men and
women off. ''Did you not also add riding to your list of
achievements while I was gone?''

''Nay, I chose to learn the sea and swimming. 'Tis much
easier on the bones. And so much more ... pleasurable.''

FitzHugh grinned and stroked the slant of her nose with
one curled knuckle. ''I see I must show you all the pleasures one can experience in the saddle.''

''Stop diddling with your wife, FitzHugh, and let's be
gone.''

Beauchamp's amused summons rang across the mass of
impatient hunters, restless horses and excited, yipping dogs.
FitzHugh responded with a good-natured insult, kissed
Mellisynt on the nose and moved to the mounting block.

As the throng shifted, preparing to depart, Isabeau's
restive horse skittered sideways, bumping into Beauchamp's. His stallion reacted with a fearsome show of yellow teeth and a quick lunge. Cursing, Beauchamp sawed
back on the bit and stilled the beast. Reaching down, he
took Isabeau's reins in a strong hand.

''If you can't control your mount, you have no business
in the hunt.''

She glared across her horse's neck. ''I'm well able to
manage my horse. Loose my reins, sir!''

A mocking light leapt into his eyes. He let his gaze drop
slowly from her haughty face, down the long column of her
throat, to the ripe bosom displayed to perfection by a fig-
ure-molding red silk bliaut.

"Nay," he drawled. "I think mayhap a tight hand on the reins is exactly what you need, girl."

Isabeau's eyes blazed. She shot him a poisonous look and jerked the leather strap free.

How she loathed that man! He seemed to miss no chance to mock her. Even that one kiss, which had kept her awake long into the night, had lacked the reverent admiration she was used to. She didn't understand why Beauchamp should be so resistant to her charms. There wasn't a man in the keep she couldn't twist around her finger if she truly wished to. Nor was there a man she couldn't conquer if she chose to. Her eyes fell on FitzHugh's broad back, just ahead. Desperate for attention and admiration, she urged her horse forward, alongside his.

By the time the riders reached the glade where they would picnic while the huntsmen and their hounds tracked and dislodged the deer, Isabeau had regained a semblance of her composure. FitzHugh's lighthearted gallantry during the ride had restored her self-confidence. When he spread his cloak on the forest floor for her to share, she settled herself beside him with a fluid, languid grace.

"Do you think the limners will raise a stag?" she asked, accepting a horn cup of wine. She really cared little if the silent, sharp-nosed stalking dogs chased down deer or goat. She just wanted to keep this man's attention and exclusive company for a while longer yet.

"They should," FitzHugh answered with a shrug of his massive shoulders. "My uncle says the mild winter didn't thin the herds as usual. With luck, we'll have a good chase and kill. If you come to the Quarry, I'll present you with the heartbone."

"Oh, I'll most assuredly be there for the kill," Isabeau told him, nodding. Not for a bagful of silver pennies would she have missed the ritualistic quarry ceremony, in which the animal was cut and quartered in a rigidly prescribed order. The lord of the hunt would receive the right forefoot with great ceremony and trumpeting of hunting horns, but the much-prized heart cartilage would go to the fairest lady present.

"I intend to follow the chase," she told FitzHugh. "I rode out often at home, with my father. Many women can't take the rough ride, claiming it bruises their bones. I can't understand such weakness, can you?"

A soft glint came into his silvery eyes, as if some private thought pleasured him. Isabeau preened under the look, expecting praise for her daring.

He smiled down at her and chucked her lightly under the chin with one huge fist. "Don't mistake a lack of skill for weakness, little one."

Isabeau returned his smile with one of her own, reveling in his attention. A movement over his shoulder caught her gaze, and she glanced across the glade to see Beauchamp watching them with narrowed eyes. Deliberately she deepened the curve of her lips into a sultry invitation and lowered her chin until it rested in FitzHugh's hand, as if in a warm caress.

At that moment, the head huntsman rode into the clearing. FitzHugh jumped up and strode over to take the man's report, leaving Isabeau curled on his cloak like a sleek purebred feline. She wet her lips and kept her back to Beauchamp.

The riders left the glade a few minutes later, following the trail of pointed branches the huntsmen had left to mark the way. A second pack of hounds was brought forward and divided into small groups, to be posted in relays along the trail in case the quarry doubled back and outran the hounds chasing him. Within moments, they arrived at the spot where the hart, reportedly full-grown, with a massive rack of antlers, had last been seen. The huntsmen unleashed the dogs, and the riders surged forward.

As her horse thundered alongside the men's, Isabeau grew too excited to mind her graceful carriage. She didn't notice the wind tugging her carefully arranged veil loose from its moorings or the branches tearing at her silk skirts. Leaning forward in the saddle, she felt the thrill of the chase rush through her veins. Shouts of *Cy va! Cy va!* rose all around her as the handlers called to the hounds, and the pure, golden notes of a horn cut across the air to signal the course of their pursuit.

Her breath scraped in her throat and her heart hammered painfully by the time the hounds cornered the stag, forcing it to turn and stand its ground. A single long note on the horn sounded the blowing of the death, and the hunters moved in to make the kill.

When FitzHugh presented her the heartbone some moments later, Isabeau forgot that the primary purpose of the hunt was to feed the keep's residents. She disregarded the fact that warriors and would-be warriors used the exercise to keep their horsemanship skills honed and their vigorous energies channeled. In that moment, she felt as though FitzHugh had arranged this whole expedition for the sole purpose of honoring her. When he bowed and handed her the glistening sliver of bone, Isabeau accepted it with her most stunning, provocative smile.

The hunters returned to Edgemoor just as the sun began to sink below the far horizon. The hart and several hinds filled the carts. Dirty, disheveled, and high-spirited with their success, the noisy party clattered through the gates.

Mellisynt met them in the bailey, duly praising their skill and directing the servants to remove the take to the kitchen sheds for processing. After a day of vigorous exercise and only a light meal in the open to sustain them, she knew they'd be ravenous. She smiled when the group spilled into the hall, chattering and laughing and describing the chase with swooping gestures. Even Isabeau sparkled with more color and animation than she'd shown in a long time.

Mellisynt sighed in relief. Of late the girl's restlessness and irritability had grated on everyone's nerves. In desperation, she'd consulted Dame Hertha, who had pinpointed the source of Isabeau's dissatisfaction with unerring accuracy. She was ripe for bedding, Hertha had snapped. More than ripe. The girl burned with her need.

The two older women had both prayed Geoffrey would
bring word that Isabeau's hand was settled. Mayhap when
the duke reached Richmond he would remind the duchess
to attend to the matter. Mellisynt shrugged and turned her
mind to more important concerns. Her eyes swept the table once more to ensure that there were adequate cold meats
and bread for the hungry crowd. Seeing empty platters, she
frowned and signaled to the senior page.

"Send the boys to bring more platters."

Her brow furrowed as she looked about the room once
more. "Why do so few pages serve? Where is Robert, and
Bartholomew?"

A look of disgust crossed the older boy's face. "They fell
into a sulk because they could not accompany the hunt this
morn. Out of mischief, they sneaked away and climbed the
apple trees in the orchard. Now they are both in the stables, puking and crying from bellies swollen with green
fruit."

Mellisynt worried a corner of her lower lip with her teeth.
She glanced over to where Beauchamp and her lord sat side
by side, deep in animated conversation. They had full
platters before them, at least. Moving to where Hertha sat
in comfortable companionship with the other ladies, she
begged the older woman to take charge of the table for a
few moments.

The warm, musky odor of horses filled her nostrils when
she slipped into the stables. She had no difficulty locating
the two miscreants. Their moans drew her to the far stall,
where an impatient squire and a slatternly house servant
attended the boys. The huge, shaggy hound sat on his
haunches in the straw beside Bartholomew's head, adding
a low, mournful whine to every groan the boys issued.

"How do they fare?" Mellisynt asked, kneeling to place
the back of her hand against first Robert's, then Bartholomew's, face.

"Poorly," the squire replied. "They heaved so much they
soiled the floor of the keep, so we brought them out here to
the straw."

"Ooooh, my lady, it hurts!"

Bartholomew's cry tore at Mellisynt's heart. When he curled into a tight ball and wrapped his arms around his middle, a pain spread through her, as well.

"I know it does," she murmured. "Rest a moment, and I'll go mix a purge to relieve your distress."

"No, don't leave me!" The boy clutched at her hand, tears streaming down his cheek. The dog echoed his pathetic cry with a long, wavering whimper.

"I'll return immediately," she promised, wiping the sweat-drenched curls back from his brow. "I just go to get my herbs."

Bartholomew's tearstained brown eyes filled her vision as she hurried across the bailey and reentered the keep. Distracted, she headed down the hall toward her chamber and the chest of precious herbs kept there.

"What's amiss?"

FitzHugh caught her hand when she would have brushed past him and Isabeau, who stood beside him. His dark brows drew together as he studied her face.

"'Tis naught but a couple of naughty pages who sampled the apples before they ripened," she assured him.

"Bartholomew," he stated with wry certainty.

Mellisynt bit back a smile and nodded. "And another."

Isabeau sniffed. "'Twas Bartholomew who led them both into mischief, I'll warrant. That imp of Satan is ever a pest."

Mellisynt interrupted before Isabeau could warm to her continuing list of grievances against the mischievous page. Their months together had not brought them closer.

"I must brew a concoction to ease their pains. I promised the boy I would return to the stables with it immediately."

"Why not bring them into the keep and tend them here?" FitzHugh asked.

"They've been most violently ill, and are more comfortable in the straw. Besides," she added innocently, "the

hound will not leave Bartholomew's side and is most...
vocal in his concern for the boy."

FitzHugh groaned. "By all means, keep them in the stables."

"I will. They have a long, unpleasant night ahead. I must
change and see to their needs."

"It'll be lonely without you in our bed," FitzHugh murmured, obviously forgetting the presence of the girl beside
him.

Mellisynt felt a blush rising and sent him a warning
glance. Then, muttering something incoherent, she hurried away.

After their long day, the hunters soon dispersed to their
pallets. Tallow torches sputtered low in their holders as the
keep prepared for the night. FitzHugh and Beauchamp,
more used to long, hard hours on the march, settled themselves in comfortably padded chairs beside the fire, a jug of
wine close at hand. Servants moved in the shadows behind
them, unrolling pallets, pushing dogs aside with knees and
elbows. FitzHugh listened to the sounds with half an ear,
his disgruntled thoughts on the stables. He stretched his
long legs out toward the fire, wondering at his discomfort.
Could he not pass one night without his wife's warm body
curled beside him? His mind wandered as he listened to
Beauchamp's low-voiced tales of the king's court.

"I think Henry's patience with Geoffrey runs thin at
last," Beauchamp said quietly, catching FitzHugh's full
attention.

"Why?" FitzHugh asked, pouring himself more wine.

"He suspects Geoffrey is about to throw in with the
French king."

FitzHugh heard a rustle behind him and waited for the
stirring to die before he replied, his voice low.

"What cause has the king to think his son would betray
him?"

"He has spies at the French court. He knows that Philip
corresponds regularly with Geoffrey and teases him with

promises of independence if he will but throw off his father's yoke.''

"King Henry has promised the duke full rule in Brittany."

Beauchamp shrugged. "And if Henry doesn't keep his fingers out of the duchy? If he interferes again, as he did when he threatened not to ratify the reforms of the grand assize?''

FitzHugh stared down into the ruby depths of his wine. "That was Geoffrey's grandest moment," he mused, remembering those hot, sweltering days at Rennes. "The stubborn Breton lords fought him every step of the way, but he forced them to accept the same code Henry himself imposed on England."

"Yet the king was most displeased. He almost stepped in and disbanded the parliament outright." Beauchamp shook his head. "I tell you, FitzHugh, 'tis dangerous the way Henry plays his sons. Even now he won't give Richard Lionheart the Lady Alice, after nigh on two decades of betrothal. The king makes no secret that he enjoys plowing between the lady's soft white thighs. He won't give her up."

FitzHugh grunted at the sudden image that flashed into his mind, one of another lady's slender white thighs. He muttered a low curse at all rascally pages.

When Beauchamp's brows rose in query, he shook his head with wry self-mockery.

"Let's talk of something other than plowing and planting. I've yet to sow all the seed I stored up while in France, and with my lady in the stables this night, I'm not like to."

"What! Do you try to cozen me into believing you plant only in one field these days? You? The same man who knocked me senseless to take the woman we both lusted after at Limoges? And that after you had her sister!"

"'Twas not me who knocked you out, you sot. 'Twas the two skins of wine you downed.''

FitzHugh rose and stretched.

"And who supplied the wine? Here, I'll return the favor." Beauchamp pushed a leather-covered jug into

FitzHugh's hands. "Take it with you to the stables. Even sick pages must sleep sometime."

A wide grin split FitzHugh's face. "Aye, so they must. I'll take the wine, and you may take my bed. 'Tis softer by far than the pallet spread for you."

Beauchamp watched while his friend made his way down the darkened hall, stepping over sleeping bodies en route. A smile tugged at his lips. FitzHugh was more smitten with his lady than Beauchamp had realized. Than the man himself seemed to realize. And, as unlikely as it seemed, the lady appeared as taken with his rough-faced, oft-distempered, overlarge friend. Stifling a twinge of envy, Beauchamp rose. He might as well enjoy the comfort of the lord's bed this night, since no one else appeared likely to occupy it.

Not wanting to disturb the sleeping servants, Beauchamp made his way to the far chamber in darkness. He groped for the door latch and let himself quietly into the shadowed room, lit only by the glow of a banked fire. As he turned toward the huge, curtained bed, his shin whacked solidly against the edge of a wooden chest.

"Aagh!"

At his startled exclamation, a dim figure beyond the fireplace jumped up, knocking over a stool in the process. Before Beauchamp could discern much more than its outline, the figure darted toward the door.

His fighting instincts honed by years of battle, Beauchamp reacted without thinking. One hand flew to the dagger sheathed at his belt, and he threw himself across the room. He wrapped a thick forearm around the intruder's throat and pressed the blade to his side.

"Who are you and what do you here, in the lord's room?"

A muffled squawk sounded against his arm.

"Speak," he ordered harshly, forcing the dagger through layers of cloth.

"I—I cannot!"

Fingers clawed his arm, and he loosened it a fraction.

"Do not hurt me!" Sobbing gasps tore from the throat under his bunched muscles.

"Holy Christ!"

Beauchamp sheathed the dagger in a swift, sure movement and spun his terrified prisoner about. Taking her in a brutal grip, he hauled her into the light of the fireplace.

"What do you here, girl?"

Isabeau tried to shake off his hand, still sobbing for breath. He took her other arm and pulled her up on her toes.

"Were you waiting for Sir Richard, you little whore?" A raging fury seized him. "Did you think to follow up on the invitation issued in the glade?"

"N-no!"

"Don't lie to me!" He punctuated each word with a hard shake. "You thought to take advantage of Mellisynt's preoccupation to satisfy the itch between your legs."

Isabeau's mouth fell open. "How dare you speak so to me!" she gasped, between gulping sobs. "No true knight would ever utter such—such crudities to a lady."

"No lady would await a man in the dark, ready to spread herself for him, while his wife labored just a few feet away."

"I didn't! I'm not! I—I—" Isabeau burst into fresh tears.

Beauchamp's fury slowly subsided as he watched huge, crystalline drops pour down her white face and splash against the red silk bliaut. The fact that she was wearing a gown at all sank into his consciousness. Belatedly he realized that if she'd really planned to whore herself, she would have shed her many layers before this. His hands gentled on her arms.

As fresh tears spilled down her cheeks, Beauchamp gave a disgusted grunt and pulled the girl to his chest. Wrapping his arms about her shuddering, sobbing frame, he held her while she cried out her fright.

He felt like the biggest dolt in Christendom. Not only had he come near to skewering a helpless girl, but he'd been all but swamped by a raging tide of jealousy when he'd

thought of her in FitzHugh's arms. He stroked her unbound hair with a soothing hand, discovering anew the feel
of generous breasts against his chest and the musky scent
that was Isabeau's alone.

When her sobs finally subsided, he tipped her chin. His
gut clenched at the shimmering wash of aquamarine, surrounded by wet, spiky lashes, that met his gaze. Resisting
the urge to sweep her into his arms once more, he ad-
dressed her sternly.

"What do you here, Isabeau?"

After several hiccuping attempts, she found her voice.
"I...I just wanted to talk. Sir Rich—Sir Richard gave me
the stag's heartbone, and made me feel beauteous
and...and desirous...and much a woman. I wanted to feel
like that again."

Slow tears rolled down her cheeks.

With a crooked smile, Beauchamp caught a silvered drop
on one finger. The bead of moisture shimmered on his skin,
as lovely and luminescent as the woman who produced it.
After a long moment, he flicked the drop aside and stepped
back. With unhurried movements, he began to remove his
clothes.

Isabeau's eyes widened. "What—what are you doing?"

"'Tis obvious, girl. I'm undressing. When I finish, I'll
undress you, as well."

Isabeau stumbled backward. "You're mad," she whispered.

"Nay." He smiled, shucking his braies, then pulling his
linen shirt off with a swift tug. "Just willing to make you
into the woman you're so eager to become."

As he stalked her, step by step, Isabeau's wide eyes raked
his naked body. Her blood began to drum in her veins. She
gave a quick look over his shoulder, searching for the door
in the dim shadows. Before she could run, Beauchamp
reached out and tumbled her into his arms. Her palms
flattened against the smooth velvet of his skin, and fiery
sensations shot from her fingertips straight to her belly. She
opened her mouth, not knowing whether she meant to

scream or to suck air into her suddenly breathless body. She did neither, for Beauchamp's lips covered hers in a hard, demanding kiss.

With skilled mastery, he bent her back. She clung to the roped muscles of his arms to keep from falling to the floor. All the while, his mouth plundered hers and filled her with a heat so intense she thought she would melt. Hardly realizing her own intent, she'd lifted her arms to lock them behind his neck and hold his mouth on hers.

After long, shattering moments, Beauchamp raised his head and struggled for breath.

"Jesu, girl, if you kiss me like that again, you'll find yourself stretched out right here, on the floor."

Isabeau lifted a long, slim finger and traced the line of his lips. "I'm not a girl," she whispered, and pulled his head down once more.

Chapter Thirteen

FitzHugh leaned against the wooden half wall enclosing the stall and watched his wife wipe Bartholomew's face with a soft, damp cloth. Tucking a stray strand of hair behind one ear, she murmured low nothings to the fretful boy as she worked. The other page, Robert, slept soundly in the next stall. The hound rested its massive head on two outthrust forepaws, anxious eyes sweeping from mistress to child and back again. Every few moments, a low, unhappy whine whistled through its lips.

The night lay heavy around them. Far down the stable, horses shuffled in their stalls, blowing softly through their nostrils, as if welcoming the companionship during the long, still hours. Except for the horses and boys—and dog—they were alone in the long building. FitzHugh had sent the other attendants away when he first arrived, thinking to follow through on Beauchamp's suggestion. That notion had been put to rest immediately. 'Twas apparent Mellisynt would have none of him while the child fretted.

FitzHugh watched her gentle hands stroke the boy's face and thought of her desire for a babe. Seeing her with Bartholomew, he understood her need. She'd make a most tender mother. The urge to plant his seed in Mellisynt's womb surged over him, hot and fierce. In that moment he wanted with all his being to see her swell with child, to watch a babe nursing at her breast. He shifted uncomfortably at the sudden ache in his loins.

"He seems to know your hand," FitzHugh commented, as much to distract himself as to share the night with her.

"Aye, I think he does. He's a good lad."

FitzHugh's snort caused the boy to start and the dog to lift its head in warning.

"Shh!" Mellisynt commanded. "He sleeps but lightly."

"Aye. Unfortunately."

Her brows rose at the dry comment, but FitzHugh just shrugged and came around the wall.

"Never mind. What can I do to help?"

As he hunkered down on his heels, his bulk crowded the small stall. The hound lifted one side of its lip in a low growl at the intrusion. FitzHugh growled back, deep in his throat.

"That beast and I will settle affairs one of these days."

"Hush," Mellisynt whispered. "Don't provoke him."

"Me? Provoke him?"

A mischievous grin tilted the corners of her mouth. "You did attack his mistress but short days ago. Now you must hover over his friend like a huge, irritated bear. Get you gone before he feels the need to defend us once again."

"Nay, I would stay and keep you company."

She sat back on her knees, smiling warmly. "I thank you, my lord, most truly. But there's no need for you to stay awake this night, especially after a day's hunt. You need your sleep."

"And what if I have other, more important needs?"

Her glance slid down to his tumescent manhood, clearly outlined against the fabric of his braies. Heaving an exaggerated sigh of regret, she shook her head.

"You must contain your needs, my lord, or find release elsewhere."

"What?"

Mellisynt blinked, confused at his startled exclamation. She swallowed and began again. "I know men can be most irritable when they swell with want and don't achieve release. Henri was wont to use his fist during those times I had my monthly courses.''

''He used his fists? On you?'' FitzHugh hoped the old degenerate was roasting in hell.

''Nay. On himself. Though it rarely brought relief, since he couldn't get his rod to stiffen for any length of— Why do you laugh? Hush, you'll waken the boy!''

FitzHugh stifled the mirth rumbling in his chest and bent to kiss his wife's pert nose. ''I'll find some way to ease my discomfort,'' he promised.

He left her then, sending the sleepy squire and stable-hands back inside to aid her with the boys. Standing alone in the yard for a few moments, he drank in the richness of the night. Sweet Jesu, it was good to be home again. The air carried a tang of the sea, even above the familiar odors of penned animals and piled manure. Stars shimmered over-head against the black-velvet sky and formed a lustrous canopy above his head. Despite the late hour, FitzHugh felt alive with the night and with the need to couple.

He wondered briefly why he felt no urge to go back to the hall and rouse the kitchen maid who'd serviced him most willingly in recent years. Since his return, the girl had in-dicated her eagerness to resume their activities. But the thought of burying his face in her warm, generous breasts and breathing in her earthy scent of garlic and sweat didn't draw him as it once would have. Instead, he found himself thinking of a long, slender body with trim hips and pink-tipped breasts that just fit his palms. The ache in his groin thrummed with a steady, pulsing need.

FitzHugh strode across the inner yard, trying to relieve his discomfort with vigorous exercise. Christ's bones, when had his wife become such an obsession that just the image of her naked form would harden him so? He kicked an overturned bucket left by a careless servant out of his path and winced when the clatter broke the night's stillness. Hastily reassuring the guard who called down a challenge at the noise, he smiled to himself in wry derision.

What was it about Mellisynt that drew him so? She wasn't beautiful, as Isabeau was. Her skin had warmed to a golden glow, but her nose was still too short and her chin too determined for the aristocratic standards of the age. And her body, much as he'd come to crave it, lacked the curves and lush earthiness of others who'd shared his bed in the past. Mayhap it was her eyes that drew him, those thick-fringed pools of green that sparkled with laughter and deepened to dusky velvet with passion. Or her smile, hesitant and restrained when first they'd wedded, now more likely to lift at the corners in an impudent grin. Or mayhap her tenderness with boy and beast, displaying so clearly her loving heart.

FitzHugh's long stride faltered. He slowed to a halt a few paces from the stairs leading to the ramparts. Thinking of Mellisynt's tenderness caused a strange ache to rise in a part of his body he'd not hitherto connected with the act of coupling, and certainly never with his previous wife. A queer tightness lodged in his chest, a half-formed longing to have her lay her hands softly on his face and whisper sweet, husky words of...

The solid tread of a guard's footsteps sounded overhead. FitzHugh shook his head, embarrassed to be mooning about in the dark like a lovesick squire, and glad that none had seen him. With a low call to alert the man above to his presence, he climbed the stairs to the wooden ramparts. He made a leisurely circuit of the upper walk, stopping to talk with the guards posted at intervals along the wall.

When he pushed open the gatehouse door, several men scrambled to their feet in surprise, sending stools clattering to the floor. A fire burned in the stone hearth in the center of the floor, illuminating the room with a cheerful glow. Swords, bowls of sand and old rags lay scattered about the floor, indicating that the men were engaged in the age-old pastime of soldiers—polishing their weapons. Shaking off the last of his strange preoccupation with the woman who was his wife, FitzHugh took refuge in the familiar. He settled himself on a stool and accepted an ale horn from one of his men. Leaning forward, elbows on knees, he prepared to pass what was left of the night in the comfortable companionship of other men of war.

Fingers of fog drifted through the bailey when Mellisynt left the stable early the next morning. She paused in the yard, putting both hands to the small of her spine and arcing back to ease the strain. Bartholomew had finally slipped into a sound sleep, after passing the last of the ill-gotten fruit in a series of discharges that mortified him as much as they left him weak and teary-eyed. After cleaning the boy and singing low, silly songs to lull him to rest, Mellisynt had given him back into the care of the squire. She smiled, thinking that after this night Dame Hertha's fruit trees would be safe for the foreseeable future, at least. She lifted her face to the mist, letting it wash into her pores and ease her weariness.

Gradually, awareness of the yard's busy occupants penetrated her tired senses, making her conscious of her stained gown and disheveled hair. More than one maid scurrying to and from the kitchen sheds cast her a curious glance, or a timid smile. Two men carrying thatch to repair the roof of the mews bobbed their heads respectfully, their eyes wide.

Mellisynt returned their greeting and smoothed her hands down the front of her robe. Sweet Mother, she couldn't go into the great hall in such a state, with all the guests most likely still taking ale and bread to break their fast. She hurried around to the back of the main building and climbed narrow stairs to the upper floor. She would cleanse herself in the bower room the maidens shared and send one of them to fetch a fresh robe.

"Well, she all but threw herself at Sir Richard on the hunt. 'Tis little wonder he'd avail himself of the slut."

The malicious, spiteful words drifted out just as Mellisynt reached for the latch to the half-opened door of the bower.

"But to go to his room! Such brazenness! I didn't believe it when a servant told me she'd seen Isabeau slip inside the lord's chamber. With the Lady Mellisynt at the stable, only a few yards away!"

Mellisynt's hand froze on the metal latch. She identified the Lady Katherine, St. Bressé's plain, unhappy wife, as one of the women inside the room. Even as a corner of her mind registered that fact, a slow, insidious hurt began to curl in her belly.

"What did the bitch say when she returned to the bower at dawn? Did you challenge her?"

"Nay, I dare not. She has sharp claws. But I watched her wash the blood from her legs and shift. I would never have believed Isabeau a virgin, but if she was before, she is no longer. Not after a night in the lord's bed." Vicious satisfaction laced the speaker's voice.

"The little whore! Where is she now? Does she dare show her face below?"

"I think she went to the sewing room. I wouldn't have the nerve to face Lady Mellisynt this morn, either, were I her."

The pain in Mellisynt's stomach spread, gathering intensity as it lanced through her chest. She stepped back from the door and leaned against the wall, both arms wrapped tight around her body. No, her mind cried, no! Surely he would not! Not with Isabeau, not here, in what she'd come to consider her own home!

Pushing herself off the wall, she whirled and ran down the dim hallway. She flung open the sewing room door. Three faces turned toward her in wide-eyed surprise.

"I would speak with the Lady Isabeau," Mellisynt told the other two women in a low, furious voice. "Leave us."

The blood drained from Isabeau's face as she scrambled up from her weaving stool. She gripped both hands together and stood, tense and fearful, while the other women left hurriedly.

Mellisynt slammed the door closed behind them. She struggled to contain the rage that coursed through her at the

frightened guilt on Isabeau's face. Fury and pain closed her
throat, and her first attempts to speak came out as inartic-
ulate gasps. Fists clenched, she moved across the room until only two feet separated her from the white-faced girl.

"So, 'tis true," she managed to croak through stiff lips.
"I can see it in your face. You lay with him!"

Isabeau lifted a wobbly chin, as if she would try to bra-
zen her way out of the charge.

"Do not lie to me!" Mellisynt snarled. "Do not dare!"

The girl's false bravado died aborning. Tears filled her
eyes, and she backed away.

"I . . . I did not mean to . . . I don't know how it . . ." She
broke down, sobbing. "I never thought he would make me
feel so . . . so wanton."

Every gasping word sent another spear of anguish
through Mellisynt's heart.

"You whey-faced slut!" Her hand arced out and cracked
against the girl's cheek.

Isabeau's cry of pain and wrenching sobs followed her as
she turned and stumbled toward the door. Outside, she
leaned a shaking hand against the wall and bent over, agony
tearing at her gut. Holy Mary, Mother of God, help me,
Mellisynt prayed. Help her what? her frantic mind raged.
Help her accept that the man she'd come to love couldn't
pass one night without plunging his accursed shaft into any
available female? That he'd tumble a virgin in their own
bed, with his wife but a few feet away?

"My lady, are you all right?"

Mellisynt straightened and tried to focus on the worried
face floating before her.

"My lady!"

After a few seconds, the face resolved itself into one of
the upper maids.

"I'm . . . I'm fine," she managed shakily. "I'm but
overtired this morn."

"Aye, we heard you spent the night in the stables with the
boys," the maid offered with a shy smile. "'Twas most kind
of you."

It wasn't kind, Mellisynt wanted to scream, it was most stupid. She'd chosen to care for the boy instead of satisfying her husband's needs, and now faced the result. She dragged in a deep, unsteady breath.

"Would you take word to Dame Hertha to see to our guests this day? I am indeed most tired and would be alone to rest."

Mellisynt waited until the girl nodded and left, then retraced her steps down the back stair to the outer yard. Gathering her soiled skirts, she slipped out of the postern gate and raced into the mist. The beach. She'd go to her private beach. There, among the rocks and gray fog, she'd try to put her shattered soul back together.

"I would speak with you, Richard."

FitzHugh glanced up from the sleek, brown-feathered falcon he held on one gauntlet. A piece of raw meat dangled from his other hand. He gave Beauchamp a welcome grin, glad of the company.

He'd spent the drizzly, fog-swept morning in the mews with his hunting birds, although he would much rather have spent it in his bed with his wife. Hertha had stopped him when he returned from his long vigil with the gate guards, however, and informed him that Mellisynt was overtired from her labors in the stables and would rest. Amused by his aunt's stern, forbidding frown, he'd retreated in good order. But even his prized birds had failed to banish thoughts of his wife, whose feathers he'd much rather be stroking. Glad of Beauchamp's distracting company, he fed the falcon the bit of meat, then passed it to the keeper.

"Speak away, Beauchamp," he said, moving toward the door where his friend waited. Ducking under the low lintel, he stepped into a fine, gray rain.

"Well, Roger?" he asked, when the man beside him hesitated, as if at a loss for words. "What matter brings you out into the rain? Do you seek me out to complain about my bed? Wasn't it soft enough for your brittle bones last night?"

To his surprise, a slow flush crept up the thick column of Beauchamp's neck.

"Aye," the other man muttered. "I found it most soft and accommodating."

FitzHugh's eyes narrowed, then slowly widened. A wicked grin lifted one corner of his mouth.

"Oho! You rogue, did you entice one of the maids to join you between the sheets? Do you fear my lady's anger when she hears you diddled one of the servants in her own bed? And hear she will, you know. There are no secrets in a keep."

"I know." Beauchamp squared his shoulders and looked FitzHugh in the eye. "I did have company last eve. I will tell you that it was most…pleasant. And that I plan to take the girl to wife."

"What? Did the wench suck out your brains, as well as your sap?"

"Cease your crudities, man."

"You pork a serving wench and accuse me of crudities?" FitzHugh gibed.

"'Twas no serving wench," Beauchamp ground out. "'Twas the girl, Isabeau."

The mocking grin on FitzHugh's lips slipped, then disappeared altogether. He stared at the man opposite, anger and disbelief rising in his veins.

"You tell me you despoiled a virgin given to me for keeping?"

"Aye."

"In my own bed?"

"Aye."

FitzHugh's hands curled into fists. "You lecherous whoring knave."

"Save your insults, Richard. You can't call me anything I haven't already named myself. I leave immediately for Richmond to petition Geoffrey for her hand."

"You leave immediately for hell," FitzHugh roared, then slammed his fist into Beauchamp's belly. Sir Roger doubled over. Another fist smashed into his chin with bone-crunching savagery.

Beauchamp's head flew up. He staggered backward, blood streaming from his nose. FitzHugh lunged forward, throwing all the force of his body into a vicious punch that landed just below Beauchamp's breastbone. The wind rushed out of the man's lungs with a whoosh, and he went down.

"Get up, you craven cur."

FitzHugh reached down and grabbed the other's tunic, hauling him to his feet. His arm swung back, then forward. Beauchamp raised a forearm, deflecting the blow. Before FitzHugh could swing once more, he wrested himself loose and staggered back.

"Hold!" he snarled. "Do not raise your hand to me again, or I'll break it off!"

"Not before I take your head from your stinking body!" FitzHugh launched himself forward, propelled by his unleashed fury. The two men crashed to the earth, arms locked around each other, rolling over and over on the hard-packed dirt. Clenched knuckles beat against face and arms, as first FitzHugh and then Beauchamp gained brief mastery.

People poured from mews and stables and granaries and gardens, their shouts filling the air.

"Jesu, what goes on here?"

Alymer, FitzHugh's uncle, pushed his way through the surging crowd surrounding the combatants, St. Bressé at his heels. The squire, Ian, came running from the armory. They jumped back as the two twisting, pummeling fighters rolled toward them.

"Christ, 'tis Sir Richard! And Sir Roger!"

An agonized grunt rose above the noise as Beauchamp's knee connected with FitzHugh's groin. Taking advantage of his adversary's momentary stunned pain, Beauchamp wrenched himself free and rolled aside. Panting, his eyes murderous, he pushed himself to his feet. FitzHugh dragged himself to his knees and started to rise.

Beauchamp swung his foot back, blood surging through his veins, his every fighting instinct screaming at him to disable his attacker, to smash his ribs and follow up with a boot to the face. His leg muscles bunched, his foot surged forward. At the last second, he twisted, and his boot sliced through the air beside FitzHugh's head. Taking advantage of the movement, his adversary leapt forward, thrusting his shoulder against Beauchamp's thigh. Both men hit the dirt once more, grunting and twisting and struggling for dominance.

FitzHugh's burly uncle watched their furious combat for some moments more, then shook his head. "We'd better separate them before they kill each other."

Sending Ian and St. Bressé to take hold of Beauchamp, he and two others grabbed at FitzHugh.

"Let go!" FitzHugh bellowed, shaking off their hold.

Alymer threw himself at his nephew once more and wrapped both arms around his chest. At his furious shout, the other two took hold of FitzHugh's flailing arms.

"Cease!" Alymer shouted. "This is no way for two knights to settle their differences, whatever they be!"

When FitzHugh tried to break his hold with a quick elbow jab backward, he grunted "Do that again and I'll whack your head with the flat of my sword."

His pained wheeze penetrated the red haze of fury behind FitzHugh's eyes. While the three men held on for dear life, he fought to bring his rage under control. He sucked air into his lungs in harsh, shuddering gulps. Never taking his eyes from Beauchamp, similarly restrained, he straightened slowly.

"Get out of my keep and off my lands," he growled. "If you dare to show your face here again, I'll slice out your gut and feed it to the dogs."

Beauchamp shook off the other's loosened grip. "I'll return within the week, to claim my bride."

"She'll be a widow before she is a bride, if you set foot on Edgemoor again."

Beauchamp's brown eyes blazed with fury. "I'll return," he promised. Dragging his sleeve across his face, he smeared blood and dirt in equal parts over his cheek. With a last glare at FitzHugh, he turned and crossed to the stables. A furious order sent his squire running for his gear.

FitzHugh spit a stream of blood to the ground and stalked into the keep. Ignoring the maids' frightened gasps and Hertha's openmouthed astonishment, he strode to his chamber and flung open the door.

"Is this how you care for a girl in your household, wife?"

He yanked open the bed curtains, then swore viciously when he saw the empty bed.

"Where is she?" he barked at Hertha, who was peering through the open door, with a crowd of wide-eyed maids at her shoulder.

His aunt's generous chins dropped. She glanced from the unoccupied bed to the man beside it and shut her mouth with a snap.

"Don't shout at me. I swatted your dirty backside more than once in your misspent youth, and I'm not loath to do it again."

She slammed the door on the goggling maids and advanced on her nephew. The sight of this rotund little woman bristling like an angry hedgehog, obviously willing to carry out her absurd threat, lessened some of FitzHugh's fury. He relaxed his iron hold on the bed curtains and wiped a hand over his aching jaw.

"Where is my lady wife, aunt?"

"I thought her here, asleep," Hertha responded, brows puckering. "Mayhap she went back to the stables, to see to the boys. What goes on here, nephew? Why is your face battered and bleeding?"

"I would speak with Mellisynt first. She can explain the matter to you later, if she wishes. Please, send a man to the stables to fetch her. And heat some water so I may bathe my jaw."

Hertha gave him a disgusted look, but turned to do his bidding. FitzHugh saw the door shut behind her with some relief. He had no desire to bring shame down on Isabeau if he could avoid it. He'd send Mellisynt to find the girl and ascertain her state. If she wasn't opposed to Beauchamp, and Geoffrey agreed to the match, mayhap they could bring it off without destroying Isabeau's name. They *would* bring it off, he vowed savagely, forgetting that just moments ago he'd sworn to kill the man he even now determined to see wedded before the next full moon.

The hot water arrived within minutes, carried by his squire. Stripping away his torn and bloody clothes, FitzHugh let Ian bathe his bruises. He was sitting on a stool, clad only in his linen braies, cursing Ian's clumsy hands, when Hertha bustled back into the room. Brushing aside the squire, she picked up the soap and a linen rag and took over the duties of attending to the lord of the manor.

"The Lady Mellisynt is not at the stables," she told her nephew, dabbing at a cut over his eye.

FitzHugh pushed her hand away. "Where is she?"

"I know not." Hertha retorted. She took a fistful of hair and yanked his head back.

"Ouch!"

"Hold still. You've opened the wound on your pate in your little brawl. It'll have to be stitched again." She poked at the half-healed scar on his forehead with ungentle fingers.

"Damn it, aunt," FitzHugh ground out, "forget the wound. Where could Mellisynt be?"

"In any one of two dozen outbuildings, seeing to her duties! You men! You think that just because you come riding back after being gone a half a year and more, your wife can forget the soap-making or cooking or gardening or any other of the chores that demand her attention. I've sent the maids scurrying to find her. She'll be here forthwith."

But Mellisynt did not arrive while Hertha finished tending FitzHugh's wounds, nor even while he pulled on fresh garments with impatient hands. Nor had anyone found a trace of the lady in any of the keep's many outbuildings.

Even Hertha's brow was furrowed in worry by the time the last of the men sent out to search the grounds reported back.

"Has no one seen her this day?" FitzHugh snapped to his aunt and uncle.

Alymer shook his head.

"Mayhap the Lady Isabeau," Hertha suggested tentatively. "I asked among the women earlier. When I queried the girl, she only shook her head and burst into tears."

"Bring her here," FitzHugh ordered. He paced in front of the hearth, a scowl etched across his features, until the two women returned. Isabeau sent him a frightened glance through red-rimmed eyes, but held her chin proudly.

"Leave us. Please, aunt," he requested when Hertha would have protested. Alymer took her arm and drew her away, shooing the servants down the hall, as well.

"Have you seen my lady wife?" FitzHugh began brusquely.

"Aye," Isabeau whispered. "Earlier. This morn."

"Where?"

"She…she came to the sewing room just after we broke our fast."

FitzHugh leaned forward to catch the girl's soft words. "She's not there now. Do you know where she is?"

"Nay."

A gnawing worry curled in FitzHugh's stomach. He turned, thinking to dismiss the girl and mount a search himself, but her tragic face held him. He'd been careless enough of his duty to protect the child; he couldn't leave her in such distress.

"Beauchamp came to me this morn," he told her.

"Aye. He said he would." Isabeau swallowed. "I heard that you beat on each other most fearsomely. Is…is he hurt?"

"Not as much as he should be. Are you all right?"

The gruff kindness, where she'd expected only blows or scorn, nearly undid Isabeau. Tears trembled on her lids, but she blinked them back furiously.

"I am become a watering pot of a sudden," she murmured, shamefaced.

FitzHugh took pity on her. "'Tis not the end of the world. Sir Roger goes to petition Geoffrey for your hand."

"I know. He told me he would do so before he... before he sent me... before I left the..."

"Before you left his bed," FitzHugh finished bluntly. "Did he force you?"

Isabeau's great sea-green eyes widened. After a long moment, she shook her head. "Nay." She sighed, with a hint of her old smile. "I all but forced him."

Despite himself, FitzHugh grinned. "Then 'tis well you're to wed. Don't look so sorry, Isabeau. None but Beauchamp and I know why we fought. You'll be married with your dignity intact, if not your virgin's shield."

"Lady Mellisynt knows," Isabeau confessed, her tentative smile fading. "She slapped my face and called me slut. And I am." Her voice wobbled, tears threatening once more.

FitzHugh frowned, unable to reconcile the Mellisynt he knew with one who would slap a suffering young woman. Worry ate at his insides. Where was his wife? He patted the girl's arm absently.

"Nay, you're no slut. You're but a pretty little morsel, too sweet for Beauchamp to resist. Rest, child, and all will be well."

"I'm not a child!"

Isabeau's wail fell on deaf ears as FitzHugh turned and hurried out.

Chapter Fourteen

Mellisynt huddled on a flat sweep of rock, her arms locked around her knees. Mist swirled about her, obscuring all but a narrow view of the sea. Below, gray waves crashed against fog-shrouded boulders, while overhead the gulls whirled and swooped, their raucous cries echoing eerily through the thick haze.

Coming here to lick her wounds had been a mistake, she realized. Every so often the mists cleared, as they did now, and gave her a view of the beach below. She stared down at the strip of sand and rock, her heart aching as her eyes sought the spot where she'd fallen headlong into love at the same moment the hound had tumbled both her and FitzHugh into the sea. Where she'd shed the last of her inhibitions as she shed her clothes and welcomed her lord home so shamelessly. Where his rough hands and hungry mouth had taken her beyond physical craving, beyond lust, beyond passion. A drift of soft drizzle obscured the beach once more, shutting off her view. Just as a few malicious words had shut off her dreams short hours ago.

She rested her chin on her knees, letting the dew wash the residue of tears from her cheeks. How could she have been so foolish as to think herself in love? How could she have opened her heart and allowed FitzHugh inside? Just because he was most skilled with his hands and most generously endowed between his well-muscled thighs? Because he seemed to take as much pleasure in their coupling as did she? Because occasionally his eyes gleamed down at her with a soft light she'd mistaken for affection?

Fool, she berated herself, fool! She closed her eyes against a fresh wave of pain. The troubadours were right, she decided when the ache subsided. Love had no place in marriage. 'Twas best to bestow one's affections on some distant knight, to play a measured game, in which a man could not sweep a woman into his arms and break her heart, did she not allow it. She sighed, thinking that this business of love rightly belonged in song and not in real life. It was too painful, too tormenting.

Settling her head more comfortably on her knees, Mellisynt let the muted roar of the sea soak into her soul. Fog blanketed the air, narrowing her world to a gray patch of rock and sea. Once she thought she heard a muffled voice calling, far off in the distance, but the sound drifted away on the thick mist. Exhaustion, both physical and mental, washed over her.

She woke some time later with a stiff neck and cramped legs. She had no idea how long she'd dozed, since the fog had deepened and now hid all but a faint haze of sunlight. Straightening her stiff limbs, she rose slowly, like an aged, tired woman. Her gown was damp clear through, and her hair hung in wet tangles from loosened braids. Pushing the thick strands back with a weary hand, she stepped off the rock ledge and began to trudge up the long, sloping path of the cliff. She would not stay and mope here like a moon-struck lackawit. She was chatelaine, with a house full of guests to see to. And a husband to attend. Mellisynt drew in a ragged breath and curled her nails into her palm.

By the time she'd climbed to the top of the cliffs, she'd buried her hurt deep inside.

Not far from the keep, a muffled thunder sounded somewhere behind her. Mellisynt turned and peered into the gray mist, trying to discern the sound. Suddenly, without warning, a rider broke through the haze, bent low in the saddle, galloping hard and fast straight at her. With a frightened shriek, she threw herself off the path, landing on hands and knees in rough gorse.

The horse was pulled to a dancing, whinnying halt.

"My lady!"

St. Bressé slid from the saddle and scrambled to her side. Urgent hands grabbed her arms and lifted her to her feet.

"Are you hurt?"

"Nay!" Mellisynt gasped, pushing her wet hair out of her eyes.

"Where have you been? Sir Richard has turned out the entire keep to search for you. We've been looking for hours."

"For me? Why?"

St. Bressé blinked at her openmouthed astonishment. "Why? Well, because . . . because Sir Richard ordered it."

"But I often walk the shore, you know that!"

"Aye, but not when our lord is here, and the keep full of guests."

Mellisynt bit her lip, mortified to be reminded of her discourtesy. With all the turmoil she'd endured last night and this morning, she dreaded having to face the crowded keep.

"Here, mount my horse, and I will lead you in," the knight offered.

"Nay, I'll walk," she muttered, not about to add the discomfort of the saddle to her other, inner hurts.

She trudged beside St. Bressé up the steep path to the gates, then into the courtyard. A chorus of shouts greeted their arrival. Before they'd crossed half the yard, Hertha rolled out of the keep and threw herself at Mellisynt. She staggered back a few paces at the enthusiastic, weighty welcome.

"We've been so worried, girl." Hertha sniffed, wiping a corner of her eye with a long sleeve.

"But why?" Exasperation drew Mellisynt's brows together in a fine line. "I don't understand all this consternation. You've not fretted when I walked before."

"But then we didn't have your lord pacing about like a snarling bear, worried at your absence."

"He should rather worry at my presence," Mellisynt muttered to herself as Hertha shooed her into the hall. She allowed herself to be hustled down the length of the great room, to the privacy of her chamber. Hertha left her with instructions to strip immediately while she sent maids for hot water and men to find Sir Richard and advise him of her return.

Alone in the bedchamber, Mellisynt stood rooted to the floor. Her eyes fastened on the huge curtained bed that dominated one wall. An image of FitzHugh's long, powerful body crushing Isabeau into the mattress seared her mind. She was still standing, unmoving, when Hertha and a string of maids hastened in with water and a bowl of soft soap. Clucking, the older woman pushed her over to the fire and began to remove her sodden clothing.

Without a word, Mellisynt allowed herself to be stripped, folded into the copper tub and scrubbed. She felt drained, like one whose body had overextended itself and now longed for nothing more than to sink into oblivion. Hertha's scolding chatter fell unheard upon her ears. She bent forward, resting her forehead on her knees, while the maids soaped her tangled hair and rinsed it with fresh water. A lethargy spread through her limbs, only to shatter as the chamber door crashed open.

The maids jumped and squeaked in surprise. A full bucket of water sloshed over Mellisynt's head, streaming into her eyes and open mouth. Gasping, she lifted her head and tried to push aside the curtain of wet hair.

"Leave us!" FitzHugh thundered.

Hertha shook her head and approached the furious man. "Now, nephew, your lady is safe and—"

FitzHugh lifted his aunt by her dimpled elbows and deposited her outside the door. He jerked his head at the openmouthed maids, then slammed the wooden panel behind them and slid the bolt into place. Pushing his glistening, rain-soaked mail hood off his equally drenched head, he approached the copper tub.

Mellisynt gasped. "What happened to your face? And your eye? 'Tis all but swollen shut!"

"Never mind my eye, lady wife," he responded, his voice grim. Leaning over, he grasped both of her bare arms. With one swift tug, he hauled her, naked and shrieking, from the tub.

"Are you mad?"

She tried to wrench her arms loose, desperate to cover herself. Her lethargy fled, and a fury fueled by hurt fired in her blood. "How dare you storm in here and handle me so?"

FitzHugh's hands tightened on her arms. "I'll handle you far worse ere this day is over. How dare *you* disappear like that, with no word to anyone? I've had men out searching for hours."

"Why?" Mellisynt spit. "Why should you look for me?"

FitzHugh stared down at her, dumbfounded. The confounded woman actually glared at him, as if angry that he should care whether she'd been abducted, or slipped off the cliffs and broken her bones on the rocks. Or lost her way in the accursed fog and fallen into one of the bogs that dotted the moors. Thinking of the many horrible fates he'd envisioned in the last hours, and of the cold fear that had lodged in his belly like a stone, his rage surged back.

"I could not believe it when the St. Bressé found me and said you'd *gone walking!*" His voice rose to a furious shout. "Have you no idea of the dangers in this land for a woman alone? Have you no sense at all?"

"I've sense enough to find my way back unassisted and unmolested!" Mellisynt screeched. "Unmolested until you returned, that is!"

FitzHugh's long night of wanting and even longer day of worry came together with the force of two chargers colliding. A tide of need swept over him, and he began to drag her toward the bed.

"I'll do more than molest you, wife. I'll make sure you don't have the strength left to *go walking* for many a day!"

Mellisynt resisted, twisting in his hold, clawing at the hands clamped like iron bands around her arms.

"Nay!" she screamed. "Nay! I will not be taken in the same bed as your whore. You will not use me so!" She bent, trying to bite his wrists.

Her savagery pierced his pounding desire before her words even registered. Frowning, FitzHugh released her arms. Mellisynt darted across the room and snatched up her damp shift, holding it over her front with shaking hands.

His eyes narrowed as she trembled before him. Folding his arms across his chest, he forced his voice to a semblance of calm. "Explain your words, lady wife."

Her lips twisted in a sneer. "What, were they not clear enough for you? I know not how else to say them! I'll not lie with you in the same bed, on the same sheets, where you fornicated with Isabeau!"

The heat drained from FitzHugh's veins like blood from an open wound, slowly, drop by drop, until he was left with a cold, hard core of disbelief.

"You think *I* sported with the girl last night?"

"I know you did! She herself admitted it!"

"She said she lay with me?"

"She didn't say your name, mayhap, but she didn't need to. She was seen coming to this room last night, and washing the blood from her thighs this morn."

FitzHugh saw the hurt behind the fury in his wife's eyes. He tried to tell himself that circumstances gave credence to her distrust. His rational mind acknowledged that she knew not all the facts. Yet a fierce pride overrode these logical reasonings. In all his years, he'd never compromised his honor. He'd lived by and was known for his word. That his wife, his own wife, would question his integrity was like an iron spike in his belly.

"I would be sure I understand this." His jaw clenched and unclenched with each word. "You think me so lacking in honor that I would deflower a virgin given into my keeping, in the same bed I share with my wife?''

Mellisynt's brows drew together. A faint cloud of doubt edged the anger in her eyes, only to be chased away with a toss of her head. ''I misdoubt honor entered into it. More like Isabeau climbed astride your shaft before you could turn her away, had you even wanted to.''

His mouth tightened into a grim line. ''So now I not only lack principle, I also lack the will to turn aside an untried girl who would steal my virtue.''

Mellisynt's frown returned. She gnawed on her lower lip, as if suddenly unsure how to proceed.

''What's the matter, wife, have you no other flaws in my character to bring forth?'' FitzHugh uncrossed his arms and moved toward her, one deliberate step at a time. ''No other slurs to cast against me, or against the girl whose behavior you were charged to govern?''

''Do not think to turn this on me,'' Mellisynt cried, goaded. She stepped back, the shift clutched to her breast. ''And do not dare to touch me, you bastard!''

A cold, icy rage filled FitzHugh's veins. ''I'll do with you as I please. You forget yourself in your accusations, lady wife. Bastard I may be, but you are mine to use, in this bed or any other, no matter how many women I take before you or after you.''

FitzHugh saw pain flood her eyes, and almost halted. But hurt pride drove him forward, and something deeper, some last, lingering trace of his confused feelings of the night before. The woman whose touch he'd longed for thought him a lowborn bastard, without honor, without principle. Even when she discovered the truth, he'd know she'd doubted him. An aching sense of loss lanced through him, only to be dismissed contemptuously. If he couldn't have the woman's trust, he'd take what else he pleased.

He halted before her. ''Get you into bed.''

''Nay,'' she whispered, her eyes huge, mossy pools.

''To bed, lady wife.''

She drew in a harsh, ragged breath. ''Nay.''

FitzHugh's fists clenched. A lifetime of absolute authority rose within him. His every instinct raged at him to reach out, to take the woman and shake her, to drag her to their bed and subdue her once and for all. No soldier who dared defy him so would live to see the light of day. No mount that refused the command of his spurs or hands would survive in his stables. Nor would any wife of his refuse him.

"If I must force you, I will."

Mellisynt heard the implacability in his voice and felt her heart shatter into a thousand tiny splinters.

"Do not do this, my lord."

Her plea didn't pierce the coldness in his eyes. The last vestiges of her anger drained, and only hurt was left. Swallowing painfully, she moved around his body and crossed to the bed. The wet shift dropped from her numb hands, and she slid between the wool-filled covers.

FitzHugh moved to stand beside the bed frame. For a long moment he stared down at her, his lips pressed together in a grim white line.

Forcing herself to meet his hard look, Mellisynt resisted the urge to pull the covers over her chilled flesh. Shivers racked her, and despite her most determined efforts, a ragged sob escaped her lips.

With a curse, FitzHugh turned and strode out of the chamber.

Not until late in the afternoon could Mellisynt bring herself to stumble out of the bed chamber. Her eyes were red-rimmed with unshed tears, and her throat felt raw.

Isabeau had been waiting, 'twas obvious. The girl caught her as she emerged from the chamber and begged private speech. Mellisynt wanted to scream at her to go away, but couldn't force a sound through her tight throat. Perforce, she listened to Isabeau's stumbling confession. When the girl mumbled Beauchamp's name, Mellisynt's heart seemed to stop in her breast.

"I don't know why I lay with him," Isabeau whispered, her head bowed. "Most times, I don't even like him! He... he belittles me and... and teases me and thinks me yet a half-grown child. But when he kissed me, my lady, I seemed to... to lose all reason."

Mellisynt wouldn't have believed she could hurt more than she already did, but the knowledge that she'd driven her husband to near-violence by her own accusations and jealousy stabbed through her with every breath. Too shattered to deal properly with Isabeau, Mellisynt signaled to Hertha.

"Don't... don't fret, Isabeau," she croaked. "Beauchamp is an honorable man, and will return for you."

She pushed the girl into Hertha's ample arms with a silent plea to the older woman. Hertha led Isabeau away, clucking and murmuring curses on men who couldn't keep their codpieces laced.

When FitzHugh returned late that evening, Mellisynt had composed herself and her words of apology. She waited while he stripped and washed and changed into clean, soft robes. He heard her out with a cold courtesy that knifed through her, gave a curt nod, then strode out for the evening meal. Mellisynt trailed after him, miserable and resentful and ashamed.

Thus was set the pattern for their days, and their nights. Ever polite, FitzHugh accorded her the dignity of her position as chatelaine. He included her when reviewing the accounts with Alymer and the cleric who kept their records, and when discussing the strength and weaknesses of the vassals who owed him service. He took her with him when he rode to the villages and farmsteads to meet with tenants. But the smile that had lightened his eyes when he looked at her was gone, as was the warmth from his voice.

While the days were misery for Mellisynt, the nights became sheer torment. Despite his seeming indifference, FitzHugh kept her in his bed. Lying beside him in the darkness, feeling the heat of his body next to hers, hearing the soft rasp of his breathing, Mellisynt grew ever more wretched.

Hesitantly, unused to taking the initiative in their relationship, she tried to bridge the growing gap between them. She took great care with her dress each morn, and went about with a calm, smiling demeanor. Still, he held himself distant.

Finally, taking all her courage in hand, she turned to him in bed one night. To her relief, he accepted her tentative caresses and rolled atop her willingly enough. But while his skilled hands and hard body brought her to pleasure, they did not bring fulfillment. 'Twas as if he held a part of himself back, as if he felt the heat they generated in his body, but not his soul. Mellisynt turned away from him afterward, shamed. She would have slipped from the bed, had he not brought her back down to the mattress with a low, growled reminder of her place.

Though they coupled frequently after that, 'twas without the passion she craved. Each time FitzHugh played upon her body and brought her to peak, then spilled his seed into her with deliberate, paced movements, another corner of her soul curled in despair. She began to hate her treacherous body for its involuntary response, as much as she hated herself from the lack of trust in her husband that had brought them to this pass.

The rest of the residents of the keep were quick to sense the changed atmosphere. Hertha frowned and fussed and queried Mellisynt until the younger woman snapped at her to cease, to leave her be! And then crumpled into an abject heap and wept on Hertha's comfortable shoulder.

Bartholomew, his indomitable spirits fully recovered from his ordeal, took to tagging at Mellisynt's heels whenever he could slip away from his tutors and training. As if sensing her discomfort, the hound would come up at unexpected moments and plop his huge, shaggy head down in her lap. Mellisynt forced herself to laugh with the boy and scratch behind the dog's lopsided ears with a knowing hand, but the joy she found in their company was overshadowed by the ache in her heart.

Isabeau quickly recovered from the fright of losing her virginity and her value as a marriage pawn. Regaining a semblance of her former self, she joined the other maidens in sewing or weaving or singing, with her head held high and the same sultry smile on her lips whenever a man passed near. But Mellisynt knew the smile was forced, and saw that her sea-green eyes held shadows not there before.

When a courier from Richmond arrived, Mellisynt watched FitzHugh read the stiff parchments with mingled dread and relief. She knew the message offered a change from the confused void her life had become.

"Constance sends you greetings and asks that you come to Richmond as soon as you may. Her time is near."

Mellisynt laid aside the woolen shirt she'd been darning. "I can leave in the morning, if that suits you."

FitzHugh shrugged. "As you will."

She bit her lip, then nodded. "Does the duchess say anything of Isabeau, and Sir Roger?"

"Aye," FitzHugh responded, his jaw tightening. "Beauchamp is in the north, carrying messages to King William of Scotland from Geoffrey about the raids across the border."

"In the north! But he was to come here, to claim the girl!"

"I see the duchess's fine hand in this." A hint of acid roughened FitzHugh's voice. "She must ever meddle. I've known her to refuse Geoffrey her bed until she got her way. Most likely she invented this mission for Beauchamp to keep us from spilling more blood."

Mellisynt lifted her eyes to his, a challenge in them. "'Tis good to hear that some husbands recognize a woman's right to refuse them anything, including their bed."

"You have many rights, wife," FitzHugh told her softly. "That's not one of them."

For a moment, the air crackled with tension. Mellisynt rejoiced in the first real emotion between them since that disastrous night. She felt a surge of hope, but then the hardness in his eyes defeated her. Swallowing a sigh, she lowered her lashes.

"Isabeau is to travel with you to Richmond and celebrate her betrothal when Beauchamp returns. I'll go and make arrangements for your escort."

"Do you not accompany us?"

"Birthing is women's business. I'll come for the baptism, or the betrothal, if it should occur first. Until then, there's much yet at Edgemoor that requires my attention."

She glared at FitzHugh's broad back as he strode down the hall and closed her lips tight against the cry that she needed attention more than the keep! A familiar ache simmering in her breast, she rose to tell Isabeau of her fate.

"You look even worse than I feel!"

Mellisynt slid from the pillion with a weary lack of grace and smiled as the duchess waddled down a flight of shallow steps.

"I have a passing aversion to the saddle, as you might recall, but the roads were too broken to allow a litter."

She leaned over to embrace the tiny, dark-haired Constance. Both women laughed when a protruding bulge of stomach kept their lips from meeting in the kiss of welcome.

"How does the babe?" Mellisynt asked, trying not to envy the duchess's radiant bloom.

Constance grimaced. "Much better than his dam." She placed a supporting hand under her stomach and walked forward a few more steps to greet Isabeau.

"Welcome, lady. I'm pleased that you've taken the interest of one of the finest of my husband's knights. Do you serve him well, Sir Roger will make you a fine lord."

Isabeau swept her a respectful curtsy, then dimpled. "Does *he* serve *me* well, he'll make me a fine lord."

Mellisynt smiled, glad of the girl's returned spirits. Her lively chatter and excited speculation about the betrothal ceremony had helped pass the three-day journey to Richmond.

Constance laughed and hooked a hand through each woman's arm. "Come inside and rest from your travels. Beauchamp should return within the week. We must plan the betrothal festivities."

She led the way inside the rambling castle, first built by Alan the Red, a Breton follower of William the Conqueror, and added to many times in the generations since. Perched high on a rocky eminence above the river Swale, Richmond Castle was swept by cooling breezes that dispelled the summer heat, but undoubtedly caused much suffering and chilblains in winter.

They passed through Scolland's Hall, famous throughout the north for its arched, oak-beam ceilings, its cavernous fireplaces, and the intricately carved screen disguising the minstrel's gallery. After a brief stop to catch her breath, Constance threw open the door of a suite of rooms with wide windows opening on a view of the river and town below. Scattered ribbons and veils and silver brushes proclaimed the airy bower a lady's sanctuary.

"You'll be comfortable here with the other women, at least until FitzHugh arrives. I'll find private rooms for you then."

Mellisynt merely nodded. For a moment she was tempted to tell Constance that she would stay in the women's chambers for the length of her visit, that FitzHugh could be housed with the men when he came. She dismissed the thought before it reached her lips. She'd not draw anyone else into the silent war between them.

Both she and Isabeau soon found themselves caught up in the inevitable swirl of gay amusements, lively entertainments and simmering politics that surrounded Constance. Geoffrey was absent most days, seeing to the demands of his holdings, so Mellisynt was spared the strain of his presence except at evening meals.

Isabeau regained her sparkle and her court of admirers as she rode to the hunt, or played at bowls on the grassy

west lawn or tried her hand at archery with the other giggling maidens.

Mellisynt fell into her old pattern of sitting quietly, her
hands busy embroidering gowns for the duchess's babe and
her ears filled with the courtiers' chatter. She listened with
amused interest to the cases brought before the court of
love. Constance heard all arguments in each case and then
issued her ruling with ruthless logic. In one instance, when
a knight complained that his mistress would not love him
unless he beat her, yet his own chivalry forbade such violent use of the woman he revered, Constance ordered him
to obtain a stout birch switch immediately.

Another day, while the ladies and their chevaliers
grouped around the reclining duchess in the sunshine of a
walled garden, they took up a heated discussion of the
thirty-one rules of love. First codified by Queen Eleanor
while she was yet the wife of King Louis of France, the law
caused much argument. Golden-haired Guy de Claire, who
had followed Constance from Nantes, teased her blatantly
about the first rule, *Marriage is not a just excuse for not
loving*.

Mellisynt plied her sewing and half listened to the courtiers' bantering arguments, enlivened by personal anec-
dote, sweeping generalities and ribald interpolations. But
at the nineteenth law, when de Claire's smooth voice stated
that *If love diminishes, it soon ends and rarely revives*, her
head snapped up.

It wasn't true, she wanted to cry. If it were, why didn't
the pain in her heart lessen? Even if she had made the
grievous error of falling in love with her husband, why did
his continued coolness not end her silly infatuation? Why
could she not accept his casual possession of her body and
go about her life?

Mayhap 'twas all he was really capable of. Hadn't he said
himself he'd known nothing of love in his life, that he
doubted its existence? Mayhap she'd only imagined the
tenderness in his blue eyes before her disastrous accusations. Mayhap she'd just become so enthralled with the

sexual pleasures FitzHugh gave her that she'd fancied herself in love. At the thought of how he kept her in his bed, yet denied her the closeness she craved, Mellisynt jabbed the needle into the linen with a vicious stab. The sharp steel pierced her thumb, and a bright red flower blossomed on the fine fabric. She sighed and lifted the injured finger to her mouth.

A teasing voice sounded in her ear. "Would that I was offered such a treat."

"Beauchamp!" she squeaked, dropping the linen and jumping up to clasp his hands. Her eyes widened at her first sight of his face, considerably rearranged since his visit to Edgemoor. His long, aquiline nose, now flattened at the bridge, was still slightly swollen. A deep, healing cut slashed through one eyebrow, giving him an even more rakish appearance than before. And he sported a yellowish bruise high on his forehead, close to the line of curly brown hair.

"You look remarkably like my husband when last I saw him," she remarked.

"Nay, don't wound me so," he protested. "Did I think I resembled that stone-faced monolith, I'd dip my noggin into a bowl of alchemist's brew and let it eat away the rocky ledges and rough crags."

Mellisynt laughed and tapped his nose with a light, playful finger. "It looks to me like one or two of your ledges have already been eaten away."

A flash of color caught her attention, and she looked over Beauchamp's shoulder to see Isabeau glaring at them. The girl's eyes slitted, and then she turned her back. Mellisynt's hand dropped immediately. She was too intimately familiar with the fruits of jealousy to wish it on another.

"Your betrothed awaits you on the other side of the garden," she told Beauchamp with a quiet smile. "I know you want to greet her. Go, and take with you my best wishes on your marriage."

Beauchamp glanced across the group of bright-plumaged courtiers. His eyes lingered on Isabeau for a moment, and then he turned back to bow over Mellisynt's hand.

"Thank you for your good wishes, my lady," he replied, a roguish smile spreading across his battered face. "I suspect I'll need them once I take that little vixen to wife."

"Aye, you will," Mellisynt muttered to his retreating back. "You most assuredly will."

Chapter Fifteen

FitzHugh and the duchess's babe appeared at Richmond on the same night, at almost the same hour. Mellisynt was too wrapped up in the drama of birth to take even a few minutes to greet the husband whose arrival she'd both dreaded and desired. With an impatient hand, she brushed aside a page's whispered message that her lord awaited below.

"Tell him I'll attend to him later."

She pushed a strand of sweat-dampened hair out of her eyes and turned back to the woman dragging herself back and forth across the room, leaning on the midwife's arm.

Constance endured the indignities of the birthing process with her usual indomitable spirit. She allowed neither the heat, nor the crowd that invaded her chamber, nor even Geoffrey's well-meant, booming advice on how to pass the babe to distract her from her fierce concentration on the task at hand. She walked, and panted, and stiffened with each pain. As her time neared, she curled on her side in the huge bed while the women took turns rubbing her back and whispering encouragement.

When the perfectly formed infant slid from between her thighs, she closed her eyes against the disappointment of a girl, then opened them immediately and demanded her daughter. Sweaty, white-faced, triumphant, she held the babe, oblivious of the swarm of nurses waiting to clean and swaddle.

Mellisynt lingered long after Geoffrey and the others had left, long after the women had washed Constance and given her herbs to heal her torn flesh.

Under the nurse's jealous eye, she approached the cradle and brushed a bent knuckle down the babe's red, mottled cheek. She looked so small and helpless, with her puckered mouth and wrinkled eyelids. Mellisynt ached to lift the tiny bundle, to hold it to her breast. After a moment, she heaved a quiet sigh and left the royal chambers.

Having no desire to join the revelries in the great hall, nor yet to meet with her husband, she slipped back into the ladies' bower. She picked her way through the litter of scattered trunks and discarded gowns and settled herself on the wide casement window seat. Leaning back against the stone wall, she let the late-summer night wash over her. Far below, torches flickered in the streets of the town crouched against Richmond's massive walls as the citizens celebrated the maid's birth. Above, wispy black clouds scudded across a round silver moon. Crickets chirped in the climbing vines that clung to the outer walls, sounding a light, sweet counterpoint to the singing and laughter from the hall below.

Mellisynt rested her hands over her stomach and stared up at the full moon. She should have flowed with her monthly courses before the silvery orb had waxed half-full. She'd never missed her time before. In her heart she knew that she'd achieved her greatest desire. So why did the knowledge that she at long last carried a babe not fill her with joy? Why did she feel her eyes even now prickle with unshed tears, she who never cried?

With a wrench of pain, Mellisynt realized how misplaced her dreams of just a year ago had been. Immured within Trémont's gray walls, all she'd prayed for was a babe to love and a chance to breathe the open air. Now she had both, and they didn't fill the emptiness inside her. Now she cringed in shame each time the husband she would love took her in casual possession. She hated the way he could manipulate her, stroke her, fire her blood. He'd trained her to his hand as he had his falcons and his steeds.

Mellisynt wondered if she'd ever be forgiven for her lack of trust. If FitzHugh's eyes would ever again fill with the glinting warmth she'd seen the night he wrapped the pearls around her throat. When she'd thought, for one breathless moment, that he might feel the same burgeoning, wondrous love that filled her breast. Mayhap someday, she thought, but could she bear this ache until that distant day?

Wearily Mellisynt slid off the window seat. She was too tired to ponder the problem, or think of any solution. She knew FitzHugh would be up the whole night, celebrating with Geoffrey. This night, at least, she would sleep by herself.

As it happened, she slept several nights by herself. The revelries continued well into the next day, then spilled over into the tourney. Knights who should have been abed nursing sick heads climbed onto war-horses to demonstrate their virility. The tourney carried them far afield, so Geoffrey sent word that they would bed down at one of his vassals' keeps instead of returning immediately.

Both Constance and Mellisynt welcomed their lords' absences. In a rare moment of near privacy, the two sat on the duchess's bed some days later with the gurgling, naked babe between them.

"Do you believe something so delicate and sweet sprang from Geoffrey's loins?" Constance rubbed the baby's tummy with soft, stroking fingers.

Mellisynt smiled. "'Tis a wonder what the sire and the dam pass on. I marveled when I met FitzHugh's son, that he should be so merry."

"The Lord only knows where that comes from," Constance said. "FitzHugh's cheeks crack every time he smiles, and I misdoubt Alicia ever laughed in her life."

"Did you know her well?"

"The Lady Alicia? Aye, I knew her, though I was but a child being raised in Queen Eleanor's household when she and FitzHugh wed. A haughtier bitch never walked the earth! Her father was just a minor knight, but she held herself above her station. She was most unhappy to be given to a bastard. You'd think she conferred the Holy Grail upon FitzHugh every time she spread her legs. 'Tis a wonder she ever bedded with him at all.''

"Mayhap she had no choice in the matter." Bitterness laced Mellisynt's soft words. She reached out to play with the babe's waving foot.

"Do you say FitzHugh forces you?" The sharp disbelief in the duchess's voice brought Mellisynt's head up with a snap.

"Is that so unlikely?"

Constance narrowed her eyes to violet slits. "I've never known him to have to do so. Although he's not the most handsome of knights, his very size usually has the maids in a dither. He has the endowments of a blooded stallion, and knows well how to use them."

At Mellisynt's shocked look, she added a hasty "Or so Geoffrey tells me!"

She laughed and reached out a finger to push up Mellisynt's sagging jaw. "I swear there are more stories of FitzHugh and Beauchamp and their conquests than were ever sung of Beowulf or King Arthur. Geoffrey thinks that if he keeps me amused with tales of their exploits, I'll not question his. It gives me great satisfaction that both his rutting companions are now bound to women who will keep them on short chains!"

The smug satisfaction in her voice faded at Mellisynt's thin smile. Reaching across the babe, Constance took hold of her hands.

"Tell me true, are you so averse to the marriage bed that FitzHugh must force himself upon you? If so, I can give you herbs to ease your discomfort or simulate a most realistic passion."

Despite herself, Mellisynt grinned. "Nay, I need no aids. My lord is as skilled with his...endowments as Geoffrey told you."

"So what troubles you?"

She bit her lip and studied the gamine face across from her. Never having had any women friends, she was embarrassed to be sharing such intimate details of her life. Yet Constance had known this man who was her husband far longer than she had herself. Mayhap the duchess could help her deal with him.

"I . . . I lacked trust in my husband, and made a false accusation. I disparaged his honor. He has yet to forgive me."

Constance whistled low and long. "I'm not surprised. FitzHugh wears his honor like a buckler, ever forward. 'Tis all he had in the world for so many years, it's become a damned second skin. So in punishment for slighting his precious honor, he's denied you his attentions?"

Hot waves of red washed up Mellisynt's neck and cheeks. "Nay, he insists I share his bed and uses me most . . . most thoroughly. 'Tis the using I object to."

Nonplussed, Constance dropped her hands. "You object? Is he rough? Hurtful?"

She shook her head.

"Does he expect you to service him in unnatural ways?"

Not quite sure which of their activities Constance might consider unnatural, Mellisynt shook her head once more.

"Does he fail to bring you to pleasure?"

"Nay," she cried, goaded. "'Tis most pleasurable. But I would have more. I would have his love."

Constance stared across the short distance, her hand automatically reaching to soothe the babe when it gave a fretful cry. As if she were searching for words, her mouth opened, then closed several times. Finally, she sighed.

"I cannot advise you in this, Mellisynt. We each must find our own way to love. But think on this—FitzHugh would skewer any man who dared question his honor. If he keeps you in his bed and in his arms, despite your lack of trust, 'tis certain he feels something special."

"Aye," Mellisynt muttered. "He feels the same as when he mounts his prized war-horse!"

Constance laughed and scooped up the babe. "Not quite, I'm sure."

She nestled the child at her breast, and a hovering nurse came forward. Mellisynt slipped off the bed to give the mother and child privacy and returned to the women's dower.

When a clatter of hooves and muffled shouts heralded the return of the men the following evening, Mellisynt was ready to face her lord. He swept into the chamber given over to their use, and her heart thudded painfully in her chest. Huge, begrimed from the ride, his dark hair plastered to his forehead with sweat, he was the most magnificent male she'd ever beheld. She could see the excitement of the tourney still brimming in his eyes and feel it in the way he wrapped his arm around her waist and gave her a kiss that held a promise of the night to come. He lifted his head, only to have the half smile forming on his face twist into a grimace of pain.

"Have you taken an injury?" Worry sharpened her voice and hid the tremor his kiss had caused.

"'Tis naught." FitzHugh set her aside and turned to hand his sword and buckler to his squire.

Mellisynt sent Ian a swift inquiring look.

"A mace struck his shoulder," Ian explained, helping to pull off FitzHugh's stained surcoat. "But my lord held on and trounced Sir Guy. Again!"

FitzHugh's dark head emerged from the folds of material.

Mellisynt gaped at him. "De Claire? You unseated Guy de Claire?"

"Not just unseated," Ian bragged. "My lord took him in the melee and all but pounded him into the dirt. He won't be spouting his pretty poetry for some time."

Lord and squire exchanged smug masculine grins.

Mellisynt couldn't help feeling a twinge of satisfaction at the thought of de Claire's arrogant nose ground into the dust. Chiding herself for her uncharitable thoughts, she rummaged through the chests for the supply of herbs and medicaments she'd brought with her. When FitzHugh had stripped and seated himself on a stool, she knelt and probed his swollen discolored shoulder. Satisfied that the muscles were bruised, but not torn, she physicked it with what she had at hand and bound it with strips of linen.

"I should send to the stables for your horse poultice," she commented tartly.

FitzHugh shook his head. "Nay, wife. I would not stink up our bed this night. Not when I have been without you and without ease these weeks."

A clutch of pain tightened Mellisynt's heart. She busied herself putting away her salves while FitzHugh rose and rolled his shoulders experimentally once or twice. With a satisfied grunt, he moved to the table holding a pitcher of water and splashed some into an enameled bowl.

Mellisynt watched while he washed himself, knowing she should go to him and do that duty, but reluctant to move. In the fading light, his body showed long and tan and incredibly powerful. Several vicious bruises stained his chest and arms where he must have taken other blows. Wordlessly she handed him thick, rough linens to dry himself with. She stood rooted to the floor as he walked across the room and stretched himself out on the velvet coverlet with a heartfelt sigh.

"Come, wife. Much as I want you, I ache in so many places that you may have to use some of old Henri's tricks this night."

Mellisynt buried her clenched fists in the folds of her skirts and didn't move. After a moment, FitzHugh turned his head on the pillow and surveyed her still form.

"Come."

"Nay." Her whisper barely carried across the wide room.

"I thought we settled this between us, before you left Edgemoor. Did your weeks here with Constance give you the mistaken idea that because she leads Geoffrey around by his rod, you may do so with me?"

Mellisynt gasped. "I have no desire to lead you around by...by anything. But neither do I desire to lie where there is no love."

She stiffened in anticipation. All her years of service as a wife screamed that it was a sin to deny her lord, that she would suffer for it. Her stomach fluttered as she awaited his reaction.

When it came, it totally disconcerted her. Having steeled herself for icy anger or physical domination, she wasn't expecting the amusement that flickered across his face.

"Did we not settle this, as well, months ago, when first we wed? I thought we were agreed such emotion exists only in song." He swung his legs over the side of the bed and started toward her. "Come, no more of this foolishness. I'm too tired to play games. I want you."

She took a hasty step back. "Nay."

The lazy amusement slipped from his face. His jaw firmed ominously.

"Do not try my patience. I'm not in the mood to school you gently this night."

"You will not school me at all," she hissed. "I'm not some dog to be trained, nor horse to be broken. Nor will I lie with you."

For a long moment, they glared at each other, his blue eyes boring into her furious green ones. Mellisynt watched, tension rising in her throat, as the shadows played across his stubble-darkened face. Finally, he gave a curt nod.

"As you will."

He went back to the bed and stretched himself out once more.

She stood in the middle of the room, too stunned to move. Now that she had girded herself emotionally for battle, FitzHugh's capitulation left her floundering. She listened with a disbelieving ear to the rustling of the mattress as he settled himself. Was this a ruse? Did he think to trick her into bed and then attack her?

As soon as the thought entered her mind, she dismissed it. Such was not her husband's way. If he wanted her, he'd take her without resorting to such trickery, overcoming her stiff resistance with his knowing hands and mouth. The memory of just how often he'd done so sent waves of shame through her. Not this night, she swore. Not ever again.

As twilight darkened into dusk, she began to feel foolish standing like a gatepost in the middle of the room. Yet she couldn't move. Her legs felt wooden, and her mind refused to tell her what she should do next.

"Get you in bed," he growled through the descending darkness. "I'll not take you if you do not wish it."

FitzHugh lay on his side, one arm bent beneath his head, and listened to the low sounds behind him as she moved forward and slowly undressed. With every rustle of her clothes, he cursed himself for a fool.

When she'd tilted up her chin and defied him yet again, he'd been tempted to teach her once and for all the foolishness of challenging him thus. But he'd stared down into her white, set face and sensed that this time she would well and truly fight. And at that moment he'd known he could neither hurt her nor try to force her.

In truth, he was tired of wringing a response from his stubborn wife. Although loath to admit it, even to himself, he got only hollow pleasure from their coupling of late. It lacked the wild, sensual explosion of passion he'd tasted with her before. Before her suspicions and accusations had disgusted him. Before his anger had replaced passion with lust.

Since her departure from Edgemoor, he'd had time aplenty to regret his furious reaction to her lack of faith. She was only a woman, after all. It was foolish to expect her to hold the same standards of trust and respect as men. He'd banished the last, lingering regret for what might have been and hoped the time apart would ease the strain between them, as it had eased his anger. Instead, it appeared to have fueled hers.

His every sense tingling, FitzHugh felt Mellisynt slide into bed behind him. Her distinctive scent, the one that always reminded him of spring and soft blue flowers, drifted across the darkness. His ear picked up the uneven pitch of her breathing, and he smiled grimly. She was as disturbed as he by their confrontation. He wondered if she felt the heat of his nearness, as he did hers. If the fine hairs on her arms stood on end, as his did.

Deliberately he closed his eyes, willing sleep to come. His way of dealing with the strain between them had left him less than satisfied these last weeks. He'd see if her way was any better.

If the lack of physical release bothered Mellisynt in the weeks that followed, she hid it well. FitzHugh himself struggled with a growing frustration and aching need. By night, he called upon reserves of restraint he had never known he possessed to keep from rolling over in the darkness and burying his rigid shaft in his wife's soft body. By day, he spent his pent-up energies in the hunts and tourneys held in celebration of the birth of the Maid of Brittany. He and Beauchamp found themselves paired as partners in list, Roger with the mace and he with the sword. In the furious battle that ensued, the two men lost the last remnants of their enmity in the sweet thrill of victory.

As the day of the babe's baptism drew near, nobles from across England and the Angevin domains in France converged on Richmond. Just days before the ceremony, Queen Eleanor arrived with all her queenly dignities restored. She'd been released from captivity some months earlier to pacify Aquitaine's hot-blooded lords after Richard Lionheart's stern rule had incited them to rebellion. Her return to power showed clearly in her regal, arrogant manner. She represented the king, who was away battling the stubborn Irish lords to force them to accept Prince John as their titular king. Geoffrey deserted the tourneys to attend his mother, a most singular occurrence for someone as sport-mad as he, one that gravely concerned both FitzHugh and Beauchamp.

They stood at the edge of the great hall together one night, Mellisynt between them and Isabeau in the dance with one of her admirers.

"I like this not," Beauchamp murmured, his eyes on Geoffrey's red head, bent over the velvet darkness of his mother's.

As she followed the line of his gaze, Mellisynt's own brows drew together. She'd been at court long enough to understand his meaning. She glanced up at FitzHugh to see him watching the royal pair with a worried frown.

"'Tis said the king's refusal to give up the Lady Alice eats at her soul." Beauchamp's low murmur barely rose above the noise of the crowd. "'Tis not just that Henry keeps a mistress, but that she is his son's betrothed, the woman promised to Eleanor's favorite."

FitzHugh's blue eyes locked with Beauchamp's over Mellisynt's head. "Lady Alice is Richard Lionheart's concern. Geoffrey would not champion his brother's cause."

"The lady's become a pawn in this game of kings," Beauchamp argued, his voice low. "Philip of France has sworn to avenge his sister's dishonor, but he knows better than to try to use Richard Lionheart to do it. Richard is too intelligent, too strong-minded, to be used by anyone. Nor does he much care what happens to the lady," Beauchamp finished dryly.

The two men exchanged knowing glances. Rumors of the prince's lack of interest in women had floated about for years. Few were surprised that he'd made no move to end the protracted betrothal.

Slowly, reluctantly, FitzHugh nodded. "Of all the sons, Geoffrey is the bravest, and the weakest. He's been hard put to refuse Philip's offers of assistance to throw off his father's heavy hand. With his mother's encouragement, it will be even more difficult for him to resist."

"And the fool will plunge us all into war again."

Both men looked down at Mellisynt in astonishment, as if realizing for the first time that she stood between them.

Whatever FitzHugh would have said in reply to his wife's impetuous remark was lost when Isabeau glided up to claim her betrothed for a dance.

* * *

The men's fears sat uneasily within Mellisynt as she bade goodbye to Beauchamp and Isabeau some days later. The couple was returning to Normandy, where Beauchamp's principal holdings lay and their wedding would take place. The duke and duchess planned to leave Richmond, as well, traveling to Brittany as soon as Constance recovered sufficiently. She wanted to be across the Channel before autumn storms swept in to make the crossing unpleasant.

Mellisynt cast a last look over her shoulder at Richmond Castle as she passed through its gates, atop a pillion behind FitzHugh. High above the tallest tower, the duke's pennant fluttered bravely in the late-September breeze. Its golden lion, rampant on a bloodred field, forcibly reminded her of the man himself. Geoffrey was as golden and bold as the lion, and just as bloodthirsty. A shiver racked her, and her arms tightened around FitzHugh.

Mellisynt ran her eyes over her husband's broad back, so close she could lean her cheek against it if she wished to. And the Lord knew she wished to. No more than FitzHugh did she like this unsettled state between them. Surely in the coming winter months, when dark descended early and shut them within Edgemoor's walls, she could bridge the gap between her husband and herself. Surely she could find the means to win back his regard.

These nights beside him in their bed had been torture. The mornings were even worse. She lay abed while he rose and dressed, then left to hunt or joust or ride with the men. Watching him through half-shuttered lids, fighting the sickness that now crept over her each morn, Mellisynt had grown more miserable with each passing day. Somehow she hadn't expected her victory in winning the right to her person to taste so vile.

Just thinking about the bouts of nausea she'd endured made her feel queasy. Of a sudden, the horse's easy gait beneath her legs took on a sinister roll. Mellisynt swallowed and stared resolutely at the roofs of the city buildings as they passed through the narrow streets. Once they left the garbage-strewn streets behind and gained the open road, she'd be fine, she told herself. She only needed to hold on till then.

She did. Barely.

"Stop!" she gasped as their small cavalcade rounded a bend in the road and entered the leafy shade of a thick forest.

FitzHugh twisted in the saddle and frowned down at her. "Why do you wish to stop? Surely you're not sore already?"

Mellisynt swallowed desperately. "I'm beyond sore. Get me down, my lord, and quickly!"

She pushed herself out of his hold as soon as her feet touched the road and dashed for the underbrush. Sinking to her knees behind a stand of willowy ash, she bent over and gave up her breakfast. Finally, trembling and wretched, she leaned back against a tree trunk.

"Here."

To Mellisynt's mortification, FitzHugh hunkered down on his haunches and held out a damp cloth.

"Wipe your face, then take some water to wash your mouth.

He passed her the cloth, then lifted a bulging bladder so that she could hold the spout to her lips. The cool liquid washed away the rank remnants of her meal. She leaned back against the slender trunk and closed her eyes.

"Are you all right?"

Her lashes flew up to see him regarding her with a steady gaze. She nodded, unable to speak. She knew she should tell him about the babe, but couldn't bring herself to the point. Not yet. Not while this tension hung between them and kept them lying awake at night, so close and yet so far apart. He'd know soon enough, in any case, if she couldn't control her stomach better.

"'Tis but a troubled stomach," she said. "I'm still a most reluctant rider."

"Are you sure that's the cause of your distress?" He reached down a hand to help her up.

"Wh-what do you mean?" She scrambled to her feet with a sad lack of dignity.

"I've felt you tossing and turning these nights, my lady wife. You've not enjoyed this enforced celibacy any more than I."

Mellisynt gaped up at him. "You think I pine so for your touch that my stomach is in knots?" she asked indignantly.

"Mine surely is," he said with a grim nod. "Or, if not my stomach, certain other parts of my anatomy."

A slow simmering anger rose in her veins. "I hate to disappoint you, my lord, but I do not crave your rod so much that its very absence curdles my breakfast."

She whirled and would have stomped back to the waiting men if his hand hadn't gripped her arm and held her in place. Mellisynt saw her anger mirrored in his glinting blue eyes.

"How much longer do we play this game? How long do you think to deny me? And yourself?"

"I don't know! Until... until..."

"Until your own need overcomes these silly woman's whims?"

She felt her heart constrict. He truly didn't understand. She wasn't sure she could explain her confused emotions, either to herself or to him. Still, here in this copse of ash, with the leaves fluttering gold above them and the stillness of the forest granting them a cloak of privacy, she felt the need to try.

"There should be more, my lord. More than just need between us."

"There is," he snapped. "There is respect. You have the dignities of your position as lady of Trémont and Edgemoor. You have your own revenues and rents."

She shook her head. FitzHugh's hand tightened on her arm.

"You have my constancy. I don't shame you by taking other women to bed."

"I know," Mellisynt whispered, hating the reminder of her own lack of trust.

"Then what in the names of all the saints do you want from me, lady?"

She stared up at him helplessly. "I want you to look at me as you do Geoffrey, or Beauchamp."

FitzHugh stepped back with a jerk, as if she'd struck him. "What? Do you now call me sodomite? I think I'd prefer you thought me a seducer of young virgins!"

"Nay! Nay! Of course I know you're not like that. I...I just want the bond, the love, the companionship, such as you have with these, your friends."

He gave her a disgusted snort. "If you expect me to share the same relationship with you as I have with my companions-at-arms, you're more addled than I thought. You're fashioned for an entirely different purpose, lady wife. One I'm hard put not to use."

Clearly out of patience, he propelled her toward the waiting men and horses. "You'd best resign yourself to your lot in life, my lady. 'Tis all you're like to get, after all."

He settled Mellisynt on her pillion with a decided plop. She glared at the broad expanse of his back when he swung onto the stallion and kicked it into a slow canter. She could feel the tension coiled in the hard muscles under her fingertips. Despite her high dudgeon, though, she had plenty of opportunity to ponder his words as they continued their journey.

As the miles passed, she felt her anger dissipate and a weary resignation begin to fill her heart. Mayhap she should accept what FitzHugh offered—respect and constancy and the pleasure they took in each other's bodies. That was more, much more, than many women got from their husbands. Mayhap friendship would grow eventually from such feelings, or something close to it. The thought gave her little comfort, and a heaviness settled in her heart. She knew that once they reached Edgemoor, FitzHugh's uncharacteristic restraint would fast dissipate. She wondered how long her own resolve would last before she did what he advised and accepted her lot in life.

As it turned out, she had little occasion to test either FitzHugh's restraint or her own resolve. They were not back at Edgemoor a day before a courier came pounding across the moors. He brought word that the duke had left for the Continent. He went not with the duchess, however, nor did he head for Brittany. Instead, he accompanied his mother, the queen, back to Aquitaine, and bade FitzHugh join him at Poitou as soon as possible.

"'Tis madness." Alymer stomped back and forth in front of the fire. "Do not go, nephew. The duke but seeks to draw you into the web his mother weaves about her sons."

"He is my sworn liege, uncle."

"He's a weak man. His head is turned by the last one who whispers in his ear."

"For that very reason, I must go."

"Nay, nephew."

"Do not, Richard."

He ignored the simultaneous exclamations of his aunt and uncle. Fixing his gaze on Mellisynt, he raised one brow.

"You do not speak, lady wife. What think you?"

Mellisynt took a deep breath. A hundred arguments tumbled through her head and trembled on her lips.

"You will do as your honor decrees."

She met his eyes squarely, then spoiled the effect of her noble words with a disgusted grimace. "Although I think it beyond stupid that one hot-tempered, hardheaded ruffian should drag us all into his intrigues and wars."

FitzHugh laughed and stretched his muscles. "Mayhap I can yet knock some sense into his hard head."

"When do you go?" Alymer asked the question that burned in Mellisynt's mind.

"On the morrow, I suppose. Unless something unforeseen occurs to delay my departure."

FitzHugh's eyes settled thoughtfully on Mellisynt's face. She met his gaze with a wide, steady one of her own. "I'll go talk to the cook about provisions for the journey, my lord."

Chapter Sixteen

Ever afterward, Mellisynt would rue the stubbornness that made her send her lord off with no sign of her regard other than a cool kiss. She stood beside him in the outer bailey, his men and the keep's occupants crowding around them in the early-morning mists.

"Is that the kind of salute to give a departing husband?"

His low, teasing voice held a trace of its old warmth. Her heart began to thump.

"'Tis the best I can do, my lord. Mayhap I will manage something better when you return."

"You will, wife, you will."

He traced a finger down her cheek and was gone. Mellisynt watched him ride out, the mists dulling the shine of his silver mail and darkening the red of his surcoat to wine. No sooner had his troop disappeared from view than sickness roiled up in her belly and she stumbled to the stews to retch and heave. Dame Hertha fussed and scolded and pushed Mellisynt into a wooden chair before the fire. The hound promptly stuck his muzzle into her lap.

"When is the babe due?"

She laid her head against the chair back. "I'm not sure. May, I think, or June."

"'Tis early days, then." Hertha smiled sympathetically. "I tossed up my breakfast for months with each of my boys."

"Oh, no," Mellisynt groaned.

"And that's the least of all your problems, child. You've much to look forward to. Swollen ankles, an aching back, piles, lack of sleep..."

"Stop! You make me want to curl up in my bed and not come out till spring."

Hertha took her hand and pulled her from the chair. "Nay, you'll do better on your feet. Hard work or a hard man are the only cures I know for breeding ailments. Since you've just lost the one, I'd best get you to the other."

True to her word, Hertha kept Mellisynt so busy through the cold autumn and dark winter months she scarce had time to miss her husband. The harvesting and milling and winemaking took many hours, as did the trenching and ditching around the keep's walls and gardens. Privies and stables were cleaned, their muck spread on the castle garden to prepare it for spring, with a goodly portion being carted to the outlying farms for their use. As the days shortened and the winds grew colder, Mellisynt oversaw the butchering of animals fattened through the fall, ensuring that the haunches and sides were salted or pickled with spices and hung on the great hooks in the vaulted storeroom in the great hall.

Gradually all activity moved indoors, as early snows swept down and blanketed the earth. The women spun and sewed and wove tapestries, while the men repaired horn and leather implements or carved wooden platters and spoons. Reeds and rushes gathered earlier, before the frosts, were plaited into baskets and harnesses and fish creels by the servants.

FitzHugh sent sporadic messages. Fall storms had delayed his departure from Portsmouth for weeks, and he wasted further weeks tracking Geoffrey's erratic movements. The duke had decided to celebrate Hallowmas with Constance in Rennes, FitzHugh wrote, disgust in every line, after having summoned all his knights to Poitou. Now they kicked their heels and waited for their lord to reappear. He was expected back before Christmastide.

Mellisynt's own Christmas, her second at Edgemoor spent without her lord, gained considerable liveliness with the arrival of both FitzHugh's sons. William and Geoffrey came to celebrate the birth of Christ with their father's lady, they told her, eyes sparkling with mischief. And their father had written to threaten them with death, Geoffrey confided, did they not behave most respectfully.

The keep soon rang with shouts of laughter as the boys organized all kinds of entertainments to keep themselves occupied. Mummeries and singing and chess tourneys occupied the nights, while squads of squires and pages and village boys battled with balls of snow and oaken staffs beating upon wooden shields during the day.

Wrapped in a thick woolen mantle, Mellisynt stood at a second-floor window watching them. Her heart leapt into her throat every time William dashed into her field of vision. So tall and muscular and dark of hair. So like his sire. Even his voice, carrying across the crisp winter air, held the same low timbre, although it occasionally still cracked with youth. Sweet Mother, she prayed, give me a son such as this. Or like Geoffrey, whose high-pitched shrieks of laughter she could hear clearly. And give me back their sire, she prayed most fervently. Soon.

In the dark winter nights, alone in her bed, she'd come to the realization that FitzHugh was right. What they had together was more than most husbands and wives found. So it was not the sweet, delicate love the troubadors sang of? So it was compounded of equal parts respect and lust? 'Twould do well enough, she decided. The longer she was without her husband's strong body beside her, the less she was concerned with respect, and the more with lust. The child growing within her kept her awake and restless with strange longings. Her breasts itched and burned and ached for the feel of his hands. Her womb fluttered with the babe's first movements and sent a tingling awareness of her womanhood through her body.

She tried to write FitzHugh of her feelings, but could find neither the words nor the courage to put them to paper.

Instead, she settled for telling him of the babe, and his sons' visit, and the business of the keep. And for begging him to return, whole and sound, as soon as he might.

But FitzHugh didn't return with the coming of spring. As the weeks passed, his messages became less frequent and more terse. The duke had returned to Poitou, he finally wrote in early March, and Eleanor became more strident in her criticisms of the king. She whipped her barons into a froth of hatred, and Geoffrey with her.

After the last terse missive, no word came at all.

"What you plan is treason."

"Be careful, FitzHugh. Even our friendship is not proof against such accusations."

"'Tis no accusation, 'tis simple fact."

The duke pushed himself away from the table. His chair crashed to the tiles as he surged to his feet.

"I will not have you harp at me on this anymore!"

With every fiber of his being, FitzHugh resisted the urge to grab Geoffrey by his velvet surcoat and beat his head against the wall. He glanced around the ring of men crowded into the duke's chamber, but saw no help on any of the faces he surveyed. Some, like Guy de Claire's, held outright hostility. FitzHugh sucked in his breath and tried again.

"Listen to me, Geoffrey. Even now your father prepares to sail from Portsmouth. He's heard of your schemes, and your mother's."

"One wonders where he got his information. And where you get yours, FitzHugh."

At de Claire's sneering drawl, FitzHugh straightened and turned slowly. He knew his prolonged and strenuous opposition to Geoffrey's proposed trip to Paris to align himself with the king of France had begun to grate on these knights. Breton lords all, they saw in the duke's schemes a means to free themselves from King Henry's heavy hand. The muttering and cold looks directed at FitzHugh had become more pointed and more frequent. Of late, he'd heard his name cursed, his power over the volatile duke decried.

"If you have something to say, say it, de Claire. Else take your ugly nose elsewhere. I would speak with my lord without your distracting presence."

A hot tide of red swept up de Claire's face, which bore the visible marks of his last confrontation with FitzHugh, in the tourney just after the birth of Geoffrey's daughter. His nose, which had once been long and aquiline, was now flattened and pushed sideways. His mouth gaped where several teeth were missing. That same mouth now twisted with rage.

"I'll say it, you puling bastard. 'Tis you who fears to lose your lands to King Henry's ire. 'Tis you who sends dispatches to England advising him of what goes on here. 'Tis you who is the traitor to your lord."

FitzHugh's lunge across the crowded room took all but Geoffrey by surprise. The duke threw himself between the two men and held them apart by the sheer force of his bulk.

"Hold!" His bellow rattled the panes of leaded glass. "Hold, I say!"

One massive arm wrapped around FitzHugh's neck in a wrestling hold that he'd used many times before, though never in earnest. His choke-hold tightened when the furious knight tried to wrest himself free. Short of wrestling his liege to the floor, FitzHugh had no choice but to stand, his breath strangling in his throat.

"I have proof," de Claire spit out, his eyes narrowed and feral with hatred. "My men intercepted a courier leaving the city. In his bag was a letter advising the king of your negotiations with Philip. Although unsigned, there were other letters in the pouch, as well, with FitzHugh's seals."

FitzHugh stiffened, his muscles suddenly rigid as tempered steel. Geoffrey's arm loosened, then slid away.

"You lie, de Claire." The flat, cold denial made the other knight's red face deepen in hue. "Produce this courier and let him say where he got this letter, if it even exists."

"It exists, bastard."

Sir Guy turned to Geoffrey, an ugly sneer twisting his features. "I didn't tell of this sooner, my lord, as I hoped to get more information from this messenger. Unfortunately, he died under my men's questioning. I have the documents he had with him in my quarters."

"Get them! And the rest of you, get out. Wait outside my chambers."

Geoffrey whirled as soon as the door shut behind them. For long moments, the two men stared at each other, friendship warring with mistrust in golden and blue eyes alike.

"You can't believe de Claire," FitzHugh finally said.

"Damn you, Richard, I don't know what to believe anymore. You've been against me since the day you arrived. Why will you not support me? Why do you harass me?"

"Because I would save your accursed hide," FitzHugh snarled. "Listen to me, Geoffrey, this isn't a game. Your father won't slap your hands and send you back to play in the provinces if you forswear your oaths to him and England."

"How do you know what the king will do?" Geoffrey shouted. "I don't. His lady wife doesn't. My mother swears he's mad, that he's been ensorcelled by the bitch he fornicates with against all the laws of God and man."

FitzHugh's own voice rose as he gave in to his own rage and frustration. He'd seen his friend pulled in so many directions in the last months, and waver so many times, he'd lost every shred of his limited patience. "Just because your father lusts after the Lady Alice doesn't mean he can't hold his dominions. He's done so for twenty years and more."

"He won't hold them much longer," the duke raged. "I will have Anjou and Maine before this month is out."

"You fool! You'll have a cell, next to your mother's."

Incensed, Geoffrey thrust out his arm. The power of that huge limb rocked FitzHugh back on his heels.

"What you do is treason, Geoffrey! It will mean war to the death."

"I've never known you to be so afeard of battle, bastard. Has that little red-haired wench you wed finally turned you against me? Is that why you play the traitor to my cause?"

"Geoffrey, for God's sake, Mellisynt has naught to do with this."

"Has she naught? Ever since you plowed the little widow, you've changed, Richard. Has she drained your manhood, as well as your man root? She looked to be a juicy enough morsel to do so. I may have to try her myself, if she's that good."

"I'll see you in hell first."

Even as he said the words, FitzHugh knew Geoffrey had spoken only out of the accumulated fear and frustration of the last weeks.

Geoffrey straightened and threw back his shoulders. "Aye," he said slowly, each word a painful rasp. "Aye, mayhap you will."

"I tell you, Mellisynt, I cannot help." Constance paced the spacious chamber, her long skirts swirling with each impatient step. "I've argued and cajoled and screamed until I've driven Geoffrey from the palace many times over these past months. He won't listen."

Mellisynt leaned forward in her seat as far as her swollen belly would allow. "I don't understand, my lady. Why does he refuse all offer of ransom? Why will he not at least discuss any terms of release?"

Constance slowed her agitated pacing, then stilled completely. For a moment she stood, a tiny figure clothed in shades of amethyst and lustrous black, shoulders slumped, as if she were too old and far too tired to carry the burdens she did. Finally she turned and crossed the tiles, sinking to the bench beside Mellisynt.

"I fear Geoffrey has lost all power to reason over this. 'Tis as if by losing FitzHugh, he's lost his last tie to a world of order and honor."

"But he hasn't lost him," Mellisynt cried, grasping the duchess's hand in both of her own. "The one message my lord was allowed to send bade me hold true to our allegiances until this matter should be resolved and he is . . . free."

She stumbled over the last word, still unable to grasp the reality of FitzHugh in a prison cell. To one so strong and so used to roaming the broad fields and plains of Europe, three months and more of confinement had to be unbearable. Her fingers tightened convulsively on the duchess's hand as she recalled the growing frustration and fear of these months. The messages and pleas to Geoffrey, to Constance, to the king himself. The frustrating inability to learn FitzHugh's location, or even the exact reasons for his incarceration. The futile offers of ransom, of bounties, of lands she could cede to the crown in return for her husband's release.

She'd agonized over pledging FitzHugh's lands and fees along with those of Trémont, not knowing if he would praise or curse her for yielding his holdings. She'd been allowed no contact with him, except that one brief message. Yet all her entreaties and promises had been refused. The king, still embroiled in the morass that was Ireland, had replied through one of his ministers that he would attend to the matter when he returned if 'twas not resolved by then. Geoffrey had not replied at all.

Constance tugged her hand free of Mellisynt's painful grip and reached up to stroke her cheek.

"Geoffrey refuses to discuss this matter with me. 'Tis as if he must cut himself off, from FitzHugh, from me, from any that would be his conscience. I think it pains him," she admitted, then gave a low, hollow laugh. "Although my lord duke does not seem to mourn the loss of my bed as much as he does the loss of FitzHugh."

Mellisynt's stomach knotted at the bitterness in the duchess's tone. Her last hope, that Constance could yet use her influence over the duke, died a slow, withering death.

She slumped, feeling her body sag with the weight pulling at her middle.

"I'm sorry, my lady," she finally managed.

"I, too," Constance said, with a sigh. "Our union has been turbulent at best, but at least Geoffrey made a pretense of being faithful before. Now he follows his father's lead and flaunts his mistresses in my face. If I did not need a son from his loins to hold Brittany, I would slice off his root with my own hand."

Mellisynt swallowed her instinctive sympathy for the flat misery in the violet eyes that had once sparkled with life and laughter. She knew Constance would little appreciate commiseration. Nor would it help with the more urgent problem at hand.

"Do you know where FitzHugh is held, my lady?"

Constance shook her head. "I heard once 'twas at Bâlfour, but Geoffrey would not confirm it. I think he feared I would order FitzHugh's release, did I know where to send the order."

Mellisynt drew in a shaky breath. Bâlfour was a day's journey south from Rennes, close to the border. Not far from Trémont.

"Will you help me gain an audience with the duke, my lady? He wouldn't answer my letters or petitions."

"'Twill do no good," Constance stated flatly. "He's... he's changed. He's not the man he was."

Mellisynt bit back the retort that she had little enough respect for the man he'd been before. She would deal with him, however he'd changed. Her throat too tight to speak, she sent the duchess a silent plea.

After a moment, Constance sighed. "All right. He's due back late this eve. I'll arrange for you to go to him—if he's not engaged with one of his whores," she added with a touch of acid.

She stood and helped Mellisynt to her feet. Her violet eyes rested on the bulge of Mellisynt's belly, almost indiscernible in the flowing folds of her robes.

"You carry the babe well," she commented with a little smile, as if sharing their women's burden could hold at bay the troubles darkening her world a few moments longer. "You didn't swell up like a bloated pig, as I did."

"Nay, I've gained little in weight. If my stretched skin didn't itch like a dog with ticks and my bladder need emptying but twenty times a day, I would scarce know it's there."

Constance laughed with a trace of her old liveliness. "Well, at least your travails will soon be over."

"I hope so, my lady, I hope so."

Their eyes met in silent determination. Constance nodded and gave her a gentle kiss.

Mellisynt stretched her aching body on the thick velvet coverlet and willed the nagging pain in her lower back to perdition. The journey from England had taken its toll, she admitted to herself, remembering Alymer's protests and Dame Hertha's dire predictions of harm to the babe. But she'd had to try *something,* after months of fruitless, frantic dispatches.

The sea voyage hadn't been difficult. But when she and FitzHugh's lieutenant, St. Bressé, had docked at Dol-de-Bretagne and hired horses for themselves and their escort for the trip to Rennes, the journey had become a nightmare. Even her modest bulk would not allow her to hook her knee around a pommel to ride sidesaddle, nor could she keep her balance on a pillion behind St. Bressé. Teeth clenched, she'd mounted astride a docile mare and ridden the distance to Rennes in acute discomfort. The fact that they had to stop with embarrassing frequency for her to relieve her pressured bladder had only made the long ride worse.

She would have endured the discomfort ten times over, however, if it resulted in FitzHugh's release. Sweet Mother, she ached to see him. Ached to feel his strong arms around her. Ached for the passion she'd thrown aside in her silly quest for love. Although she doubted they could do much to assuage that passion when she did secure his release, not for some weeks yet. She couldn't imagine his desiring to lie with a woman whose breasts had begun to leak and whose legs cramped with increasing frequency. As one was doing even now.

Mellisynt groaned and bent her leg, massaging the aching muscles. Although she'd not swelled to gigantic proportions, as had many other women she'd seen in this state, she'd endured most of the other irritating effects of such dramatic stress on her body. Still, her aches and irritations were minor and easily dismissed. She folded protective hands over her belly, searching for movement under the layers of robe and shift. She was rewarded with a gentle undulation as the taut skin dipped, then bowed, then dipped again under her fingers. A tired smile tugged at her lips. 'Twas indeed FitzHugh's child in there, not the least daunted by the long ride aboard a swaying, jolting mare. Her lord has passed his own endurance to the babe. Mayhap his blue eyes, as well, she mused. And his thick, dark hair. She drifted into a light doze, dreaming of the child and its sire.

"The duchess sent me to fetch you, my lady."

Mellisynt swallowed and nodded to the servant who stood at her door. His flickering torch battled the darkness of the hall beyond, sending eerie shadows against the walls. Pitch hissed and spit, the small sounds loud in the stillness of the night.

Lifting her trailing skirts, Mellisynt followed the man through twisting corridors.

"Lady Constance wished you to know she sent a message to the duke's apartments, requesting a private meeting at this hour on a matter of some urgency."

Mellisynt nodded, sending a silent prayer of thanks to Constance for arranging a private audience. The duke might be more amenable to changing his mind if he did not have to do so in front of an audience of retainers and chamber attendants.

"Through here, my lady." The servant opened an arched door and ushered her into a luxuriously appointed ante-room. She thanked him, drew in a deep breath, and approached the guards posted at the inner door. Tilting her chin, she used her haughtiest tone.

"I am here to see Duke Geoffrey."

The guard flicked a knowing glance over her face, then down the length of her body. His eyes lingered overlong on the swell of her breasts, round and heavy and pushed into high mounds by the square cut of her gown. Of a sudden, Mellisynt wished she hadn't dressed in her finest robe, a rich forest-green velvet embroidered with gold at neck and sleeves. It was meant to give her confidence, but she realized belatedly it also emphasized the lushness of her ripe body.

"Your master is expecting me," she told the guard, her voice dripping ice.

The man flushed and tore his eyes from her neckline. "Aye, my lady." He lifted the iron latch and pulled open the heavy wooden door.

Geoffrey sat in a huge carved chair drawn close to a low fire. He paused in the act of lifting a silver goblet to his lips and glowered at the open door.

"Do you come to plague me yet again, Con—?" His querulous words broke off as he discerned who stood on the threshold. For a moment his face registered surprise, and then settled into an angry scowl.

Mellisynt stepped into the room quickly, before he could order her away. The door swung shut behind her with a thud that she barely heard over the pounding of her heart.

Constance was right, she thought. He has changed. The singers had once heralded Geoffrey as the handsomest of the Plantagenets, the possessor of a figure of elegant symmetry, a man of most winning manner. Yet now he slumped heavily in his chair, his body gross with added weight, his face etched with lines of dissatisfaction. Mellisynt felt all her buried resentment for the duke surge up. Stripped of his facade of charm, he looked like a man who would laugh as he gave a child to a withered old lecher to use. Like a man who would incarcerate his best, his only, friend.

"What do you here?" he growled.

Mellisynt buried her clenched fists in the folds of her gown and lifted her chin. "'Tis obvious, is it not? You would not answer my petitions or letters, so I come in person to secure my lord's release."

A slow tide of red crept up his neck at her tone, and Mellisynt knew at once her mistake. She swallowed, and injected a humbler note into her voice.

"My lord duke, I beg you listen to me. I know not why you hold my husband, only that he angered you most grievously. You must know that FitzHugh is your truest vassal. Your truest friend."

Geoffrey stared down into the goblet he held. "He is a traitor, to me and to his oaths."

"What? Never!"

Mellisynt caught herself as his head snapped up and an angry light gleamed from his golden eyes. "Whatever else FitzHugh may have done, he would not betray you," she offered in a low, pleading voice.

Geoffrey stood and slammed his goblet onto the table beside his chair. Red wine splashed onto the fine silk covering the table and spread in a slow, bleeding stain.

"He would, and did, betray my cause. I have evidence, and will hold him to trial."

"You cannot," Mellisynt gasped. "He is a knight, a titled lord. You cannot try him like a common felon."

"He's but a bastard," Geoffrey replied with a sneer. "He earned his knighthood through my graces, and will lose it in the same manner."

Mellisynt fought the panic wrapping its insidious coils around her heart. This man had stood in their hall, his arm wrapped about FitzHugh's shoulders, the glow of friendship in his eyes. Those same eyes now gleamed with a light that sent cold shivers of dread down her spine.

"My lord, let me buy his release. I'll pledge all I have, all I inherited from Henri of Trémont."

"You have naught to pledge," Geoffrey snarled. "The estates of a traitor are forfeit to the crown."

The duke seemed to take great pleasure from her shocked gasp. "That surprises you, you haughty little bitch? Why? Did you think I would allow him, or you, to keep such wealth?"

He sauntered forward and gripped her chin in a hard hand. Mellisynt held herself rigid, unwilling to give him the satisfaction of pulling free.

"Do you think I didn't notice your veiled insults? Your cool reserve whenever you were in my presence? The scorn in your eyes you couldn't quite disguise? Do you think I don't know who turned FitzHugh against me?"

He leaned his face close to hers. The sweet, sickening scent of wine and a heavily perfumed body assaulted Mellisynt's senses.

"Do you think I don't know how you whispered your woman's spite into his ear every time he plowed between your thighs?" His breath thickened and beat against her face in heated waves. "What do you have there, between those slender legs, that would turn a man from his lord, his friend? What milk does he draw from your breasts that would sour him on his oaths?"

His other hand lifted and curved on her breast. His fingers dug cruelly into her swollen flesh.

She didn't flinch, didn't betray by so much as a flicker of an eyelash the disgust roiling in her stomach. His golden eyes narrowed to tawny slits. "How much do you wish your lord restored to you?"

His words sent a spiraling wave of dread down her spine. Mellisynt could feel her muscles tighten, her skin crawl with prickles of revulsion.

"How much do you want the bastard back in your bed?" Geoffrey rasped.

Her hands curled into claws, her nails bit into her palm. Bitter, angry curses welled up in her throat, trembled on her tongue. She bit them back, but could not keep the scathing disgust from her eyes.

He dragged the fabric of her robe down and took the full weight of her breast in his palm. "Do not look so proud and scornful!" he ground out. "You're a whore, for all your fine robes and haughty airs. I saw you romping in the waves those months ago at Edgemoor. I saw your naked skin under that wet shift. And I saw how you were carried into the keep, flushed and reeking with the scent of Fitz-Hugh's spend."

"You vile, lecherous pig! 'Twas my husband I lay with!"

Restraint crumbling, Mellisynt tried to wrench herself away from his groping hands. The rough fingers holding her chin whipped down to circle the back of her neck. He jerked her close, his strength keeping her easily in place.

"Mayhap if you please me mightily, wench, you might lie with him again someday."

The hand crushing her breast released its hold and moved downward. "Mayhap if you spread your legs and share this—"

His hand batted against the bulge concealed under her flowing robes. He sucked in a sharp breath, his red-gold eyebrows snapping together.

"Aye," Mellisynt told him, her voice low, and vibrating with scorn. "I carry his babe, the child of he who was once your friend above all others. If you try to mount me, I'll not fight you. I'll not risk hurt to my babe. But when you finish, you'd best guard well your person, my lord duke. If I don't skewer you myself, FitzHugh will, someday, somehow."

With a vicious oath, Geoffrey released her and turned away. Mellisynt gulped in a deep, ragged breath.

"Get out of here," the duke snarled. "Get out of here, or I swear you'll join your lord in Bâlfour and whelp your spawn in the dungeon's filthy straw!"

Chapter Seventeen

Mellisynt's small cavalcade crossed the river Vilaine at dusk the following day. In the gathering dimness, the walls of Trémont were barely visible on the high cliff above the river.

She had not dared linger in Rennes to hire a larger escort or allow her men time to rest. If Geoffrey hadn't yet taken her lands in forfeit, he would no doubt try to do so now he knew she was in Brittany once more. She'd slipped out of the city while it was yet dark, covering the bruises on her breast and the despair in her heart. Urging St. Bressé to an ever-faster pace, she'd covered the distance in good time. With every jarring step of her horse's gait, she'd prayed for the safety of her babe and the loyalty of her people.

'Twas strange and most ironic, she thought as the troop began the slow, tortuous climb to Trémont's gates. When she'd left so many months ago, she'd wanted only freedom and a babe. Now she returned, risking both, and praying to find safety and strength in Trémont, where before she'd found only a prison.

"My lady! Holy Father, what do you here?"

Mellisynt slid awkwardly from the mare's back. Her unsteady legs quivered under her, and she would have crumpled to the cobbles had not Sir Bertrand slipped an arm around her waist.

Giving the old knight a grateful smile for his support, she picked her way across the uneven stones.

"I've come to gather the men of Trémont. We ride to rescue our lord."

The old man's eyes blazed in the fading spring light. The remembered taste of battle flavored his voice. "When and where do we go?"

"To Bâlfour."

His step faltered, and the eagerness faded from his face. He shook his head at her questioning look.

"Nay, 'tis not a matter for discussion here, in the darkness of the bailey. Come inside and rest, and we'll discuss how our half-strength garrison is to besiege the duke's strongest, best-manned castle."

Mellisynt fought off waves of hopelessness as she and St. Bressé listened to Sir Bertrand's succinct recital of the few men and sparse weaponry left at Trémont. Most of the able-bodied men-at-arms had been sent in response to the duke's summons weeks ago, taking with them a full complement of stores. They were to serve in the army Geoffrey was amassing, for what purpose Sir Bertrand didn't know, although he had a shrewd guess.

"I'm sorry, my lady. We dared not refuse the duke's summons." Sir Bertrand reached out a gnarled, arthritic fist and patted her hand. "I would gladly lead the men left against Bâlfour, but I fear 'twould be a hopeless cause."

Mellisynt took comfort from the warmth of his grip, even as her mind struggled to accept his words.

"'Tis what you should have expected when you tied yourself to that baseborn knight."

Father Anselem's spiteful voice came out of the dimness at the far end of the hall. He waddled forward, even more portly than before. 'Twas obvious the priest had made even better use of the castle's provisions under FitzHugh's dominion than he had under Henri of Trémont's miserly rule.

Mellisynt surveyed her old nemesis with a dispassionate eye. To think she'd once let this mean-spirited little man have such sway over her. The petty transgressions and verbal battles of her past life seemed so far away, and so unimportant.

"You should have gone to the nunnery, as Henri had planned," the priest continued, his pale eyes filled with malice. "At least you'd have your widow's dower. Now you lose all."

"Nay, Father, not all." Mellisynt rested a hand on her stomach.

"You foolish woman, what good does it do to produce an heir at last if you have naught to leave it?"

Sir Bertrand stiffened and rose from his seat. "Watch your tongue, friar. A priest can as easily lose his living as a knight his estates."

The little man blanched at the steward's bristling approach. He stepped back quickly, stumbling over the hem of his robe.

"I but seek to help! I would save Trémont!"

"You would save your own fat hide and comfortable larder."

"Wait, Sir Bertrand." Mellisynt stepped between the two men, her brow furrowed. "How could you save Trémont, Father?"

The priest cast a nervous glance at the old knight and licked his lips. "You could yet have your estates, lady. If you have your marriage to the bastard declared null."

Mellisynt gave a disbelieving laugh. "How could it be null? I carry evidence of its fruitfulness."

"Queen Eleanor had already borne two daughters when her marriage to King Louis of France was annulled because they shared too close a degree of kinship," the priest argued. "Eleanor retained all her honors and inheritances and brought them to the Angevin king, Duke Geoffrey's own father. If you did the same, Geoffrey would have to recognize your claim."

A waft of garlic and nervous sweat assaulted Mellisynt's nostrils. It barely penetrated her consciousness. Her eyes thoughtful, she stared at the priest.

"I have no kinship with FitzHugh," she commented softly. "On what grounds could my marriage be annulled?"

"You and your widow's estate were pledged to the Church. Henri so decreed in his will. The documents were signed, and the entry fees paid, when the FitzHugh came to claim you. Your pledge to Christ comes before any bonds to man."

"You putrid little—"

Mellisynt cut off St. Bressé's angry interruption with a quick wave of her hand.

"How is it done, Father? How would such an annulment be obtained?"

He leaned forward eagerly. "'Tis simple, my lady. You have to appear before an ecclesiastical court, as did Eleanor and Louis, and convince three bishops of the Church's prior claim. Once you are free of the bastard, you could petition the Church to release you, as well. Since you carry a child, they would not force you into a nunnery."

"You've thought this through most carefully."

Her quiet, considering tone encouraged the priest.

"Aye," he said, eagerness running his words together. "When first I heard the FitzHugh was taken and charged with treason to our duke, I—I wrote the bishop of Rennes. He sent a reply that he would hear the case."

"God's bones!" St. Bressé stood, his face flaming with anger. "My lady, you must not listen to this craven's mad schemes. He but seeks to protect his soft living!"

Mellisynt's gaze flicked from FitzHugh's livid lieutenant to the perspiring Father Anselem. Her mind whirled with dazed, half-formed thoughts. Unconscious of the act, she crossed her arms protectively over her belly.

"My lady, you must—"

Mellisynt's trembling voice interrupted St. Bressé's anguished one. "Bring me the bishop's documents, Father. I would see them. And bring me parchment and ink, as well."

Over the heads of the two men, she met Sir Bertrand's steady gaze. He gave her a long, considering look, then nodded slowly.

* * *

"You would go? Just like that? She bids you come, and you go?"

"Isabeau, I must."

Isabeau tossed her sewing onto the table beside her chair and glared at her husband. He crowded the small *solar* given over to her private use. His shoulders blocked the light from the mullioned windows, and his long legs ate up the short distance from wall to wall as he paced impatiently.

"*Why* must you go?" she asked, struggling with a hot surge of jealousy. Not yet wed two months, and her lord would leave her at another woman's summons. "Fitz-Hugh and the duke will resolve their differences. They always do. You need not succumb to Lady Mellisynt's hysterical fears."

Beauchamp stopped pacing, a familiar look of exasperation settling over his handsome features. Isabeau ignored it. She often provoked such looks, and she had her own ways of dealing with them.

"Listen to me, woman, and try to understand. Fitz-Hugh is in prison and stands to lose all his titles and holdings. Geoffrey would bring him to trial like a common felon. Lady Mellisynt asks my aid, and I would give it."

"I know naught of felons and trials," Isabeau answered, shaping her lips into a sulky pout. "I only know that you had ever an eye for the lady."

"Isabeau, for pity's sake, she is wife to my friend."

"And passing fair, is she not?" Her wide eyes lifted to his in an expression both innocent and knowing.

She bit back a smile as Beauchamp's lip lifted in a rueful grin. Her coquette's tactics never failed to amuse him. Or to rouse his interest. He crossed to take her hands in his. Tugging her out of her chair, he wrapped his arms around her waist, his palms shaping the lushness of her bottom.

"The lady is not near as fair as a certain overripe piece of baggage, one who has claimed all my attention of late and drained my energies."

Isabeau snuggled in his arms, fitting her curves to his long, lean torso. A rush of sweet, sudden desire shot through her belly as she felt his rod hardening. By the saints, this man could heat her blood beyond anything she'd ever imagined. These months of marriage had only fired her sexual appetites. Beauchamp was a most skilled and most inventive lover. And most attentive. She knew he craved her body as much as she wanted his. He'd not leave her to go on this fruitless mission, she vowed. The duke and FitzHugh were far away; their problems were Brittany's problems. She was here, and here her husband would stay.

"Have I really drained your energies, my lord?" she murmured into his chest. Her fingers slid down to tease the bulge between his legs. "Have you none left at all?"

"Isabeau," he warned, on a low in-drawn breath.

"Beauchamp," she teased, her voice low and sultry. She raised on tiptoe to kiss the underside of his jaw, her hand still cupping his manhood. "Do not leave me," she whispered. "You're gone enough fighting your own liege's battles. Do not fight everyone else's, as well."

He stiffened and would have drawn away, but Isabeau clung to him with one arm around his neck, one hand at the juncture of his powerful thighs. Her fingers tightened on his codpiece, loosened, then tightened once more. When he failed to respond to her blatant invitation, she lowered her voice and whispered a husky promise in his ear.

"Stay, my lord. Stay here with me, and I will make the staying most pleasurable."

After a long, still moment, Beauchamp eased back to stare down at her. His eyes, usually so filled with laughter or flaring desire, held an inscrutable expression. Piqued at his lack of response, Isabeau redoubled her efforts. She raised both arms and locked them about his neck, drawing his mouth down to hers. Her tongue darted out to trace his lips, then slipped inside to taste the dark honey. Shamelessly, she rubbed her front against his chest, wanting the friction against her breasts.

"Wait." Beauchamp grasped her wrists and pulled them down. "Wait, and let me bolt the door."

She leaned back, her hands on the sewing table behind her, a small, triumphant smile on her lips. When he finished fumbling with the bolt and turned back, she altered the smile to one of sultry desire.

Any thought that she might control the pace of their coupling fled as Beauchamp strode back to her. His brown eyes were no longer unreadable. They flamed with a fierce light that set her blood to racing. His fingers reached for the laces on the front of her bliaut, ripping them apart when they would not give. Cool air kissed her breasts, causing their peaks to harden and stiffen.

Isabeau gasped as he bent her backward, across the table. Strong, hard hands lifted her skirts, loosed her linens, then pulled her thighs apart. A hot blush stole up her neck when he stepped back, surveying her. She lay bared, vulnerable, and aching with need. She could feel moist heat welling between her legs. Her lashes fluttered down, and she quivered in anticipation.

"My lord," she gasped, when yet he waited, prolonging the foretaste. "Enough. Give me what I crave."

"If I come near you, I'll give you more than that which you crave. I'll beat you black-and-blue."

Isabeau's lids flew up. Beauchamp stood before her, his arms crossed and his face set in implacable lines. Confused, mortified, a little alarmed, she tried to scramble up.

"Nay," he said, stepping between her legs and pinning both her wrists to the table. "If you wish to play the whore, you'd best get used to being on display."

"Wh-what?"

He leaned forward, his hips forcing her thighs farther apart. Rough wood scratched at her wrists, the edge of the table cut into the backs of her legs. His chest brushed against her straining nipples, making her flush in mingled want and shame.

Protesting in small, mewling cries, she tried to twist her body sideways. Beauchamp drew her arms up, taking both wrists in one painful hold. His other had gripped her chin. Isabeau flinched at the coldness in his eyes.

"Listen to me, girl, and listen well. Those who use their bodies to gain their ends are whores, whether on the streets or in the marriage bed. I don't want one for a wife. When you are woman enough to understand that, come to me."

Stunned, furious, unable to formulate a single coherent thought, Isabeau watched him walk to the door and slide back the bolt. Giving a little squeal, she scrambled to throw down her skirts and cover herself as he flung open the wooden panel.

Fingers of gold and red streaked the dawn sky when Beauchamp strode from the great hall, pulling on his gauntlets. His squire stood at his mount's head with helmet and shield in hand. He nodded to the squire and took the proffered helmet. He paused before lifting it to his head to cast a quick look up at the tower holding their private apartments.

Isabeau had remained in her little *solar* throughout the night, alternately sobbing and ranting. He'd heard her furious sobs from their bedchamber. A dozen times and more he'd almost given in to his conflicting needs. He wanted to comfort her, to shake her, to bury himself in her honeyed heat again and again. The urge to beat her had quickly passed, to be replaced with a well of self-disgust. 'Twas as much his fault as hers that Isabeau thought she could use her body to win her way. In these last months, he'd indulged her like a child and loved her like a wanton. He gave the narrow *solar* windows one last, regretful glance, thinking that they'd both learned a painful lesson.

"My lord, wait!"

Turning, Beauchamp saw the figure of his wife run out of the keep and across the bailey. He swallowed at the sight of her long, unbound hair flying dark as a raven's wing in the gathering light. Her shift flattened against succulent curves and shadowed valleys. Her bare feet stumbled on the rough stones, and Beauchamp gripped his helmet hard to keep from reaching out for her.

Breathless, she stopped before him. He stiffened, hardening his heart to the appeal in those magnificent aquamarine eyes.

"My lord, I would bid you farewell, and Godspeed." She slipped to her knees in front of him and bent to kiss his hand.

Surprise kept Beauchamp still for long moments. Then a slow amusement filled his eyes as he stared down at this unfamiliar creature. In their months together, he'd seen Isabeau in many guises, from pouting, playful kitten to hungry cat to satiated, purring feline. Never had he seen her with her dark head bowed, kneeling in a penitent's pose.

A tender smile on his lips, he pulled her gently to her feet. "I thank you for your blessing, my lady."

"'Tis...'tis more than a blessing," she whispered, stumbling over the words. "'Tis a wife's prayer. I would be your wife, not your wh—"

He cut off her earnest plea with a light, brushing kiss. She clung to his hand, her fingers pressed against the cold metal gauntlet.

"Beauchamp, I'm sorry. Truly. I didn't mean to— Well, I did, but I won't try again, to—"

He chuckled. "Minx! You'll probably try all sorts of tricks on me before I break you completely to my hand." His eyes softened, and his hand gripped hers. "If ever I do. You are much a woman, Isabeau."

A tremulous smile hovered on her lips. "Thank you, my lord. Come back quickly. God keep you safe, and the lord and lady of Edgemoor, as well."

She stepped back, her toes curling into the stones to keep her balance. That image, of Isabeau's dainty white toes peeping out from under her shift, beguiled Beauchamp for a good portion of the long ride from Normandy. It faded as he crossed the border into Brittany and headed for the small town just north of Castle Bâlfour, where Lady Mellisynt had asked him to meet her. Instead, grim images of the castle's fortifications filled his mind.

FitzHugh grunted, whipping his head sideways to flick the beading sweat from his eyes. His knuckles showed white as his hands strained against the bars. Relaxing his muscles, he took a deep breath and then pushed once again with all his might.

"At it again, m'lord?"

The guard's amused query broke his concentration. Loosening his grip, FitzHugh turned and nodded to the gap-toothed face pressed against the grate in the door.

"Aye, 'tis the only exercise I get in this accursed place." He rolled his shoulders to ease the tension from his hour of pushing and straining. "Unless you can convince Lord Piss-for-Brains to give me access to the exercise grounds."

The guard snorted with laughter, showing the blackened stumps of his few remaining teeth. FitzHugh's arrogant disdain and crude names for the huge, beef-witted knight who governed Bâlfour had provided the entire castle much amusement over the last weeks.

"Nay, I wouldna dare to ask again. The last time you went into the yard, you knocked six soldiers flat on their arses. You were almost through the gates before they brought you down."

FitzHugh kept a careless smile on his face as he fought back a wave of frustration. He'd been so close, so damned close. Another few seconds and the horse he'd grabbed would have broken through the soldiers rushing for the gate. He swore under his breath, hearing for the hundredth time the horse's screams as a hastily thrown oak staff tangled in its legs, bringing it, and FitzHugh, crashing down. At least he'd had the pleasure of feeling his fists smash a few noses and splinter a jawbone or two before they'd fought him to the ground.

When the guard turned away, FitzHugh stretched out on the narrow cot, one leg drawn up, one booted foot hanging well over the edge. Willing his body to stillness and his mind to calm, he traced the patterns of the uneven cracks in the ceiling above. Before his abortive escape attempt, he'd had somewhat finer quarters and much better meals, as befitted a knight of his standing. In truth, he little missed the softer bed or the sauce-drenched meals. One prison was much the same, when there were bars at the windows.

Jesu, how could Geoffrey have left him here these many weeks? His jaw tightened, and anger clutched at his gut. How could Geoffrey believe him a traitor?

Because he wanted to, his inner voice replied with sardonic honesty. Because the duke would rather deny his friend than deny his own twisted ambitions. Once more, FitzHugh cursed the temper that had made him attack Geoffrey, instead of reasoning with him. They'd disagreed before, had come near to blows on more than one occasion, yet always before FitzHugh had been able to exert the discipline he needed to deal with the man's volatile temper. 'Twas his vile comment about Mellisynt that had snapped FitzHugh's own restraint. That, and the sudden lust in Geoffrey's eyes when he'd spoken of her. FitzHugh knew well the duke's carnal appetites, and that flare of hunger had filled him with rage. Even now, the thought of Geoffrey using Mellisynt made his stomach muscles knot.

He fought the fury creeping through him, forcing himself to relax with an iron will. At least he had the satisfaction of knowing Mellisynt was safe at Edgemoor while Geoffrey plotted and schemed here on the Continent. The picture of his wife basking in the sun on the rocks along Edgemoor's shore teased at his mind and at his body. He savored the memory of her long, slender body as a starving man might the remembered taste of a long-past feast. And her eyes, glowing with the new green of a spring day in the light, deepening to emerald in the dark.

A sharp pang of regret lanced through him as he thought of how those same eyes had grown distant and cool in the weeks before he'd left. Of how she'd withheld her body, withheld her love. FitzHugh shifted uncomfortably on the cot, trying to ease the ache thoughts of his wife always brought. It was as much mental as physical, and he'd wrestled with it these many weeks. He thought of all the ways to describe what he felt for the woman he'd wed, and none seemed satisfactory. He only knew he would give much to see a glow in Mellisynt's eyes once again when he...

"I'm to escort you to Lord Piss—Lord Devereaux's chambers immediately, my lord."

FitzHugh turned his head to eye the guard with only mild curiosity. He'd made the trip to the governor's rooms many times before. He had no desire to be harangued once again for a confession, nor to listen to the man's empty threats. When Geoffrey made his move, FitzHugh would act. Until then, he could only bide his time. Still, even Devereaux's thick-headed company was better than none.

Bright light streaming through the great hall's tall windows blinded him momentarily. Narrowing his eyes against the glare, he tried to make out the figures ranged around a table in front of the far fireplace.

"Come in, Sir Richard, come in." Devereaux's guttural voice cut through the stillness of the hall. "You've visitors, with business that will interest you."

The malice in the man's tone alerted FitzHugh even before his mind registered his wife's cold eyes and lifted chin. He slowed his pace for an imperceptible moment, trying to absorb the implications of her presence, then moved across the hall with a steady stride.

Roger Beauchamp stood behind Mellisynt, his protective stance as blatant as the possessive hand held under her arm. FitzHugh's gaze riveted on that hand, then sliced to Roger's eyes. The flat hardness there made him draw in a slow breath. He turned to the fourth figure, a robed and cowled monk. The priest met his piercing stare with a nervous flick of his tongue. Dragging his eyes from the cleric, FitzHugh noted the litter of documents on the table, all covered with gold ribbons and seals.

The red-faced knight who governed Bâlfour rocked back on his heels, thumbs hooked in his belt. A sneer twisted his thick lips. "You will be most interested to learn that your lady has journeyed here to—"

Mellisynt halted him in midspeech. "Please, my Lord Devereaux, I will tell him myself."

His face impassive, FitzHugh folded both arms across his chest and waited while she stepped forward. Beauchamp followed, maintaining his position behind the lady. Fitz-Hugh felt a muscle begin to tick in his cheek.

"I've come to—" She swallowed and began again. "I've come to tell you that I've petitioned the bishop of Rennes to annul our marriage."

Of all the possible reasons for Mellisynt's presence at Bâlfour FitzHugh's whirling mind had formulated, that would never have occurred to him. Stunned, he struggled to make sense of her words. As if from a distance, he heard her continue in a more urgent manner.

"We are to meet the ecclesiastical court within the week to have the matter decided. Lord Devereaux himself examined all the documents. They're in proper order, and..."

She stumbled to a halt as fury flared in his eyes.

"You are mine, wife." He raked her thickened body with a fierce, angry look. "Wedded, bedded, and ripe with the fruit from my seed. You have no grounds to annul our joining, documents or no."

"I do have grounds," she whispered. "I was pledged to the Church before you. Our vows were invalid."

Before the surprised guards could stop him, he stepped around the small table and caught her arm in a cruel grip. Jerking her against him, FitzHugh snarled down into her frightened face.

"Vows be damned. You are mine. What I have, I hold!"

She tried to twist away, her free hand splayed across her belly as if to shield it from his rage. Her weight made her clumsy and threw her off-balance. Only FitzHugh's strong grip kept her from falling to the floor.

"Take him, you fools! Take him!"

Devereaux's angry shouts mingled with Beauchamp's low curse. "Release her, bastard."

FitzHugh shook off the guard's fumbling hold, twisting Mellisynt's arm as he evaded their reach. He faced Beauchamp, fury darkening his face.

"You've tried before to come between me and my *lady* wife," he taunted, his lip curling. "Are you part of this foul scheme, Beauchamp? What do you get in reward? Do you take the next step in your game of chivalrous love and bed the bitch?"

"No!" Mellisynt gasped, clawing at his fingers. "No, I swear!"

Beauchamp lunged forward. With a sweeping chop, he brought his hand down on FitzHugh's arm and broke his punishing grip. Thrusting Mellisynt to safety, he whirled back, ducking just in time. FitzHugh cursed viciously as his blow missed its target.

Moving with lightning speed to take advantage of FitzHugh's lost momentum, Beauchamp pushed up on the balls of his feet. His fist landed with bone-jarring force on the side of the other man's chin. Staggering, FitzHugh fell back.

"Take him, take him!" Lord Devereaux danced on the tips of his pointed shoes in his excitement.

The gap-toothed guard led the charge. FitzHugh went down under the force of half a dozen men-at-arms. He struggled furiously, throwing most of them off, before a vicious kick to the ribs knocked the air from his lungs. The remaining men piled on and pinned him to the floor.

"Stop!" Mellisynt cried. "Order them to stop!"

Devereaux ignored her frantic pleas, his eyes gleaming at the muted grunts and muffled curses as the guards subdued the prisoner. When they staggered to their feet sometime later, a bound, still struggling knight between them, blood flowed from several battered noses. FitzHugh's massive chest heaved with every furious breath, and a red bruise was beginning to darken his chin.

"It will take these many guards and more to protect you, *wife*. That half man you lie with will never keep you safe from me."

Shaking loose Beauchamp's hold, Mellisynt came as close as she dared. "I did not lie with Beauchamp," she sobbed. "I swear! But I had no one else to turn to for help. Sir Roger will provide us escort to Rennes."

"He'll escort us to the grave and beyond before I give up what is mine."

"You have no choice, Sir Richard!"

The robed monk spoke for the first time, his voice throbbing with a zealot's passion. "You must provide witness at the ecclesiastic court or face excommunication."

The threat brought FitzHugh's head up with a snap. As much as any man, he feared for his immortal soul. This same threat had sent King Henry to his knees, to be scourged and made to beg forgiveness for Thomas à Becket's murder. It had held Frederick Barbarossa's hand from the territories he'd conquered when his reach came too near Rome's own vassal states. It made FitzHugh release his breath in a long, slow hiss.

For a timeless moment, no one moved or spoke. Finally, Beauchamp stepped forward, tucking a protective hand under Mellisynt's arm once more.

"We must leave at once if we're to reach Rennes before dark, my lady."

When she stumbled back beside him, he bowed to the governor. "I thank you for your offer of additional escort, Lord Devereaux, but I have sufficient of my own men."

"Are you sure?" The beefy knight cast FitzHugh a dubious glance. "This one's not been easy to handle. He cost me one of my best horses. Let me at least call the armorer to attach a set of shackles."

"Nay," Beauchamp said with a trace of scorn. "He's safe enough, bound as he is. The months without exercise have weakened him. 'Twas not always so easy to send him down."

"Please, can we not leave?" Mellisynt reached out a hand as if to lay it on Beauchamp's sleeve. She caught FitzHugh's furious glare and jerked it back as if scalded.

"Please, I would get this business over and done with as quickly as possible. Let us go."

FitzHugh tensed his muscles, testing the strength of the ropes that bound him as he was led from the great hall. The hemp cut into his wrists and gave not an inch. His eyes smoldering, he endured the grunts and heaves of the guard as they shoved him aboard a waiting mount.

Leaning heavily on Beauchamp's arm, Mellisynt was led to her palfrey. Her breath came in shallow little gasps, and she refused to meet FitzHugh's piercing stare.

Even with the aid of a mounting block, she had difficulty gaining the saddle. Her mouth was set in grim, determined lines, and she clung to the pommel with white, straining fingers. Jumping onto the block, Beauchamp placed her foot in the stirrup. His hands cradled her hips and lifted her gently. She settled against the hard leather with a little grunt.

FitzHugh felt his teeth grinding, one against the other. His eyes bored into his wife's back as the other men mounted. At length the cavalcade rode through Bâlfour's gates. Beauchamp's standard-bearer in the lead, and a double column of mounted men-at-arms behind.

With every step of the plodding horses, FitzHugh's skin crawled. He resisted the urge to glance back over his shoulder at the sprawling castle. At any moment he expected a shout, an order to halt and return the prisoner. Even this brief taste of open air made him shudder at the thought of returning to his cell. He swallowed and forced himself to focus on the road ahead.

Beauchamp waited until they'd covered a good five miles before he halted the troop. Riding to the prisoner's side, he sliced the ropes with a quick slash of his dagger.

FitzHugh brought his stiff arms forward with aching slowness, and lifted one hand to rub the bruise on his chin. His mouth twisted in a wry grimace.

"You need not have hit with quite so much force, Beauchamp."

Chapter Eighteen

Beauchamp threw back his head, shouting his laughter to the leafy trees overhead. The sound was rich with relief.

"You're lucky I didn't have the guards knock you unconscious and carry your damned carcass out," he managed finally. "I swear, Richard, I couldn't tell whether you had tumbled to our ploy."

"Do you think you could've landed that blow if I had not?"

The two men grinned, sharing a moment of comradeship that transcended words. FitzHugh leaned forward, and they grasped each other's forearms in a hard grip.

"There's a ship waiting at Dol-de-Bretagne to carry you back to England," Beauchamp told him. "If Lady Mellisynt can stand the pace, we should make the evening tide. Your best—your only—hope is to get to King Henry and plead your case. Geoffrey is beyond listening."

He paused, and his rogue's grin faded. "The time nears when we will all have to chose sides once more. This time, I fear, for good."

FitzHugh nodded, his eyes somber. Releasing Beauchamp's forearm, he greeted Peter St. Bressé, then turned at last to the two figures waiting, still and silent, in the road. His heart pounding, he nudged his horse forward. With each step closer to Mellisynt, FitzHugh felt his chest tighten, but he forced himself to address the man beside her first.

"You make a most convincing friar, Sir Bertrand. You set my knees to knocking with your threat of excommunication."

The old knight nodded, grinning. "I'm much better with a sword in my hand than a Psalter, but I thought that bit was rather a good stroke."

"It was. I thank you, sir."

A slow red suffused Sir Bertrand's face, and he shifted uncomfortably in the saddle.

"Harrumph! 'Tis not me you should thank. 'Tis your lady. She thought the whole scheme out."

"Aye, I thought mayhap she did," FitzHugh said softly, his gaze swinging to the trembling figure of his wife. Throwing his leg over the pommel, he slid out of the saddle. In two strides, he was at her side.

For a long moment, neither moved. FitzHugh stood beside her stirrup, his thirsty mind drinking in the details he'd not let himself dwell on during the tense scene at Bâlfour. She looked pale, with lines of strain etching the corners of her mouth. Her veil was coated with dust of travel, and she once again wore loose, baggy gowns, to accommodate her pregnancy. FitzHugh thought he'd never seen anything more beautiful in his life. He lifted his arms.

Mellisynt gave a little sob and eased from saddle into his strong hold. Her shoulders heaving, she wrapped both arms around his neck and buried her face in his chest. FitzHugh carried her into a copse of trees beside the road and settled on a fallen log, cradling her on his lap. He ached to crush her against him, to taste her mouth and skin, to feel the press of her body against his. Instead, he held her while she sobbed out her fright and accumulated strain. When she shifted and her rounded stomach butted against him, he sucked in a ragged breath.

At length her storm of tears passed. Rubbing her nose against his chest, she sniffled, then raised her face to his. She managed a weak, tremulous smile when he brushed a knuckle against her tear-streaked cheek.

"That's the first time I've ever seen you cry," FitzHugh commented in bemused wonder.

Mellisynt swallowed a hiccup. "I've never had to win my husband free of prison through lies and deception before. 'Twas most unnerving."

"Aye, I expect it was."

"And you frightened me. You were so fierce!"

"Aye, I was."

His calm rejoinders stilled her lingering terror. With the lessening of her fear came the first prickle of indignation. After all she'd endured, the man could at least show a modicum of gratitude. Or give some sign he was pleased to see her! She straightened on his lap.

She sniffed. "You, at least, are most composed, my lord."

"Oh, no, my lady," he murmured. "I'm not the least composed. 'Tis all I can do to restrain my own emotions at this moment."

Mellisynt felt her pulse begin to race at the sudden intensity in his eyes. This was much better.

"Don't restrain them, then," she whispered.

"Nay, this is not the place, nor are you in any condition for me to serve you as I would."

A slow, feline smile curved her lips. This was better by far.

"But when we're back in England, and you've delivered of the babe, you may be sure I intend to beat you soundly."

"What?"

Astounded, she gaped at him. His arm tightened on her shoulders, and he brought her around to face him fully.

"My God, Mellisynt!" he growled. "How could you make such a journey! How could you take such risks!"

"I thought the prize worth the risks," she said, sputtering. She jerked in his hold, incensed. "Obviously I was mistaken! Of all the ungrateful, thankless, churlish louts. Of all the—"

"Be still, before you bounce off my knee."

"I'll bounce off your head, you obnoxious oaf."

FitzHugh caught her fist as it raised in a wide, swinging arc. Despite himself, he grinned. The fear that had begun churning in his belly the first moment he'd seen her in Bâlfour's hall swelled once more, and spilled over into a rush of sensation so intense he all but shook with it.

She looked so indignant, so furious. Her eyes blazed with a green fire that sent a shaft of heat straight to his loins. An aching need swamped his own lingering fear for her and the babe.

With a groan, he wrapped a hand around her neck and brought her lips to his. His kiss possessed, devoured, demanded. Her scent and her sweet, honeyed taste filled his senses and fed his hunger.

After a startled moment, Mellisynt shook her fist loose of his hold and wrapped both arms around his neck. She strained against him, her mouth as fierce and ravenous as his. Her breasts tingled when they rubbed against him, their tips beading and dewing against her shift. Her fingers tangled in the dark hair of his nape. It was longer now, and thicker.

She forgot the constant, piercing ache low in her back. She ignored the bulge of her stomach that bowed her toward him at an awkward angle. Shivery, fluttering waves of sensation undulated through her, and she gave herself up to his kiss.

"Well," she gasped, when at last they separated to draw in harsh, ragged gulps of air. "That's more the response I had hoped for!"

He buried his face in her hair, groaning. "I near died when I saw you in that hall, so white-faced and frightened."

"I *was* frightened," she admitted, burrowing into the warmth of his neck. "And you didn't help, my lord. I was afraid you'd ruin all by getting yourself killed!"

"I was but playing the role you gave me," he muttered into her hair.

"You played it fearsome well! You fooled me!"

"Nay," he protested, lifting his head. "Surely you knew I would guess what you were about."

"How could you guess? The annulment grounds were valid. The documents are real, you know. Lord Devereaux examined them most carefully, and was convinced."

"That one took a crack on his head when he won his spurs that spilled half his brains," FitzHugh snorted, rubbing his chin against her forehead as if he could not allow their contact, once made, to be broken.

"Nay, I knew at once what you were about. Even if I hadn't recognized Sir Bertrand right away, I knew you could never play me false, nor repudiate your vows."

Mellisynt eased her head away from his chin, a slow, painful hope building in her breast. "How could you know that?"

"Your heart is true, my lady."

His breath bathed her cheek, as soft and caressing as the words he spoke. A slow smile lit his eyes.

"You told me so. That day in the forest, when Beauchamp tried to steal you before we wed. You swore then you'd hold to your vows, and you have."

His gaze softened and took on a silvery glow, one that Mellisynt had despaired of ever seeing there again. 'Twas enough, she told herself, enough and more. She needed not the words, the songs, the silly love tokens. She needed only this look, this warm glow. Her hand lifted to stroke the line of his jaw.

FitzHugh felt a queer tightening in his chest. He opened his mouth to speak, then closed it as Mellisynt stiffened, her eyes widening in surprise. Her hand left his jaw to splay across her stomach.

"Holy Mary!" she breathed.

With gathering alarm he watched as her teeth came down hard on her lower lip and a low, hissing grunt issued from her mouth.

"Mellisynt! Sweet Jesu, is it the babe?"

FitzHugh fought an urge to crush her to his chest. After a long, tense moment, she lifted her lids. Thick black lashes framed rueful eyes.

"Aye. At least, I think so. 'Tis either that or a very different set of saddle aches."

"Christ's bones," he swore, "how long have you had the pains?"

"They've come and gone since before Bâlfour."

He gave a disbelieving groan, then stood and stalked toward the road, Mellisynt tight within his arms.

Beauchamp met him halfway, striding through the underbrush with undisguised urgency.

"The advance guard just rode back. There's a troop ahead of us on the road. He thinks they carry the duke's pennant."

Mellisynt clung to the safety of FitzHugh's arms as their band pulled off the road and plunged deep into the woods. The men covered their horses' muzzles with shirts and cloaks to keep them still and held themselves rigid and unmoving in the dappled sunlight. Gradually the thud of pounding hooves and jingle of harness penetrated the stillness of the woods. Mellisynt buried her face in FitzHugh's chest once more and forgot to breathe. Within moments, the troop passed.

"'Tis the duke himself," Beauchamp confirmed in a grim voice. "With a full company of men."

FitzHugh nodded. "They'll be back at full gallop when he hears I'm gone from Bâlfour."

Both men glanced down at Mellisynt.

"I'm all right. Truly. The pains come and go, with long intervals in between. I can ride."

A gleam of laughter lightened the worry in FitzHugh's eyes. "You could not ride when you were whole, wife."

"I got here, didn't I?" she reminded him, a tilt to her chin.

He grinned and shifted her weight in his arms. "Can you make it to Trémont? 'Tis closest. We'll hold there while you attend to this business of birthing."

"Nay, not Trémont," Sir Bertrand said urgently. "There's but a skeleton force there. Most of our men were drawn to the duke's levy after you were taken. I expected Duke Geoffrey to garrison the castle with his own men at any time. 'Tis likely they're there now."

"You must make the ship," Beauchamp urged. "I'll take part of the force and head for Rennes. I can leave enough signs to convince Geoffrey to follow us, and make enough speed that he doesn't catch us. You must take Mellisynt and circle around the city to the coast."

Mellisynt held her breath at the conflicting emotions chasing across the sharp planes of FitzHugh's face. He glanced down at her once more, his jaw tightening, then back at Beauchamp.

"It galls me greatly to leave you risking capture and fighting my battles for me," he growled. "But I thank you, Roger. I will see my lady safe."

"There'll be no battle," Beauchamp tossed out with his usual insouciance. "I'll turn east at Rennes and be back across the border before Geoffrey knows who it is he follows. With luck, I'll reach my own keep in time to catch Isabeau before she tumbles out of bed tomorrow morn. God keep you, Richard, and you, my lady."

He swooped down to plant a hearty kiss on Mellisynt's lips and was gone.

The next hours passed in a blur of clawing, wrenching spasms and heart-stopping fear. Cradled in FitzHugh's hold, cushioned against his thighs, Mellisynt endured the ride with a stoicism that surprised her as much as it did him. He slowed whenever the pains seized her and let her find what ease she could within his arms. When they passed, he gripped the reins again and sent the horse forward. Beads of sweat rolled down his brow and traced lines in the dust coating his lean cheeks.

Resisting the urge to press forward with all haste, FitzHugh stayed off the main roads and kept the pace as slow as he dared. They skirted two smaller towns and gave the walls of Rennes a wide birth. As the sun passed its zenith and Mellisynt's spasms grew more regular, he gritted his teeth. They stopped but once, to water the horses and allow Mellisynt to walk about a small clearing, her face set, her hands clutching FitzHugh's arm.

"Ahhh..." she breathed. "That helps."

She leaned against a sapling and turned her face to the sun. Perspiration rolled down the tendons of her neck and slipped below the line of her shift. With gentle fingers, FitzHugh untied the laces and peeled the linen back above her bodice to give her air.

"Who did this?"

Her eyes flew open at the rasp of cold fury in his voice. She saw his gaze fastened on the ugly bruises marking the swell of her breast.

"Who did this?" he repeated, his jaw clenching.

"It matters not."

"Who marked you, lady wife?"

When she refused to speak, he knew.

"'Twas Geoffrey, was it not?"

His gut knotted at the thought of the man who had been his friend putting his hands on her. Or mayhap more. He started to ask, but took one look at her wide, steady eyes and did not.

"He'll not hurt you again, Mellisynt," he promised.

"Nay, my lord," she replied with a quiet dignity that belied the sweat on her brow and the streaks of dust on her cheeks. "Such a one as he can't hurt me."

She took her lower lip between her teeth, staring up at him with troubled eyes. "His heart—nay, his soul—is twisted in his breast, my lord. He's let the dark side of his being leach the good away, if good there ever was."

FitzHugh dragged a hand down his face, his palm rough against the tightness of his jaw. "There was, once."

He fought the anger that coiled, hard and cold, in his belly. He would settle with Geoffrey at the right time and place.

"Come, if you're ready, we'll press on."

They traveled several more miles before she stiffened in his arms once more and bit down on her lip so hard, droplets of blood ran down her chin. Cursing under his breath, he reined in. His hands covered hers on the swell of her stomach, feeling the roiling, rolling flesh beneath the layers of gown.

"This is madness," he told her when the paroxysm had passed. "We must stop and get you a midwife."

"No!" She gripped his hand with a desperate strength. "No, we won't stop. It's not yet time! Hertha told me I would feel the need to push at the end. It may be hours yet."

"Jesu, woman, it *may* be any minute! Do you want to drop the child in an open field, like a mare?"

She met his angry look with a determined one of her own. "As I recall, you've a steady hand with the horses and are most knowledgeable of treatments and poultices. If the babe should come, I trust you to ease its way. Now go!"

Gritting his teeth, FitzHugh spurred his horse forward once more. Where did this remarkable female spring from, he wondered? The thin, pale little widow, who had trembled in their marriage bed, who couldn't even read her betrothal documents, had blossomed into a woman of incredible strength and indomitable will. His hands still shook at the thought of her crossing the sea, braving Geoffrey's wrath, and brazening her way into Bâlfour to free him. And now she'd put herself and her babe in his hands, trusting him implicitly.

With a silent vow to see her and their child safe, he urged the horse into an easy, loping canter.

FitzHugh would gladly have exchanged a day on the rack for the hours that followed. With each spasm, he could feel the taut flesh of his wife's belly stretch and roll, then tighten under his arm. She never cried out, never asked him to stop.

His jaw ached from clenching it so hard, and his arms were
leaden from holding her, by the time they crested a hill and
saw the sea far off in the distance. The sun hung just above
the waves, painting them a deep blood red.

"An hour more, Mellisynt. Can you make it?"

Her lids lifted, and the fearlessness he saw in the depths
of her eyes struck at his soul.

"Aye, we can make it. Only... only hurry."

"My lord!"

At St. Bressé's low call, FitzHugh lifted his head. His
nostrils flared, like those of a lion that has scented danger.
Far down the hill, he saw the patrol. The mounted troop
had come around a bend in the road, heading their way.
Even from this distance, he could recognize their pennants
rippling in the breeze, and knew the golden lions on a
bloodred field.

"We must go back!" St. Bressé urged.

"Nay," FitzHugh said, his voice cold as steel. "They've
seen us. We can't outrun them." He shifted in the saddle
and turned to face the young knight. "Take your lady to the
ship."

"FitzHugh, no!" Mellisynt clutched at FitzHugh's arms.
"No! Don't let them take you again. Go! Ride away, now.
Without me, you can escape them."

"Nay," he told her gently. "Without you, I have no wish
to escape. You know in your heart this meeting was meant.
Go with Sir Peter, my lady, and take our child home to
Edgemoor. God be with you."

He kissed her cheek, drinking in the tang of musky
sweat, the taste of dust, and the faint, sweet scent of gillyflowers. Over her protests, he passed her into St. Bressé's
strong arms, then kicked his horse into a gallop.

By the time FitzHugh hauled back on the reins and
pulled his mount to a pawing, rearing stop, Geoffrey had
ridden forward. They measured each other as the swirling
dust settled, like two strangers chance-met on the road. The
jingle of harness and shuffle of hooves faded from Fitz-

Hugh's consciousness. There was only him, and the man he would kill.

"So, Richard!"

"So, Geoffrey."

FitzHugh sat easy in the saddle, one hand holding the reins, the other resting lightly on the hilt of his sword.

"The diversionary force you sent out led us a merry chase," the duke said, his golden eyes gleaming. "I assume 'twas Beauchamp. The dolt at Bâlfour said he escorted your lady on her onerous duty."

FitzHugh shrugged, not revealing his relief that Beauchamp had made good his escape.

Geoffrey's lip twisted in a wry smile. "'Twas a good ploy, that business of the bishops' court. I might've wasted hours riding into Rennes and missed you altogether if I didn't know you—and your lady—better."

"Aye," FitzHugh told him softly, "you do know better. The Lady Mellisynt would not avail herself of a bishop's decree. She holds to her vows, as I do."

Geoffrey flushed at the scorn in his eyes. "Are you so sure, bastard? Did she tell you she came to my rooms? Did she tell you what she offered for your release?"

"She didn't need to. I saw the marks you left. Your manhood must have shriveled apace with your honor, Geoffrey, that you must needs force a gentlewoman."

A slow tide of red washed up the duke's bull-like neck.

"What, have you no answer?" FitzHugh swung his leg over the pommel and slid to the road. "Have these weeks and months of skulking like a gormless knave, swinging from one cause to the other as a rotten carcass swings on the gibbet, totally unmanned you? Have you lost your balls, as well as your integrity?"

A grim smile tightened Geoffrey's mouth, and he dismounted with a semblance of his old grace. His hands were steady as they undid the clasp holding his cloak and flung it aside. Drawing his sword in a slow, unhurried movement, he held it, blade out, hilt to his chest.

"Despite all, it will pain me to kill you, FitzHugh."

"Despite all, I'm glad you will try. 'Tis better to settle this here, and now."

FitzHugh drew his own sword, his eyes never leaving the duke's face. The knights behind them stirred at the sight of drawn weapons, and several pushed forward.

"Hold!" Geoffrey roared over his shoulder. "Hold! This is between me and Sir Richard. Any man who dares interfere will feel my blade in his gut!"

For a brief instant, their eyes met, regret and resignation mingling. This had been long in coming, but now it was here. They both knew full well the love that had once been between them could end only in death.

At the first clash of steel on steel, a shock ran up Fitz-Hugh's arm and a cold, deadly satisfaction sang through his veins. The wild rush that soldiers feel when they charge into battle surged through him. He had a moment's wonder that he should feel no remorse, no hesitation, and then he swung once more.

The blades sliced through the air, to ring against each other with each swing. His world narrowed to a patch of dusty road, a grunting, heaving, flame-haired man, a swish of air with each vicious stroke.

He overreached, and his sword cut air. Geoffrey lunged up on the balls of his feet and thrust. Icy heat seared FitzHugh's side, and the force of metal against bone thrust him back. He smelled blood, saw it dripping from the edge of Geoffrey's blade. His side was afire, but a quick glance down, beneath his arm, showed that the wound had glanced off the rib, slicing flesh but not penetrating.

He felt no pain, only a raw, burning heat that fueled his utter determination. Lifting his sword, he swung and slashed and began the dance of death.

Step by step, he beat Geoffrey back. The horsemen behind the duke pulled on reins, and hooves shuffled in the dirt as they edged out of the way. FitzHugh neither saw nor heard them. His sole focus was the rasping, grunting man before him. Sweat spiraled down, stinging his eyes. Blood soaked his tunic and ran down his leggings.

Pulling on the last of his reserves, FitzHugh threw his shield aside and grasped his hilt with both hands. Swinging the blade with all his strength, he crashed it into the gold-coated embossing on Geoffrey's shield. The protective barrier dropped for a vital instant, and FitzHugh followed with a sideways thrust against the duke's mailed gauntlet that sent his sword flying from a numbed hand. Using his body's forward momentum, FitzHugh slammed his shoulder against Geoffrey's chest. The duke crashed to the ground.

"Do it, damn you! Finish it!" Geoffrey's voice rattled against the hissing, sucking gasp for air. A fearless gleam lit his golden eyes, and a slow, taunting smile curled his lips as Fitzhugh's sword pressed against his throat. Blood welled, flesh yielded.

FitzHugh's knuckles tightened around the hilt. He had but to lean forward a fraction, exert the smallest pressure.

"It's done," he said finally, the tip of his sword lifting. "You're dead to me, as a man, as a friend."

He straightened slowly, painfully. And walked away. The wound in his side made mounting difficult, but he pulled himself into the saddle. He expected at any moment to hear Geoffrey call to his men, to feel hard hands dragging him back down. Silence rang in his ears.

"Is he come yet?"

Mellisynt lifted one hand to push her sweat-slicked hair back from her face. She knelt on all fours, a mound of piled rags beneath her.

"Nay, my lady." St. Bressé's grim face swung from her to the shipmaster at the door of the small cabin.

"We must cast off," the weathered seaman said again, as he had repeatedly the last twenty minutes. "We're losing the tide."

"Go, look again," Mellisynt ordered St. Bressé. "I won't leave yet."

Her head drooped as Sir Peter's feet pounded up the steps. She drew in shallow, panting breaths. A violent spasm wrenched her lower stomach, and she arched, bowing her back against the pull. Her fingers curled into the rags, her nails dug into the bare wood beneath. For long moments she lost herself in the wrenching pressure, forgetting to breathe, conscious only of the need to push. She spread her knees, the bones grinding against the hard floor. Her hair fell forward, blocking the dim light, shutting out all sound. There was only her, and the babe.

The spasm passed, and she sat back on her heels, breath racing into her lungs. Before the mists even cleared from her eyes, another swell began, a wave of sensation that brought her to her knees once more. Head hanging, she clamped her lips down over the rush of air that beat against them and pushed.

"That's it, push down."

She heard his voice as if from a distance, barely discernible through the roaring in her ears. Yet her heart recognized him instantly.

"Push, Mellisynt."

She felt a clean, sharp pain, and a bulge between her legs.

"Sweet Mary, Holy Mother!" she gasped. "It comes!"

The floor seemed to heave under her. FitzHugh took her arms and laid her on her side. She tried to focus on him, to understand the blood that stained his shirt, to ask what had occurred. She couldn't push the words through her constricted throat, and thought they didn't matter, in any case. He was here, his strength flowed around her. She felt him push up her skirts, then bunch the rags under her to ease her hips and cushion the babe.

Mellisynt's eyes widened as she felt the bulk of her child slide forth—first the head, then the protrusion of a shoulder. She looked down, but couldn't see over the robes mounded at her waist. FitzHugh held her leg up in strong, sure hands, his face fierce with concentration.

"'Tis almost done, little one," he crooned. "'Tis almost done."

Mellisynt felt a wild laugh bubble in her throat at the incongruous sight of her husband, his massive frame bent over her, his deep voice singing to the babe between her legs. Swallowing the laugh, she bit down on swollen lips. A last great heave. A slippery, slithering rush. She fell back in triumph.

FitzHugh shouted as the babe slid into his hands.

Mellisynt closed her eyes as a wave of weariness washed over her, sagging her stomach, collapsing her legs. At the first, tentative cry, her lids flew open.

A girl. A tiny, perfect girl, cradled in her husband's huge hands, still anchored to her by the cord of life. Mellisynt reached out, not tired anymore. A need to hold her babe surged through her, sharp and strong. Leaning on one elbow, she nestled her child against her body and used a corner of a rag to wipe the stains of birth from her eyes.

The tiny mouth puckered, and a lusty wail issued forth.

Smiling, Mellisynt looked up. "Thank you, my lord."

Chapter Nineteen

"How can you sit there so calmly?"

Mellisynt stopped her furious pacing to glare at her lord. He sprawled in a huge, carved chair, his long legs crossed at the ankles. He looked completely at ease, for all the world like a farmer sitting before a comfortable fire instead of a knight about to meet his king.

"Our fate was decided weeks ago, when we left Brittany. We'll find out what it is soon enough."

"I cannot stand this uncertainty! King Henry could've given some indication of how he'll rule on our petitions. Instead he sent just that one short summons!"

"Most like he's been awaiting word from Geoffrey, to see whether he will come forward."

"That puling catiff," Mellisynt sniffed. "I wish you'd skewered him when you had the chance."

FitzHugh shook his head, a rueful smile tugging at his lips. "I thought motherhood was supposed to make women soft and gentle. You've grown more fierce with each passing week."

She stopped beside his chair, slicing through the air with an angry hand. "Why did you let him live? When you had him down, your sword at his throat?"

"I told you, lady wife, many times over. Must we argue this yet again?"

FitzHugh sighed as she turned away and resumed her pacing. She couldn't accept that he'd spared Geoffrey's life.

In truth, at times he found it hard to accept himself. His rational mind told him he'd live to rue the moment when he'd wiped the sweat and blood from his face and stared down at the duke, sprawled defenseless in the dirt.

"We shouldn't have surrendered so tamely to the king's men when they came." Mellisynt picked up the thread of the argument. Her skirts brushed against the stone flooring as she measured the length of the chamber, then back again.

FitzHugh studied the Flemish tapestry above the cold hearth, refusing to be drawn into another area of contention. His wife had wanted to close Edgemoor's gates when the king's summons came, and hold the keep against all comers. As if he could hold out against the king's forces.

By all the saints, he'd never understand women, at least not this particular one. This last month, she'd been so unlike herself, full of irritation and despondency. Instead of rejoicing over their escape and the birth of the babe, Mellisynt had seemed to fall into a black humor.

She passed his chair, her stride agitated. FitzHugh's gaze followed her, sliding down the slender frame outlined in emerald silk. The tight bodice lacing emphasized her swollen breasts, ripe and full for the babe. The thought of those white breasts, threaded with a fine tracery of blue veins and tipped with nipples wet and slick from little Meridyth's suckling, sent a shaft of heat lancing through him.

Christ's blood, he wanted her. Had wanted her for weeks. His aunt's stern admonition that his lady needed time to repair her body humors after birth, and Mellisynt's own uncertain temper, had stayed his hand, if not stilled his wants.

Many women went through swings in their temperament, Dame Hertha had confided to him after one long, frustrating night. His wife had seemed healed and willing that day, yet turned from him that night with a snapped comment that she was not ready. FitzHugh had gritted his teeth, taken as much of her in his arms as she would allow, and waited.

Only the babe seemed to bring them together, the tiny scrap of gurgling, smiling humanity that even now slept in a cradle beside the bed. FitzHugh found himself drawn to the laughing infant, dawdling beside her cradle at odd moments in the day. Many times Mellisynt joined him, cooing and murmuring in the manner of all parents, and for a few moments, at least, they were at peace.

When the king's summons had come, Mellisynt would not leave the babe behind, nor would she allow him to come alone to Kenilworth, where the king would wear his crown at the Feast of Saint John and hear petitions. FitzHugh had resigned himself to the commodious, slow-moving horse-drawn litter that carried mother, babe and tiring nurse, but protested vehemently the three-legged mongrel that loped beside the wagon, fangs bared whenever anyone dared approach. Luckily, the little page Bartholomew had been away on a visit to his parents, or FitzHugh doubted not that Mellisynt would've brought him, as well.

Perforce the journey south had been slow and wearisome, as had the waiting once they arrived at Kenilworth. They'd been two days now awaiting the king's summons.

"Do you think Henry will allow you to keep Edgemoor?"

FitzHugh schooled his patience and answered, as he had many times in the last days, "I don't. Although Edgemoor isn't part of the honor of Richmond, and thus not Geoffrey's to dispose of, I pledged to him when I first won the keep. The king may see it as his son's rightful fief and want to install a knight loyal to Geoffrey to hold it."

Mellisynt whirled and faced her lord, a hand on either hip. "How could he support Geoffrey, even now? How much evidence does he need of his son's treachery? The queen herself admitted their plotting and scheming when she was brought back from Aquitaine!"

Heaving himself out of his chair, FitzHugh moved to stand beside his wife. Her clear eyes glowed with indignation and frustration.

"I know 'tis difficult for one such as you, who holds true to her oaths, to understand these Angevins."

"I know only that they would use you, and I like it not!"

"Mellisynt, there's naught to like or dislike. King Henry has ruled these lands for thirty years and more. He's curbed his sons' power before, and thinks to do so yet again. But they're his blood, his line. Where he can, he'll support them."

"Bah!" Mellisynt threw up her hands. "Damn all these Angevins! You should've skewered Geoffrey when you had the chance! You've lost all because of him."

"Does the thought of losing Edgemoor distress you that much?" FitzHugh asked, folding his arms across his chest and watching her with thoughtful eyes.

"'Tis our home, your sons' patrimony. 'Tis all you have, now that Trémont is lost."

"Nay, I have you, and strong, healthy children. And my sword arm. I earned my way before with the strength of my arm, and can do so yet again."

A troubled frown marred her brow, and she stepped forward, laying her hand on his. Whatever she would have said was lost as a sharp rap sounded on the chamber door.

From where it rested on the floor beside the cradle, the hound lifted its massive head and growled low in its throat.

Mellisynt stood stock-still, the hairs on the back of her neck lifting. It had come, the moment she'd dreaded since their ship touched the shores of England. Her frantic glance darted from the door to her lord's face.

He covered her hand where it rested on his. "Don't worry so, my lady. Trust me to care for what is mine."

The knock sounded once again. The hound's growl deepened in pitch to a rumbling, reverberating snarl. The baby began to fret, making the little mewling, sucking sounds that preceded her full awakening.

"My lord, listen to me. I have yet the documents from Trémont. You could use them."

"What documents?"

"The petitions of annulment. You could put me aside and take another wife, one with lands in the king's holding." Both her hands gripped his arms now, the fingers digging into his hard flesh. She ignored the frown that settled like dark thunder on his brow.

"I've thought much on this since we returned. I know you wed me for Trémont, and now 'tis gone. The castle's garrisoned by the duke's men, the revenues reverted to Brittany's treasury. You've lost all you gained by our joining."

FitzHugh's eyes gleamed silvery blue as he stared down at her. "For God's sake, woman, is this what's been troubling you these weeks?"

She swallowed, forcing the words through her dry throat. "You fulfilled your part of our bargain. I have Meridyth. If I can't give you Trémont in return, I would give you the chance to—"

"My lord, the king awaits!"

The herald's voice called through the wooden door, accompanied by another, louder rap on the panel. Responding to the threat, the hound surged up, its feet spread protectively. A deep, ear-splitting bark rolled across the room and bounced off the walls, accompanied by the lusty wails of the babe.

"Jesu, woman! I disbelieve you wait until this moment to throw such arrant foolishness at me."

He pried her fingers loose and took both wrists in a hard grip. "We'll discuss this later, when I return."

Mellisynt watched him stride from the room, then responded instinctively to the baby's lusty cries. Settling herself in the chair FitzHugh had so recently vacated, she unlaced her bodice and put the child to her breast. The hound hunkered down beside the chair and rested his muzzle on her foot.

Her heart aching, Mellisynt curled her hand around her daughter's dark head. The familiar tug and pull as the child suckled drew at her very soul. Ever since the babe's birth, she'd felt a heaviness of spirit she could not throw off.

Dame Hertha had clucked and scolded and prepared cool, moist foods to soothe her choler. But even such delicacies as veal soaked in vinegar and cucumber hadn't lightened her bleak humor.

FitzHugh had been first confused, then concerned, over her moods. He alternated between a gentleness that made her want to weep and an imperfectly disguised impatience to resume the activities of their marriage bed. But as much as she ached to take his body into hers, to feel the thrust of man to woman, husband to wife, once more, Mellisynt couldn't seem to cast off the dark melancholy that held her back.

When the summons had come for FitzHugh to meet with the king, she'd plummeted into a deep despondency. He would lose Edgemoor, she knew, as he had lost Trémont. That was when she'd dug out the creased and weathered annulment documents. She'd used them once to free him from bondage, and would use them again. She'd release FitzHugh from the marriage bargain that had gained her all and him naught.

The babe gurgled and kneaded her fists against Mellisynt's tender breast. She shifted the child to her other nipple, wiping the dribble of thin milk from the tiny rosebud mouth with a loving finger. While the babe suckled contentedly, Mellisynt leaned back and made her plans.

FitzHugh strode through the high-ceilinged halls with a heavy tread. Of all the addlepated, idiotic, vaporish, *female* notions! To think he would set her aside to take another heiress! To imagine he would care more for lands and rents than for his wife and child!

"Wait here, my lord. I'll advise the king of your presence."

He threw the herald a look of such irritation that the man blinked in surprise. Several courtiers lounging in the anteroom started forward, smiles of greeting on their lips, only to fall back at his fierce scowl.

All these weeks! All these weeks he'd handled her so gently, trying to help her through this uncharacteristic melancholy. Gentleness be damned, he fumed. When this audience with the king was through, he might not have a holding to call his own, but he would have his wife.

"The king will see you now, my lord."

With a start, FitzHugh recalled himself to the business at hand. Forcing down his irritation, he followed the man into the king's private audience chamber.

At fifty-three, Henry was in the full vigor of his middle age. He'd lost none of his legendary frenetic energy to advancing years. His hair was yet more red than white, and he traveled like the wind. To his courtiers' dismay, he still crammed twenty hours or more of hunting and work into every day, and rarely sat down. As FitzHugh knelt on one knee before him, Henry waved an impatient hand and strode about the chamber.

"Get up, man, and tell me in your own words what this insanity is with you and Geoffrey."

FitzHugh rose and quickly surveyed the three men in the room. The king's chancellor, the lord of the exchequer, and the most powerful baron in England, Lord Ranulf, earl of Chester, stood around a table scattered with parchments and maps. They could not sit while the king paced. Ranulf, who had taken FitzHugh's youngest son into his household for training, nodded in greeting.

Taking a deep breath, FitzHugh responded to the king's question. "I have abjured my vows of vassalage to your son, the duke."

"Abjured! Christ's blood, man, I heard you all but sliced off his head. And this after he kept you imprisoned. What happened between you?"

Familiar as he was with the king's constant motion, FitzHugh nevertheless found it disconcerting to be addressing his shrewd face one moment, his back the next, as he circled and paced. Henry stopped to sign a document on the wooden table with a quick flourish. Throwing the quill pen down, he whirled and faced FitzHugh once more.

"Well? What caused two men who've fought and wenched and spilled blood together for twenty years and more to fall out so?"

Looking into the king's golden eyes, eyes that were so like Geoffrey's, FitzHugh tried to shape the words that would tell him that his son sought to betray him. A sour taste filled his mouth.

"The king knows of Geoffrey's discourse with Philip," Lord Ranulf put in, easing the way.

FitzHugh nodded and faced the king. "Then you probably know, as well, Geoffrey thought I had betrayed his schemes."

"But you did not."

"The duke thought he had evidence to the contrary."

Henry turned, his motion stilled for once.

"Would you? Would you have come to me with word of what my son plots?"

FitzHugh drew in a deep breath. "Nay, my lord. Not while I was pledged to him."

The men at the table stiffened, but the king didn't move, nor speak. FitzHugh met his look squarely.

"I tried to dissuade him, my lord king, with all the power of our friendship. But I would not betray him while yet I owed him homage."

He paused, and a silence descended, broken only by the light trilling of a small bird on the window ledge. The earl of Chester stepped forward, his shaggy brows drawn together over an angled face that reflected his years and his heavy responsibilities. Many feared this man, who was advisor and confidant to the king. He held dominion over vast lands in England and on the Continent, and wielded a heavy sword hand. FitzHugh had fought with him more than once, and found him honest, if harsh. His youngest son could have no better man to foster with.

The earl's deep bass rumbled across the stillness. "I will take Sir Richard's homage, my lord king. I will have any man who stood true to his oaths until they were honorably dissolved."

The king's eyes narrowed on FitzHugh. "I've spawned rash, hot-tempered sons. But for all their bullheadedness, they dance yet to my tune. I'll bring Geoffrey within bounds, right enough. He'll need you then, Richard. He'll need your friendship and counsel, as he has before. Hold to him, and let me ease these troubles between you. I'll restore your holdings in Brittany, and give you new honors, as well."

For a long moment, FitzHugh stared at his king. The thought occurred to him that each man, king or peasant, knight or priest, had some fatal weakness. Some blindness that obscured his vision. For all Henry's wisdom in ruling his domains, for all his military daring and natural shrewdness, he couldn't see his weakness in handling his own sons. Geoffrey would not come back, nor would he dance any longer to the king's tune.

FitzHugh wondered briefly what his own blindness was, then thought he knew. It awaited him even now in the chamber they shared. His jaw firming, he shook his head.

"Nay, my lord king. I cannot serve as Geoffrey's vassal."

Henry measured him for interminable seconds. "So be it!"

"And he shall pledge his knight's duties to me?" the earl prodded.

The king waved a weary hand. "Aye. I've not enough honest men in this realm to scorn one who holds true. Put your sword and Edgemoor's men in service to Chester. I'll have the articles of enfeoffment drawn up and subscribed."

Already Henry's mind had moved to another matter. He strode back to the table and took up a document. Lord Ranulf nodded once more to FitzHugh and turned to join the ensuing discussion.

Bowing to the king's back, FitzHugh turned and left the chamber. The crowd of courtiers waiting outside had swelled in number, drawn by hopes of conducting their business at this wearing of the crown. Squeezing through the mass of bodies, he was hailed by more than one acquaintance. FitzHugh returned their courteous greetings, but precluded any lengthy discussions by the simple expedient of pressing forward at a determined pace.

At length he reached the far doors to Kenilworth's great main hall and escaped into the dim corridors. He strode forward, his step lengthening, feeling as if a great burden had rolled off his shoulders. He was free of Geoffrey and all oaths to him at last. He had but one problem left to resolve, one irritating, stubborn, achingly desirable problem.

"Mellisynt!"

The door to their chamber crashed open before he remembered the sleeping babe. He winced as the wooden panel banged against stone and swung back to jar against the frame.

No wails greeted him, no deafening bark, no instant demand for quiet. Frowning, FitzHugh moved into the room. A quick glance told him they were gone, and the child's nurse, as well, if the empty adjoining room was any indication. His eyes fell on the rolled parchments left neatly in the center of the table. Knowing well what they contained, he disdained even to open them.

Within the space of twenty minutes, he'd summoned his bewildered squire, assembled his troop, and ascertained through liberal distribution of silver pennies Mellisynt's direction. Grim-faced, armed only with his sword, he led his men south, clattering over the uneven cobbles of the great road leading from Coventry to London.

They made uneven progress against the tide of travelers streaming into the city for the festivities to be held this eve. Freedmen driving livestock and carts piled high with farm goods to sell at fairs thronged toward the city. Penitents and pilgrims on their way to the holy observances brushed shoulders with traveling jugglers and itinerant tinkers. The Church celebrated the Feast of Saint John with much pomp. After the solemn church services, the citizens would continue the festivities with much more abandoned midsummer's eve rituals.

Cursing the crowds and slow progress, FitzHugh reined in. The way was blocked by a shouting, gesticulating, immovable crowd. The remains of an accident, an overturned farm cart, spilled over the roadway into the ditches on either side. Cabbages lay strewn across the cobbles, providing fodder for the animals caught in the milling mass and convenient balls for the small boys who kicked them back and forth, shouting and laughing.

"Stand aside!"

His squire's shout was lost in the din.

Exasperation tore at the last shreds of FitzHugh's temper. Somewhere beyond this heaving mass of humanity, farm animals and spilled vegetables was his lady wife. Turning his mount's head, he set his spurs to its flanks. The great war-horse cleared the ditch in a flying leap, then pounded across the open field. Ian and the rest of his men scrambled to follow.

He cut back toward the roadway when he'd passed the bulk of the crowd. Ignoring the gawking travelers, he spurred his horse forward. His eyes and attention were concentrated on the road ahead when a reverberating, rolling barking penetrated his consciousness. Sawing on the reins, he hauled his mount to a dancing, skittering stop. Stunned, he saw Mellisynt standing beside a litter, babe in one arm, hound baying at her side. His mind barely registered the fact that the wagon was headed north, back toward Kenilworth and Coventry, as he pounded across the short distance separating them.

"By all that's holy," he bellowed when his horse thudded to a stop beside her, "how dare you leave me so!"

Heedless of the milling troops or gawking crowd, Mellisynt laughed up at his thunderous face. "I thought 'twas right and honorable to leave. I'd gone but a few miles when I decided 'twas neither, only stupid."

"Those are the first sensible words out of your mouth these last weeks and more," FitzHugh growled, clearly not appeased. His black brows were drawn together in a scowl so familiar Mellisynt's heart ached with a mix of crazy joy and relief. He'd come. He'd come for her, even as she was heading back to him. He'd come for her, disdaining lands and the chance to remarry.

"You will ride with me, lady wife. Give our daughter into Dame Ellen's care."

With a happy smile, Mellisynt passed her babe to the wide-eyed nurse.

FitzHugh turned to his squire. "Lead the escort for Dame Ellen and my daughter back to Kenilworth. We will join you at the castle."

"Aye, Sir Richard."

Mellisynt held her breath as FitzHugh nudged his horse forward until it, and the man astride it, filled her vision.

"Take my hand."

She stared at the fist held down to her, seeing the strength in the curled fingers, the tracery of scars among the dark hairs. With a tiny, breathless sob of happiness, unheard by any except her and the man above her, she took his hand with both of her own and was swung up onto the saddle before him.

The hound whined and padded to stand before the horse. FitzHugh's destrier shuffled uneasily, rolling its eyes at the shaggy beast blocking the way.

"Take care of your lady, and I will take care of mine," FitzHugh commanded softly.

Great, liquid brown eyes surveyed them both for the space of several heartbeats. Finally the hound returned to the litter and plopped its muzzle onto the cushions beside the babe.

An iron arm banded Mellisynt's waist, and the powerful stallion whirled and headed for the open fields. The wind whipped away her veil. She threw back her head against the solid wall of shoulder behind.

A wild exhilaration filled her, and her blood began to pound in rhythm with the horse's hooves. The darkness of the last month faded. The gripping hurt that had dogged her short journey from Kenilworth, had set her weeping, and at last had made her order the men to halt and turn around, fled. As much as she wanted this man, he wanted her.

They left the open fields behind and entered the leafy darkness of the forest. The horse shuddered to a halt, its great withers twitching and quivering beneath her legs. Rough hands took her waist and turned her on the saddle. She floundered against FitzHugh's broad chest, struggling to draw her leg over his thighs and regain her balance. A hard hand on her rear helped her settle, and brought her into direct and intimate contact with his body.

Mellisynt's eyes widened as she felt the rigid hardness beneath her bunched skirts. Her gaze flew up, and her breath stopped at the blue flame in his eyes. With a savage groan, FitzHugh covered her mouth with his.

Her nerves screamed with need. Her need flamed into aching want. And as his mouth gentled on hers, drawing out her taste with tongue and teeth, her want melted into love.

He dragged his head up and framed her face with two huge hands.

"Listen to me, wife. You are mine. Now and always. There is no document, nor man, nor priest, who can take you from me."

"Aye," she whispered.

"Nor will you escape me. If you try to leave, I'll track you down, wherever you may think to go."

"Aye."

"What I have, I—"

He stopped and drew a slow, ragged breath.

"I know not the pretty words sung by troubadours, Mellisynt. I can only tell you that what I have, I hold. And I hold you in my heart."

A soft smile curved her lips.

"And I you, my lord."

She leaned forward and touched her mouth to his, drinking in his warmth, giving of her own. He claimed to have no poet's skills, but Mellisynt knew she'd heard the sweetest song of love ever sung.

His left arm wrapped around her waist once more and brought her up against his body. Beneath her legs, Fitz-Hugh's thigh muscles bunched as he kicked the stallion into a slow, rolling walk.

Mellisynt looked with regret at the cushion of green beneath the trees.

"Do we not stop here, my lord?" she murmured against his mouth. "For even just a little while?"

"Nay," he replied, his voice husky. "But I remember promising to show you all the pleasures one can experience in the saddle. 'Tis time you learned to ride, lady wife."

* * * * *

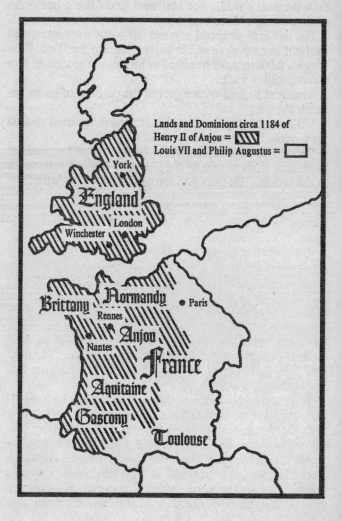

Lands and Dominions circa 1184 of
Henry II of Anjou = ▨
Louis VII and Philip Augustus = ☐

York

𝕰𝖓𝖌𝖑𝖆𝖓𝖉

London

Winchester

𝕭𝖗𝖎𝖙𝖙𝖆𝖓𝖞 𝕹𝖔𝖗𝖒𝖆𝖓𝖉𝖞   • Paris

Rennes

𝕬𝖓𝖏𝖔𝖚

Nantes   𝕱𝖗𝖆𝖓𝖈𝖊

𝕬𝖖𝖚𝖎𝖙𝖆𝖎𝖓𝖊

𝕲𝖆𝖘𝖈𝖔𝖓𝖞

𝕿𝖔𝖚𝖑𝖔𝖚𝖘𝖊

Author's Note

Have you ever had the perfect vacation? I have—several in fact! But one that stands out above all others was when my husband and I took a badly needed break from our military duties and jumped on a plane headed for Europe. We had no reservations, no itinerary and only a vague intention of exploring parts of France we'd never seen before.

What we discovered was Brittany. Wonderful, stormy, sea-washed Brittany. Cities marked by narrow, twisting medieval lanes. Ancient castles perched high atop inaccessible crags. Thick, creamy fish stew sopped up with crusts of mouth-watering bread. And a proud, fiercely independent people with a rich history. It was while reading about the Bretons that I became fascinated by the story of their duchess, Constance, and her rogue of a husband. I had no idea then that I'd someday write a novel that featured this extraordinary woman as one of the characters!

You may be interested to know that Duke Geoffrey finally did rebel against his father's iron hold. In 1186, a year after the conclusion of *Sweet Song of Love*, Geoffrey forswore his oaths, fled to Paris and allied himself with his father's arch enemy, Philip of France. While the two kings girded for war, the incorrigible duke died from a wound taken in a jousting tournament. Constance subsequently gave birth to his posthumous son, Prince Arthur, and was later forced by King Henry to wed the dark, brooding Ranulf, Count of Chester. She agreed to speak the marriage vows, but in their wedding night...

Well, that's another story!

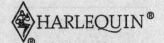

® HARLEQUIN ®

Weddings, Inc.

**Harlequin Books requests the
pleasure of your company this June
in Eternity, Massachusetts,
for WEDDINGS, INC.**

For generations, couples have been coming to
Eternity, Massachusetts, to exchange wedding
vows. Legend has it that those married in
Eternity's chapel are destined for a lifetime of
happiness. And the residents are more than
willing to give the legend a hand.

Beginning in June, you can experience the
legend of Eternity. Watch for one title per
month, across all of the Harlequin series.

**HARLEQUIN BOOKS...
NOT THE SAME OLD STORY!**

Harlequin® Historical

LOOK TO THE PAST FOR FUTURE FUN AND EXCITEMENT!

The past the Harlequin Historical way, that is. 1994 is going to be a banner year for us, so here's a preview of what to expect:

* The continuation of our bigger book program, with titles such as *Across Time* by Nina Beaumont, *Defy the Eagle* by Lynn Bartlett and *Unicorn Bride* by Claire Delacroix.

* A 1994 March Madness promotion featuring four titles by promising new authors Gayle Wilson, Cheryl St. John, Madris Dupree and Emily French.

* Brand-new in-line series: DESTINY'S WOMEN by Merline Lovelace and HIGHLANDER by Ruth Langan; and new chapters in old favorites, such as the SPARHAWK saga by Miranda Jarrett and the WARRIOR series by Margaret Moore.

* *Promised Brides,* an exciting brand-new anthology with stories by Mary Jo Putney, Kristin James and Julie Tetel.

* Our perennial favorite, the Christmas anthology, this year featuring Patricia Gardner Evans, Kathleen Eagle, Elaine Barbieri and Margaret Moore.

Watch for these programs and titles wherever Harlequin Historicals are sold.

HARLEQUIN HISTORICALS... A TOUCH OF MAGIC!

DESTINY'S WOMEN

Sexy, adventurous historical romance at its best!

May 1994
ALENA #220. A veteran Roman commander battles to subdue the proud, defiant queen he takes to wife.

July 1994
SWEET SONG OF LOVE #230. Medieval is the tale of an arranged marriage that flourishes despite all odds.

September 1994
SIREN'S CALL #236. The story of a dashing Greek sea captain and the stubborn Spartan woman he carries off.

Three exciting stories from Merline Lovelace, a fresh new voice in Historical Romance.

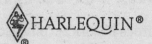